COLD PARADISE

G·K
Hall
&Cº.

Also by Stuart Woods
in Large Print:

Heat
Dead Eyes
L.A. Times
Santa Fe Rules
Grass Roots
Under the Lake
Deep Lie
Chiefs

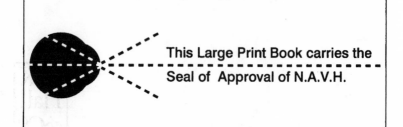

This Large Print Book carries the
Seal of Approval of N.A.V.H.

COLD PARADISE

Stuart Woods

G.K. Hall & Co. • Waterville, Maine

Published in 2001 by arrangement with G. P. Putnam's Sons, a member of Penguin Putnam Inc.

G.K. Hall Large Print Core Series.

The text of this Large Print edition is unabridged.
Other aspects of the book may vary from the original edition.

Set in 16 pt. Plantin by Christina S. Huff.

Printed in the United States on permanent paper.

Library of Congress Cataloging-in-Publication Data

Woods, Stuart.
    Cold paradise / Stuart Woods.
      p. cm.
    ISBN 0-7838-9470-8 (lg. print : hc : alk. paper)
    ISBN 0-7838-9471-6 (lg. print : sc : alk. paper)
    1. Barrington, Stone (Fictitious character) — Fiction.
    2. Private investigators — New York (State) — New York —
    Fiction. 3. New York (N.Y.) — Fiction. 4. Large type books.
    I. Title.
PS3573.O642 C65 2001b
  813'.54—dc21   2001024175

This book is for
Marvin and Rita Ginsky.

1

Elaine's late.

Stone Barrington finished his osso buco as Elaine wandered over from another table and sat down.

"So?" she asked.

" 'So?' What kind of question is that?"

"It means, 'tell me everything.' "

Stone looked up to see Dino struggling to shut the front door behind him. Dino was his former partner, now a lieutenant, head of the detective squad at the 19th Precinct.

Dino came over, sloughing off a heavy topcoat. "Jesus," he said, hanging up his coat, muffler and hat. "There's already six inches of snow out there, and there's at least thirty knots of wind."

"How are we going to get home?" Stone wondered aloud.

"Don't worry, my driver's out there now, putting the chains on the car." Dino now rated a car and driver from the NYPD.

Stone shook his head. "Poor bastard. It's tough enough being a cop without drawing you for a boss."

"What do you mean?" Dino demanded, offended. "The kid's getting an education working for me. They don't teach this stuff at the academy."

"What, how to put chains on a lieutenant's car?"

"All he has to do is watch me, and he learns."

Stone rolled his eyes, but let this pass. They drank their champagne in silence for a moment.

"So?" Dino asked, finally.

"That's what I just asked him," Elaine said.

"So, I'm back." Stone had returned from an extended stay in LA a few days before.

"I knew that," Dino said. "So?"

"Can't either of you speak in complete sentences?"

"So," Dino said, "how's Mrs. Barrington?"

"Dino," Stone said, "if you're going to start calling her that, I'm going to start carrying a gun."

"I heard," Elaine said.

"I'm not surprised," Stone replied. "Dino has a big mouth."

"So, how is she?" Dino demanded.

"I talked to Eduardo today," Stone said. "Her shrink doesn't want me to see her. Not for a while."

"That's convenient," Dino said.

"You bet it is," Stone agreed.

"You feeling guilty, Stone?" Elaine asked.

"Sure he is," Dino said. "If he had just taken my advice . . ."

8

"Mine, too," Elaine echoed.

"All right, all right," Stone said. "If I had only taken your advice."

"Arrington is for you," Elaine said.

"Arrington isn't exactly speaking to me," Stone said.

"What does that mean?"

"It means that if I call her, she's civil, but if I try to reason with her, she excuses herself and hangs up."

"How's the boy?" Dino asked.

"Peter's fine."

"Does he know who his father is yet?"

"Look, Dino, *I* don't know who his father is. It could just as well have been Vance as me. Not even Arrington knows. Nobody will, until we do the DNA testing."

"And when does that happen?"

"Arrington won't discuss it."

"Keep after her."

"I don't know if it's worth it," Stone said wearily. "I'm not sure it would make any difference."

"Give her time," Dino said. "She'll come around."

"You're a font of wisdom, Dino. Know any other relationship clichés?"

"Every eligible man in the country is going to be after her," Elaine said.

"What?" Stone asked.

"She's Vance Calder's widow, dummy, and as such, she's very, very rich. Not to mention gorgeous. You'd better get your ass down to Virginia and win her back."

"She knows where to find me," Stone said.

Elaine rolled her eyes.

Another blast of frigid air blew into the room as the front door opened again.

"It's your pal Eggers," Dino said, nodding toward the door.

Bill Eggers came over to the table. He didn't unbutton his coat. "Hi, Elaine, hi, Dino," he said, then he turned to Stone. "I've been calling you all evening. I should have known I'd find you here." Bill Eggers was the managing partner of Woodman & Weld, the extremely prestigious law firm with which Stone was associated, in a very quiet way.

"My home away from home," Stone said. "What's up?"

"I've got a client in the car that you have to see tomorrow morning."

"Bring him in. I'll buy him a drink."

"He won't come in."

"Who is he?"

"No names, for the moment."

"You have secrets from us, Bill?" Elaine asked.

"You bet I do," Eggers replied. "Ten o'clock sharp, Stone?"

"Ten o'clock is fine; sharp depends on the snow. Your office?"

"Penthouse One, at the Four Seasons. He doesn't want to be seen with you."

"Tell him to go fuck himself," Stone said.

"Stone," Eggers said, "get this thing done and get it done right, and you could end up a rich man."

"Ten o'clock, *sharp*," Stone said.

2

Stone left his house in Turtle Bay early. Eighteen inches of snow had fallen the night before, and the city was a mess. Cabs were few, and he would have to hoof it to 57th Street and the Four Seasons Hotel.

He was clad in a sheepskin coat, cashmere-lined gloves, a soft, felt hat and rubber boots over his shoes. The sidewalks on his block had not been cleared, but the street had been plowed, and he walked up the middle of it all the way to Park Avenue, unmolested by any traffic. The city was peculiarly quiet, the silence punctuated only by the occasional blast of a taxi's horn and, twice, the sound of car striking car. He made it to the Four Seasons ten minutes early.

It was said to be the most expensive hotel in the city, a soaring, very modern skyscraper set on the broad, crosstown street between Madison and Park. A gust of wind propelled him into the lobby, and he was immediately too warm. He found a checkroom and unburdened himself of his outer clothing, and shortly, the elevator deposited him on a high floor. He rang the bell beside the double doors and, immediately, a uniformed butler opened the door.

"Yes, sir?"

"My name is Barrington. I'm expected."

"Of course, sir, please come in."

Stone was ushered through a foyer into a huge living room with a spectacular view of the city looking south, or what would have been a spectacular view if not for the clouds enveloping the tops of the taller buildings.

Bill Eggers came off a sofa by the windows and shook his hand. "Sit down," he said, "and let me brief you."

Stone sat down, and immediately he heard another man's voice coming from an adjoining room through an open door. "Bill?" the voice said. "Come on in."

Eggers stood up. "I'm sorry," he said to Stone, "but there's no time. Just listen a lot and follow my lead. Say yes to anything he says."

"Not if he propositions me," Stone said, but Eggers was already leading the way into the next room. Stone followed, and a very tall, very slender man in his mid-thirties came around a desk and shook Eggers's hand. "How are you, Bill?"

"Very well, Thad," Eggers replied. "Let me introduce a colleague of mine. This is Stone Barrington. Stone, this is Thad Shames."

"How do you do?" Stone said, shaking the man's hand. He knew just enough about him to know who he was, but no more than that. Software came into the equation and multimillions.

Stone didn't follow finance or business very closely.

"Good to meet you, Stone," Shames said. "Bill says you can solve my problem?"

Stone glanced at Eggers. "Yes," he said, more confidently than he felt. Shames was dressed in a nicely cut dark suit, but his shirt seemed to have been laundered but not pressed. His tie was loose, and the button-down collar's tips were not buttoned. Shames waved them both to a pair of facing sofas and, as he sat down and crossed his legs, revealed that he was also wearing a battered pair of suede Mephisto's, a French athletic shoe. His blond, nearly pink hair was curly and tousled and had not been cut for months. He was clean-shaven, but Stone doubted that he could raise a beard.

"I've got a press conference at the Waldorf in an hour," Shames said, "so I'll make this as quick as I can."

Stone and Eggers nodded automatically, like mechanical birds.

"I've met this spectacular woman," Shames said, then waited for a reaction.

"Good," Eggers replied.

"Yes," Stone said.

"I think I'm in love."

The two lawyers nodded gravely.

"Congratulations," Eggers said.

"Yes," Stone echoed.

"This is a lot more important than I'm making it sound," Shames said, grinning. "I've never

14

been married, and, well . . ."

Not getting laid, Stone thought. *Horny. Vulnerable rich guy.*

"Anyway, she's just spectacular. I feel so lucky."

He doesn't realize yet she's taken him, Stone thought.

"What's her name?" Eggers asked.

"That's just the thing," Shames said, blushing. "I'm not sure I know."

"When did you meet her?" Eggers asked.

"Last weekend."

"Where?"

"In the Hamptons."

"At this time of the year?"

"Oh, it's getting awfully chic out there in winter, now," Shames replied. "All the most interesting people go out there on winter weekends. You don't have to put up with the summer tourists and all their traffic."

"Sounds great," Eggers said. "Who introduced you to, ah, her?"

"Nobody, actually. We met at this big party at some movie guy's house — I get those guys mixed up — and after talking for a few minutes, we got the hell out of there and went to Jerry Della Femina's for dinner. We had a great time."

"Good," Eggers replied.

"Yes," Stone said.

"She said her name was Liz," Shames said.

"Maybe that's her name," Stone chanced, but shut up at a glare from Eggers.

"I'm not sure," Shames said.

"Do you have some reason to think her name might not be Liz?" Eggers asked.

"Not really, just a feeling. She wouldn't give me a last name or even tell me where she lives."

"How can Stone and I help, Thad?"

"I want you to find her for me."

This time, Stone glared at Eggers, but Eggers avoided the look.

The butler appeared at the door. "Excuse me, Mr. Shames, but your office is on line one."

Shames stood up. "I'd better take this in the other room," he said. "Please excuse me for a moment." He left, closing the door behind him.

"I know you have some questions," Eggers said.

"Just one," Stone replied. "Are you out of your fucking mind?"

"Now, Stone . . ."

"What am I, some seedy shamus, tracking down women for rich men?"

"Stone . . ."

Stone stood up. "Call me when you've got something of substance, Bill."

Eggers didn't move. "The press conference he's holding is to announce an initial public offering of stock in a new company he's started. Shames has taken two other companies public in the past eight years, and they're both multibillion-dollar, worldwide corporations now. How would you like to have ten thousand shares of the new company at the opening price?"

16

Stone looked at him warily. "Tell me about it."

"I don't know all that much, except that it's supposed to be an astonishing new technology for the Internet, and that Thaddeus Shames is doing it."

Stone knew enough to know how spectacular a lot of Internet stocks had been in the market. "What's it going to open at?"

"The price hasn't been set yet; probably around twenty dollars a share. Last week an Internet IPO happened, and the stock went up eight hundred percent the first day."

Stone sat down.

Shames returned to the room, and Eggers stood up.

"Thad, Stone is going to take this on. I've got a meeting back at the office, so I'll leave the two of you to continue." He shook hands with Shames and Stone and left.

"Bill told you about my new IPO?" Shames asked.

"Yes," Stone said. You bet he did. Stone had already calculated how much of his portfolio he'd have to liquidate to buy the new stock.

"This girl is really wonderful," Shames said.

"I'll help you in any way I can," Stone said.

"Walk me to the car, and I'll tell you everything I know on the way."

I'll bet we'll have time left over, Stone thought. "Sure. And, Thad?"

"Yes?"

"Why don't you let me walk you across the

17

street and get you a new shirt for this press conference."

"Across the street?"

"Turnbull and Asser is right across from the
hotel. Won't take a minute."

Shames looked down at his shirt. "Guess it
couldn't hurt," he said.

"They have shoes, too."

3

As they passed through the living room of the huge suite, a woman's voice rang out.

"Thad?"

Shames and Stone stopped and turned. An attractive young woman wearing a chef's smock was waving from the adjacent dining room.

"Yes, Callie?" Shames replied.

"Do you have any idea how many for lunch, yet? I'm turning it over to the caterers, and they'd sure like to know."

"Oh, I don't know. Tell them to plan for a hundred. If there are leftovers we can donate them to a good cause."

"Right," she said. "See you in PB."

Shames rang for the elevator. "Now, about Liz," he said to Stone. "What do you want to know?"

"Describe her appearance."

Shames held a hand across his chest. "She comes up to about here."

"Five-five, five-six?"

"I guess."

"Was she wearing heels?"

"I'm not sure."

"Hair color?"

"A dark brunette."

"Long? Short?"

"To her shoulders; maybe a bit longer."

"How old was she?"

"Thirtyish, I guess."

"Weight?"

"Mediumish, I suppose."

"Body?"

"Attractive."

"Anything else distinctive about her appearance? Nose?"

"Turned up."

"Eyes?"

"Blue, I think."

Jesus, Stone thought, *I'm glad the girl didn't commit a crime; she'd get away with it.*

The elevator arrived, and they got on.

"Let's talk about her name again, Thad. What made you think that Liz might not be her real name?"

"Just a feeling."

"Try and remember if she said anything specific about her name."

"I asked her, 'What's your name?' And she said, 'Liz will do.' And I said, 'What's your last name?' And she said, 'Just Liz.' "

"Well, she's pretty cagey. Do you think she knew who you were?"

"If she did, she didn't give any sign of it. She asked me what I did, and I told her."

"What did you tell her?"

"I said I was a software entrepreneur. She

said, 'Like Bill Gates?' And I said, 'Well not quite on that scale.' That was the only time we talked about work."

"You didn't ask her what she did?"

"Oh, yeah, I did. She said, 'I'm retired.' And I said, 'From what?' And she said, 'From marriage.'"

"So she divorced well?"

"I guess."

"How was she dressed?"

The elevator reached the ground floor, and they went to the checkroom.

"She was wearing this sort of dress."

"Did it look expensive?"

"I guess. I mean, she looked beautiful in it, and it was a pretty expensive crowd at the party."

"How about jewelry?"

"I think she was wearing earrings. Yes, diamond earrings. Those little stud things, you know? Except they weren't all that little."

"Wedding or engagement ring?"

"A big diamond, but not on her left hand."

"So she didn't return her engagement ring after the divorce."

"I guess not."

"Necklace? Bracelet?"

"A gold necklace and a gold bracelet, I think with diamonds. Nothing flashy, though."

"How about her speech; any sort of accent? Southern? Midwestern?"

"American. No accent that caught my attention."

Stone got into his coat, and they left the hotel. "Right across the street, there," he said, pointing to the shop. He led the way, avoiding ice patches and slush in the gutters. "Don't you have a coat?" he asked.

"It's in the car," Shames said, nodding at a stretched black Mercedes that was making a U-turn, following them.

Stone held the shop door open for Shames, then pointed the way upstairs. They emerged onto the second floor and went into the shirt and tie room.

"Gosh!" Shames said. "I've never seen so many colors. You pick out something for me."

"What size?"

"Sixteen. The sleeves usually aren't long enough for me."

"These will be pretty long," Stone said. A salesman showed them the sixteens. Stone riffled through them and picked out a blue-and-white narrow-striped shirt. "How about this?"

"Fine."

Stone picked out a tie and a complementary silk pocket square and handed them to a saleslady. "Send these down to the shoe shop, please." He led the way back downstairs to the shoe shop.

"This is a really nice place," Shames said, looking around.

"You'd never heard of it?"

"No, and it's right across the street from the hotel, too."

A salesman approached, and Stone helped the man choose some dignified oxfords and some socks.

Shames handed the man a credit card.

"There's a dressing room," Stone said, pointing. "Why don't you put those things on?" He waited, and when Shames returned, he had made a mess of tying the tie. Stone retied it for him and stuffed the silk handkerchief into his breast pocket. "You could pass for a captain of industry," Stone said. "That's a really nice suit."

"I had it made in London. This is the only time I've worn it." Shames signed the credit card chit and checked himself out in a mirror. "Something doesn't look quite right," he said. "What is it?"

"There's a barbershop at the Waldorf," Stone replied, glancing at his watch. "Make the crowd wait for you."

"Okay, I guess I could use a trim."

They stepped back into the street, where the Mercedes was waiting. "Ride down to the Waldorf with me," Shames said. "You can drop me, and the car will take you to your place to pack and then to the airport."

"Sorry?" Stone said, getting into the car. He wasn't sure he had understood.

"To Teterboro. My airplane is out there."

"I don't understand."

"Well, you'll have to go to Palm Beach."

"Why?"

23

"Because that's where she is. Didn't I mention that?"

"I don't believe you did," Stone said. "Why do you think she's in Palm Beach?"

"I ran into a guy I know at dinner last night who was at the party in the Hamptons. He recognized her at LaGuardia yesterday. She was boarding a flight for Palm Beach."

"You think she lives in Palm Beach?"

"I've no idea."

They drove down Park Avenue, then the driver made a U-turn and stopped in front of the Waldorf.

"Oh," Shames said, reaching into an inside pocket and extracting an envelope. "Here's some expense money."

Stone took the envelope. "Thanks."

"You can stay at my place down there," Shames said, handing him a card. "Not in the house; the house is being renovated, and it's a complete mess."

"Guest house?" Stone asked.

"No, my boat is moored out back. You can stay aboard. There's some crew aboard, I think. They'll get you settled. Anything else I can tell you?"

"I can't think of anything," Stone said. "If you think of something, please call me."

"Okay. You can reach me through my office. The number's on the other side of the card. I'll be down to Palm Beach in a few days. See you then." He offered Stone his hand, grabbed a ratty-looking overcoat from the front seat, got out of the car and walked into the Waldorf.

"Where to, sir?" the driver asked.

Stone gave him the address. "I have to pack some clothes, then I guess we're going to Teterboro. Jesus, I didn't ask him *where* in Teterboro."

"Atlantic Aviation," the driver replied.

"Thanks," Stone said. He wished he'd had time to find Shames an overcoat. His had been awful.

He sat back in the seat and thought about his first move when he got to Palm Beach. All he could think of at the moment was to stop every thirtyish brunette he saw and ask if her name was Liz and if she had had dinner in the Hamptons last weekend with an extremely tall geek. Stone sighed.

4

When he got home, Stone ran upstairs and started packing. He'd never been to Palm Beach before, but he assumed it would be warm, so he took tropical-weight suits and jackets. He thought about a dinner jacket and threw it in, just in case. He changed into a lightweight suit, took his bags back downstairs, opened the door and waved the driver to come and get them, then he went downstairs to his office. His secretary, Joan Robertson, was working at her desk.

"Oh, good, you made it in," he said.

"My husband drove me. Otherwise, I wouldn't have. Why are you wearing that suit? You'll freeze."

"I'm off to Palm Beach."

Joan rolled her eyes. "Just back from LA a couple of weeks ago, and now off to Florida. Why don't *I* ever get to go where it's warm?"

"Someday," he said. He looked into the envelope Thad Shames had given him; a thick stack of hundreds, at least ten thousand dollars. He counted off two thousand, stuck them in a pocket and tossed Joan the rest. "Put this in the safe for hard times." He jotted down the address and phone number from Shames's card and handed it to her. "This is where I'll be."

"How long?"

"Who knows? No more than a few days, I hope."

"Have fun. Oh, I almost forgot." She handed him a slip of paper. A Mrs. Winston Harding the Third called this morning, wants to talk to you?"

Stone looked at the paper. "Who is she?"

"I've no idea. She sounds terribly upper class, though. She said she needed to talk to you about an important legal matter, and that you came highly recommended."

"Did she say by whom?"

"Nope, but she sounds like money to me. I wouldn't waste any time getting back to her."

Stone stuffed the paper into a pocket. "I'll call her from Palm Beach." He ran for the car.

At Teterboro, the car drove him up to the airstair door of a Gulfstream V, and the driver carried his bags on and stowed them.

"Mr. Barrington?" a uniformed crewman asked.

"That's me."

"We're ready to taxi. Please find a seat and buckle up."

Stone chose from a dozen comfortable chairs and fastened his seat belt. As the airplane started to move, the young woman he'd seen in

Shames's Four Seasons suite came out of a compartment and sat down near him.

"Hi," she said. "I'm Callie Hodges."

"I'm Stone Barrington." They shook hands.

"I heard you were coming to Palm Beach with us," she said.

Stone looked around the airplane. "Who's 'us'?"

"The pilots and me. We're all that's aboard today."

"What do you do for Thad?" Stone asked.

"I'm his chef and party planner. I pretty much go where he goes. I'll fix you some lunch after the seat belt sign goes off."

"Thanks, I haven't eaten."

The big corporate jet taxied to runway 24, paused for a minute, then rolled onto the runway and started moving faster. Shortly, they were climbing into a thick overcast, and in less than five minutes they broke out into sunshine and clear skies.

Callie unbuckled her seat belt. "Would you like something to drink before lunch?"

"A glass of wine with lunch will be fine."

"Be right back." She disappeared into the galley.

Stone picked up a *New York Times* and leafed through it. On the front page of the business section there was an article about Shames's coming press conference, with speculation about the announcement.

Callie returned with a tray bearing a large lobster salad and a glass of white wine, then she went and got a tray for herself. "I'll join you, if you don't mind."

"Please do. How long have you worked for Thad?"

"A little over four years," she said. "You?"

Stone looked at his watch. "Less than three hours. I'm doing a legal investigation for him."

"Thad's a character," she said. "You'll like working for him."

"I hope so. I don't know much about him, except that he's in computer software, in a pretty big way, I gather."

She smiled. "A pretty big way, yes. The last *Forbes 400* put his net worth at five point eight billion dollars."

Stone blinked. He had spent a lot of time around the rich, but not *that* rich. "So this new venture of his is a pretty big deal, then?"

"I hope so," she said, "because I've got a nice little bundle of stock options."

"So what's it like, working for the superrich?"

"Insane," she said, "but I've gotten used to Thad's quirks."

"He has a lot of them?"

"Thad is *all* quirk," she laughed. "The superrich are one thing, but the *newly* superrich are something else entirely. Thad's a big child, really, and he's grown accustomed to instant gratification. Whatever you're doing for him, my advice is to do it in a hurry."

"I'll try," Stone said. "The salad is delicious;

wonderful dressing."

"Thank you, kind sir."

"Have you spent a lot of time in Palm Beach?"

"Oh, yes. Thad's had his place there for a couple of years, and he's mostly back and forth from there to New York. Of course, the house has been under construction for all that time, so we live on the boat."

"That's what he told me."

"You're staying aboard, then?"

"I am."

"Good. I'll cook you dinner tonight."

"Why don't I take you out?" Stone asked. "I should get to know the lay of the land."

"I'd love that."

"Book us at some place you like."

"Will do." She turned her attention to her lunch.

She was very attractive, Stone thought. Late twenties or early thirties, tall, slender, a blond ponytail, nice tan. He finished his lunch and she took their trays away.

"Is there a phone on the airplane?" he asked her.

"In the arm of your chair," she said. "It's a satellite phone, but it works like a cell phone." She headed for the galley.

Stone dug the slip of paper from his pocket and looked at it. Mrs. Winston Harding III, in the 561 area code. Where was that? He dialed the number.

"Hello," a low female voice said immediately.

"May I speak with Mrs. Winston Harding, please? My name is Stone Barrington."

"Oh, Mr. Barrington, this is Mrs. Harding. How good of you to ring me back so promptly. You sound a little funny. Are you in a car?"

"In an airplane," Stone said. "Tell me, where is the five-six-one area code?"

"Palm Beach, Florida," she said.

"Oh. Oddly enough, that's where I'm flying to."

"How convenient," she said. "I wonder if we might meet while you're here? I'm in need of some very good legal counsel."

"Of course. Who recommended me, may I ask?"

"No one, really. It was something I read about you once. Let's have lunch tomorrow. Do you know a restaurant called Renato's?"

"No, this will be my first visit to Palm Beach."

"It's in the heart of town, in a little cul de sac off Worth Avenue, right across the street from the Everglades Club. Anyone can tell you."

"I expect I can find it."

"Twelve-thirty, then, in the garden?"

"Fine. How will I recognize you?"

"I'll recognize you," she said. "See you tomorrow." She hung up.

Stone replaced the phone in the arm of the chair. Winston Harding. Sounded faintly familiar, but he couldn't place the man. Hard to tell much about Mrs. Harding from her voice, even her age. He pictured her as in her fifties,

31

but she could be younger, he supposed. Or older.

He settled back into his chair and returned his attention to the *Times*. Soon, he dozed off.

5

Stone was wakened by a slight jar and the screech of rubber on pavement. He opened his eyes to see airport buildings rushing past the airplane's windows as the pilot deployed the thrust reversers.

"You slept very well," Callie said. She was back in her seat.

"It's one of the things I do best," he replied.

"I guess I'll have to figure out the other things for myself," she said, with a little smile.

The airplane taxied to a stop in front of a terminal, and the copilot came out of the cockpit and lowered the airstair door. A lineman entered the airplane, and the copilot showed him where the luggage was stored.

Stone followed Callie down the stairs to a waiting car, a Jaguar XK8 convertible, top down. The lineman was stowing their luggage in the trunk and behind the seat.

"Hop in," Callie said.

Stone got into the passenger seat, and a minute later they were out of the airport, rolling east. The temperature was in the mid-seventies, and the sun was shining brightly.

"Quite a difference from New York, huh?" Callie said.

"Where are we now?" Stone asked.

"We're in West Palm, and in a couple of minutes we'll cross onto the island of Palm Beach, if traffic isn't too screwed up on the bridge. They're replacing it, and it's taking forever."

Traffic was screwed up on the bridge, and it took forever before they were waved across and Callie was able to drive quickly again. They passed between a double row of very tall royal palms.

"This your first trip here?" she asked.

"Yes, it is. In fact, the only place I've ever been in Florida is Miami — twice, both times to pick up people in handcuffs."

She looked at him. "What kind of lawyer are you?"

"One who used to be a cop."

She made a few quick turns and suddenly, they were on the beach, driving past huge, ugly stucco mansions. "Thought I'd give you a little tour on the way to the house," she said. "That's Mar a Lago over there — the home of Marjorie Meriwether Post, now owned by the awful Donald Trump. He's turned it into a club. Some of these palaces have tunnels to the beach." She turned down Worth Avenue. "This is the shopping heart of Palm Beach," she said. "All the famous stores are here." They drove past Saks Fifth Avenue, Ralph Lauren and dozens of smaller shops.

"Where is the Everglades Club?" he asked.

"Down at the end. Why do you ask?"

"I have a lunch date for tomorrow at a place called Renato's, which is supposed to be across the street."

"Here comes the Everglades Club on the left," she said, "and on the right is a little alley full of shops, and Renato's is at the end."

"What's the Everglades Club?"

"Palm Beach's most desirable club, or the snottiest, depending on your point of view."

"And what is your point of view?"

"It's the snottiest. Not only are Jews not allowed as members, they can't even visit as guests, and I'm half-Jewish."

"I didn't know that sort of thing still existed in this country."

"You've led a sheltered life," she said. She turned left and began driving through a series of quiet streets, lined with large houses and sheltered by tropical vegetation.

"This is beautiful," he said.

"Certainly is. The most desirable houses are either on the beach or on the Inland Waterway, which in Palm Beach is called Lake Worth. Thad's place is on Lake Worth. It's more sheltered for the boat." Shortly, she turned the Jaguar through a large gate into a circular drive and stopped before a palazzo that seemed to have been airlifted from Venice. "Here we are. Leave the luggage. Somebody will get it."

Stone followed her to the huge double front

doors. She pushed and a door swung back to reveal a central hallway that ran straight through the house. The hall was a gallery, hung with large oils. Stone recognized a Turner.

"Oh, good," she said. "They've finished redoing the hall." She led Stone out the back door and into gorgeously planted gardens.

Stone looked back. "You'd never know the house was under construction," he said.

"The outside is all finished, now, so all the equipment and tools are inside." They passed through the gardens and onto a broad lawn, beyond which Lake Worth gleamed in the sunlight.

Blocking most of the view, however, was a very large, very beautiful old yacht.

"That's *Toscana*," Callie said.

"She's glorious."

"She was built in Italy in the thirties. Thad spent two years both restoring her to her original condition and almost invisibly modernizing every system on board."

"How big is she?"

"Two hundred and twenty-two feet, but with only seven cabins, so everyone aboard can be comfortable. Thad gives me the smallest one, but that's bigger than the big cabins on lesser yachts."

A small Hispanic young man wearing a smart uniform of white shirt and shorts came down the gangplank to meet them.

"Stone, this is Juanito, *Toscana*'s chief

36

steward. Juanito, this is Mr. Barrington."

"Welcome aboard," Juanito said. "Mr. Barrington is in cabin number two. Mr. Thad phoned to say he was coming."

"I'll show him aboard," Callie said. "Our luggage is in the Jag."

Juanito found a handcart and ran off toward the house.

Stone followed Callie into the main saloon, and it was as if they had stepped into a much earlier decade. "My God," he said, "it might have been launched yesterday."

"Yes, Thad did a really good job on the restoration. Come on, I'll show you to your cabin. Thad has given you the best one, after the master stateroom." She led the way down a central passage off the saloon and opened a heavy mahogany door on the starboard side. "Here you are."

Stone stepped into a cabin paneled in mahogany, with white painted trim. There was a carved marble fireplace on one side of the room, with a sofa and a pair of chairs facing, and behind them, a large bed with a canopy, trimmed in nautical-looking fabric. Out the large porthole was a view of the water. "Marvelous," he said.

"Your bath is in here," Callie said, switching on a light.

More marble, with a large tub and a separate shower stall. "I've never seen anything like this vessel," Stone said, "although I once sank a yacht nearly as large."

"Run her on the rocks?"

"No, I was just angry with her owner."

Callie looked at him, unsure whether he was serious. "I wouldn't mention that to Thad," she said. "You might make him nervous."

Juanito appeared with Stone's luggage. "May I unpack for you, Mr. Barrington?"

"Thank you, Juanito, yes."

"And would you like your suits pressed?"

"Thank you again."

"My cabin is down the hall," Callie said, grabbing the single small duffel that had accompanied her. "Why don't you poke around, take a look at *Toscana*? Dinner at eight all right? I booked from the airplane."

"Fine. How are we dressing?"

"It's an elegant place, and the crowd will be elegantly dressed, at least, as they define elegant."

"See you a little before eight," Stone said. He left Juanito to do his work and began to explore the big yacht. There were two other cabins on the starboard side, and another three on the port side. Stone took a narrow staircase up a deck and emerged under a broad awning covering an expanse of teak decking. The superstructure was forward, and a set of doors led to what he suspected was the master stateroom. He took another staircase and came to the bridge, where a man in his mid-thirties, wearing the same white uniform as Juanito, except with more stripes on his shoulder boards, was sitting at the chart table.

"G'day," the young man said with an Australian twang. "You must be Mr. Barrington."

"That's right," Stone said, offering his hand.

"I'm Gary Stringfellow, the captain," he said.

"Good to meet you."

"Juanito show you to your cabin?"

"Yes, I'm just having a look around. This is quite some bridge." It was all mahogany and brass.

"Yes. In the rebuilding, we tried to keep it much as it was when the yacht was built, except, of course, we have every piece of modern gear known to man."

"I can see that."

"Wander at will," Gary said. "I have some work to do. Just let Juanito know if you need anything."

"Thanks, I will." Stone continued his tour, working his way forward to the stem, then aft to a broad sundeck, where he shucked off his coat, loosened his tie and collapsed into a chair.

Juanito appeared, as if by magic, bearing a silver tray and a frosty glass. "I thought you might like a gin and tonic," he said.

"Thank you, Juanito. You're psychic." Stone took the drink, and Juanito disappeared, only to return a moment later with a cordless phone.

"A call for you, Mr. Barrington," he said.

Stone accepted the instrument. "Hello?"

"It's Bill. How was your flight?"

"You're full of surprises, Bill, I'll give you that."

"I had meant to brief you before you met Thad, but there was no time. I take it you understand his problem?"

"Yes, it's sort of like being back in high school — the geek wants to date the beauty queen."

"Thad is impulsive, but he takes these things seriously. Do the best job for him you can, and it will react to your benefit."

"It already has," Stone said. "After all, I'm sitting on a yacht in Palm Beach with a gin and tonic frozen to my fist, while you're in New York, freezing your ass off."

"That was unkind."

"It's no fun being in Florida in winter if you can't gloat a little."

"Yeah, yeah. Listen, Stone, take this assignment seriously, all right? Thad is very important to the firm. We're doing all the legal work on his IPO, and I'm his personal attorney. Clients don't get any bigger than Thad Shames."

"I get the picture," Stone replied.

"Keep me posted," Eggers said, "and don't let anything go wrong." He hung up.

Stone put his feet up, sipped his drink and watched the yachts sail by. This was wonderful. Tomorrow he'd find the girl and she and Shames would live happily ever after. What could possibly go wrong?

6

Stone reappeared on the afterdeck just before eight, showered, shaved and wearing a gray linen suit, a cream-colored silk shirt, a yellow tie and black alligator shoes. He took a long look at the lights of West Palm, and then he was joined by Callie.

"Good evening," she said.

He turned to look at her and was stunned by the transformation. Her hair was loose around her shoulders, and she was wearing a tight-fitting, short dress of a dark brown espresso color. It was cut fairly low, showing off handsome breasts and a good tan. When she smiled, her teeth practically glowed in the dark. "Good evening," he said, when he got his breath back.

"Shall we go?" She led him back through the gardens, their way lighted by low lamps along the path, through the house and to the car. "Would you like to drive?" She held out the keys.

Stone took them. "Sure. I haven't driven one of these." He opened the door for her, then went around to the driver's side. The engine purred, rather than roared, to life, and he pulled into the lamplit street and accelerated. "Nice. What kind of power?"

"A two-hundred-and-ninety-horsepower V-eight."

"Very smooth, too. Is it yours?"

"Yes."

"Cooking must pay better than I thought."

"Well, I don't have rent, utilities or any other household expenses to worry about, and it helps when your boss gives you an interest-free loan."

"Sounds as though you've made yourself important to Thad."

"I try." She directed him through a number of turns and shortly they pulled up before a restaurant called Cafe L'Europe. A valet took the car.

"I would have thought the 'el, apostrophe' was a little much," Stone said as they entered.

"A great deal about Palm Beach is a little much," she said.

They were shown to a table near the center of the room. "What would you like to drink?" Stone asked.

"A Tanqueray martini, please."

"And a vodka gimlet," Stone told the waiter. "This is a very good table," he said to her.

"I booked it in Thad's name," she replied.

"Smart move." Menus and a wine list were brought.

Callie closed her menu. "I'm sick of thinking about food," she said. "Order for me."

"Anything you don't eat?"

"I can't think of anything."

The waiter returned. "Are you ready to order, sir?"

"Yes," Stone said. "We'll start with the beluga caviar and iced Absolut Citron," he said. "For the main course, the rack of lamb, medium rare." He opened the wine list. "And a bottle of the Phelps Insignia 'ninety-one."

"Very good, sir." He went away.

They sat back and sipped their drinks until the caviar came, then they ate it slowly, sipping the lemon vodka and making it all last. A couple came into the restaurant, the young woman wearing a sleeveless sweater with the name "Chanel" emblazoned across her chest, in two-inch-high letters.

"A billboard," Stone said.

"Typical of Palm Beach," Callie replied.

"Eurotrash?"

"Just trash. There's a lot of it about. Oh, there are still some old-line families around, living quietly, if grandly, but mostly it's what you see here — people who somehow got ahold of a lot of money and want everybody to know it. They've bid up the real estate out of sight. A nice little house on a couple of acres is now three million bucks, and last week I saw an ad for what was advertised as the last vacant beach-front lot in Palm Beach — all one and a half acres of it — and they're asking eight and a half million."

Stone nearly choked on his vodka.

The waiter had just taken away the dishes

when three people, two women and a man, entered the restaurant and were shown to a table by the street windows. Stone followed their progress closely. One of the women, a redhead, had something very familiar about her.

Callie kicked him under the table. "I thought that in this dress, I might get your undivided attention."

"I'm sorry," Stone said, "but I think I know one of the women. Except she's a redhead, and the woman I knew was a blonde, like you. Well, not as beautiful as you."

"She must have been important," Callie said. "Tell me about her."

"It's not a short story," Stone said. "More of a novella."

"I've got all night."

"All right."

Dinner arrived, and Stone tasted the wine. "Decant it, please," he said to the waiter.

When that was done, Callie said, "Continue."

"Oh, yes. A few years back I scheduled a sailing charter out of St. Marks. You know it?"

"Yes, we've been in there on *Toscana*."

"My girlfriend was supposed to follow, but she got snowed into New York, then she got a magazine assignment to interview Vance Calder."

"Lucky girl," she said. "My favorite movie star."

"Everybody's favorite. That's why she couldn't turn it down. Anyway, I was stuck there alone, and one morning I was having breakfast in the cockpit of the boat, and something odd happened. A yacht of about fifty feet sailed into the harbor, the mainsail ripped, and nobody aboard but a beautiful blonde. After customs had cleared the boat, the police came and took her away.

"The following day I was passing the town hall and there was some sort of hearing under way, and I went in. Turned out to be an inquest. The girl, whose name was Allison Manning, had been sailing across the Atlantic with her husband, who was the writer Paul Manning . . ."

"I've read his stuff," she said. "He's good."

"Yes. Anyway, her testimony is that they're halfway across, and he winches her up the mast to fix something, then cleats the line. She finishes the job and looks down to find him lying in the cockpit, turning blue. She's stuck at the top of the mast, but eventually she manages to shinny down. He's dead, probably of a heart attack. He's the sailor, and she's the cook and bottle-washer, and now she's in the middle of the Atlantic Ocean, alone, her husband starting to rot in the heat. She buries him at sea and, in a considerable act of seamanship for somebody who isn't a sailor, manages to get the yacht across the Atlantic to St. Marks."

"This is beginning to sound familiar. Wasn't there something about it on *Sixty Minutes* a while back?"

"Then you know the story?"

"No, go on. Tell me everything."

"St. Marks's Minister of Justice doesn't buy

45

her story, and he charges her with murdering her husband. Stone to the rescue. I offer to help. She's tried. With the help of a local barrister, I represent her. Long story short, she's convicted and sentenced to hang."

"Jesus."

"Yes. I call New York and pull out all the stops on publicity. *Sixty Minutes* shows up, and many telegrams are sent to the prime minister, demanding she be released. On the day of the execution, fully expecting a pardon, I and the barrister and a priest visit her in her cell. Suddenly she's taken out, and the three of us are locked in. A minute later, we hear the trap sprung on the gallows."

"That's horrible," she said. "I don't think I knew the end of the story. I must have been traveling at the time."

"There's more. Turns out her husband wasn't dead; it was all an insurance scam. He'd lost a ton of weight and shaved off a beard and was unrecognizable, and he was there, in St. Marks, posing as a magazine writer covering the story."

"And he didn't stop the hanging?"

"No. What's more, in order to cover up his new identity, he engineered a light airplane crash in which his ex-wife and two others died."

"And he got away with it?"

"Fortunately, no. He turned up in New York a few weeks later, demanding his yacht."

"What?"

"Didn't I mention that Allison, by way of my fee, gave me the yacht?"

"No."

"Well, she did."

"And now Paul Manning wanted it back?"

"He did."

"What did you do?"

"I'd been expecting him to show up, so I made a phone call, and the police came and took him away. He was extradited to St. Marks, where he was tried, then hanged for the three murders."

"God, what a story. And what made you think of it tonight?"

"I thought of it because Allison Manning is sitting right over there by the windows."

Callie's head spun around.

Stone tapped her on the arm. "Don't stare. I don't want her to see me."

"You're sure?"

"She's dyed her hair red, but that is Allison in the flesh, and very nice flesh it is."

"How could she possibly be here if she was hanged in St. Marks?"

"I didn't finish my story. Unbeknownst to me, Allison had, through the local barrister, arranged to deliver a cashier's check for one million dollars into the prime minister's hands. Accordingly, the execution was faked, and Allison departed the island in a fast yacht she had chartered for the purpose."

"That didn't make it into the *Sixty Minutes* report, did it?"

"It did not. And I may have violated attorney-client confidentiality by telling you."

"Where did Allison get a million dollars?"

"Paul Manning had been insured for twelve million dollars, and the insurance company had already paid."

"So she skipped St. Marks with all that money?"

"Much to the annoyance of her husband."

"But he got his comeuppance."

"He did."

"And you got the yacht."

"I did."

"Do you still have it?"

"No. I sold it in Fort Lauderdale."

"You said you'd never been anywhere in Florida except Miami."

"I forgot about Lauderdale."

"How much did you get for the yacht?"

"A million, six."

"And what did you do with it?"

"I gave the IRS a large chunk, and the rest is in a sock, under my mattress."

She threw back her head and laughed. When she had recovered herself, she asked, "Why do you suppose Allison Manning is in Palm Beach?"

"I have no idea."

They got back to *Toscana* around eleven and stood on the afterdeck, watching the moon come up.

"If you will forgive me," she said, "I'm going

to turn in. It was a long day, and I've had a lot to drink."

"I'm hurt," he replied, "but I'll get over it."

She leaned into him and kissed him, just long enough to be interesting; creamy lips, warm tongue. "Sleep well."

"Now I won't sleep at all," Stone said.

"Oh, good," she replied, then walked off toward her cabin.

7

Late the following morning, Stone borrowed Callie's Jaguar, drove downtown and found a parking space on Worth Avenue. He arrived at Renato's five minutes early and presented himself to the headwaiter. "I'm meeting a Mrs. Harding," he said.

"Oh, yes," the man replied. "We have you in the garden." He led Stone to a table under overhanging bougainvillea and left a pair of menus. Stone sipped some mineral water and waited for Mrs. Winston Harding to appear. When she arrived, Stone choked on his mineral water. This, he had not been expecting.

She was only fashionably late, wearing blue slacks and a matching cashmere sweater, pearls at the neck, the very picture of the fashionable young matron. He tended to remember her in short shorts, with a shirt tied below her breasts, revealing an enticing midsection, and he tried to make the adjustment.

Stone stood to greet her. "Hello, Allison," he said.

"Shhh," she whispered, hugging him, her breasts pressing against him for an extra moment. "We don't use that name here."

He held her chair and ordered a cosmopolitan for her. "Brad," she said to the headwaiter, "this is Stone Barrington. I'm sure you'll be seeing more of him."

The headwaiter shook Stone's hand, then went to get her drink.

"So what is this Mrs. Winston Harding business?"

"That, my love, is my name these days. It's good to see you." She smiled, leaning forward to allow her breasts to be seen down the V-necked sweater.

"And you," he said. "You disappeared over the horizon in that rented yacht, and I thought I'd never see you again. I've often wondered where you got to."

"Oh, all over," she said, smiling. "I've seen the world since last I saw you. I started with a cruise in the Pacific and the Far East, and I just kept going. A year later, I met Winston Harding in London, and a few weeks later we were married in Houston, his home. Winston was a property developer."

"Was?"

"I'm a widow now."

"My condolences. Was there insurance involved?"

She blushed a little. "That was an evil thing to say. He died of a heart attack. He was fifty-five."

"My apologies."

"But there was insurance involved, and a great deal else. Let's order."

She chose the poached salmon, and Stone the rigatoni with a sauce of wild boar sausage and cream. He ordered a bottle of Frascati.

"Well, Palm Beach must be the perfect spot for a wealthy widow," Stone said.

"We bought the house the year after we were married," she replied. "I hardly chose it for widowhood; it just worked out that way. Funny, it's worth three times what Winston paid for it."

"I've heard the market is hot."

"And so am I," she said. She stopped talking while their lunch was served. "In a manner of speaking," she said, when the waiter had left.

"I should think you would have cooled off considerably," Stone said. "After all, you're dead."

"Being dead has its advantages," she said, "but if you run into someone you used to know, it can come as a shock to them."

"Has that happened to you?"

"From time to time, but I've always managed to duck out before we came face-to-face."

"I think I prefer you as a blonde, though."

She laughed. "I'm probably the only redhead in Palm Beach with blond roots."

"So you're finding it a strain, being dead?"

"I'd rather be alive."

"Well, there is the insurance company," Stone said.

"That's why I called you. I want you to represent me in squaring things with those people."

Stone blinked. "You mean you want to give them back their twelve million dollars?"

"Of course not," she said. "Well, not all of it. I thought you might negotiate a settlement. What do you think the chances are of that?"

"I think the insurance company would be very surprised to get *any* of their money back."

"How little do you think I could give them?"

"Who knows? After they get over their initial shock, they'll probably begin to wonder who wants to give it to them. After all, both the culprits are dead."

"I read about your part in sending Paul back to St. Marks," she said.

"I hope you derived some satisfaction from that," Stone replied. "After all, he could have stopped your 'execution' at any time, and he didn't."

She shrugged. "Well, that's all in the past, isn't it?"

"Apparently not, if you're still suffering the aftereffects."

"Stone, I've always been an honest person. You mustn't think I'm some sort of career criminal."

"I don't. I've always thought it was Paul's idea to screw the insurance company."

"It was. Of course, I went along with it, after he'd spent a few months persuading me. Who knew it would end the way it did?"

"Did you love him?"

"Oh, God, did I love him, and for years! It had begun to wear off, though, by the time we hatched the plot. My plan was to take half the money and kiss Paul goodbye." She smiled. "That's when I fell into your bed."

"As I recall, it was *your* bed, but it hardly matters. I had just had the shock of my girl running off with somebody else, so I was easy."

"Yes, you were," she said, her voice low. "Maybe, now that I'm going to be legal again, we could see something of each other."

Stone shook his head. "For the moment, all I can do is represent you in trying to put things right with the insurance company. If I spend any more time with you than that, then I'm a part of a criminal conspiracy."

"But once I'm legal again . . ."

"That's different."

"I mean, I don't want to start using my old name again, or anything like that. I just want to know that I can cross a border without popping up in some computer."

"Not much chance of that, since you're supposed to be dead."

"I still have my old passport. I used it, until I married Winston, then I used my old birth certificate to get a new one."

"Did he know about your past?"

She shook her head. "Not the bad part. I reinvented my life without Paul Manning, and he believed me. He was a dear soul. He never doubted me."

"Well, I think you're right to want to settle this thing with the insurance company. How high will you go?"

She looked thoughtful. "Five million?"

"I should think they'd be *delighted* to get that much back. They wrote off the money a long time ago. Can you afford it?"

"Oh, yes. I still had ten million when I met Winston, and he had a considerable estate. Also, the market has been *very* kind to me."

"You'd need to square things with the IRS."

"How?"

"I don't know, maybe file an amended return. Get a good accountant and let him handle it. It's worth the money to be righteous again."

"Yes, I suppose it is."

"Well, Allison . . . I'm sorry, what do you call yourself these days?"

"Elizabeth."

"That's nice. I . . ." Stone stopped. No, it couldn't be.

"I've had to be so wary all the time. Only last weekend, I met the most interesting man, but he's apparently pretty well known, and I just didn't want to get into anything like that until I had my life in order, so I got all nervous and just walked away from him."

Yes, it could be. "And where were you last weekend?"

"In Easthampton."

"Did you dine at Jerry Della Femina's?"

Her jaw dropped. "How could you know that?"

55

"You're Liz," he said.

"You know Thad, what's his name?"

"Shames."

"Well, I'll be damned."

"Not if I can square things with the insurance company." Stone got out his cell phone and notebook and dialed a number. "This is Stone Barrington. Is he available?"

"Who are you calling?" she asked.

"Yes, tell him it's important."

Shames came onto the line. "Stone? Anything to report?"

"There's someone here who'd like to speak with you," Stone said. He handed the phone to Liz.

She took it, baffled. "Hello? Yes, this is Liz. Oh, it's you! We were just talking about you. Well, yes, I'd like to see you again. Saturday? I believe I'm free. All right, I'll look forward to seeing you then." She handed the phone back to Stone.

"Stone, bring her to the party on Saturday night, aboard *Toscana*. Seven o'clock."

"All right."

"See you then. Gotta run."

Stone returned the cell phone to his pocket.

"So, you're a matchmaker, as well?"

"Glad to be of service."

"He is well known, isn't he?"

"Yes, in the worlds of computer software and Wall Street, he's something of a celebrity."

"I don't know about these things. I never read

the *Wall Street Journal.*"

"Neither do I."

She frowned.

"Anything wrong?"

"There is something else."

"What's that?"

"Paul Manning."

"He's dead."

She shook her head. "No, he's not."

"But he went back to St. Marks and was . . ." Stone stopped. "You bought him out, didn't you?"

She nodded sheepishly. "I called Sir Leslie, the barrister, remember?"

"Oh, yes. How much did it cost you?"

"Half a million."

"You got a volume discount?"

"Stone, I couldn't just let him be hanged."

"Why not? He's a triple murderer. And, when he thought you were going to be executed, he didn't lift a hand to save you from the gallows."

"That's true, of course, but still . . ."

A terrible thought struck Stone. "Please tell me Paul doesn't know you're alive."

She slumped. "I'm afraid he does. Sir Leslie let it slip."

"Good God. Where is Paul?"

"I don't know, but he was in Easthampton last weekend."

"You saw him?"

"I was in a shop on Sunday afternoon, and he passed by in the street."

"You're sure it was Paul?"

"Absolutely sure. He's kept all that weight off, and he's had a nose job, but I recognized him just by the way he walked."

"Did he see you?"

"No. I mean, I don't think so. Still, I got the hell out of the Hamptons, and as soon as I got to Palm Beach, I changed my hair color. What can I do about this, Stone?"

"It's the money he wants, isn't it? You could try buying him off."

"Will you deal with that for me?"

"Well, there are two problems with that. First, I don't know where to find him. Second, the last time he saw me, he wanted to kill me, and since I got him arrested, imprisoned and nearly hanged in St. Marks, I doubt if he feels any more kindly toward me. In fact, it makes me nervous just knowing he's out there somewhere."

"Apparently, he wants to kill me, too," she said. "At least, that's what he told Sir Leslie."

"Grateful, isn't he?"

"Stone, what am I going to do?"

"Well, Allison — excuse me, *Liz* — since we don't know how to find him, I suppose we're going to have to wait for him to find you."

She nodded. "Or you."

8

After lunch, when Allison, now Liz, had left him, Stone took a drive around Palm Beach before returning to the yacht. He thought about Paul Manning and how he would not like to renew his acquaintance with the man. During his career as a police officer, Stone had known a number of people who would have preferred to see him dead, rather than alive, but all of them were either dead themselves, or safely locked away in prison. Except Paul Manning. He flipped open his cell phone and dialed his office number.

"Stone Barrington's office," Joan said.

"Hi, it's me."

"Hi. How's Palm Beach?"

"Sunny and warm."

"Oh, shit."

Stone laughed. "Joan, have you told anyone I'm in Palm Beach?"

"No," she said.

"Has anybody inquired about my whereabouts?"

"I don't think anybody cares," she said archly.

"Thanks. Will you check my old files for one on the Boston Mutual Insurance Company.

There's an investigator there I'd like to speak to, and I can't remember his name."

"You want to hold? I've got most of that stuff scanned into the computer."

"Go ahead and look." Stone made a couple of turns. He was now in a handsome residential neighborhood off North County Road, which pretty much served as Palm Beach's main street.

"I've got it," she said. "He's the chief investigative officer for Boston Mutual."

"That's the guy. Name and phone number?" He pulled to the curb and got out his notebook.

"Frank Stendahl." She gave him the number.

Stone wrote it down. "Any other calls?"

She read him a short list, and he gave her instructions on handling them, then he hung up and dialed Frank Stendahl's number. He had met Stendahl in St. Marks, when the man had come to investigate the claim on Paul Manning's insurance policy and had ended up testifying at Allison's trial. Stone had involved him in the capture of Paul Manning later, but the murder charges against Manning had taken precedence over Boston Mutual's insurance fraud charges, and, since Allison had made their twelve million dollars disappear before she was "hanged," Manning had had no money left for them to go after.

"Stendahl," a gruff voice said.

"Frank, it's Stone Barrington."

Stendahl's voice warmed. "Stone, how are you?"

60

"Very well, thanks. How's the weather in Boston?"

"Don't ask."

"I won't. Tell me, Frank, how do you think your company would feel about getting back some of the money you paid out on the Paul Manning policy?"

"You planning to reimburse us, Stone?" Suspicion had crept into the investigator's voice.

"Certainly not," Stone replied. "But it might be possible to recover a part of the sum."

"How?"

"Let's just say that I have a client who is interested in clearing up the matter. Not the whole twelve million, of course, but a decent fraction."

"How decent a fraction?"

"How about a million dollars?"

"How about six million?"

"It's not going to happen, Frank."

"And what do we have to do to get this money?"

"Nothing, really. Just agree to a settlement and sign a release."

"Releasing who from what?"

"Releasing anybody from any liability connected with the fraud."

Stendahl was silent.

"Frank?"

"I'm just trying to figure this out," he said. "Who's your client?"

"I'm afraid that's confidential and will have to remain so."

"I just don't get it, Stone," Stendahl said. "Both the people responsible for the fraud are dead, and the money vanished into thin air, or at least into some offshore account we could never find. Who would want to give us a million bucks out of the goodness of his heart?"

"I'm afraid I can't help you there, Frank. I was contacted and instructed to contact your company and make the offer. That's all I can tell you."

"I just don't get it," Stendahl said again.

"You want me to tell my client you said no?"

"Of course not," Stendahl nearly shouted. "I'll have to take this upstairs, see what they have to say."

"I can have the money in your account twenty-four hours after I receive the release."

"I'll tell them that."

"And, Frank, it's going to be an iron-clad release — broad and deep, covering anything anybody could ever have done to Boston Mutual in the matter of this policy."

"Stone, do you have any idea how hard it would be for an insurance executive ever to sign such a document? It would turn his liver to rock candy."

"Maybe a million dollars would melt it."

"Where can I reach you?"

Stone gave him the cell phone number. "I'm in Florida," he said.

Stendahl groaned and hung up.

Stone called his office again and dictated a release. "Type that up, leaving the amount blank, and have it ready to fax to Stendahl," he said.

"Will do," Joan replied.

Stone pulled back into traffic. On the way back to the yacht, he passed West Indies Drive, where Elizabeth Harding's house was. He was going to have to get used to that name.

"Liz," he said aloud. "Liz, Liz, Liz." He thought about the nights he had spent with her aboard the yacht in St. Marks, and the memory stirred more in him than he was comfortable with. After all, he was pimping — well, that was too strong a word — *representing* Thad Shames in the matter of Liz Harding, and sleeping with the woman his client was chasing would probably violate *some* canon of legal ethics.

He was back on board *Toscana*, sipping a rum and tonic on the afterdeck, when his cell phone rang.

"Stone Barrington."

"It's Stendahl. I'm with our CEO and CFO, and I'm going to put you on the speakerphone."

"Okay."

Stendahl's voice became hollow. "Now, Stone, our people are not willing to enter into this transaction without knowing more about your client and his reasons for making this offer."

"Frank, gentlemen, client-attorney confidentiality prevents me from telling you any more than I already have about my client's identity or motives. This is a very simple proposition: I will wire-transfer one million dollars into Boston Mutual's account, in return for a release of criminal and civil liability in the matter of the Paul Manning policy for anyone who ever had anything to do with it."

Another voice spoke. "This is Morrison, CFO of the company," it said. "Five million, and that's our best offer."

"Mr. Morrison," Stone said, "*I'm* doing the offering, and while I'm at it, I'll give you our last, best offer to settle this matter. One million, five hundred thousand dollars, and that's it. You have only to accept or reject, but I must tell you, that if you reject this offer, when this phone call is over, you will never hear of this matter again. You simply have to decide whether you'd rather be out twelve million dollars or ten million, five." Stone stopped talking and waited.

"Hang on," Stendahl said, and the call went on hold.

Stone waited, tapping his fingers against his glass. If they stood firm, he could always come back with five million later. After all, that's what Liz Harding had said she would pay.

"We're back," Stendahl said.

"This is Shanklin, the CEO of the company," a new voice said. "We accept, pending a legal review of the form of the release."

"Give me a fax number," Stone said, then wrote it down. "Gentlemen, you'll have the release in five minutes. Sign and fax it to my office, along with your bank account number, and

FedEx the original. Upon receipt of the original, I will wire-transfer the funds to your account."

"We're waiting," Stendahl said.

Stone punched off and speed-dialed his office. When Joan answered, he said, "Insert the amount of one million five hundred thousand dollars in the document, print it out and fax it to Stendahl pronto; he's waiting for it." He gave her the number, then hung up.

Stone sat and sipped his drink, watching the afternoon grow later. Half an hour later, his cell phone rang. "Hello?"

"It's Joan. They signed the document and faxed it back to us."

"Great," Stone said. He found Juanito, got the yacht's fax number, gave it to Joan and asked her to fax the document to him, then he called Liz Harding.

"It's Stone," he said when she had answered. "I have news."

"Tell me," she said.

"Boston Mutual has accepted an offer of one point five million to settle the matter and release you from any civil or criminal liability."

"Oh, Stone," she gushed. "I can't tell you how wonderful it is to hear that."

"Now listen," he said. "It's three-thirty. I want you to call or fax your bank right this minute and instruct them to wire-transfer the funds to my firm's trust account in New York. It's too late for them to do it today, but instruct them to

65

wire the funds immediately upon opening on Monday morning. That way, I can have the funds wired to Boston the same day, and this transaction will be complete."

"Then I'm a free woman?"

"I've no doubt that you're a very expensive woman, but you'll be free when that money hits their bank account. I have a copy of the release being faxed to me, and I'll give it to you tomorrow night, when I pick you up. And I want you to fax a copy of the instructions to your bank to me aboard the yacht." He gave her the fax number. "Now get moving."

"Okay!"

Half an hour later, he had both faxes in hand. He took a long swig of his drink and reflected on a good day's work. There was some small doubt tickling the back of his brain, but before he could summon it up, the rum flushed it away.

9

Stone was taking a nap in his cabin when there was a knock on his door.

"Come in," he called out.

The door opened and Callie Hodges stuck her head in. "Sorry, I didn't mean to wake you."

Stone sat up on his elbows. "It's all right. How are you?"

"I'm good. You free for dinner?"

"Sure."

"I'll cook for you, then."

"Sounds wonderful."

"Find the galley when you're awake," she said. "I'll be the one in the apron."

"Be there shortly," he said. "I'd like to grab a shower."

"Half an hour is fine," she said, then closed the door.

Stone went into the bathroom, a little groggy, and inspected his face. The shave was okay. He stripped and got into the shower, and by the time he emerged, he was awake again. He dried his hair, slipped into a polo shirt and chinos and made his way forward. He found the galley a deck below the bridge, off the dining room. Callie was, indeed, wearing an apron, and, it appeared, nothing else.

"Hi," she said. "Make us a drink?" She pointed to the butler's pantry, and when she turned back to the stove he was a little disappointed to see that she was wearing a strapless top and shorts under her apron.

"What would you like?" Stone asked.

"You were drinking vodka gimlets last night, weren't you?"

"That's right. Would you like to try one?"

"Love to."

Stone measured the vodka and Rose's sweetened lime juice into a shaker, shook the liquid cold and strained it into two martini glasses. He took them back into the galley and handed one to Callie. "Try that."

She sipped the icy drink. "Mmmm . . . perfect!"

"What are you cooking?"

"Risotto," she said, stirring a pot with her free hand. "It has to be constantly stirred until it's done."

"I love risotto," he said.

"Any kind of food you don't love?"

"I never eat raw animals," he said, "or anything that might still be alive, like an oyster."

"You don't like oysters? You don't know what you're missing."

"Last time I saw somebody eat oysters, he squeezed some lemon juice onto them, and they flinched. I never eat anything that can still flinch."

"Anything else?"

Stone thought. "Celery and green peppers. I think that's it."

"There's a bottle of chardonnay in the little wine fridge, there," she said, nodding. "Will you open it? This is almost ready."

Stone found a bottle of Ferarri-Carano Reserve and opened it. "Where are we dining?"

She was spooning risotto onto two large plates. "Follow me," she said, picking them up. She led the way through a swinging door into a small dining room, where a table was set for two. "The big dining room is through that door," she said. "We can seat up to sixteen in there."

"This is lovely," Stone said, sliding her chair under her and taking his own. He tasted the wine and poured two glasses.

"Dig in," she said. "Don't let it get cold."

Stone tasted the risotto, which contained fresh shrimp and asparagus. "Superb. Where'd you learn to cook?"

"At my father's knee," she said. "My mother preferred his cooking to hers, so she never entered the kitchen if she could help it. Later, I did a course at Cordon Bleu, in London, and I worked for a while for Prudence Leith, who has a London restaurant and catering service there. I learned a lot from Prue."

"How'd you come to work for Thad Shames?"

"Last summer I was cooking for a movie producer and his wife in the Hamptons, and Thad came to dinner. The producer was a real shit. He enjoyed ordering me around and complaining about my attitude."

"Did you have an attitude?"

"Probably. Anyway, he was particularly bad that night, complaining about the food, when everyone else was complimenting it. Finally, I'd had enough. I put dessert on the table and told him I was quitting, and he could do the dishes, then I walked out. I went to my room and packed my suitcase and started walking toward the village, up the dark road. Then Thad pulled up in a car and offered me a lift. He asked where I was going, and I said I didn't know. He offered me a job cooking for him, drove me back to his place, installed me in the guest house, and I've worked for him ever since. The job has grown to include lots of other duties, and I've enjoyed it."

"What would you be doing if you weren't working for Thad?" Stone asked.

"Probably working in a restaurant and hating it. I don't like a big kitchen, and you have no social life at all. This job is perfect for me. You aren't married, are you?"

"No."

"Ever married?"

"No. Well, once for about fifteen minutes. It was sort of annulled."

"And where is the ex-wife today?"

"Under full-time psychiatric care. I have that effect on women."

She laughed. "I won't pry. I just wanted to know if you were free before . . ."

"Before what?"

"Before I seduced you."

"If I weren't free, would it matter?"

"It certainly would," she said. "I've learned not to get involved with married men."

"I won't ask how. Where are you from?"

"I was born in a small town in Georgia, called Delano, but I grew up mostly in Kent, Connecticut."

"I have a little house in Washington, Connecticut."

"Nice town."

"Your folks still there?"

"Both dead. Daddy was a small-town lawyer and banker; my mother wrote short stories and poetry, sometimes for *The New Yorker.*"

"One of them was Jewish, you said?"

"Mother. She was a New York girl through and through. They met in the city at a party, and she married him and moved to Connecticut with him. She always missed living in New York. How about you?"

"Born and bred in the city. My father was a cabinet and furniture maker, my mother, a painter."

"Were they good at it?"

"They were. Dad has work in some of the city's better houses and apartments; Mother has two pictures in the permanent collection of the Metropolitan Museum. Mother and Dad are both gone, now."

"So we're both orphans?"

"We are, I guess."

They finished the risotto, and Callie served them a salad, then dessert — old-fashioned chocolate cake.

They took their coffee onto the afterdeck and settled into the banquette that ran around the stern railing.

"So, did you have a productive day?"

"I did."

"How did your lunch with the dead lady go?"

"Very well. I believe I solved her problem."

Callie set down her coffee cup. "Now," she said, "how do I go about seducing you? Do I just stick my tongue in your ear, or what?"

"It's easier than that." Stone took her face in his hands and kissed her for quite a long time. Their temperatures rose quickly.

"There may be crew about," she breathed between kisses. "We'd better go to your cabin."

"Oh, yes," Stone said.

She took his hand and led him forward. In less than a minute they were standing at the end of his bed, undressing each other. In Callie's case, it was quick; she was wearing only the two pieces. She sat on the bed and watched him peel off his clothes.

He knelt before her and began kissing the inside of her thighs, as she ran her fingers through his hair. He pushed her back on the bed and explored her delta, kissing the soft, blond fur at the edges. She gave a little shudder as he took her into his mouth. It took only a minute for her to come, and when she was finished, she pulled him onto her by his ears and felt for him, guiding him in.

"I love the first time," she said, as they made love. "It's always so . . ."

"So new," Stone panted.

"And exciting."

"Sometimes it gets better as it goes along," he said, thrusting.

She thrust back. "We'll see," she said, and they both came together.

10

When Stone awoke his cabin was filled with sunshine, and it was past eleven o'clock. He never slept that late, and he was surprised. Callie was gone, and her side of the bed had been made. He shaved and showered, got into some slacks and a polo shirt and, since the palms outside were moving with the breeze, tied a light cashmere sweater around his shoulders.

He found Callie on the afterdeck in a bikini, reading a novel.

"Good morning," he said, kissing her.

She kissed him back. "You slept late," she said.

"Something I rarely do. I must have been tired."

She chuckled. "I should hope so."

"You look awfully fresh," he said.

"I've only been up for half an hour."

"Good book?"

"Starts really well. A writer I haven't read before, but I saw a good review in the *Times Book Review* last week. Fellow named . . ." She looked at the cover. "Frederick James."

"I don't know him, either."

"A first novel, the review said. You had break-fast?"

"No, I was considering waiting for lunch."

"How about brunch? I'll take you to the Breakers."

"Isn't that a hotel?"

"Yes, and it has a nice beach club."

"Am I dressed properly?"

"Very." She stood up. "I'll get into some real clothes." She put down the book and walked off toward her cabin.

Stone sat down and picked up the book. He read a couple of pages, and by the time she returned, he had read thirty. "You're right," he said, "it starts well." He looked up at her. "You look wonderful."

"Thank you, sir." She was wearing a yellow shift that set off her tan.

They walked through the main house, and as they were about to get into her car, a small procession of Mercedes convertibles pulled into the driveway behind them, and a man got out of one and came toward them, carrying a clipboard.

"Where could I find Mr. Shames?" he asked.

"He's on his way to Palm Beach, but he won't be arriving until this afternoon."

"Are you Ms. Hodges?"

"I am."

"Oh, good. You can sign for the cars."

She looked at the three convertibles. "Sign for them?"

"I'm delivering them from the dealer," the

man said. "Mr. Shames ordered them some time ago."

"Sure, I'll sign," Callie said, and did so. "Just leave the keys in them."

"They're all registered. You want me to show you how everything works?"

"We'll figure it out," she said, getting into her car. She pulled out of the drive and headed toward the beach.

"Thad has bought *three* Mercedes convertibles?"

"He does things like that. Come to think of it, he mentioned this a few weeks ago, and I had forgotten. He bought them for himself and the guests on the yacht to use."

"I'm unaccustomed to people who buy expensive cars three at a time."

"Well, if you're going to work for Thad, you'd better get used to that sort of thing."

"Actually, my work here is nearly done," Stone said. "I thought I'd fly home tomorrow."

She glanced at him. "Whatever your work was, it seems to have been conducted in restaurants. You haven't been anywhere else here, have you?"

"I guess I haven't," Stone replied, "and you're right."

"Can you tell me about it now?"

"Afraid not."

"This is all very mysterious."

"It isn't, really, or at least, it wasn't until I got here."

"This has to have something to do with the lady in the restaurant the other night."

"Could be."

"What's her name again?"

"Elizabeth Harding."

"That wasn't what you told me the other night. It was Alice, or something like that."

"Allison. Allison Manning."

"Oh, yeah, Paul Manning's wife."

"Widow." Then it occurred to Stone that she wasn't Manning's widow, since he was still alive. He made a mental note to think about that later.

A guard let them through a gate and they drove down a narrow road beside a golf course.

"The Breakers has golf, tennis, the beach, the works," Callie said. She parked the car. "Come on, I'll show you the inside of the place before we eat." She led the way into a huge, twin-towered building and into a lobby that looked like some part of an Italianate cathedral.

"Jesus," Stone said.

"Yeah. It was built by Henry Flagler, the railroad magnate, who seems to have built just about everything on the east coast of Florida. Come on, let's get some lunch." She led him out of the hotel and through another security gate, where she flashed a photo ID. A minute later, they were seated on a broad terrace, overlooking a huge swimming pool and the sea.

The sun shone brightly, but the breeze made it cool, and Stone put on his sweater.

"You dress well," she said.

"Thanks. So do you."

"Are your suits, by any chance, made by Doug Hayward?"

"Yes. How did you know?"

"I've met a number of men who go to him, and I dragged Thad in there once and made him have a suit made. Doug's a nice man, isn't he?"

"I've never met him."

"Oh? How can he make your clothes without meeting you?"

"I inherited a lot of stuff from a friend who died last year. It was all from Hayward."

They ordered lunch.

"Nice friend," she said.

"Well, I've known his wife for a while. She insisted I take the clothes. In fact, she just shipped them to me and said I could send them to the Goodwill, if I didn't want them. She was afraid they'd end up in some celebrity auction."

"Celebrity? Who was he?"

"Your favorite movie star, Vance Calder."

"Holy mackerel. I've been dining with Vance Calder's clothes?"

"You have, indeed."

"Who killed Vance Calder, anyway?"

"Good question. There were suspects, but no conviction."

Their lunch came, and Stone dove into a chicken Caesar salad. "How much time do you spend here?" Stone asked.

"Quite a lot, it seems. Thad does more entertaining here than in New York, so I've just camped out on the yacht."

"Does he have a New York apartment?"

"He keeps that suite you saw at the Four Seasons."

Stone shook his head.

"Yes, I know, it's a lot of money. Thad would really prefer to live in hotels full-time, but he thought he ought to have a home somewhere, so he bought the Palm Beach house. I think he bought it as much for dockage for the yacht as for the house, but he's got a big-time designer doing the place up. There's a warehouse in West Palm already bursting with stuff that's ready to move in, as soon as the builders are gone."

"Which is when?"

"Shouldn't be long, now. What will happen is, the painters will finish, and the next day a parade of moving vans will arrive, and by nightfall, the place will be furnished."

Stone laughed. "When I think of how long it took me to get settled in my house."

"And where is your house?"

"I inherited one in Turtle Bay from a great-aunt, and I spent a couple of years renovating it. Did a lot of the work myself."

"You seem to inherit everything — clothes, houses."

"Just those things, nothing else."

"What sort of work did you do on your house?"

"Carpentry, mostly, but a little of everything."

"And where did you learn to be a carpenter?"

"Same place you learned to cook: at my father's knee."

"Oh, right, I forgot; he was a cabinetmaker."

"He was more than that, really; he was a kind of artist in wood."

Somewhere, a cell phone rang. Callie picked up her straw handbag and rummaged in it, finally coming up with a phone. "Hello? Oh, hi. Where are you? Okay, I'll be back at the house by the time you get there. Oh, and the cars came. The Mercedes convertibles? Remember? See you shortly." She hung up. "That was Thad. He's just landed." She laughed. "He'd forgotten all about ordering the cars. Come on, eat up and let's get back."

Stone ate up, wondering about the kind of man who could order three Mercedeses, then forget about it. The longer he hung around Thad Shames, the more bizarre things got.

11

Stone and Callie arrived back at the house simultaneously with Thad Shames, who climbed out of the back of a limo and tossed two briefcases to Juanito.

"Hey, Callie, hey, Stone!" Shames called out.

"Hey, boss," Callie said. She pointed at the convertibles. "There are your cars."

Shames looked them over. "Nice," he said. He bent over, removed the keys and tossed them to Stone. "Use it while you're here," he said.

Stone walked along with him toward the house. "Actually, I was hoping to get a lift back to New York with you on Sunday," Stone said. "Not much more I can do here."

"Sorry, I'm headed to the Coast on Sunday," Shames replied. "Why don't you stick around for a few days and relax a bit? Callie could use the company, and I can tell she likes you. You got anything urgent waiting for you in New York?"

"Nothing that couldn't wait a few days, I guess," Stone admitted.

"It's settled, then."

They walked through the house, and Shames inspected the work done on the central hallway.

"Oh," he said to Callie, "I think we'll have cocktails and dinner in the house. Big buffet, okay?"

"But Thad, the house isn't finished being painted," Callie replied.

"It will be by morning," he said.

"But there's no furniture."

"It's on its way; I called from the airplane. The painters will work straight through the night, the furniture comes at eight A.M., and tomorrow evening we'll turn our party into a housewarming."

"Whatever you say, boss."

"It's black tie, right?"

"That's what I put on the invitations."

"How many acceptances?"

"Fifty couples, give or take."

"Nice-sized group. Feed them well."

"I thought Maine lobster, a bourride — that's a garlicky French fish stew — and tenderloin of beef for the carnivores. Lots of other stuff, too."

"Whatever you say, Callie." They had reached the yacht, and Shames led the way aboard, followed by Juanito with the two briefcases. He had apparently brought no other luggage. "Let's talk a minute, Stone," Shames said, beckoning to him to follow.

Stone followed him to the owner's cabin, the first time he had seen it. They walked into a large, gorgeously furnished sitting room. Juanito deposited the two briefcases on a big desk and left.

"What do you think of *Toscana*?" Shames asked.

"She's a dream," Stone replied. "I've never seen anything like her."

"Neither has anybody else," Shames laughed. "She's my favorite thing. If I had to give up everything but one, I'd keep her."

"I can understand that."

"I wish we had time for a cruise out to the Bahamas this weekend, but I really do have to be on the Coast by Sunday night. We're having another announcement shindig out there on Monday morning."

"Just what is this new technology your company is going to make?" Stone asked.

"It consists of a circuitboard that replaces the modem in a computer, plus some extraordinary software we're developing for both e-companies and users that gives every customer what very nearly amounts to a T-1 Internet connection over ordinary telephone lines, twenty-four hours a day, for a monthly fee of less than fifty dollars."

Stone knew that a T-1 was the fastest Internet connection, and that it required a special phone line to be installed. "That's very impressive," he said.

"Don't worry, I've already allocated your shares. Bill Eggers will buy them for you the day before the initial public offering."

"Thank you, Thad. That's very generous."

"You'll be tempted to sell them the first week, but don't; hang on to them."

"I'll take your advice."

Juanito appeared with two frosty gin and tonics. They touched glasses and drank.

"Now," Shames said, "tell me about Liz Harding."

"I had lunch with her yesterday," Stone replied. "She was apologetic about rushing away from Easthampton, but she had to come back here."

"She lives here?"

"Here and in Houston. She's a widow, not a divorcée."

"How long?"

"Last year sometime. She seems excited about seeing you again."

Shames grinned like a schoolboy. "That sounds good."

"Thad, I have a lot else to tell you about Liz," Stone said, adopting a serious mien.

"That sounds bad."

"It's not, necessarily, but there are things that, since you're my client, I have to tell you about her."

"I'll just shut up and listen," Shames said.

Stone started at the beginning and told Shames the story of Allison/Liz — all of it, leaving out nothing except his own affair with Allison. When he had finished, he polished off the rest of his drink, sat back and waited for questions. There weren't any.

"That's extraordinary," Shames said. He got to his feet. "I think I'll have a nap before dinner.

Will you excuse me?"

Stone got up. "Of course. Thad, I want to be sure you understand about the husband, Paul Manning."

"Ex-husband, isn't he?"

"Ex–Paul Manning. She doesn't know what he's calling himself these days."

"Well, if he's legally dead, she's twice-widowed, isn't she?"

"In a manner of speaking. I'm not sure what the legal ramifications are. I've never run into anything quite like this before."

"She considers herself single?"

"Yes, she does."

"Then as far as I'm concerned, she's single, and that's an end to it."

"It is," Stone said, "unless Paul Manning turns up. I think you have to consider him a dangerous man."

"Well, he doesn't sound stupid, so I don't think he's dangerous. He's gotten away with a triple murder and major insurance fraud, so I think he has to count himself lucky, don't you?"

"I suppose."

"Don't worry about Manning, Stone. He's not going to risk screwing up his life by exposing his own past."

"I hope you're right," Stone said.

"You will pick up Liz tomorrow night? I have a lot on my plate, what with all these guests coming."

"Of course."

85

"Thanks." Shames disappeared into the bedroom and closed the door behind him.

Stone went back to his own cabin. Thad was right, of course. Paul Manning wasn't stupid, and, if Stone could just find him and talk to him, he'd be a rich man from the settlement Allison/Liz wanted to make with him. And then, he thought, sighing, he'd be free of this whole business, Thad Shames would have the girl of his dreams, and everybody could get on with the business of living happily ever after.

Sometime after midnight, Stone was wakened from a deep sleep by someone crawling into bed with him. He had been dreaming, and what was happening seemed an extension of his dream.

"Arrington?" he said sleepily.

"Whoa!" Callie said, sitting up and crossing her legs.

Stone shook himself fully awake. "Callie? What's happening?"

"You were about to get made love to," she said, "but you spoke to the wrong girl."

"I'm sorry. I was dreaming. I thought you were . . . somebody else at first."

"Stone, I know very well that Arrington is Vance Calder's wife — rather, widow. The whole world knows. Why would you be dreaming of her crawling into bed with you?"

"I don't remember exactly what I was dreaming," Stone said, sitting up in bed and dragging a couple of pillows behind him.

"That doesn't answer my question," she said. "But if it's none of my business, tell me so, and I'll get out of here."

"No, no," he said, stroking her hair. "Arrington and I were . . . close, before she married Vance. We don't have a relationship now, at least not a very good one."

"You're sure about this? I don't want to intrude where I'm not wanted."

He pulled her head down onto his shoulder, and she stretched out beside him. "You're wanted," he said.

She ran a hand down his belly until it stopped at his penis. She held it in her hand. "Oh!" she exclaimed, "it's alive!"

"Alive and well," he replied.

She rolled on top of him, sat up and guided him inside her. She bent down and put her lips close to his ear. "You'd better be telling the truth about Arrington Calder," she whispered, "or this will never happen again."

12

Stone was awakened by conflicting smells — one chemical, one culinary. He sat up in bed in time to see Callie enter his cabin, bearing a covered tray, kicking the door shut behind her.

"Smells good," he said. "But what's the other odor?"

"Paint," she replied. "The painters finished their work last night, and all the windows in the house are open. The decorators and moving people are in there now, working like beavers." She set the tray on the bed between them and whipped off the cover. "Voilà!" she said. "Brie omelettes!"

Stone picked up a plate and dug in. "Fantastic!" He sipped some orange juice.

"We've got the yacht to ourselves this morning," she said. "Thad has already made a lot of phone calls and had a business breakfast aboard and has taken a party into town for some shopping."

"I can't believe he's putting that house together in a day," Stone said.

"Oh, he's had the designers shopping for a year. They've planned out every room, right down to the pictures on the walls."

"It took me a year to get my house to that state."

"You must not have been newly superrich," she said.

"Good guess."

"What are your plans for today?"

"Plans? Me? I never have plans. I just sit back and let you and Thad do it for me. I don't think I've made a decision of any kind since I met the two of you. What do you have planned for me today?"

"Absolutely nothing. I plan to get some sun, do some reading and rest up for tonight."

"Oh, that's right. You're going to be pretty busy, aren't you?"

"Not if the caterers don't want to get fired. They're turning up at five, and I'll show them the kitchens and where to set up. After that, they'd better not bother me because I'll be partying."

"Well, I think your plan for the day sounds good. I'll join you, if that's all right."

"It's all right," she said. "By the way, do you need to rent a dinner jacket? I know a place."

"Nope. I brought one, just in case."

"Always prepared, aren't you?" She finished off her omelette, took his plate, poured him a large mug of coffee and stood up. "I'll get this stuff back to the galley, and I'll see you on the afterdeck, later."

"Okay." Stone watched her go, then he got up,

showered, put on a swimsuit, grabbed a terry robe from the closet and walked back to the fantail. Callie was already stretched out on a chaise, wearing only her bikini bottom, reading.

"Hi, want something good to read?"

"Sure."

She tossed him a book. "I just finished it. It's great."

Stone looked at the book: *Tumult,* by Frederick James. "Oh, yes, I read some pages yesterday. Starts well."

"Ends well, too. Enjoy."

Stone read through the morning, broke for sandwiches and closed the book at five.

"Good?"

"Good."

"Thad liked it, too. He had me send the author an invitation to the party tonight, but we never heard from him. I guess his publisher didn't forward it." She looked at her watch. "I've got to get over to the house and brief the caterers," she said. "I'll see you at the party."

"Think I'll have a nap," Stone said. He went back to his cabin and slept for half an hour, then he shaved, showered and dressed in Vance Calder's ecru raw silk dinner jacket, a silk evening shirt and black tie. He walked back to the house and through the central hallway, dodging frantic caterers and decorators, got into his borrowed Mercedes E430 convertible and drove into town. Shortly, he pulled up in front of Liz Harding's house. He walked across the driveway, his evening shoes crunching on the pea gravel. The doorbell was set in an intercom box. He pressed it and it made a noise like a telephone ringing.

"Hello?"

"It's Stone."

"Oh, Stone. The door's unlocked; let yourself in, and I'll be down in a few minutes."

"Okay." She clicked off, and Stone opened the door and walked into the house. It was quite beautiful, Queen Anne in style, not terribly large, but made of good materials — marble floors, walnut paneling, beautiful moldings. He found the living room and continued to explore, ending up in a handsome little library with many leather-bound volumes. A small bar had been set up on a butler's tray, and he poured himself some chilled mineral water, then he wandered around the room. A collection of silver-framed photographs rested on the mantel, and Stone inspected them. They were all of Liz Harding with a handsome, silver-haired man, clearly Winston Harding, taken in various cities and on various beaches.

"He was handsome, wasn't he?" she said.

Stone turned and found her standing in the doorway, wearing a white silk dress and a gorgeous diamond necklace, with matching earrings. Her hair was blond again.

"Yes, he was, and you are very beautiful," Stone said.

She came and gave him a little hug, careful not to muss her makeup. "And so are you," she said. "That's the most beautiful dinner jacket I've ever seen."

"Thank you," Stone replied. He decided to stop telling people that the clothes were Vance Calder's, and to start taking credit himself.

"Would you like a drink before we go?" she asked.

"I think we're already fashionably late," he replied. "Why don't we just go to the party?"

She took his arm, and he led her out to the car.

"Drive slowly," she said. "The hair."

"I like it blond."

"So do I. It's my natural color."

"I remember."

"Stone!" she said, laughing and blushing.

"That wasn't what I meant, but I remember that, too."

"You're awful."

"I know."

"Still, we had some good times, didn't we? You were getting over a girl, as I recall."

"And you were helping."

"I did what I could," she said.

Stone drove slowly through the town and finally turned into the driveway of Thad Shames's house. Or tried to; there were half a dozen cars ahead of him. Music wafted through the open windows. Finally, he gave the keys to a valet and extracted Liz from the car. He was beginning to think of her as Liz by now. They walked through the open doors of the house and into the living room. A big band was playing Rodgers & Hart at the other end, and people were dancing.

"How spectacular!" Liz said. "I mean, in spectacular good taste!"

"It certainly is," Stone agreed. "Would you believe that twenty-four hours ago, this was an empty, unpainted house?"

"No, I would not," she replied. She sniffed the air. "Still, there is that faint odor."

Stone spotted Thad Shames across the room, towering over his guests. "I think there's someone over there who'd like to see you," he said, taking her arm and leading her across the room.

Shames spotted them coming and went to meet them, or rather, Liz.

"Well, hello," he said, taking both her hands and kissing her on both cheeks.

"Will you excuse me?" Stone asked. They didn't seem to notice, so he left them and made his way across the large room to where the bar had been set up on a long table. "A gin and tonic," Stone said to the bartender.

"Coming up," the bartender replied.

Stone saw Callie across the room and waved to her. She waved back, but seemed to have no interest in joining him.

"Here you are," the bartender said.

"Thank you," Stone replied, accepting the drink.

"You know," a voice behind him said, "I think you may look better in that dinner jacket than the original owner did."

Stone turned around and found Arrington Carter Calder standing there, looking gorgeous. Before she put her arms around his neck and kissed him, he could see, over her shoulder, Callie Hodges making her way toward them.

13

Her lips melted into Stone's, and her body was against his, and only the thought of Callie approaching made him take hold of Arrington's shoulders and hold her back. He smiled broadly for effect. "It's good to see you, Arrington."

Then Callie was upon them. "Well, Stone," she said, "who's this?"

"Callie, I'd like you to meet Arrington Calder," Stone said, trying not to dab at his lips.

"Well, clearly, you two have met before tonight," Callie said. "How do you do, Arrington?"

"Very well, Callie. I believe we talked on the phone this morning."

"Yes. Thad very much wanted to have you here. Have you seen him yet?"

"Yes, when I arrived."

"I hope your room is comfortable."

"It is, indeed, though it smells a little of paint."

"We apologize," Callie said. "I understand you and Stone know each other."

"We're old friends," Arrington said.

"Yes," Stone echoed, wanting somehow to guide this conversation, if he could. "And how did you manage to get Arrington here so quickly, Callie?"

"We sent the airplane for her this morning," Callie said sweetly.

"Twenty-four hours ago," Arrington said, "who knew I'd be in Palm Beach tonight?"

"Yes," Stone replied, casting a sharp glance at Callie. "Who knew?"

Callie suddenly seemed flustered. "Please excuse me, I have to welcome somebody," she said. She had not even glanced at the door, but she made off in that direction.

"And how do you know Thad Shames?" Stone asked.

"Vance and I met him in Los Angeles early last year. Vance was an early investor in some of his companies. And how do you happen to be here, Stone?"

"I've been doing some work for Thad, which involved coming to Palm Beach."

"What sort of work?"

"I'm afraid it's confidential."

"Show me around the house, will you?" she said.

"We'll explore together," Stone said. "This is the first time I've been inside, except for the central hallway. I'm staying on the yacht, out back."

"Then follow me," Arrington said, taking his hand and starting out. She led him among handsome couples of various ages, beautifully dressed and coiffed. They walked across the central hall and into a large, two-story library, stocked with matched sets of books, some of them, apparently, quite old.

They found the dining room, which had been set up for a buffet, then climbed the central stairs to the second floor.

"Where are we going?" Stone asked.

"Just exploring," Arrington replied, towing him along. "That must be the master suite," she said, pointing at a large set of doors. They walked on farther. "Let's see what a bedroom looks like," she said, suddenly opening a door, tugging him inside and closing it behind her.

They were in a large, sumptuously furnished room with a huge, canopied bed, elaborate draperies and antique furniture. Stone saw a stack of luggage in a corner, and as they walked toward the windows, he saw the initials *ACC* stamped on the cases. "This is your room?" he asked.

"Oh, look, there's the yacht," she said, standing at the window. The moon was coming up and a streak of its light fell on the vessel. In the foreground, the gardens were lit with Japanese lanterns. She turned, took Stone's face in her hands and kissed him again.

Stone felt her against him, the familiar curves of her body, the cool tips of her fingers against his skin, and he responded appropriately.

"Oh, I can feel you," she whispered, moving her hips forward. She tugged at his bow tie, and it came undone.

Suddenly, Stone was uncomfortable, and he

held her away. "I can't do this," he said, "not with the way things have been between us."

"I'd like for things to be as they were," she said.

"A lot has happened since then."

"Most of it to me," she said.

"I'm aware of that. But every time something happens to you, it seems to happen to me, too."

"Poor baby," she cooed.

"Which brings up the matter of Peter," Stone said.

She stepped back from him. "Do we have to talk about that now?"

"Now is as good a time as any, and better than most."

"Why do you have to be certain who Peter's father is?" she asked. "I'm not sure *I* want to know."

"I don't understand that, but I'm sure you can understand why I want to know," Stone said. "If you put your mind to it."

She turned away from him. "Men!"

"Do you find it so odd that a man would want to know if he had a son?"

"I don't want to talk about it anymore," she said. "Let's go back downstairs." She headed for the door.

Stone followed close behind her. Two couples were coming down the hall toward them, apparently touring the house. They smiled knowingly at Stone as they passed. What the hell was that about? he wondered, then he realized that his tie was untied and hurriedly retied it. He ran down the stairs after Arrington, caught up with her on the landing overlooking the living room and stopped her.

"Listen to me," he said. "You and I cannot have a normal relationship until we settle the question of Peter."

"Why can't you just leave it alone?" she said. "I really don't want to know."

"Then you don't want to know me," Stone replied.

She ran down the stairs, and he followed more slowly. People were looking up at them, among the crowd, Callie. Stone let Arrington make her way across the room, and he turned toward the bar and ordered another drink.

A moment later, Callie appeared at his side. "Oh, your tie is all mussed," she said. "Let me fix it for you." She tugged at the bow until she was satisfied. "Well, it didn't take the two of you long, did it?"

"What?" Stone asked, distracted, then he caught her meaning. "Oh, don't be ridiculous."

"Am I being ridiculous?" she asked. "A woman scorned, I suppose."

"Scorned? You invited her here, didn't you? Not Thad."

"I suggested it to Thad," she said. "I wanted to know where I stood."

"If you wanted to know where you stood, you could have simply asked me," Stone said, trying to keep the anger from his voice. "There was no need to send a jet to Virginia and haul her down here; no need to pull the scabs off old wounds."

"I'm sorry," Callie said sheepishly.

"You should be. You shouldn't interfere in other people's lives, especially when you don't have a clue what's going on."

"Listen, Stone," Callie said, now sounding angry herself. "I don't know about you, but I don't sleep casually with people, especially when there's something else going on in their lives. If you and Arrington are in love with each other, I'd rather know it now, not later."

"I didn't bring her down here," Stone said, "*you* did. I'd be grateful if you'd stop meddling in my life." He set down his drink, turned and walked out of the room. He made his way past couples in the gardens, then to the yacht, where he made himself a large drink at the bar in the saloon and sat on the afterdeck, drinking it, watching the moonlight on the water, trying to banish the thought of both Arrington and Callie from his mind.

Later, the music stopped and the sound of slamming car doors and diminishing voices told him the party was ending. He knew he couldn't sleep for a while, so he made himself another drink.

Then Juanito was at his elbow with a cordless phone. "Mr. Barrington, Mr. Thad is calling for you," he said.

Stone took the phone. "Hello?"

"Stone, please come over to Liz's house right

away," Shames said. "I've already called the police."

Stone started to ask why, but Shames had already hung up.

14

Stone drove quickly, but not too quickly, through the streets of Palm Beach. It was well after midnight, now, and traffic was light, but he did not wish to attract the attention of a traffic cop at this moment. He swung into West Indies Drive and, shortly, into the driveway of Liz's house. One of Thad Shames's Mercedes convertibles was parked outside and, beside it, what was obviously an unmarked police car. The front door of the house stood wide open.

Stone walked quickly inside and looked around. No one was in sight. "Hello!" he called out.

"In here," came a man's voice through the living room and to his left. Stone followed the sound and arrived in the study. Shames and Liz, who appeared to be unharmed, and a man in a police officer's uniform with stars on the shoulders stood in the center of the room, which was a mess. All the pictures on the mantel had been swept onto the floor, a large mirror on one wall had been shattered and much of the furniture had been overturned, reducing some small porcelain figurines to shards.

"What's happened?" Stone asked.

"We're not sure," Shames replied. "Stone, this is Chief Dan Griggs of the Palm Beach Police Department. Chief, this is my and Mrs. Harding's attorney, Stone Barrington."

The chief offered his hand. "I thought I knew all the attorneys in town," he said. "Good to meet you, Mr. Barrington."

Stone shook the man's hand. "And you, Chief. I'm based in New York; that's why we haven't met. What's happened here tonight?"

Shames spoke up. "Liz and I arrived to find the front door open and the place a mess."

"The whole place? The living room looked all right."

"I've had a look around," the chief said. "This is the only room that was disturbed."

"Anything missing?" Stone asked.

Liz spoke up. "I can't find anything gone, just broken."

"What about the door? Was it forced?"

Griggs shook his head. "Either it wasn't locked, or somebody had a key."

"I'm afraid it may not have been locked," Liz said sheepishly. "I tend to forget. Anyway, Chief Griggs and his men take such good care of us all that it hardly seems necessary."

"I thank you, Mrs. Harding," the chief said, obviously pleased, "but we'd really prefer you to lock your doors."

"I'll make a point of it from now on."

"So this is vandalism?" Stone asked.

"Looks that way to me," Griggs replied. "Nothing taken, only this room messed up; nothing else to call it."

"Chief, have you had other incidents like this in town?"

Griggs shook his head. "We might get some spray paint on a building or a bridge sometimes — teenagers, you know — but I can't recall an incident of vandalism in a private home, unless it was connected to a burglary."

"No known perpetrators of this sort of thing around town?"

"None in our files."

"Chief, why don't you and I take a walk through the house. Liz, Thad, will you excuse us for a couple of minutes?"

"Of course," they said together.

Stone and the chief left the room, and Stone led him toward the stairs. "Let's take a look up here."

Griggs followed him, but at the top, stopped. "I've already walked through here with Mrs. Harding," he said.

"I know," Stone replied, "but I wanted to make you aware of a situation."

"Go right ahead," Griggs said.

"Mrs. Harding was formerly married to a man named Paul Manning, a well-known writer. Her name was Allison Manning, at the time."

"Why'd she change it to Elizabeth?"

"To get away from Manning."

"And you think he did this?"

"Very possibly. The photographs on the mantel were of Mrs. Harding and her late husband. Looks like a jealous rage to me."

Griggs nodded and wrote something in his notebook. "Mr. Barrington, your name is familiar. Were you ever on the police force in New York?"

Stone nodded. "For fourteen years."

"I've got it," the chief said. "The Sasha Nijinsky case."

"That's right. I retired about that time; disability."

"You look pretty healthy to me."

"Bullet in the knee."

"Hope you got the son of a bitch."

"My partner did."

"Allison Manning," the chief mused. "Something about an island?"

"That's right. She was accused of murdering her husband, but, of course, he wasn't dead."

"Saw something about it on *Sixty Minutes*."

"Yes. It got a lot of press at the time."

"You're a pretty high-profile lawyer up there, aren't you?"

"Not when I can help it."

"You got a card?"

Stone handed him one, and he pocketed it. "About this Paul Manning. You think we're going to hear from him again?"

"I wouldn't be surprised."

"You think he might harm Mrs. Harding?"

105

"That's a possibility."

"I'll look into it."

"Chief, I hope you'll keep all this background information in confidence. I'm sure Mrs. Harding wouldn't want people to connect her with a past incident that was very traumatic for her."

"We have a lot of well-known people in Palm Beach, and I run a very discreet department," Griggs said.

"I'm sure you do, and I appreciate your discretion."

"Can we go back downstairs, now?"

"Yes, I just wanted to discuss all this with you privately."

They started down the stairs.

"Tell you what," Griggs said. "I'll put a man on the house for a while. Nobody'll notice him, not even Mrs. Harding."

"I'd be grateful for that," Stone said.

"Of course, I can't keep people on this forever, if nothing happens."

"I understand completely. I'm going to suggest to Mr. Shames that he invite Mrs. Harding to stay at his house. He's going out of town for a while, but I'm sure his staff could make her comfortable there."

"Good idea," Griggs said.

"Maybe your man could stay in the house?"

"With Mrs. Harding's permission, sure."

"I'll have a word with her."

They reached the study.

"Liz is going to come back to the house with

me," Shames said. "She'll stay with us, at least until I get back from the Coast."

"Good idea," Stone said. "Liz, the chief would like to have one of his men stay in the house. Is that all right?"

"Oh, yes," Liz said. "That would be wonderful." She went to a desk drawer, found a spare key and gave it to the chief, along with the alarm code.

"Well, if you folks don't need me anymore, I'll be going," the chief said. "I'll have a man here in half an hour."

Hands were shaken all around, and the chief departed.

"I'd better pack some things," Liz said, and left the room.

Shames turned to Stone. "It's this Manning guy, isn't it?"

"Very likely," Stone said. "This has none of the markings of a random crime — nothing taken, only one room disturbed."

"So, he's tracked her down."

"It looks that way."

"I'm glad you're staying on for a while, Stone. I feel better knowing you're here to take care of her."

"I'll let Woodman and Weld know."

"I'll call Bill Eggers and arrange everything."

"Thank you."

Shames was quiet for a moment. "Stone," he said finally, "you think he's going to try to kill her?"

"I think if that's what he had in mind, he'd already have tried. This was obviously to frighten her."

"It worked," Thad said. "She was a mess for a few minutes after we got here. There are some guns on the boat. I'll have Juanito make them available to you."

"I hope I won't need a gun," Stone said. "But you never know."

Stone followed Thad and Liz back to the house, and when they were safely inside, he walked back to the yacht and his cabin. His adrenaline was still a little high, and he got out of his dinner jacket and the rest of his clothes and into a hot shower. He was drying himself when he heard a soft knock at the cabin door. He got into a robe and went to answer it.

He opened the door to find Callie Hodges standing there, in a silk dressing gown, holding a 9mm semiautomatic pistol.

15

Stone stared at the armed young woman. "My money or my life?"

"Don't be ridiculous," she said, handing him the gun. "Thad wanted you to have this. I can't imagine why. What's happened?"

"Nothing serious," he replied. He checked that the safety was on, then tossed the gun onto the bed.

"May I come in for a minute?" she asked.

"Sure." He stood back and allowed her to enter.

She went and sat on the sofa before the fireplace. "Would you like a fire?" she asked. "It's cool tonight."

"All right." He went and sat on the sofa beside her, keeping some distance between them.

She found a box of long matches, checked to be sure the flue was open and lit the fire. The kindling caught, and the fire blazed cheerily. She switched off the ceiling light and sat down on the sofa again. "I want to apologize to you for my behavior today."

Stone didn't say anything. He was still annoyed with her.

"I was interfering in your life without any idea of the consequences. I hope having Arrington here didn't make things worse between you."

"They were already pretty bad," he replied. "I suppose I had a chance to make it up with her, but I didn't like the terms."

"You accept my apology?"

"I do," he said, his voice softening, "and I appreciate it."

"You don't have to explain anything to me. I don't have the right to ask."

"I'll explain anyway," Stone said. "I told you about my trip to the islands, where I met Allison Manning, now Liz Harding, but I didn't tell you that, at the time, Arrington and I were living together in New York. We were supposed to fly down together, but she was delayed and missed the flight, and then there was a snowstorm, and she was stuck there for another day. She was a magazine writer, and the *New Yorker* asked her to do a profile of Vance Calder, whom she already knew. She accepted, and the next thing I knew, she had gone back to California with him, and they were married, almost overnight."

"That must have come as a shock."

"It did. A bigger shock came later, when she told me she was pregnant."

"With your child or Vance's?"

"She didn't know. It could have been either of us. In due course, she had the child, I supplied a blood sample, and so did Vance. She called to say that the boy was Vance's, and that was that."

"I'm sorry."

"There's more. When Vance died, I went out to help Arrington handle the situation, and in so doing, I learned that Vance may have been in control of the test results."

"So, you're the father?"

"It may be that the results showed that Vance really was, but if not, he could have had the report changed."

"So you may be the father and you may not?"

"Right."

"So why don't you do the test again?"

"Arrington doesn't want it done."

"Why not?"

"I don't know."

"You'd think she'd want to know for sure who the father of the child is."

"You'd think."

"Who does he look like?"

"He looks like both Vance and my father." She laughed. "I'm sorry, but it's a little . . ."

"Yes, I know, funny." He smiled himself.

"So that's how you left it with Arrington?"

"That's it."

"Let me ask you something," she said. "If the test were done, and the child turned out to be yours, what would you want to do about it?"

"I'm not sure, except I'd want him to know, eventually, and I'd like to have some part in his life."

"What about Arrington? Wouldn't you want her back?"

"Arrington and I seem to be . . . I think the expression is 'star-crossed.' She's a volatile person, and every time we have seemed to be getting close to each other again, something happens to blow it up."

"And that's what happened tonight?"

"I told her that if she didn't want to know who the boy's father is, then she didn't want to know me."

"Then how, may I ask, did your tie get mussed up?"

Stone laughed. "Arrington had just pulled it loose when I made my little speech, and she stalked out."

"Out of where?"

"Out of her room."

"And how did you get to her room?"

"On foot."

Callie laughed again.

"I thought we were touring the house. I didn't know where her room was."

"So you were led down the garden path?"

"In a manner of speaking."

Callie stroked his cheek with the backs of her fingers. "Poor Stone," she said. "Between Arrington and me, you've had a rough time tonight, haven't you?"

"Beset from all sides," Stone said, kissing her fingertips.

"Can I make it up to you?" she asked, sliding

across the sofa toward him.

"You can try," Stone said.

She put her hand on his leg under the robe and slid it up his thigh. "How's this?" she asked.

"It's a start," he replied.

She untied his robe and took it away, then untied her own robe, letting it drop to the floor. She pressed him back on the sofa, knelt beside him and kissed his penis.

Stone made a little noise.

She took him into her mouth and played gently with him, rubbing a nipple, getting the response she wanted at both ends. She held his testicles in one hand, doing inventive things with her tongue, then she stopped for a moment. "This is just for you," she said. "You don't have to wait for me."

"I want you now," Stone said, panting a little.

"Maybe later," she said, taking him into her mouth again. She pushed his legs apart and pulled his knees up, then began exploring the cleft of his buttocks with her fingers.

"I'm going to explode soon," Stone said.

"Not yet," she replied, then began again. She moved her head slowly up and down, beginning with the tip, then pressing until nearly the whole length of him had disappeared.

Stone couldn't find words, only noises.

Then Stone exploded, and she stayed with him for another minute, prolonging the orgasm, keeping him going until he could only cry out and collapse back onto the sofa.

Finally, cradling his testicles in a hand, she laid her head on his belly and kissed it softly. "How are you?" she asked.

"I can't make a fist," he replied.

"You hardly need to," she laughed.

They remained that way for a moment, then she climbed onto the sofa with him and lay on top of him, nestling her head into his shoulder.

"There's something else I should tell you," he said, "just so you won't think I'm keeping anything from you."

"I'm listening."

"When I heard about Arrington and Vance — I was on the island of St. Marks, at the time — Allison Manning and I had . . ."

She raised her head. "Each other?"

"Yes. I was angry with Arrington, and Allison . . ."

"Was there?"

"Yes."

She laid her head back down. "Well, Allison is somewhere down the road, and I'm here, so just stay away from her."

"That may be difficult," he said.

"What do you mean?"

"Somebody broke into her house this evening and trashed a room. Thad has brought her back here. He's asked me to look after her while he's on the Coast."

She raised her head again. "Where's that gun?"

He pulled her head back down. "Not to worry."

"How do I know that?"

"Let me show you," he said. He rolled her onto her back and knelt beside the sofa, the way she had. With his tongue, he explored her soft fur. "How's that for reassurance?" he asked.

She pulled his head back into her lap. "It's a start," she said.

16

Stone was still sleeping soundly when he was awakened by the sound of his cabin door opening. He lifted his head and saw Callie approaching with a breakfast tray. She was fully dressed.

He sat up on his elbows. "What time is it?"

"A little after nine," she said, setting down the tray on the bed. "I've been up since six, seeing that everybody got breakfast before Thad and Arrington left for the Coast."

"They're gone?"

"Half an hour ago. After our conversation of last night I didn't think you'd want to get up early to say goodbye."

Stone laughed. "After our, ah, 'conversation' of last night, I don't know that I *could* have gotten up. I may spend the day in bed."

"I'd spend it with you, but there are some odds and ends with the painters and builders that I have to deal with. And, by the way, your friend Allison — sorry, Liz — is moving onto the yacht, into Thad's cabin."

"Why?"

"She complained that the odor of drying paint

gave her a headache. I'd like to give her a permanent one."

"What have you got against Liz Harding?"

"Her past with you, of course, and now she'll
be right down the corridor. See that your door is
securely locked before retiring, please."

"Then how will you get in?"

"I have a key," she said smugly, "and I know
how to use it."

"Fear not, you've rendered me incapable with
another woman. I'm not sure I can walk."

"Don't walk, eat," she said, stuffing a croissant into his mouth. She walked to the door,
then turned back. "You're going to need your
strength," she said. "See you tonight."

Stone bit off a bite of the croissant and lay
back on the bed, chewing.

At mid-morning, showered, shaved and
dressed, Stone ventured out of his cabin and
found Liz Harding sitting on an afterdeck sofa,
reading a book about Palm Beach.

"Good morning," he said. "Feeling better today?"

"Feeling safer," she said, "since I'm here with
you." Her voice was kittenish.

"You're not here with me," he said. "You're
here with Thad."

"But you'll protect me while he's gone."

"Yes, but I'm not expecting anything unto-
ward to happen. Are you?"

She closed her book and tossed it onto the

coffee table. "I don't know anymore," she said. "It took me a year after I left St. Marks before I began to relax, and the marriage to Winston before I felt really safe. But after last night . . ."

"It may just have been some teenaged vandal," Stone said. "I wouldn't worry about it."

"I hope you're right," she replied. "Now, I want to do some shopping, and I don't think I'd feel safe unless you were with me."

"All right, I'll tag along. Since I'm staying longer than I'd planned, I could probably use a few things myself."

"I'll get my purse," she said.

They found a parking spot on Worth Avenue and strolled slowly down the street. Stone glanced around occasionally, looking for anyone resembling Paul Manning. Liz had said he'd had a nose job, so Stone concentrated on tall men. Manning was at least six-three, he remembered. Everyone he saw was comfortingly short.

He sat in the husband's chair in a shop as Liz tried on dresses, while he flipped idly through one of several Palm Beach magazines, which featured grinning people in lavish clothes, photographed at parties, and many shots of overdecorated interiors of huge houses. There were ads for Rolls-Royces and Ferraris and many for jewelry.

They went into the Polo Ralph Lauren shop, where Stone bought some extra underwear and socks, along with a spare cashmere sweater for the cool evenings he had not anticipated.

He followed Liz into a jewelry shop and looked at a Cartier Tank Francaise wristwatch, while she tried on a diamond bracelet.

"You like?" she asked, holding out her wrist.

"I like."

"I like your watch, too."

Stone gave it back to the saleslady. "It's beautiful, but . . ." The "but" was twenty grand, he thought.

Liz bought the bracelet, which came to nearly thirty thousand dollars, Stone noted. "I'll wear it for Thad, when he comes back," she said.

"When is he coming back? He didn't tell me."

"Tomorrow or the next day, depending on how his business goes."

"Don't forget to call your insurance company to put the bracelet on your policy."

"Thank you. I would have forgotten. I did call my bank about the settlement with the life insurance company. The funds will be wired to your bank today."

"Good. I'd like to get that settled as soon as possible."

"Me, too," she said.

"I'll call my office when we get back to the yacht." As he spoke, he felt his cell phone vibrate in his pocket. "Excuse me," he said, answering it. "Hello?"

"Hi, it's Joan."

"How are things in the big city?"

"Running smoothly. The bank called. Mrs.

Harding's money is in your trust account. You want me to complete the transaction with the insurance company?"

"Please."

"I'll get the wire off now, and we should have a confirmation today, I expect."

"Great. What else is happening?"

"One or two calls; I put them off. When are you coming back?"

"Thad Shames has asked me to stay on a few days. I'll let you know later in the week."

"Okay. Remember, sunshine causes skin cancer."

"Thanks for reminding me." He punched off and turned to Liz. "The money's on its way to the insurance company."

"Wonderful. Can I buy you lunch to celebrate? We can go back to Renato's."

"Sure. I liked it there."

They ate pasta and chatted. "Now that you're going to be a truly free woman, what are your plans?" he asked.

"Well, I think that depends on how it goes with Thad," she said. "So far, so good. He's very sweet . . . and virile." She smiled.

Stone laughed. "He'd have to be to keep up with you, as I recall."

"We were quite something for a short time, weren't we?"

"I guess we were, at that."

"You were the first man I'd slept with besides

120

Paul for a very long time, and I found the experience, well, liberating."

"I'm glad."

"I have the distinct impression that you're liberating Callie Hodges, at the moment."

"I didn't say that," he blustered.

"You didn't have to. I took one look at her this morning — or rather she took one look at me — and I knew. She knows we slept together, doesn't she?"

Stone nodded and sipped his wine. "I thought it best to tell her."

"You getting serious about this girl?"

"Too soon to say," Stone said, uncomfortable.

She placed her hand on his. "I'm sorry to embarrass you, Stone. It's just that I think I envy her a little. Maybe more than a little."

Stone didn't know what to say.

"But," Liz said, "we must learn to be content with our lot, mustn't we? Lord knows, I have no complaints. I was just feeling a little greedy."

"I'm flattered," Stone said.

They walked back to the car, and as Stone opened the door for Liz, he noticed that the rear tire on the curb side had gone flat. He squatted and examined it. There was a large hole in the tread, too big a hole for a slow leak. It was as if somebody had plunged a knife into it.

Stone shrugged off his jacket and tossed it into the rear seat. "I'm afraid we've got a flat," he said. "It'll just take a couple of minutes to change."

"Why don't you call the Mercedes service people?" she asked. "They'll come and change it."

"It'll only take a minute." He opened the trunk and went to work. He thought about it as he cranked the jack. Was somebody really crazy enough to slash a tire in broad daylight in the middle of Worth Avenue?

17

Stone spent the afternoon reading, and late in the day Joan Robertson called from New York.

"We've closed with the insurance company," she said, "and I've wired the funds. Want me to fax you a fully executed copy of the document?"

"Please," Stone replied. "I expect Mrs. Harding would like to have it."

"Right away." She paused. "Stone?"

"Yes?"

"There's something I think I ought to mention. It seemed like nothing, really, but I just have a feeling . . ."

"What is it?"

"You've had some phone calls the last few days, from a man who wouldn't give his name."

"What did he say?"

"He wanted to speak to you; then, when I told him you were away, he wanted to know where you were."

"Did you tell him?"

"No, I felt uneasy about it. I just told him that I'd have you call him, but he wouldn't leave a number."

"How did he sound?"

"Nice, at first, then insistent. He was very annoyed that I wouldn't tell him where you were."

"And he wouldn't leave a number?"

"No, but I nailed him on caller ID. The first two times he called from the Brooke Hotel, on Park Avenue."

"Did the readout give a room number?"

"No, just the phone number. I called it and got the hotel operator. Then, after that when he called, the caller ID didn't report a number, said it was outside the area or something."

"When were the first phone calls?"

"Thursday and Friday."

"Okay, if he calls back again, give him my cell phone number."

"You sure? I have this creepy feeling."

"I'm sure. He won't know where I am."

"Okay."

"Anything else?"

"Everything else seems normal," she said.

"Talk to you later, then." He hung up and thought about the calls for a few minutes, then he dialed the number of Bob Berman, an ex-cop who sometimes undertook investigative work for him, particularly work that Stone could pretend not to know about.

"Hello," Bob said.

"Hi, it's Stone."

"How you doing?"

"Pretty good. I'm in Florida at the moment."

"You're just trying to hurt me, aren't you?"

"Yes. You up for some work?"

"Sure. What you got?"

"I've had a couple of phone calls that are worrying Joan. The first two came from the Brooke Hotel, on Park — she got that from caller ID. You know anybody at the Brooke? Maybe somebody in security, an ex-cop?"

"Nah, not a soul. You got a room number?"

"No."

"Could the calls have come from a pay phone?"

"No, the number reported was the hotel's."

"Would the guest list for that time help?"

"Maybe," Stone said. "How hard would it be to get it?"

"I might be able to hack into their computer," Bob replied. "Depends on how tough their security fire wall is. My guess is, if a travel agent can get in to check availability, I can get in. I know a guy at the phone company. He can give me a list of all their lines. Probably cost five hundred, though."

"Spend the money," Stone said. "At least I can see if there's a familiar name on the list."

"What day did the guy call?"

"Thursday and Friday. I suppose the guest list for either day would do. See if you can get the home addresses of the guests, too."

"I'm on it," Bob said.

"Call me on my cell phone when you get something."

"Will do." Bob hung up.

Juanito appeared with an envelope. "A fax for you, Mr. Barrington," he said.

"Thank you, Juanito," Stone said, accepting the envelope. He opened it to find the fully executed agreement with the insurance company.

"And you have a telephone call," Juanito said, handing him a cordless phone.

"Hello?"

"Mr. Barrington?"

"Yes?"

"This is Dan Griggs, from the Palm Beach Police Department."

"How are you, Chief?"

"Okay, I guess. I ran a check on this Paul Manning fellow. He's dead. He was hanged for murder on a Caribbean island called St. Marks a few years ago."

"I'm sorry, Chief, I should have given you a heads up on that."

"You knew he was dead?" The chief sounded annoyed.

"He's not dead. St. Marks is a small, independent nation with a strange justice system and a greedy prime minister. He was bought out."

"Bought out of a hanging?"

"For half a million dollars."

"I never heard of anything like that," Griggs said.

"There are some places where it happens."

"So you think we might have a murderer loose around here?"

"It's possible. I still don't have any concrete evidence of that, but if I come across any, I'll let you know."

126

"How many people did he kill?"

"Three."

"Well, I think I'd like to see him in my jail."

"I'm afraid there's nothing to arrest him for, yet," Stone said.

"Three murders isn't enough? Isn't there any evidence against him?"

"It happened in another country, and my guess is the evidence no longer exists. According to the record, he was tried, convicted and executed, so, in a legal sense, he's not only protected by the law on double jeopardy, he no longer exists."

"Except he does."

"He does."

"You got a description of this man? I'd like to distribute it to my people."

"Tall, six-three or -four, on the slender side when I knew him, although he used to be a lot heavier, I'm told. Hair could be any color. He had a prominent nose when I knew him, though he's apparently had a nose job, so I'm not sure I'd recognize him on sight."

"So, tall is all we've got?"

"That's about it. He might have gotten heavier, but I doubt if he's gotten any shorter."

The chief laughed. "I guess not. Okay, he's tall and dead. I'll let my people know."

"I'll call you if I learn anything else," Stone said. The two men said goodbye and hung up.

Liz appeared on the afterdeck in a bikini, looking fetching.

"I've got something for you," Stone said, handing her the envelope.

She took out the agreement and read it swiftly. "My get-out-of-jail-free pass," she said, smiling.

"Well, not exactly free," Stone reminded her.

"It's worth every penny." She put her arms around him and gave him a big kiss, reminding him, for a moment, how much he had enjoyed her embrace in the past.

Stone looked over her shoulder and saw Callie coming up the gangplank. "All in a day's work," he said, gently removing her arms from his neck.

She tucked the document into her purse. "I'm going up on the top deck and catch some sun," she said.

"See you later." He watched her climb the stairs, then turned to greet Callie.

"I can't leave you alone for a minute, can I?" she said, poking him in the ribs.

"Just her sincere thanks for a job well done," he replied.

"What kind of job?" she demanded, her eyes narrowing.

"A professional job," he said, giving her a kiss.

"If she does it again, *I'm* going to do a professional job on *her*," Callie said.

"Say, have you, by any chance, seen a tall man hanging around the house or the neighborhood?"

"No, but . . ."

"But what?"

"There was a tall man at the party I didn't know and didn't invite."

"How tall?"

"Real tall; taller than you."

"Hair color?"

"Dark, going gray."

"Nose?"

"Straight. Rather nice-looking man. I started to work my way over to him to find out if he was a crasher, but at that moment you arrived with Liz, which distracted me, and when I looked for him again, he was gone."

"Would you recognize him if you saw him again?"

"Yes."

"If you see him again — anywhere — I want to know about it."

"Okay," she said. "But why?"

"Let's just say that I'd like to speak with him."

18

Callie cooked dinner for the three of them, taking her time about it, and it was nearly ten when they sat down.

"You're a superb cook, Callie," Liz said, tasting her sweetbreads.

"Thank you, Liz," Callie replied. She turned to Stone. "Compliments, please."

"Wonderful," Stone said. "Everything is wonderful."

"A little quicker about it next time, if you want to continue to dine so well."

"I could not be more grateful," Stone said, tugging an imaginary forelock.

"Praise accepted," Callie replied.

They ate in silence for a while, not even bothering with desultory conversation. Callie finished, got up and went for dessert.

"Callie is very attractive," Liz said.

"Yes, she is."

"I think I'm a little jealous. I had an awfully good time in your bed — or rather, in mine — and I haven't forgotten a moment of it."

"Neither have I," Stone said, "but if quoted, I'll deny I said that."

"She's very attractive," Liz said, looking across the room at Callie.

"You said that before."

"Why don't we try . . ." She stopped.

"Try what?"

"Oh, what the hell — why don't we try a three-some?"

Stone nearly choked on his wine.

"What, do you find the idea so repulsive?"

"Hardly," Stone said, recovering himself. "It might just be too much of a good thing."

"Are you afraid she won't?"

"I've no idea how she would react, and I'm not going to find out."

"I'll feel her out," Liz said. "So to speak. Don't worry, I'll be subtle."

"Now listen," Stone said, but then he looked up to see Callie returning with dessert. He shot Liz a glance and turned to receive a warm crème brûlée. "Looks wonderful," Stone said.

Callie sat down. "So what have you two been talking about?" she asked, looking at Liz, then at Stone.

"Sex," Liz said.

Stone gulped.

"What about sex?"

"Are you for it, or agin' it?"

Callie laughed. "I'm all for it," she said.

Stone felt panic rising in his chest. This conversation was out of control — out of his control, anyway. At that moment, Juanito appeared with the cordless phone. Stone could have kissed him.

"For you, Mr. Barrington," the steward said. Stone took the phone. "Hello?"

"Stone, it's Dan Griggs. I'm sorry to call you so late."

"That's all right, Dan. What's up?"

"One of my men — a plainclothesman — has spotted somebody matching the description of this Paul Manning."

"Where?"

"Downtown, at a bar and restaurant called Taboo." He gave Stone the address.

"He's still there?"

"At the bar, talking to a woman. You want me to have him picked up?"

"No, Dan, I'll go down there myself."

"Okay. My man will be around if you need backup. His name is Detective Riley — short, good-looking, wears sharp suits."

"I'll call you later," Stone said. He hung up and turned to the two women. "Something's come up. I have to go downtown," he said.

"I'll come with you," Callie said.

Stone had to think only for a nanosecond. He didn't trust the two of them alone together. "All right," he said. "Liz, do you mind?"

"No, go ahead. I'm going to have a brandy and turn in."

"Let's go," he said to Callie. He led the way off the yacht and to the car.

"Where are we going?" Callie asked.

"You know a bar called Taboo?"

"Sure."

"Get me there."

"Okay, but why are we going there?"

"A man answering the description of the man you saw at the party is there. I want to know if it's the same man."

"Who is he?"

"I can't really answer that until I've talked to Liz."

"He's part of the legal matter?"

"Yes."

"Take a left, then a right," she said.

Stone followed her directions.

"Is that why you wanted me to come along, so I could identify him?"

"Yep."

"I got the feeling you didn't want Liz and me talking about sex."

"I can't imagine how you got that idea," Stone said.

"Well, you were obviously uncomfortable with the turn the conversation was taking. What was Liz talking about?"

"Nothing, really."

"Well, I suppose I'll have to ask her, if I want to know."

"Oh, all right," Stone said. "She suggested that she and you and I have a threesome. I want to point out that it was *she* who raised the subject, and I said absolutely nothing to encourage her."

"Turn right again," Callie said.

Stone turned.

"So what did you tell her?"

"I didn't tell her anything. I was too surprised."

"What were you *going* to tell her, after you'd recovered from your surprise?"

"I wasn't going to tell her anything."

"Why? Did the idea not appeal to you?"

Stone turned and looked at her.

"Keep your eyes on the road," she said. "And take the next left."

Stone turned left.

"Have you ever been in a threesome?" she asked.

"No," he said.

"I have, once."

"Really?" he asked, surprised.

"In college, with two guys. We were all good friends. It was just a one-time romp."

"You astonish me."

"For such a sophisticated man, you can be so . . . naive. Didn't you think I would enjoy having two men?"

"Did you?"

"Very much, although we were all so embarrassed the next morning, we never repeated the experience."

"Why were you embarrassed?"

"We were very young," she said. There was a long pause. "I'm older, now, but I've never been in bed with a woman — in a threesome, I mean."

"And not in a threesome?"

"Oh, sure. Most girls have tried that. It's not such a big deal as it is with men."

"I've heard other women say that."

"So, what do you think?"

"About what?"

"About a threesome, with Liz and me?"

Stone looked up ahead and saw an awning, with the restaurant's name emblazoned on it. "There's Taboo," he said, grateful for an excuse to avoid answering.

A valet took the car, and Stone and Callie went inside. The bar was straight ahead, and Stone saw Paul Manning immediately.

19

The bar was up front, the restaurant at the rear. The place was subtly lit, and a pianist was playing quiet jazz underneath the conversation at the busy bar. Stone spotted Detective Riley leaning against the piano, holding a glass apparently filled with mineral water. Riley motioned toward the bar, but Stone was already staring at Manning's back.

He nodded at Riley and turned to Callie. "See the tall man at the middle of the bar, talking to the brunette?"

"Yes."

"Is that the man you saw at the party?"

"Looks like him from behind, but I can't see his face."

"Come on." Stone took her arm and guided her toward the couple. The brunette, looking past her companion, flicked an eye toward them, then turned back to her conversation.

Stone stopped a pace from the couple. "Paul!" he said, loudly enough to be sure he could be heard.

The man's head jerked around in an instantaneous reaction.

"That's the man," Callie whispered.

"I'm Stone Barrington. I'm sure you remember."

The man turned fully around and regarded Stone, his brow wrinkled. His hair was longish and dark, flecked with gray. "I don't believe we've met," he said, "but weren't you at the Shames party the other night?"

Stone looked at him carefully. The face was thin, the nose straight. He was the right age, and there was a resemblance to the Paul Manning he had known, but the nose seemed to change everything. "Yes, I was, but we met some time ago, in St. Marks."

"I'm sorry," the man said. "I put into St. Marks a few years ago on a sailing charter, but I don't recall meeting you there."

"I'm sure you remember your wife," Stone said.

The brunette looked up sharply at the man.

"My wife died last year," he said.

"Oh, longer ago than that," Stone said.

"I think I would remember when my wife died," the man said quietly.

The brunette spoke up. "You didn't tell me, Paul. I'm sorry."

"I hadn't had time, yet, but thank you," he said to her. He offered his hand to Stone. "I'm Paul Bartlett, and this lovely lady is Charmaine Tallman," he said. "Perhaps you've mistaken me for someone else."

Stone nodded at the woman and shook the

man's hand. "Stone Barrington."

"Do you live in Palm Beach, Stone?"

"No. How about you?"

"I arrived a couple of weeks ago."

"How long do you plan to stay?" Stone asked.

"Actually, I'm house-hunting. I sold my business late last year, and I suppose I'm taking early retirement."

"What sort of business?"

"Graphic design."

"Where?"

"Minneapolis. I thought I'd try somewhere with a warmer winter. Florida seemed attractive. Where are you from, Stone?"

"New York," Stone replied. The man displayed not a hint of nerves. Could he be mistaken?

"Did you think I was another Paul?"

"Does the name Paul Manning ring a bell?"

"Writer? I read some of his stuff a few years ago, but not recently."

"How did you come to be at the Shames party?" Callie asked.

"I came with the Wilkeses," he said. "We just stopped by for a drink on the way to another dinner."

"How do you know the Wilkeses?"

"From Minneapolis. I used to do a lot of his company's design work — product packaging, mostly."

Callie nodded.

"Does the name Allison ring a bell?" Stone asked.

"I had a secretary named Allison, once."

Out of the corner of his eye, Stone saw Detective Riley moving slowly past them. He stopped a few feet behind Paul Bartlett.

"I can't get past the feeling that you think I'm someone else."

"I can't get past that, myself," Stone replied. "What was the name of your firm?"

"Bartlett and Bishop," he replied. "We were bought out by a New York–based firm. May I offer you a drink?"

"Thanks, but we have to be going," Stone said. "Perhaps I'll see you again. Where are you staying?"

"At the Chesterfield," Bartlett replied. "Call me anytime."

"Thanks. Ready, Callie?"

"Sure."

Stone gave the couple a small wave and guided Callie out of the bar.

On the sidewalk, as they waited for their car to be brought around, the policeman approached them. "Mr. Barrington? I'm Dave Riley."

Stone shook his hand. "Of course. Chief Griggs said you'd be here."

"Was that your man?"

"I'm not sure," Stone said. "He's the right size and age, but I haven't seen him for a few years, and I'm told he's had his nose altered. Did you hear any of our conversation?"

"I got his name and his story about the business."

"Can you check that out? Maybe get a photograph of Paul Bartlett?"

"I'll see what I can do," Riley said.

The car arrived. Stone thanked the detective and he and Callie got in and drove away.

"What he said about the Wilkeses rings true," she said. "He was standing near them when I saw him, and Mr. Wilkes does have a lot of business interests in the midwest."

"At first I was sure it was Manning," Stone said. "But now . . . well, let's see what the police turn up."

"Why are the police involved?"

Stone took a deep breath. "I've already told you about Allison; Manning was her husband." He told her the story.

"And you think Manning is in Palm Beach? What evidence do you have of that?"

"Nothing concrete," Stone said. "Just a hunch, brought on by the trashing of Liz's study at her house."

"Bizarre," Callie said.

"Indeed."

They pulled into the driveway of the Shames house, got out and walked toward the yacht.

"So," Callie said, "what about this threesome?"

"Well, there are problems about that," Stone said, trying to think of some.

"What sort of problems? I'm certainly not one of them. I think she's very attractive."

"She's my client, and she's the girlfriend of

another client, for a start."

"And where in the canon of legal ethics does it say you can't sleep with a client?"

"I, ah, can't quote you chapter and verse, but believe me, it's inadvisable."

"Come on, Stone, what's the real reason? You're a red-blooded American boy. You must harbor the fantasy of two women in bed with you — and with each other."

"I can't deny that," Stone said, reaching the gangplank and helping her aboard. "I suppose the main reason is that I wouldn't want to share you with anybody, not even another beautiful woman."

"Now, that was the politic thing to say," she said, smiling at him. "But is there some other reason?"

"Apart from what I've already said, it just doesn't feel right," he replied.

"Now, *that's* the best reason you've given me," she said. "Maybe another time."

"You never know," Stone replied.

"I can tell you're interested," Callie said.

"How?"

She rubbed the back of her hand across the front of his trousers. "Let's just say, it shows."

Stone laughed and pulled her to him. "Think you could be satisfied with just me?"

"I expect so," she replied, leading him toward his cabin.

20

Stone had a late breakfast the following morning and was finishing his coffee, when Juanito came aboard from the house with a Federal Express package for Stone. He ripped it open.

Joan wrote in a note: "Bob Berman brought this by for you. He said you'd know what it is."

Stone lifted a four-inch-thick stack of computer paper out of the box and looked at the first page. It was a computerized registration form for the Brooke Hotel in Manhattan. The fanfold paper opened to reveal what appeared to be the entire guest list for the Brooke on the previous Friday.

Liz came on deck looking fresh and new in a short linen dress. "Good morning," she said. "What's that?"

"I had some phone calls from a Manhattan hotel last week; fellow asked for me and wouldn't leave a number."

"You think it might have been Paul?"

"Maybe. It would be a big help if you would go through these registration forms and see if any of the names seems familiar to you — not just people you know, but names that Paul

142

might have chosen for a new identity."

"Sure, I'll be glad to."

"When you've done that, I'd like you to take a ride with me."

"Where?"

"I met a man last night who could possibly be Paul, but I couldn't be sure. The nose was different, as you said, and that seemed to change everything. Anyway, I haven't seen him for some years, and I'm not sure how good I'd be at identifying him. I'd like to see if we can spot him around his hotel and let you get a look at him."

"Okay, and I can tell you that when I saw him in Easthampton he looked very different from his old self. I spotted him as much by his walk and his body language as by his appearance."

"What sort of hair did he have?"

"His natural dark, going gray; that hadn't changed."

"How long?"

"Not too long; longer than yours, though."

"Does the name Paul Bartlett ring any bells?"

"Just the Paul. But if Paul were hiding out, I don't think he'd use his real first name. He's a lot smarter than that."

"Sit down, and let's go through this hotel list together."

"Okay. Can I have some coffee first?"

Stone rang for Juanito and ordered the coffee, then they started through the stack of fanfold paper. They had gone through only a dozen or so names when Liz stopped. "Garland," she said. "Donald Garland."

"Familiar?"

"Garland was Paul's mother's maiden name. Donald was his father's first name."

"Do you know how to contact them? Maybe he's been in touch."

"Both dead," Liz said.

"Mr. Garland is from San Francisco," Stone read from the document. "Says here he's with Golden Gate Publishing, and he lives in Pacific Heights. When it's opening time out there, I'll check him out."

They continued to read through the list for a while, then Juanito appeared with the telephone. "For you, Mr. Barrington."

"Yes?"

"It's Dan Griggs."

"Morning, Dan. I expect Dave Riley briefed you on last night's events."

"Yes, and we've checked out Mr. Bartlett. He's from Minneapolis, as he said, and he did sell his design firm last year."

"Oh," Stone said. "I guess that lets him out."

"Not necessarily," Griggs said. "He had owned the firm for only two years when he sold it, and I haven't been able to find out anything about him before that, which is unusual."

"I thought I'd take Mrs. Harding over to his hotel this morning and see if we can spot him. She thinks she can identify Paul Manning."

"It's a nice thought, but he checked out this

144

morning; said he was going back to Minneapolis on business."

"He doesn't have a business," Stone pointed out.

"I'm checking with the airlines to see if he was on any outbound flight this morning," Griggs said. "I'll let you know if I come up with anything."

"Thanks, Dan," Stone said and hung up.

Liz was still going through the guest list. "I haven't come across anything else yet," she said.

"Paul Bartlett has checked out of his hotel," Stone said. "Said he was returning to Minneapolis on business. Did Paul Manning have any connection with Minneapolis?"

"No, but he wouldn't have settled in a place where anybody knew him."

"How recognizable would he have been to his readers? Did he do a lot of book signings? Have his photograph on the book jackets?"

"The only photograph of Paul that ever appeared on a book jacket or in a press release from his publishers would have been one taken when he was very heavy and had a full beard. He would be completely unrecognizable to any reader now."

"Bartlett recently sold a graphic design business. Did Paul have any design inclinations?"

"He was a fine arts major at Syracuse," Liz said. "He drew and painted quite well."

"Did he take any design courses? Anything

that would give him the skills he would need for graphic design?"

"I don't really know," she said. "He didn't talk about college all that much."

Callie appeared on deck. "What are you two doing?" she asked.

Stone explained the stack of paper.

"And how did you get the guest list of a New York hotel?"

"You don't want to know."

Juanito came back with the phone for Stone. "Hello."

"It's Dan Griggs. Paul Bartlett didn't take any flight out this morning, and he didn't charter any aircraft on the field, but he did turn in his rental car at Hertz, at the airport."

"That doesn't make any sense," Stone said. "Why would he drive to the airport and turn in his car, then not fly out? How would he leave the airport without transportation?"

"I'll check the local cab companies and see if a driver picked up anyone answering his description," Griggs said.

"You might check if he rented a car from another company, too, and if so, what kind and what license number. Might be nice to get his driver's license info from Hertz, too."

"I got that. It lists a Minneapolis address."

"Issued when?"

"Two years, three months ago."

"Can you check with the Minnesota motor vehicle department and find out if it was a renewal or a new license, and if he turned in a license from another state?"

"Sure, that's pretty easy."

"Oh, and what's his date of birth on the license?"

Griggs told him, and he repeated it to Liz.

"Eighteen months younger than Paul," she said.

"Keep me posted," Stone said to Griggs, and hung up.

Liz was still going through the hotel list.

"Anything at all?" Stone asked.

"Just Garland so far," she said. "Pity the hotel doesn't photograph its guests."

"I'll bet it won't be long before they start that," Stone said. "That'll make it easier to track fugitives."

"And errant husbands," Liz said. "I wonder if there's a Mrs. Bartlett."

"He said she died last year."

"Might be interesting to check with the Minneapolis police department and find out if that's true and, if so, how she died," Liz said.

"You know something, Mrs. Harding," Stone said. "You'd make a good cop." He picked up the phone and called Dan Griggs.

"It's Stone. Bartlett said his wife died last year. Can you check with the Minneapolis PD and see if there was foul play suspected?"

"Sure can do that," Griggs said. "Bartlett's driver's license was issued after a driving test, not swapped for another state's."

"Now that's *really* interesting," Stone said. "How many middle-aged men take driving tests?"

"Only those who learned to drive late in life, and that's not likely — and those who haven't driven for a long time or who've been out of the country long enough for their licenses to expire."

"And people who need new identities."

"Right. Something else: I talked with the Hertz clerk at the airport, and she said Bartlett was picked up by somebody in a BMW. She could see the curb from her desk."

"So he could still be in town."

"Or on a road trip."

"Yeah. Dan, could you check with an outfit called Golden Gate Publishing in San Francisco and find out if their employee Donald Garland matches Bartlett's description?"

"Okay. They open in an hour out there. How'd you get onto this Garland?"

"You'd rather not know, but there's an outside chance he could be Manning."

"I'll get somebody on it."

"Thanks." Stone hung up and gazed across Lake Worth.

"What?" Liz asked.

"Somebody picked up Bartlett at the airport. I wonder why."

Callie was leafing through the hotel guest list.

"Callie? Where do the Wilkeses live?"

"On North County Road."

"Let's go see them."

21

"Tell me about the Wilkeses," Stone said. "What are their first names?" They were driving up North County Road. To their right, usually behind high hedges, were houses that fronted the beach.

"Frank and Margaret," she said. "He founded a chain of fast-food restaurants in the midwest, and later, he bought some other companies. He's very rich." She pointed. "The house is the next one."

Stone pulled up to a wrought-iron gate, which was tightly shut. A section of hedge prevented the house from being seen from the street.

"I think I'm uncomfortable just ringing the bell," Callie said.

Stone handed her his cell phone. "Tell them we're in the neighborhood, and we're calling at the suggestion of Thad Shames."

Callie made the call, chatted brightly with Mrs. Wilkes for a couple of minutes, then hung up. "Okay," she said, "they'll see us."

Stone pulled up to the gates, reached out the window, rang the bell and the gates opened. The driveway was longer than Stone had expected, and they emerged in a cobblestoned circle with a fountain in its center. The house was an old one, in the Florida Spanish style, and appeared to have been carefully restored. Stone and Callie got out of the car and rang the front doorbell.

The door was answered by Margaret Wilkes, dressed for golf in a plaid skirt and polo shirt. "Callie, come in," she said. "How nice to see you."

"Mrs. Wilkes, this is Stone Barrington, a friend of Thad's."

"How do you do?" Stone said, and shook her extended hand.

"Please come back to the terrace," she said. A houseman appeared from the rear of the house. "Bobby, please bring us a pitcher of lemonade."

Frank Wilkes rose from a wicker sofa on the rear terrace to greet them, and introductions were made. The terrace overlooked a large pool and a garden, with the Atlantic beyond. Both the Wilkeses were charming and unpretentious.

After the lemonade had been served, Stone got to the point. "Mr. and Mrs. Wilkes . . ."

"Please, Frank and Margaret," Wilkes said.

"Thank you. I'm here, on Thad Shames's behalf, to inquire about a Mr. Paul Bartlett, of Minneapolis. You know him, I believe."

"Yes, of course," Wilkes replied. "For several years."

"May I ask just how many years?"

"Well, let's see: He had a design business in

Minneapolis, and he and his partner made a presentation to us, oh, a little over two years ago. That's when we first met. We hired them to redesign all our paper products — plates, sandwich cartons, the hats for the counter people, that sort of thing. Why do you want to know about Paul? Is he in some sort of difficulties?"

"Oh, no, nothing like that. It's just that he bears a resemblance to someone I used to know and that Thad is interested in. We only want to know that he's who he says he is."

"I see," Wilkes said. Clearly, he did not. "Who did you think he might be?"

"Did you meet Mrs. Winston Harding at Thad Shames's party?"

"No."

"Mrs. Harding is a close friend of Thad's. The man we're interested in was someone she knew in the past, who dropped out of sight a few years ago. No one knows what happened to him, but there are indications that he might be in Palm Beach. Someone noticed that Mr. Bartlett resembled this man, whose name is Paul Manning."

"Well, why don't you ask Paul about this?"

"I did, last night, but he pretty much denied being Manning."

"But you're not convinced?"

"Thad has asked me to investigate the possibility that Bartlett and Manning are the same man."

"Then why don't you arrange for Paul and Mrs. Harding to meet? Surely that would answer the question."

"I had hoped to do that, but Mrs. Harding doesn't wish to see him. Also, Mr. Bartlett checked out of his hotel this morning."

"That's news to me," Wilkes said.

"I just wondered if you had any knowledge of Bartlett's background before you first met him."

"I saw a résumé at the time," Wilkes said. "He had a broad background in advertising and graphics design, worked for several places in New York, as I recall."

"Did you check with any of his former employers for a reference?"

"No. We would ordinarily do that with a prospective employee, but we dealt with Paul as an outside contractor, and frankly, we were more interested in the presentation he prepared for us than in what he had done in the past. We were very enthusiastic about the work, and that was all that mattered."

"Do you know anyone who has known Paul Bartlett much longer than you have?"

Wilkes thought about that for a moment. "No, I don't believe I do."

"Did you know Mr. Bartlett's wife?"

Margaret Wilkes spoke up. "Oh, yes. In fact, we introduced them. Such a shame about Frances."

"I understand she's deceased?"

"Yes, in an accident last year. Terrible thing."

"How did it happen?"

"She and Paul were out driving on a Sunday afternoon, and they swerved to miss hitting a deer. Frances was thrown through the windshield and killed instantly."

"Who was driving?"

"Paul was, but he was wearing a seat belt."

"There was no passenger-side air bag," Wilkes said, "and apparently the buckle on Frances's seat belt failed or was defective. I urged Paul to sue the car company, but he didn't have the heart. He just wanted to put it behind him. That's why he sold his company."

"Do you know if he made a lot of money on the sale?"

"I shouldn't think so; they were a fairly new company. I think the people who bought them wanted the talent they employed and me for a client more than anything else. Of course, Paul would be quite well fixed, though."

"How is that?" Stone asked.

"Well, Frances was very wealthy. She'd lost her husband a few months before she and Paul met, and he'd left a considerable fortune."

"I see," Stone said.

"Mr. Barrington," Margaret Wilkes said, "you're beginning to frighten me. Are you thinking that Paul might somehow have caused Frances's death?"

"At this moment, I have no real reason to think so, Mrs. Wilkes. I'm simply concerned with learning whether he is, or once was, Paul Manning."

"This Manning," Wilkes said, "what was his relationship to Mrs. Harding?"

"He was her first husband."

"And what sort of man is he?"

"Not a very nice one, I'm afraid."

"Was this just some domestic dispute?"

"More than that," Stone said. "Manning murdered three people."

"Good God!" Wilkes said. "He's dangerous, then?"

"Manning certainly is, but please remember, I have no evidence yet that Manning and Bartlett are the same man."

"Well, I hope to God you'll find out!" Wilkes said.

"I know this is upsetting to you and Mrs. Wilkes," Stone said, "and I apologize for that."

"No, no, if Paul is this Manning, then we certainly want to know. I assume you'll have him arrested."

"We'll take whatever measures are appropriate," Stone said.

"I'll hardly know what to say to Paul when we see him," Mrs. Wilkes said.

"Do you expect to see him anytime soon?"

"Why, yes. He's coming to dinner tonight."

"Here, in this house?"

"Yes," she said.

Wilkes spoke up. "Perhaps you'd better come, too," he said.

22

The three of them stood on the afterdeck, Stone in black tie, Callie in a silk dress and Liz in a terry robe.

"I wish you'd come with us," Stone said to Liz.

Liz shook her head. "I don't want to see him," she said.

Callie patted her small purse. "I've got a camera in here," she said. "I'll get his picture."

"All right, let's go," Stone said. "I've no idea what time we'll be back, but I've asked Juanito to keep an eye on you."

"Thank you, Stone," Liz said.

Stone and Callie walked to the car and drove north.

"What do you think is going to happen?" Callie said.

"I don't think anything will happen. I'll contrive to stand next to Bartlett, and you'll take our photograph, come hell or high water."

"Have you alerted the police?"

"No. If he is Manning, he's not charged with anything. I just want an opportunity to get him alone and to put an offer to him."

"What sort of offer?"

"Liz is willing to pay him to go away."

"Oh. And you think that will work?"

"I can only hope so."

"What if he still denies being Manning?"

"I've got a friend in New York working on Bartlett's background. Maybe we'll be able to present him with some evidence that he's not who he says he is."

"Tonight?"

"Probably not that soon, although my friend has my cell phone number."

"This is kind of exciting," Callie said, giggling.

"All in a day's work," Stone said dryly.

The gates of the Wilkes house were open, and a valet took their car. Stone and Callie walked into the house and were greeted by Frank and Margaret Wilkes in the foyer.

"Stone, Callie, welcome," Mrs. Wilkes said.

"Thank you for asking us, Margaret," Stone replied. "Is he here yet?"

"No. In fact, he called and said he couldn't make it in time for drinks, but he'd be here for dinner."

"Did he say why?"

"No. Why don't you two go on out to the terrace and have a drink. Frank and I will be along as soon as all our guests have arrived."

"Thank you, we will." Stone led Callie through the house and out to the same terrace where they had sat earlier that day. A dozen couples had already arrived and were drinking and talking to the tune of a light jazz trio, which was set up beside the pool.

Callie saw some people she knew and introduced Stone. A waiter brought them drinks, and they chatted with the other guests. Soon the crowd had swelled to around fifty, and the Wilkeses joined their guests on the terrace.

Margaret Wilkes tugged at Stone's sleeve and whispered, "I've arranged the place cards so that you and Paul are at the same table."

"Thank you," Stone said.

Conversation continued for another half hour, then they were called to dinner. The very large dining hall had been set up with tables of eight, and Stone and Callie found their place cards and Paul Bartlett's. Callie was seated next to Bartlett, and Stone was two places away. They had barely introduced themselves to their dinner partners and sat down, when Paul Bartlett entered the dining room, stopped to kiss his hostess on the cheek, then made his way to his place.

He looked surprised to find Stone and Callie there. They shook hands. "I hadn't expected to see you again so soon, Stone," he said. "How did you come to be here?"

"Callie is a friend of the Wilkeses," Stone said. "They were kind enough to ask us."

"Oh," he replied, but he didn't seem satisfied with the answer.

The first course was served, and Stone and Callie exchanged a glance and a shrug. No opportunity to get a photograph at dinner. It would have to be later.

The woman on Stone's right was deep in conversation with Bartlett, to the exclusion of Stone, who had to occupy himself with the dinner companion on his left, a handsome woman in her seventies.

"And who are you?" she asked him, with a touch of imperiousness.

"My name is Stone Barrington."

"And how do you know the Wilkeses?" There was suspicion in the question.

"My companion for the evening is a friend of theirs," Stone said, nodding in Callie's direction.

"Goodness," the woman said, taking in Callie. "One wouldn't think *she* would need a walker."

"A walker?" Stone asked.

"Isn't that what you are?"

"I'm afraid I don't understand."

"Of course you do, darling. My name is Lila Baldwin. Perhaps you could give me your card, for the future?" She nodded toward her own date, a sleekly handsome man in his thirties, who sat next to Callie. "I'm afraid I've had about all of Carlton that I can bear for one season."

Stone gave the woman his card, then the penny dropped. The woman thought he was for hire as an escort, maybe more. "If you should ever need an attorney, please call me," he said.

"Attorney?" She looked at the card, holding it at arm's length. She apparently didn't want to be seen in her glasses.

"Woodman and Weld, in New York," Stone said.

She looked at him more closely, squinting. "Your firm did my estate planning," she said. "A lovely man named William Eggers."

"I know him well," Stone said.

"You don't look like an estate planner," she said, accusingly.

"No, that's a little out of my line," he replied. "I'm more of a generalist."

"And what sort of problem would I hire you for?" she asked.

"Oh, nothing specific. If you should have a problem of any sort, call Bill Eggers, and he'll know if I'm your man."

"Oh, I think you could be my man, no matter what my problem was," she said.

Stone was trying to come up with an answer to that when his tiny cell phone, clipped to his waistband, began to vibrate silently. "Would you excuse me for just a moment?" he said. "I'll be right back." He stood up and walked toward the dining room door, fishing out the phone and opening it, but keeping it concealed in his hand until he was out in the hall.

"Hello?"

"It's me," Bob Berman said.

"Have you got something?"

"This guy's an amateur," Bob said. "His identity is paper thin. There's nothing in his credit report going back more than two and a half years. His driver's license is green as grass, and he's only got one credit card, one of those that's guaranteed by a savings account. No mortgage or bank loans on the record, only a car loan, from a high-interest loan company."

"His design company must have done business with a bank."

"Probably, but I'll bet his partner did all the financial stuff. Bartlett would never survive even the most minimal credit check for any substantial business. There's not even a history of other bank accounts, nothing in the New York credit bureaus, either."

"Anything on who he really is?"

"If you can get a fingerprint on a bar glass or something, I could run that. Otherwise, I'll need a lot more time to nail him down."

"I'll have a shot at it," Stone said. "Call me if you come up with anything else."

"Will do."

Stone returned to his table, stopping to whisper in Callie's ear. "It's looking good. When dinner's over, try to slip a glass or something with his fingerprints on it into your purse."

"Love to," she said.

Stone returned to his seat and the attentions of Lila Baldwin, glancing at Paul Bartlett, who seemed to be having a good time. Stone wanted to end his good time.

23

The woman sitting between Stone and Paul Bartlett got up between courses and went to the powder room, and Stone took the opportunity.

"Paul, I was out at the airport this morning. Did I see you leave in a BMW?"

Bartlett looked at him as if Stone had seriously invaded his privacy. "Were you following me?" he demanded.

"Of course not," Stone said. "I was at the airport, and I saw you, that's all. I didn't mean to upset you."

Bartlett waved a hand. "Sorry, I guess I'm being paranoid."

Stone wondered what he had to be paranoid about.

"I took my rental car back to Hertz. I bought a car this morning, and the salesman picked me up and drove me to the dealership."

"Oh, what did you buy?"

"A Bentley."

"Very nice."

"Were you considering one?"

"No, the Bentley is out of my league. If you're making that sort of investment, you must have decided to stay on in Palm Beach."

"Well, I am looking for a house."

Callie was on her feet, digging into her purse. "Let me get a shot of you two," she said. "Stone, move over a seat."

Bartlett waved her away. "No, please. I don't enjoy being photographed." When Callie seemed to persist, he nearly barked at her. "Sit down," he said. "Please. I take a Muslim view of photography: It steals one's soul."

"If one has a soul," Stone said.

Bartlett shot a glance at Stone, picked up a liqueur glass, downed the contents and stood up. "Excuse me," he said.

"You're not leaving," Callie said.

"Terrible headache," Bartlett replied.

"Still at the Chesterfield?" Stone asked.

"Sure, call me anytime. Good night." He strode toward his hostess's table, spoke to her for a moment, kissed her on the cheek and left the room.

Callie reached over, picked up the small liqueur glass, wrapped it in a tissue from her purse and dropped it into her bag. "Better than a photograph," she said.

Stone looked up to see Frank Wilkes coming toward them. He sat down in Bartlett's chair. "Paul has abandoned us, I see."

"Yes, he seemed uncomfortable."

"Stone, after speaking with him, do you think he may be the man you're looking for?"

"I think he may be," Stone said, "but even if

162

he's not, he's not the man he says he is."

"Then who is he?"

"I hope to know more about that soon, Frank. I'll let you know when I find out."

"I'd appreciate that. Margaret and I introduced him to Frances, his wife, and the thought that he might have had something to do with her death is, naturally, very disturbing to us."

"I can understand that. Can you tell me everything you remember about the accident?"

"It was on a Sunday afternoon, I remember. Paul and I had a golf date, and Frances picked him up at the clubhouse when we had finished — must have been around six. They were on the way home when . . ." He stopped. "No, they weren't on the way home. We played at the Manitou Ridge Golf Club, in the Minneapolis suburbs, and their house — Frances's house — is west of there. The accident happened along the shore of White Bear Lake, which is east — no, northeast of the club. After the funeral, I remember asking Paul what they were doing out in that direction. He said Frances had wanted to go for a drive along the lake. I didn't say anything at the time, but that seemed odd to me. I can't explain why, exactly, but it seemed out of character for Frances to want to do something as idle as go for a drive. She was the sort of person who would never take the long way home, if there was a shorter route."

"And what do you remember about the accident itself?"

"The papers said that they were coming around a curve when a deer jumped out of the brush, and in trying to avoid it, Paul went off the road and smashed into a tree. Frances went through the windshield and hit the tree, killing her instantly."

"You said earlier today there was something wrong with the seat belt?"

"Yes, I remember reading that. I told Paul he should sue, but he wanted no part of that."

"Do you remember anything else about the accident or its aftermath that struck you as odd?"

Wilkes thought about it. "A few weeks later I was playing golf with a friend of mine, Arthur Welch, who was Frances's lawyer. He mentioned that Paul had sold Frances's house, and that surprised me."

"Why?"

"Well, I knew that when Frances and Paul married, she insisted on a prenuptial agreement that severely limited any inheritance for him in the event of her death. The bulk of her estate was to go to a local art museum. When Arthur told me Paul had sold the house, I mentioned the prenup, and he told me that Frances had rescinded the prenup and had made a new will."

"When?"

"Less than a month before her death."

"I see."

Wilkes rubbed his forehead. "I think I see, too. I didn't want to believe it, but now . . ."

"Let's not jump to any conclusions just yet," Stone said. "Let's wait until we know more."

Wilkes nodded. "You're right," he said.

"And please don't do anything that might make Bartlett feel that your relationship with him has changed, or that you don't want to see or talk to him."

"I'll try," Wilkes said. "Margaret will, too."

As they left the party, Stone called Chief Dan Griggs.

"Dan, can you meet me at your office?" Stone asked. "There's something I need to talk to you about."

"Sure, Stone. I'll be there in ten minutes."

Stone took a minute to bring Griggs up to date on what he had learned that evening.

Griggs nodded as he heard the story. "So, if Bartlett is Manning, and if he killed his wife for her money, he *has* committed a crime, after all. We'd have grounds for an arrest."

"I think you'd have to have a long talk with the Minneapolis police department before we'd know about that," Stone said. "After all, if they'd suspected him, they'd probably have already arrested him."

"Good point," Griggs admitted.

"We may be able to confirm his identity anyway," Stone said. "Callie, the glass?"

Callie removed the liqueur glass from her purse and set it on the table.

Stone picked it up by the stem and held it

against the light. "There's at least one good print on here," he said.

Griggs picked up the phone and pressed a couple of buttons. "Sam, it's Griggs," he said. "I want you to lift some prints from a drinking glass and run them through the computer." He hung up, and almost immediately, a detective came into the room, took the glass and went away with it.

"Well," Stone said, rising, "let me know what results you get."

"Hang on," Griggs said. "This won't take as long as you think." He got up and left the office for a few minutes, then returned. "A good right thumbprint and two partials," he said. "My guy is running them through the FBI computer now. Come on, let's go see what he comes up with."

Stone and Callie followed Griggs down a hallway to another office, where the detective was sitting at a computer.

"Got anything yet, Sam?" Griggs asked.

Sam hit the return key and sat back. "Shouldn't take long," he said. "Hang on," he said, "what's this?"

The group walked around the computer and looked over the detective's shoulder. The screen displayed a message:

ACCESS TO THIS FILE DENIED.
ENTRY REQUIRES APPROVAL
AT DIRECTOR LEVEL
UNDER PROTOCOL 1002.

"You ever seen anything like that before, Sam?"

"No, Chief, I haven't."

"What's protocol ten-oh-two?"

"I don't have the slightest idea," Sam said.

"Who the hell is this guy?" Griggs muttered.

"I'd really like to know that," Stone replied.

24

The next morning, Stone called Dino. "How are you?"

"Not bad. Where the hell are you now?"

"In Palm Beach."

"You rotten bastard."

"Yeah, I sure am."

"And if I know you, you're getting paid for it."

"Right again."

"Why didn't I go to law school?"

"Listen, I want to run something by you."

"Okay, shoot."

"I'm trying to identify a guy down here who isn't who he says he is. You remember our friend Paul Manning that you arrested for me?"

"Sure, he's dead."

"Nope." Stone took Dino through what he knew about Manning/Bartlett thus far. "Then last night, I got his prints off a glass, and the local cop shop ran them for me."

"And he turns out to be the Lindbergh baby?"

"Nope. At least, I don't think so. But something weird happened: We're logged onto the FBI print database, and when we transmit the print, we get a message saying access is denied without approval from the director level, and it mentions something called 'protocol ten-oh-two.' What it sounds like to me is some sort of national security thing, like maybe he has a CIA connection."

"Nah," Dino said. "I'll tell you what I think it is, and I'll give you five-to-one odds I'm right. The guy is in the witness protection program."

This stopped Stone in his tracks. "But that doesn't make any sense. Manning's background is not that of somebody the government would want to protect. In fact, he doesn't even exist, in a legal sense."

"Maybe he testified against somebody in a criminal trial somewhere."

"I suppose it's possible, but I would think that Manning would do everything he could to avoid putting himself in such a position. Also, Bob Berman checked out Bartlett, and he says the man's identity is thin, that he has no financial background to speak of. Even his driver's license is recent. That doesn't sound like the kind of identity the Department of Justice would create for somebody in the program."

"No, it doesn't, but there's another possibility."

"What's that?"

"Let's say that Manning or Bartlett or whoever whatever the fuck his name is, gets involved in some criminal deal, and he gets busted and rats out his partners in return for immunity and the program."

"Possible, but it seems unlikely."

"Go with me, here, Stone. Anyway, they put him in the program and he finds himself stuck in Peoria or someplace, running a Burger King, and he doesn't like it. So he bails out of the program — happens all the time. Once the government gets these people in the program, the feds run their lives, and they've got fuck-all to say about it. Lots of them go overboard."

"True enough."

"So our guy is on the street, now. Maybe he sells the business and the house the government bought him, so he's got a few bucks. He finds someplace he likes, in this case, Minneapolis, though God knows why anybody would want to be stuck there in the winter, but he can't use his old name because whoever he ratted on still wants to cut his heart out and eat it for dinner. So he has to make up his own new identity, and he doesn't do the greatest job in the world. After all, he's not Justice; he can't call up the State Department and tell them to issue him a new passport, so he does the best he can. He gets a local driver's license, picks up a credit card and finds a business partner who's real and who can deal with the banks."

"Makes sense."

"Then he meets the rich widow, and pretty soon he's living in a much nicer house, and he doesn't need the business anymore, or, for that matter, the wife, so he sells one and does away with the other, and he gets away with it. Now he's rich, footloose and fancy fucking free, and he's house-hunting in Palm Beach and shopping for a Bentley."

"Okay, I buy it."

"I don't," Dino said. "I don't buy it for a minute."

"What? Why not? You just convinced me."

"Yeah, well, you're a pushover for a good story, Stone. You always were."

"What are you talking about, Dino? Have I missed something?"

"You usually do, pal, and this time it's this: If Bartlett is Manning, why would he hunt down his ex — well, his *previous* wife and start harassing her? He risks bringing himself to the attention of the local police, which he has already done, and exposing himself — in the fully clothed sense of the expression. Why would he want to do that?"

"Because he's pissed off at her for running off with all the money he stole, and he's crazy as a fruit bat, and he knows how to hold a grudge."

Dino didn't say anything.

"Well?"

"Okay, maybe you're right. After all, you can't depend on criminals to behave sensibly. I got another question, though."

"Okay."

"He doesn't look enough like he used to look for anybody to ID him, even you. You didn't get a picture of the guy, so Allison can't identify him because she won't be in the same room with him, and the FBI won't tell you who his prints belong to. How are you going to know, once and for all, who he is?"

"I wish you hadn't asked that question."

"Because you don't know the answer?"

"That's pretty much it."

Dino sighed deeply. "It looks like I'm going to have to come down there and straighten this out for you."

Stone had sort of been hoping he would; he missed Dino.

"You'll have to bring Mary Ann."

"Nah, she won't come while the kid's in school."

"How is Ben?"

"Well, his grandfather hasn't turned him into a made man yet."

"And how is Eduardo?"

"As mean as ever. He never gets older, just meaner."

"And Dolce?"

"I don't know. Mary Ann won't talk about her. I guess she's still nuts. Eduardo's got her locked up in farthest Brooklyn, and I don't see her ever getting out."

"When can you come?"

"Tomorrow, the next day, maybe. I can get the time off, I think. Can you find me a sack?"

"Sure, and a nice one, too."

"I'll call you with my flight number."

"I'll be there."

"See you."

"See you."

25

The following morning it was, to Stone's astonishment, raining, and raining hard. Juanito had put up clear curtains around the afterdeck, so Stone had breakfast alone there and checked with Joan for messages. He returned half a dozen calls, including one to Bill Eggers.

"I spoke to Thad yesterday," Eggers said, "and he is one happy client. I hope you're not thinking of coming back to New York before you clear up any remaining problems. If you do, I'll have you hit over the head in the airport and put on the next airplane back to Palm Beach."

"Oh, I'm sticking it out," Stone said, "and it has turned interesting."

"How so?"

Stone went through the whole story once again.

"You know," Eggers said when Stone had finished, "being a partner in this firm is not nearly as interesting as what you do."

"Probably not. By the way, I sat next to one of your clients at dinner last night — a Lila Baldwin."

"Oh, God," Eggers groaned. "Be careful around her. Once, during a discussion of estate tax avoidance, she grabbed my crotch."

"I'm not surprised."

"*I* was, I can tell you."

"You've led a sheltered life."

"Right, and I'd better get back to it. Call me if you need any backup."

"Will do."

Stone had hardly hung up when the phone rang. He punched a button. "Shames residence."

"May I speak with a Mr. Stone Barrington, please?" A male voice.

"Speaking."

"Mr. Barrington, my name is Ebbe Lundquist. I'm with the Minneapolis Police Department."

"How are you?"

"Okay. Earlier this morning I had a very interesting conversation with Chief Griggs of the Palm Beach PD."

"Did you?"

"Yes, and I immediately checked our records on Mrs. Frances Bartlett."

"And what did you find?"

"I found that the smashup was handled as an accident by the traffic division of the sheriff's department, and since they didn't suspect foul play, we were never brought into it. Apart from reading about it in the papers, this was the first I've known about it."

"I'm glad Dan Griggs enlightened you."

"He said that you enlightened him. You're ex-NYPD, right?"

"Right."

"Ever work homicide?"

"For many years."

"You think this was a homicide?"

"It has that distinct odor."

"What makes you think so?"

"Griggs told you about Bartlett's little identity problem?"

"Yes, we're looking at that now."

"That's a tip-off. Then there's the fact that Mrs. Bartlett rescinded a prenuptial agreement and made a new will in Paul Bartlett's favor less than a month before she was killed. And I understand she was very rich."

"First I've heard of that," Lundquist said. "I'll check it out. We're looking for the wrecked car, too. Right now, I'm not sure where it is."

"I'd be very interested in what you learn," Stone said.

"Tell me, what's your interest in Paul Bartlett?"

"He may be harassing a client of mine."

"Enough harassment to put him in jail?"

"Not yet, not unless he tries to harm her."

"So, if we arrested him for the murder of his wife, that would be okay with you, huh?"

"Sure would. But please don't think I'm trying to frame him for it to get my client off the hook. The information that Griggs and I passed on to you is just what I came up with, almost by accident. If he's a murderer, I'd like to see him nailed for it, but I'm not positive he's the guy who's harassing my client. There's a physical resemblance, and that's as far as I've gotten. Griggs told you about the FBI hold on his fingerprint file?"

"Yeah. I've run into that once before. It's not going to help."

"I don't see how it would hurt a homicide investigation. You can convict him as Bartlett or as John Doe; you don't need his real identity. I'm the one who needs that, so if you come up with something along those lines, I'd really like to hear about it."

"Can I reach you at this number?"

"Yes, and I'll give you my cell phone number, too." He recited the number.

"Got it. I'll call you."

"Thanks."

"Do you know where this guy can be found?"

"No. He checked out of the Chesterfield Hotel yesterday and didn't leave a forwarding address. He says he's house-hunting, and that he bought a Bentley. So far, he doesn't seem to have any interest in leaving Palm Beach, unless he's worried about me. I did ask him a few pointed questions."

"Do me a favor and don't crowd him. If we get something on him, I want him where I can find him."

"Our interests may diverge there," Stone said. "I have to put my client's safety first."

"Okay, okay, just try not to scare him out of town."

"I won't, unless I have to."

"Thanks. I'll call you."

"Bye." Stone hung up and greeted Callie, who was still yawning. "Sleep late?"

"It's the rain," she said. "It's like a narcotic. You had breakfast?"

"Yep, but it wasn't as good as the ones you make."

"You're sweet."

"Are you going to talk to Thad today?"

"Maybe. I can, if necessary."

"Please tell him that I've asked a friend, a New York City detective lieutenant, to come down here and lend a hand. I'd like to put him up on the boat."

"I'm sure that will be all right. We're not expecting any other guests, and anyway, the house is ready now. Who is this fellow?"

"His name is Dino Bacchetti. He and I were partners for a long time when I was on the force. He's saved my ass more than once."

"I must remember to thank him. Will I like him?"

"Probably. He'll certainly like you," Stone said.

"Should I see if I can find him some female companionship while he's here?"

"Not unless you want his Sicilian wife to come after you with a sharp instrument."

"I think not."

"Don't worry, Dino will be fine on his own. Anyway, we can pair him with Liz at dinner."

"Does he know her?"

"He knows about her, but they've never met."

"Funny, I don't think I've ever met a cop before. I mean, except for you, and you're not a cop anymore."

"You'll find Dino charming at times, and blunt to the point of rudeness at others."

"I never mind bluntness in people, unless they're insulting. Sometimes I'm not sure whether they're trying to insult."

"When Dino is trying, you'll know."

"He sounds interesting."

"He is certainly that."

Liz came out of her cabin and made her way aft.

"Oh, Liz," Callie said. "Stone has got you a date."

"Huh?" Liz asked sleepily.

"Not a date, just a dinner companion," Stone explained.

"As long as it's not Paul Manning," she said, sitting down at their table.

"It's not," Stone said. "Callie, so you know where the Rolls-Royce dealership is in Palm Beach?"

"It's in West Palm, on the mainland," she said. "Hang on, I'll show you." She dug a map out of her purse and pointed at it. "There are a whole bunch of car dealers along this stretch of road; it's one of those. You thinking of buying a Rolls?"

"No, but they sell Bentley, too."

26

Stone crossed the bridge to the mainland. The heavy rain roiled the Inland Waterway, and his windshield wipers were on full blast. The Rolls-Royce showroom was on the same lot with the BMW dealership, but separate. He put up his borrowed umbrella, strolled into the showroom and began looking at the Rollses and Bentleys, new and used, on the floor. Shortly, a man whose clothes were a cut above those of the average car salesman left his glassed-in office and approached him.

"Good morning. May I answer any questions?"

"Just looking, really. What does the new Bentley sell for?"

"It starts at two hundred fifteen thousand," the man said. "And there are some options available."

"Very handsome car," Stone said. "You just sold one to an acquaintance of mine — yesterday, I believe."

The salesman wrinkled his brow. "Yesterday? And who would that be?"

"His name is Paul Bartlett."

"Tall gentleman?"

"Yes."

"Oh, he came in and had a test drive, but he didn't buy a car. I believe he went into the BMW showroom next door, though. Perhaps they had something rather more to his liking."

"Maybe so," Stone said.

"Would you like to drive a car?"

"On another occasion, perhaps. Thanks for your time."

"Please come back," the salesman said.

Stone left and went next door. The BMW showroom was less plush than its neighbor, and the salesmen were lined up along the window at steel desks. One of them leaped up and came toward Stone.

"Hi, there. Can I show you a car?"

"Oh, I'm just window-shopping at the moment. You sold a car to a friend of mine yesterday, though."

"Oh? Who's that? We sell cars every day."

"Paul Bartlett."

"Oh, yeah. We did the deal on the phone. I picked him up at the airport yesterday. He's from Minneapolis."

"That's the one."

"Paul got the black 750i, with the V-twelve engine. I've got another one on the lot. I could put you in it inside the hour. Why don't you take a test drive?"

"Oh, I'd just be wasting your time. I'm a couple of weeks away from buying. I just wanted to have a look. Say, where is Paul staying, do you know? He was at the Chesterfield, but he's checked out."

"He's at the Colony. I sent the paperwork over there yesterday afternoon."

"Oh, yes, the Colony. Say, I don't mean to cause you any concern, but how did Paul pay for the car?"

"He gave me a cashier's check on a local bank." He suddenly looked concerned. "Why? Do you think something might be wrong?"

"Not if he gave you a cashier's check," Stone said. "Thanks for your time." He walked out of the showroom, put up his umbrella and ran back to his car, avoiding the deeper puddles. Well, he thought, Mr. Bartlett has lied about his residence and his car. He is obviously now watching his back. Stone sat in the car and called the Minneapolis police department.

"Ebbe Lundquist, in homicide," he said to the operator.

"Homicide," a man's voice said.

"Ebbe Lundquist, please."

"Lieutenant Lundquist is out of the office for a few days."

"Might he have gone to Florida?"

"That's right. Can someone else help you?"

"No, thanks," Stone said. He broke the connection and called Dan Griggs.

"Hello?"

"Morning, Dan, it's Stone Barrington. I believe you talked to a Lieutenant Lundquist yesterday?"

"Right."

"I think he's on the way down here."

"He must have found out something that got him moving," Griggs said.

"I think he wants to talk to Paul Bartlett," Stone said. "I've learned that Bartlett didn't buy a Bentley but a black BMW 750i. Also, he's moved into the Colony Hotel. I think Lundquist might appreciate it if you put a man on him. He seems to be getting slippery."

"I can do that."

"Tell him not to crowd the guy. Our friend Mr. Bartlett is getting nervous, and we wouldn't want him to bail out before Lundquist has a crack at him."

"I'll tell my man to work wide. Thanks, Stone."

"And I'd appreciate a call if there are any developments."

"Sure. You learn anything about that protocol ten-oh-two thing?"

"I talked to my old partner in New York. His guess is that Bartlett is, or rather was, in the Justice Department's witness protection program, and that he jumped ship and set up a new identity on his own."

"That's an interesting theory," Griggs said. "Has he got anything to back it up?"

"No, it's just his hunch, but I think it's a good one. By the way, he's coming down here soon, and I'd like for you to meet him. His name is Dino Bacchetti, and he commands the detective squad at the Nineteenth Precinct."

"Love to greet him," Griggs said.

"I'll bring him by. Take care." Stone hung up.

He pulled into traffic and headed back toward the yacht, and his cell phone rang again.

"Hello?"

"It's me," Dino said.

Stone could hear a police siren in the background. "Let me guess; you're on the way to the airport."

"That's right," Dino said. "My flight arrives at two-thirty." He gave Stone the flight number.

"I'll meet you. Dino, you've got to stop driving around with the siren on. A trip to the airport is not exactly an emergency call."

"It is if I say it is," Dino replied. "Traffic is hell on the FDR Drive right now."

"And the siren helps."

"You bet your ass it does. How's the weather down there?"

"Gorgeous," Stone said, peering through the driving rain at the road ahead, which was barely visible. "I hope you're bringing a swimsuit."

"Damn right I am; my golf clubs, too."

"Great. How about a tennis racket?"

"You know I'm a lousy tennis player."

"You're a lousy golfer, too, but you're bringing your clubs."

"If that sonofabitch doesn't get the fuck out of the way, ram him!" Dino shouted, apparently at his driver.

"Have you got another rookie detective at the wheel?"

"So what if I have?"

"Give the kid a break, Dino. He can't drive *over* the traffic."

"My flight leaves in twenty minutes."

"So what? You're not going through the airport; you're going to flash your badge and drive out onto the tarmac, right up to the airplane, aren't you?"

"You bet your ass, but I've still got to move to make it."

"So call the airline and tell them it's a police emergency, to hold the flight."

"Jesus, why didn't I think of that? Get off the phone!"

"I'll see you at Palm Beach Airport," Stone said, and pressed the end button. He laughed aloud at the thought of Dino holding the flight for a police emergency, then arriving at the airplane carrying his golf clubs.

He called the yacht, and Carrie answered.

"Hi. Where are you?"

"On the way back from the Rolls dealer."

"Find out anything?"

"I'll tell you later. Have you heard a weather forecast for tomorrow?"

"Rain ends late tonight; sunny all day tomorrow."

"Thank God. Dino's arriving this afternoon, with golf clubs. He'd shoot me if he couldn't play. Can you find us some golf somewhere?"

"Sure. I'll book a tee time at the Breakers. Ten o'clock okay?"

"Perfect. Dino's bringing his own clubs. I'll

need to rent some."

"You can use Thad's; he won't mind."

"Do you play?"

"I've got a twelve handicap. What's yours?"

"We'll make it a threesome, then," Stone said, avoiding an answer.

"Well," she said, laughing, "I'm glad you're interested in *some* kind of threesome."

27

Stone drove to the airport, and the rain had still not let up. At times he was driving through three and four inches of water in the street, and the wind had started to get up, as well. At the airport, he parked at the curb and ran inside, and the hell with tickets.

He found Dino in baggage claim, just getting his golf clubs off the carousel.

"You didn't tell me it was hurricane season," Dino grumbled, handing Stone two bags and hoisting the clubs onto a shoulder. "I should have brought fucking scuba gear!"

"Oh, I just wanted you to see that Palm Beach is a city of contrasts," Stone said, running for the car and getting soaked while stowing the bags in the trunk. The golf clubs had to go in the backseat. Finally, they were under way, with the windshield wipers trying hard to keep up with the deluge, and losing.

"I'm soaked to the skin!" Dino complained. "You might as well put the top down!"

"I don't understand it," Stone said. "The weather was glorious, until you decided to come."

"Oh, right, I brought the weather with me; it's all my fault."

"Thank you for pointing that out. So, how are things at home?"

"Oh, just great. Dolce is out."

Stone nearly wrecked the car. "What do you mean, 'out'?"

"Out. She set a fire in her room, which set off the alarm, and while her nurses were preoccupied with that, she got out of the house, took one of Eduardo's cars and vanished into the world."

"When did this happen?"

"This morning, apparently. Mary Ann called me on my pocket phone just as I was getting on the airplane. Eduardo is going nuts."

"She won't get far. Eduardo will have her back in no time. What, is she running around in her nightgown?"

"She packed three bags, according to the housekeeper, who counted the luggage. I'd say she has clothes for any occasion. Dolce is nothing if not organized."

"But she doesn't have any money or credit cards; she can't travel."

"Dolce has money of her own, you know, and quite a lot of it. Eduardo settled two million bucks on each of the girls when they turned twenty-one. And she took her purse, too — credit cards, even her passport. There's nowhere you can run."

"Oh, shit," Stone said, his heart sinking. He

dug out his cell phone and pressed the speed dial button for his office.

"The Barrington Practice," Joan said.

"Hi, it's me. You might get a call from Dolce sometime soon. Can you recognize her voice?"

"Sure I can. I heard it less than ten minutes ago."

"What did she want?"

"You, I expect."

"What did you tell her?"

"That you were out of town."

"Did you tell her where?"

"No."

"Thank God for that."

"Bill Eggers told her that."

"*What?*"

"As soon as she hung up I called Bill's office, but he was on the phone. I held, and when he came on the line, he told me Dolce had called, and they'd had a nice chat. I take it Bill isn't fully informed about Dolce's condition."

"Wonderful. If she calls back try and get a number where I can reach her."

"Okay."

Stone hung up and punched the button for Bill Eggers's office at Woodman & Weld.

"Bill?"

"I take it from Joan's reaction that I did something stupid?"

"It's not your fault, Bill, but just how stupid were you?"

"Stupid enough to tell her you were in Palm

Beach, before I noticed something about her. I stopped just short of telling her where you're staying."

"Thank God for small favors," Stone muttered.

"What's the matter with her, Stone? I thought she was just sick, but she sounded . . ."

"Exactly how did she sound?"

"Well, not deranged, exactly, but sort of otherworldly."

"Does she know I'm doing work for Thad Shames?"

"I didn't mention that."

"Okay, Bill, thanks, and I'll be in touch." Stone punched off. "She doesn't know where I'm staying."

"Her sister does."

"Oh, no. Mary Ann wouldn't . . ."

"No, of course she wouldn't, not if she were tortured, and Dolce is perfectly capable of torturing somebody to find out where you are."

Stone turned into the driveway of the Shames mansion.

"Hey, pretty nice," Dino said. "Do we have it to ourselves?"

"We're not staying in the house; we're out back."

"Guest house?"

"Not exactly."

"Uh-oh," Dino said.

"Come on, let's get the car unloaded and make a run for it."

189

Two minutes later they had dashed up the gangplank of *Toscana* and were standing, panting, on the afterdeck, while puddles formed around them. Juanito appeared with some towels and two thick terry robes, and took the luggage.

"Maybe you could change into the robes here?" he said, as he padded off toward Dino's cabin.

Stone and Dino emptied their pockets onto the table, including Dino's badge and gun, and stripped. They had just kicked their clothing into a sodden pile when Carrie appeared.

"Well, hi there, sailors!" she said to the two naked men.

Dino grabbed for his robe.

"This must be Dino," Callie said. "I can always recognize a naked policeman."

"Dino, this is Callie Hodges," Stone said, getting into his own robe.

"How do you do," Dino said, trying to muster some dignity.

"We have a ten-thirty tee time at the Breakers tomorrow," she said.

"Great," Dino said. "We can go there on the boat."

"Don't worry, the front will pass through tonight. Tomorrow will be beautiful, I promise. The greens may be a little slow, but Palm Beach is thirsty and will soak the rain right up. I'm surprised your plane was able to land."

"It took the pilot two tries," Dino said. "I was

ready to bust into the cockpit with my gun and order them to fly back to New York."

"I'm glad you didn't," Callie said, smiling sweetly.

Juanito came back with a tray of steaming mugs.

"We fixed you a little toddy," Callie said. "Figured that, with the temperature thirty degrees below normal, you might need it."

Everybody sat down, and Stone and Dino gratefully sipped their drinks, which were laced with rum.

"Well," Dino said to Callie, "any more at home like you?"

Callie laughed. "Don't worry, we've got you a date for dinner."

"Oh?"

"Allison Manning," Stone said. "Although she's called Liz Harding these days; you might remember that."

"I'll try," Dino said.

"Callie, have there been any phone calls for me?"

"No."

"If anyone besides Thad, Bill Eggers, Chief Griggs or my secretary, Joan, calls, will you tell them I've gone back to New York?"

"Sure. Who are you avoiding?"

"Mrs. Stone Barrington," Dino said.

She turned and looked at Stone, and her eyes narrowed. "*Who?*"

Dino set down his cup. "Well, I think I'll go

get into some dry clothes."

As soon as he was gone, Stone began explaining to Callie who Dolce was. When he had finished, he waited for a comment.

"Well," she said finally, "hanging around you is never dull."

28

Because of the weather, they had dinner in the yacht's dining room, which was a symphony of mahogany and teak. Juanito had set a small table for the four of them, and candlelight gleamed on fine silver, as he served the dinner Callie had cooked for them. Dino had taken a shine not only to Callie, but to Liz as well, and they to him.

"What, exactly, do you do on the police force, Dino?" Liz asked him.

"Well, you know how, on the TV cop shows there's always these two detectives who are out there busting their balls to solve the case?"

"Yes."

"That used to be Stone and me."

"Oh."

"And you know how the two detectives come back to the station house and report to their lieutenant, and he criticizes them and second-guesses them and ridicules them and sends them back out onto the street to do it all over again?"

"Yes."

"That lieutenant is me, now."

"Was Stone a good detective?" Callie asked.

Stone shifted his weight uncomfortably.

"He wasn't all that bad," Dino said, "but he was hard to keep alive. I was always having to shoot people so they wouldn't kill him."

"Nonsense! I was a *very* good detective," Stone said, "but that second part is perfectly true, which gives you a pretty good indication of what percentage of Dino's statements you can believe."

"Tell us about when you saved Stone's life," Liz said.

Dino took a big sip of his wine. "Well, let's see," he said. "The first time was when we had chased this guy down in a car, and he came out shooting, got Stone in the knee. I put one in the middle of his forehead."

"Goodness," Callie said. Both the women were rapt.

"Then there was the time Stone had to jump out of a helicopter because people were trying to kill him. I used a shotgun that time; didn't kill anybody. Then — oh, this is my favorite — this very strange guy had Stone strung up by his heels, naked, in this old slaughterhouse, about to cut him a few new orifices, and I put two in him."

Liz blinked rapidly. "Strung up by his heels, naked? Whew! If I had a folding fan, this is where I'd use it."

"And there were probably a couple of other times, but you get the idea."

Callie spoke up. "The idea seems to be that

Stone needs his hand held." She took his hand and squeezed it.

"That's about it," Dino said. "Stone has good instincts, but he never listens to them. He's so curious that he doesn't notice when people are trying to kill him."

"Tell us about Stone and women," Callie said.

Dino rolled his eyes. "Don't get me started."

"No," Stone said, "don't get him started. You keep this up, Dino, and I'm going to start telling them the truth about you."

Dino held up a hand. "Peace," he said. "Anything else you girls want to know about Stone, you're going to have to ask him."

"Well, Stone," Callie said. "Will you sit still for some personal questions?"

"As long as you don't expect an honest answer," Stone replied.

Juanito suddenly appeared, the cordless phone in his hands. "Miss Callie," he said, then mouthed, "It's for him," pointing at Stone.

Callie took the phone. "May I help you? And who is this? I'm sorry, Mr. Barrington left this morning. I believe he was headed for California somewhere, before returning to New York. No, I'm sorry, I don't have his schedule. Why don't you call his New York office? Goodbye." She punched the off button.

"Was it a woman?" Stone asked.

"No, a man. He wouldn't give his name. He sounded a little like Paul Bartlett, but I can't be sure about that."

"That was a nice touch, about California," Stone said. "I'll have to remember what a good liar you are."

"I was lying in a good cause," Callie replied. "Dino needs help in keeping you alive."

"Like Regis says, 'I'm only one man,'" Dino said.

The phone rang again while still in Callie's hand. "Here we go again," she said. "Hello? Oh, yes, Chief, I'll put him on." She handed the phone to Stone.

"Hello, Dan."

"Hi, Stone. Our friend from the frozen tundra, Lieutenant Lundquist, has arrived. Could we have a word with you tonight?"

"Sure," Stone said. "Give me half an hour, then come over to the Shames house. We're on the yacht moored out back."

"See you then."

Stone hung up. "Well, ladies, you're going to have a couple more cops on your hands shortly."

"I'd better finish dessert," Callie said, rising and heading toward the galley.

"What cops?" Dino asked.

Stone explained about Griggs and Lundquist, and about Paul Bartlett's sojourn in Minneapolis.

"God, I love catching murderers," Dino said, "don't you?"

"Not as much as you, Dino, but I'll admit, it's satisfying. What I don't like about murderers is that time after you've figured out what they did but before you arrest them. They tend to be touchy during that period."

"So you think Bartlett is dangerous?"

"I certainly do. Griggs has assigned somebody to keep an eye on him, but Lundquist has asked us not to crowd him just yet."

"I hate not crowding them," Dino said.

Callie returned to the table, followed by Juanito carrying a tray of flaming desserts.

"Something old-fashioned," she said. "Baked Alaska. I thought, given the weather, we could use the extra warmth."

"Mmmmmmmm," Dino said, plunging into his. "We may keep you on here."

"Why, thank you, sir."

Liz was toying with her dessert. "Stone," she said, "am I ever going to be able to leave this boat again?"

"Sure you are, but right now is not a good time. Paul doesn't know you're here, at least not for sure."

"We could stake her out, like a goat for a lion," Dino said.

"Thank you, Dino," Liz said. "That was so beautifully put."

"Don't mention it," Dino said, grinning.

29

Chief Dan Griggs and Lieutenant Ebbe Lundquist arrived, sharing a golf umbrella. They were both dripping wet.

"Sorry to get you out this late, Chief," Stone said. "Couldn't this have waited for better weather?"

"Lundquist, here, insisted," Griggs replied.

Lundquist looked around at the yacht. "You live pretty well, Mr. Barrington."

"I'm sorry to disappoint you, but, unfortunately, the yacht is not mine. And please call me Stone." Stone introduced everybody, and Callie got the visitors a hot toddy, while everyone else had brandy.

"It's like this," Lundquist said. "We dug Bartlett's car out of a junkyard, where it was waiting to go into the compactor. Couple more days, it would have been gone. We have you to thank for that, Stone."

Stone shrugged. "I just happened to get lucky."

"The car was a 1991 Mercedes station wagon, and that year, a passenger-side air bag was an option, and Mrs. Bartlett, who owned the car, had not ordered the option. Everything about the car was normal, for one that had just collided with a tree, except that the seat belt latch had been tampered with."

"Tampered with how?" Dino asked.

"There's a steel eye that sticks up on a stalk, then there's the receptor end that latches onto that. We opened up the receptor, and the spring inside had been deformed, compared with the driver's side, so that it would not hook securely when fastened. Mrs. Bartlett would have heard a click when she put it on, but it would have come undone under pressure."

"And colliding with a tree would certainly be enough pressure," Stone said.

"This guy is very clever," Lundquist said. "That was the sort of technical thing that would have gone completely unnoticed if you hadn't given us a heads up to look for something."

"This same guy once rigged an airplane engine to fail, killing all three aboard," Stone said. "He's not stupid, and he has some skills."

"*What?*" Lundquist demanded. "He's murdered three *other* people?"

"If he's who I think he is," Stone said. He explained Paul Manning's background, not mentioning that he had been Liz's husband.

"So we couldn't charge him with those three killings, then?" Lundquist asked.

"No, he was tried and convicted, then the authorities were bought off."

"He might even have a pardon," Liz said.

Stone looked at her. "Was his wife pardoned?"

"In a manner of speaking. She was given a piece of paper."

"So, Lieutenant, do you have enough evidence to arrest him?"

"I can arrest him for obtaining a Minnesota driver's license under a false name, and I can probably get him extradited, but I'm not sure we have enough evidence to convict him of murder. Still, I'd like to get him back to Minneapolis and question him thoroughly. Maybe he'll even cop to it."

"Not a chance," Stone said. "He'd lawyer up in a heartbeat. I'd be willing to bet he's got the number in his pocket right now, just in case. And it sounds like you'd have a hell of a time proving that he tampered with the seat belt. His attorney would paint it as damaged in the accident or defectively manufactured, and Bartlett as a grieving husband."

"Maybe you're right," Lundquist said, "but I'm waiting for a call from my office, and when they come up with just a little more evidence, I'm going to bust him. At the very least I can expose his false identity and let the world know who he is."

"He's not going to tell you who he is," Stone said, "and that's the only way you're going to find out. The feds certainly aren't going to admit that he was in their program."

"If he's Paul, I can identify him in court," Liz said.

"I thought you were refusing to face him," Stone replied.

"I won't while he's free, but I'd be happy to testify as to his identity, if it would help put him away."

"I don't know that it would," Stone said. "Given the evidence we've got, I'd much rather defend him than prosecute."

"This is very convoluted," Dino said. "Not only do we not know if he was in the witness protection program, we don't even know what name he was using before he went in."

"I don't understand," Liz said.

"Okay, he gets out of being hanged in St. Marks, and he returns to this country. He's not going back to using Paul Manning for a name, he's going to pick another one. Then he gets involved in whatever ends up getting him into the program, and he gives the feds that name, not Manning. They change it to another name, then he skips out of the program and changes it again. And there may be a couple of other name changes that we don't even know about."

"Holy cow," Lundquist said. "I didn't know what I was getting into when I came down here."

"You probably wanted a little nice weather, like me," Dino said. He waved an arm. "And look what we got."

Lundquist gazed through the transparent curtains as lightning lit up Lake Worth. "I might as well have stayed in Minneapolis."

"Well," Chief Griggs said, "if it's any consolation, I think we've got enough to run him out of Palm Beach."

"You sound like an Old West sheriff," Callie said.

"It's a little different," Griggs replied. "In the Old West, I'd have threatened to shoot him if he showed his face in town again. Nowadays, I'd just make sure the local and Florida papers heard the whole story, and once everybody had heard about it and gossiped about it, he wouldn't be able to show his face in town again. We had a guy down here a few years back that had kidnapped his young kids when a divorce didn't go his way. Established himself here under another name and stayed for years until his wife caught up with him. Now he's persona non grata among the people he knew best. That, I can do to Bartlett, or whatever his name is."

"It isn't enough," Liz said. "He could still try to kill me."

Lundquist turned and stared at her. "Just when I thought I had a grip on this story . . ."

"Mrs. Harding was once married to Paul Manning," Stone said. "We didn't mention that before."

"Oh," Lundquist said, tonelessly. He was massaging his temples, like someone trying to hold on to his sanity.

"Maybe your lab will come up with something else in the car," Stone said.

"Maybe, but I'm not going to count on it,"

Lundquist replied. "We do have the fact that he got his wife to cancel the prenuptial agreement and make a new will. That's motive."

"Oh, you have both motive and opportunity," Stone said, "but a good lawyer would make a conviction very difficult to obtain. It's like this: I'm his lawyer, and I stand up in front of the jury. Ladies and gentlemen, my client had no criminal intent when he changed his name. Bad people were after him, and he had to protect himself. Why, it was the government itself that changed his name first. There's no evidence that he put pressure on his wife to change her will. No, she did that out of love and affection for my client, who is a very loveable and affectionate fellow, crushed by the loss of his bride. My client doesn't have the technical expertise to tamper with a finely made piece of German engineering, and after all, he was in the same car; he could have been just as easily killed. And on and on like that."

"This is very depressing," Lundquist said.

Dino spoke up. "It might help in court if you proved he was Paul Manning, who had already murdered three other people in St. Marks, even if he got away with it."

"I could get his past ruled out as evidence," Stone said, "on the grounds that it was irrelevant and prejudicial, and if I couldn't, I'd say he was railroaded by a corrupt foreign government. No, Mr. Bartlett has crafted himself a very nice little box to live in. And, Dan, if you got him run out of Palm Beach, he'd just go to Palm Springs, or some other place with an inviting climate, and establish himself all over again under another identity. And now he's got the money to make himself credible in a place like that."

Everybody was quiet for a while.

Finally, Dino spoke up again. "Unless we staked out Liz like a goat for a lion, then waited to see what happened."

30

The four of them got out of the two cars at the Breakers Golf Club and gave three bags of clubs to the attendant. The clubhouse was modest, in comparison to the grandeur of the hotel, Stone thought. The weather, as predicted, had cleared beautifully, and it was much cooler after the front had passed through.

"But I don't play golf," Liz complained. "What am I doing here?"

"Playing chauffeur," Stone said. "You can drive a cart. Also, you're playing the goat."

"I don't think I like the goat idea," she said. "Not when Paul is the lion."

"Dino's right," Stone said, "as much as I hate to admit it. This is the only way to smoke him out. We're not having much luck any other way. If we see him, you can identify him; if not, then at least *we'll* be seen, and word may get back to him that you're still around."

"All right," Liz said.

"This is a pretty chilly paradise you got here," Dino said, zipping up his jacket to the neck.

"In more ways than one," Callie said, as another group of golfers inspected them as they passed, staring hard.

They signed in at the clubhouse, then got into carts and drove to the first tee, where the starter cleared them to tee off.

The course was mostly flat and uninteresting. "It's not the most attractive golf course I've ever seen," Stone said.

"Don't worry, they're about to rip the whole thing up and completely rebuild it to new design," Callie said.

"Ladies first," Dino said, motioning Callie to drive.

Callie took a few practice swings, displaying good form, teed up a ball and struck it solidly. It flew down the middle of the fairway.

"About two hundred and twenty yards," Stone said. He teed up and sliced his drive into the next fairway.

"Take a mulligan," Callie said.

Stone took the mulligan and got it in the fairway, a good twenty yards short of Callie's ball.

Dino teed up and hooked the ball into the rough. "Mulligan," he said, teeing up another ball. He swung at that, and it landed no more than a yard from his first ball.

"Your grip is too strong," Callie said, showing him how to turn his right hand to the left. "That should cure your hook."

"Don't count on it," Stone said.

They trundled off down the fairway in their carts, playing at a good pace, now and then crossing South County Road.

"This is the most urban golf I've ever played," Stone said. "Usually, on a golf course, you don't have to worry about being hit by a car."

"The Breakers has another course west of here," Callie said. "Maybe we'll play that one next time."

They played on, occasionally running into a foursome in which Callie knew someone. Two people knew Liz and chatted with her.

"Word's getting out," Callie said. "You shouldn't even try to keep a secret in this town, but we're advertising. Liz, you're the subject of much conversation since being seen with Thad at his party."

"Grand," Liz said.

They finished their round, went back to the clubhouse, had a beer, stowed their clubs in the two cars and prepared to depart the Breakers. Stone opened his cell phone and tapped in a number. "Okay, Dan, we've made our appearance at the Breakers, and we're ready to move on to part two of our plan."

"My guys are parked just down the road," Griggs said.

"Tell them not to crowd the girls. We don't want Bartlett picking up on cops."

"Bartlett left the Colony half an hour ago, and he's having lunch on Worth Avenue."

"They'll go shopping, then," Stone said. "Dino and I will wait back at the yacht."

"Right," Griggs said.

Stone ended the call. "Okay, ladies, you are sentenced to Worth Avenue shopping for at least two hours. Liz, if you recognize Paul, don't let on, just tell Callie so she can confirm who he is. You've got my cell phone number if you need to reach me."

"I'd feel better if you and Dino came along," Liz said.

"He knows us both, so we can't do that. We'd just scare him off."

"Oh, all right," Liz said, disconsolately. She got into the car with Callie, and they drove off.

"There goes our goat," Dino said. "But even if she makes him, Griggs isn't going to have any grounds for an arrest."

"Lundquist does, though. He can always bust him for the driver's license, and that will at least get him out of our hair."

"For the time being," Dino said. "This guy ain't going to go away easy."

"You have a point," Stone agreed.

They drove back to the yacht and waited. Dino got into a swimsuit and took up a strategic position on a chaise on the afterdeck, a rum and tonic at his elbow.

"You got anything to read?" he asked Stone.

Stone went into the saloon and came back with the novel *Tumult* that he had read a few days before. "Try this," he said, handing it to Dino. "It's very good."

Dino was soon rapt, and Stone dozed on a

nearby chaise, protecting his fair skin from the sun under an awning.

Stone woke up with Callie shaking him. "Huh?" he said, sleepily.

"We're back," Callie said.

Stone sat up. "Anything happen?"

"We saw him."

"You did?"

"Coming out of Verdura, the jewelry store."

Liz came up the gangplank.

"Liz, you saw him?"

She nodded. "Yes."

"And?"

"And I don't know."

"You don't know what?"

"I don't know if it's Paul."

"But you said you recognized him in East-hampton by the way he walked and his body language."

"It was different this time," she said. "Anyway, I only saw him for a minute."

"Liz," Callie said, "you had a very good look at him. I was there; I saw him, too."

"Well, I'm sorry," Liz said crossly, "but I just can't swear that he's Paul. He may be and he may not be."

Stone's cell phone vibrated, and he opened it. "Hello?"

"It's Dan Griggs. The two ladies got a real good look at the guy. What does Mrs. Harding say?"

"Inconclusive," Stone said, walking away from the group.

"How could it be inconclusive? She got a good look at him, and she used to be married to the guy."

"All I can tell you is what she told me," Stone said. "She seems pretty annoyed about our pressing her on it."

"I don't get it," Griggs said.

"Frankly, neither do I. I thought that if we just put Bartlett in front of her, she'd make him, and that would be that."

"You think she's not playing this straight?"

"I honestly don't know, Dan. She's protected him in the past, after all."

"But she's supposed to be scared of the guy. You'd think she'd want to be rid of him and would help us do it."

"I don't know what to tell you, Dan."

"Well, if Mrs. Harding can't identify the guy, and if Lundquist can't come up with enough evidence for a murder warrant, I'm not going to be able to keep men on this. We have other problems to deal with, you know."

"I know you do, Dan, and I don't blame you. Has Lundquist not heard from his office?"

"He's called them twice, but the lab is still working on the car."

"Okay. Ask him to call me when he gets word. If he's going to arrest Bartlett, I'd like to be there when he does it."

"I'll tell him."

Stone ended the call and stood there thinking for a moment. He was getting tired of this, too. He punched 411 into the phone, asked for the number of the Colony Hotel and waited while the operator connected him.

"The Colony, good afternoon," a woman's voice said.

"Paul Bartlett, please."

She connected him, and the phone rang and rang. Finally she came back on the line. "There's no answer. Would you like to leave a message?"

"Yes, please. Ask him to . . ."

"One moment, I'll connect you with the front desk." She did so.

"Reception," a man's voice said.

"I'd like to leave a message for Paul Bartlett," Stone said. He'd just arrange to meet the man and put Liz's proposition to him.

"I'm sorry, but Mr. Bartlett checked out just a few minutes ago, and I'm afraid he didn't leave a forwarding address."

Stone punched the end button. "Shit," he said aloud.

31

Stone couldn't believe it. He and Dino got dressed and into a car and drove to the Colony Hotel; he wanted to question the desk man. As they pulled into the parking lot, he spotted Detective Riley and Lieutenant Lundquist sitting in an idling car thirty yards away. Stone walked over and rapped on the window, startling them both.

"What are you doing here, Stone?" Lundquist asked. "You're going to spook the guy."

"What guy?" Stone asked.

"Bartlett."

"Bartlett has decamped."

"*What?*"

"Come with me." Stone started for the hotel lobby.

Lundquist caught up and fell into step with Stone. "What do you mean, 'decamped'?"

"I mean, Bartlett has checked out of the hotel, and he didn't leave a forwarding address."

"How do you know that?"

"Because I telephoned him half an hour ago, and that's what the desk clerk told me. I want to find out if it's true, or if Bartlett simply bought the desk man, and I want you to flash your badge at him so he'll talk to me."

The desk clerk stared blankly at the badge. "You're a police officer? Where? Your badge doesn't look familiar."

"He's from Minneapolis," Stone said. "I can have a Palm Beach badge here in thirty seconds, if that will refresh your memory."

"My memory about what?"

"First of all, has Paul Bartlett really checked out?"

"Yes, I saw him go."

"What forwarding address did he give?"

"I'll show you his registration card," the clerk said, riffling through a stack of them. "Here." He held it up. The space for a forwarding address was blank.

"Did you check him out of the hotel?"

"In a manner of speaking. He didn't even wait for his bill, said he had to catch a plane and I should mail it to him."

"To where?"

"To the address on the card."

Lundquist checked the card. "It's his Minneapolis address. The guy's gone home."

"How much luggage did he have?" Stone asked.

"A lot; three or four bags."

"And where did the bellman load his car?"

"Down on the street," the clerk said, pointing at the side door.

"That's why he got past you," Stone said to Lundquist. "I'd like to see his room, please."

The man pressed a few buttons on a machine, and a plastic card was spat out. "It's suite four-oh-four. Help yourself," he said.

Stone led the way to the elevator and pressed four. A moment later they were standing outside the suite, and Stone got the door open.

"Easy there," Lundquist said, pushing past Stone. "I'd better go first."

"It's not a crime scene," Stone said, following him. "Unless there's a corpse stashed under the bed."

Lundquist looked under the bed. "Nothing."

"No kidding?" Stone looked around. The room had already been cleaned that morning, and the bed had not been used since. He went around the room, looking in closets and opening drawers.

"What are you looking for?" Lundquist asked.

"I don't know," Stone replied.

"Whatever he can find," Dino said.

Lundquist started opening drawers, too.

Stone went back into the sitting room and looked around. The place was neat as a pin, the wastebaskets were empty, and there was not so much as a trace of Paul Bartlett, or whoever he was.

"What now?" Lundquist asked.

"The airport," Stone replied. "He told the clerk he had to catch a plane."

The three men left the hotel, and Lundquist

got into the rear seat of Stone's convertible.

"I should be wearing sunscreen," Lundquist said as they pulled out of the parking lot.

"Yeah, that pale Scandinavian skin will fry every time," Dino said, half to himself, chuckling. "World's whitest white men."

"That's what you call me," Stone said.

"You, too."

At the airport, they went to the nearest ticket counter, and Lundquist flashed his badge and asked about flights to Minneapolis.

"None of the airlines flies directly to Minneapolis from Palm Beach," the woman behind the counter said. "You'd have to change, probably in Atlanta."

"Will you check reservations for a Paul Bartlett?" Lundquist asked.

The woman turned to her computer terminal, tapped a few keys and looked at the screen. "I'll do a search for the name," she said, tapping more keys. "Nope, nobody by that name."

"Try Paul Manning," Stone said, because he couldn't think of anything else to do.

She tapped the keys again. "Nope, no Manning."

"Do you recall, in the past hour or so, a tall man, six-three or -four, mid-to-late forties, dark hair going gray, fairly good-looking?"

"No, and I think I'd have noticed," the woman said, smiling.

"Thanks for your help," Stone said. He turned to Lundquist and Dino. "Let's hit the charter services."

"How do we find those?" Lundquist asked.

"There's a big sign outside, pointing to them all," Stone replied.

They went outside and checked the sign; there were half a dozen.

"Ebbe, you go in the car with Riley and check the north side of the field; Dino and I will check the south side."

"Okay." Lundquist jumped into the car with Riley.

"Well," Dino said as they got into the Mercedes. "Lundquist isn't the brightest tulip in the garden, is he?"

"Tulips are Dutch, not Scandinavian, and remember, he's a lieutenant, like you."

"Well, he can't be all bad," Dino said.

They checked all four companies on the south side of the field and came up with nothing. As they left the last one, Lundquist and Riley drove up.

"Nothing on the north side," Riley said.

"Nothing over here, either," Stone said. "Where's the chief?"

"Probably in his office," Riley replied.

Stone punched the number into his cell phone and asked for Griggs.

"Chief, Bartlett has checked out of the Colony."

216

"Well, shit," Griggs said. "You think he's left town?"

"He told the desk clerk he had a plane to catch, but we're at the airport now, and he didn't fly out of here."

"I guess he could have driven to Miami," Griggs said. "It's only an hour and a half to the airport."

"Can you check the flights out of there for a Bartlett or Manning?"

"I'll put somebody on it. Where do you think he went?"

"The only address we have is Minneapolis, but I don't think he's there."

"Where do you think he is?"

"I think he's still in Palm Beach. Remember, he checked out of the Chesterfield, too, without leaving a forwarding address, and he went directly to the Colony. Maybe, before you check the Miami flights, you should alert the other hotels in town to call you if he checks in."

"Okay, Stone, I'll do that."

"It seems that every time we start to get a line on the guy, he changes hotels."

"I'll get back to you."

Stone hung up.

"You think he's in another hotel?" Dino asked.

"That's my guess," Stone said. Then he thought for a moment. "Unless . . ."

"Unless what?"

"Come on," Stone said, "let's get back to the yacht, quick."

217

32

Stone drove as quickly as he could, without getting arrested, through West Palm and across the bridge. Traffic was heavy and frustrating, and it took them nearly half an hour to reach the Shames residence. The front door stood open, and he ran quickly through the central hall and out the open back door, with Dino close on his heels.

As he came up the gangplank he was presented with an uncharacteristic sight on *Toscana*: a mess. Towels and books were scattered indiscriminately across the afterdeck. Normally, Juanito made a mess disappear as soon as it presented itself.

Stone turned around and was not surprised to see a gun in Dino's hand. He put a finger to his lips, then motioned for Dino to follow him. He walked through the saloon and down the corridor toward his cabin. His cabin door was open, and so was every other door in the passageway. He went into his cabin to retrieve the 9mm automatic from under his pillow. It was gone. He went back into the passage and climbed a few steps to the bridge, and as he approached it, he could hear music. He stepped onto the bridge, ready for anything. A portable radio rested on the dash above the wheel, softly playing rock music.

Stone crossed the bridge and left it on the other side, returning along the port corridor. Again, every cabin door was open.

He heard a footstep from somewhere aft and tiptoed toward it. Dino brushed past him, the gun out in front. He was armed, and he would lead the way; there was no talk about it. Stone followed him into the saloon.

"*What the hell!*" a man's voice shouted. "Who are you?"

Stone stepped around Dino to find Thad Shames standing in the saloon. "Thad," he said. "It's all right, Dino."

"What's going on here, Stone?" Shames demanded, clearly startled. "Who is this?"

"Thad, I'm sorry we frightened you. This is Lieutenant Dino Bacchetti, of the New York Police Department. Dino, this is Thad Shames, our host here."

Dino put the gun away, and the two men shook hands.

Thad collapsed onto a sofa. "Tell me what's happened," he said.

"I don't know what's happened," Stone replied. "We came back to the yacht a few minutes ago to find it deserted, and all the cabin doors open."

"No Callie or Liz? No crew?"

"Nobody."

"There's nobody in the main house, either," Thad said, "but the front and rear doors were open."

"I know; we just came through there."

"Do you think Callie and Liz might have gone shopping or something?"

"I don't think so; they did that earlier today."

"Did you check the pool?"

"Pool? What pool?"

"There's a pool on the property, you know."

"No, I didn't know. It must be very well concealed."

"Come on, let's take a look." Thad led the way down the gangplank and into the gardens. Instead of taking the path to the house, he turned right and appeared to be about to walk through a hedge, when he turned and disappeared.

Stone followed and discovered a gap in the hedge, concealed by a quick left turn, followed by a right. He caught up with Thad, who had stopped and, with his hands on his hips, was staring ahead.

"Isn't that lovely?" Thad said softly.

Stone looked and saw a beautiful swimming pool, completely surrounded by the high hedge. Beside it, perhaps thirty feet away, lay two women, asleep on their backs, naked.

Thad motioned them back through the gap in the hedge. "Let's give them a little warning," he said. "Callie? Liz?" he called out loudly.

"Yes?" Callie's voice replied. "We're out here."

Shames led them through the hedge a second time. Callie and Liz were tying robes around themselves. "There you are," he said. "I thought you had both decamped." He pecked Callie on the cheek, then embraced Liz at more length.

"Not likely," Callie said. "We thought we'd be safe here."

"Where's the crew?" Stone asked.

"I gave them the afternoon off. We weren't expecting you, Thad."

"And why are all the doors on the yacht open?"

"I thought it would be good to air out the cabins; keeps the mildew down."

"You gave us a scare," Stone said.

Callie reached into a pocket of her robe and produced the 9mm automatic. "We're perfectly all right," she said, handing the weapon to Stone. "Come on, let's go back to the yacht."

The group returned to *Toscana*, and Callie got drinks for everybody, except Liz, who excused herself to change. Callie followed her.

"Oh, Callie?" Thad called after her.

She turned. "Yes, Thad?"

"Book us a table someplace gaudy tonight. We'll celebrate my return."

Callie nodded and went toward her cabin.

"Where have you come from?" Stone asked.

"California. I've been sort of barnstorming LA and San Francisco and Silicon Valley, talking up the new company."

"I hope it went well."

"It did. How are things going here?"

"It's gotten complicated," Stone said. "Let me bring you up to date."

"I'd appreciate that."

Stone told him, in detail, everything that had happened in his absence. When he was through, he stopped talking and waited.

"And you still don't know if this guy is really Manning?"

"No," Stone said. "Not even Liz can be sure."

"I find that hard to believe," Shames said.

"So do I, but that's the way it is. She saw him only briefly in Easthampton, and something about the way he moved made her think the man she saw was Paul Manning. But she can't be sure that Paul Bartlett is Manning."

"And this guy Bartlett is a friend of Frank and Margaret?"

"Yes, from Minneapolis."

"And you think he killed his wife for her money?"

"It seems a strong possibility."

Shames grinned. "Well, this has certainly turned out to be interesting, hasn't it?"

"That's one way to look at it," Stone said. "I'm sorry I don't have any definite answers for you."

"I'm sure you'll come up with them," Shames said. "Well, Dino, welcome to Palm Beach. Callie told me you were coming, and I'm glad you could join us. Have you been made comfortable?"

"Yes, thanks," Dino said. "She's a beautiful yacht."

"Thank you, I think so." Thad stood up. "Well, if you'll excuse me, I'm going to go to my room in the main house and have a nap. I've been traveling for days, and I'm a little tired. I'll bounce back for dinner, though." He gave a little wave and left the yacht.

"He's a pretty easygoing guy, isn't he?" Dino said.

"He certainly is."

"I mean, if I'd come aboard my yacht and found a stranger with a gun, I'd have freaked out, but he didn't."

"I thought he behaved very well, in the circumstances," Stone said. "Looks like our goat-and-lion plan didn't work. If anything, we're worse off than we were this morning."

"Well, there's still dinner," Dino said. "If we're going someplace gaudy, *anybody* could be there, right?"

"In Palm Beach, you're right."

33

Callie's choice of a gaudy restaurant turned out to be the high-ceilinged, chandeliered, tapestried, velvet-seated La Reserve. Thad seemed particularly pleased with the choice, and he swept the group to a round table at the center of the single large room, slipping the maître d' a bill on the way, then ordering a Krug champagne for everybody.

"You have beluga, of course," Thad said to the captain.

"Of course, Mr. Shames," the man replied. "Fifty grams each?"

"Let's start with half a kilo for the table," Shames said. Glasses were filled, and Thad raised his. "To this group," he said. "I'm happy to be back with you all." He turned to Liz at his side. "Particularly you."

Everyone drank. A moment later, a crystal bowl of caviar arrived, and the waiter went around the table spooning large amounts onto each plate.

Dino tried his.

"Well?" Thad asked.

"Well, wonderful," Dino replied. "We don't

see a lot of beluga at the precinct."

"I remember once when we did," Stone said. "Somebody on the squad busted up a smuggling outfit, and, among other things, there was a lot of caviar. Most of it disappeared immediately, but I remember a few small tins found their way to your desk and mine."

"You're right, Stone," Dino said. "Funny, I remember busts involving drugs and money, but you remember caviar."

Menus appeared and everyone pored over them. Eventually, decisions were made, and the captain took their orders. Thad lingered over the wine list. "Who's drinking red?" he asked. Everyone's hand went up. "Ah, good. We'll start with a magnum of the Opus One," he said to the sommelier. "The 'eighty-nine."

The sommelier scurried away and returned with the big bottle. Thad tasted it. "Marvelous! Go ahead and pour us a glass so it can breathe."

"I like your friends," Dino said to Stone, getting a laugh.

"Ah, Dino," Thad said, "you have to spend more time in Palm Beach. The yacht is yours whenever you want it."

"Nobody ever said that to me before," Dino said, drawing another laugh.

Stone thought the evening was going particularly well. Then he looked up and saw Frank and Margaret Wilkes come into the restaurant, followed closely by a woman Stone did not know, and then, by Paul Bartlett. No one else at the table had seen them, but Stone caught Dino's eye and nodded in their direction.

Dino watched the tall man hold a chair for his companion, then sit down. "I would never have made him as Manning," Dino whispered. "He must have done something to his face."

Stone slipped the little cell phone off his belt, cupped it in his hand to hide it as well as possible, and dialed Dan Griggs's direct office number, which also rang at his home.

"Yes?" Griggs said.

"Dan, it's Stone. I'm at La Reserve, and Bartlett is here with Frank Wilkes and his wife and another woman."

"Have you talked to Lundquist?" Griggs asked.

"No."

"The Minneapolis department arrested a known car thief and insurance scam artist who, for immunity, told them Bartlett had hired him to fix his wife's seat belt. Apparently, they met in prison, during Bartlett's earlier existence, and he'll testify against Bartlett. Have they just sat down to eat?"

"Yes."

"Good. I'll get ahold of Lundquist and put some people together, and we'll take him when they leave. I don't want to cause a scene in the restaurant. Let me give you my portable number."

Stone wrote it down.

"Call that number when they get their check. That way I won't have to send people in to watch him. He's pretty edgy; he might catch on to that."

"I'll do it," Stone said. "I imagine you have a good hour and a half."

"See you later."

Stone put the phone away and saw Thad looking at him inquiringly. "It's nothing," he said.

Their dinner arrived, and everyone ate heartily, still in high spirits from the champagne. They had just finished their dessert, and their dishes were being taken away, when Stone looked up to see Lieutenant Ebbe Lundquist enter the restaurant, flash his badge at the maître d' and take up a position at the bar. Stone looked at Bartlett. He had seen the badge and was now staring at Lundquist, who in his plaid polyester suit looked out of place in the elegant restaurant.

Stone glanced at Dino, who had already taken this in.

"That's one really stupid cop," Dino said quietly.

Stone looked over at Bartlett's table and saw the waiter approaching with the check. "Excuse me a minute," Stone said to the table. "I'll be right back."

He rose and made his way across the restaurant to where the Wilkeses and Bartlett were sitting.

Frank Wilkes rose to greet him. "Stone," he said, "how good to see you."

Stone shook his hand as Bartlett, too, rose, buttoning his jacket.

"Hello, Stone," he said. "How are you?" He introduced his companion.

"How do you do? Good evening, Paul. Please sit down." Stone caught sight of the bulge under Bartlett's jacket.

"Frank, Margaret, I just wanted to thank you for such a delightful dinner the other evening," Stone said. "It was very kind of you to ask Callie and me."

"We were very glad to have you," Margaret Wilkes said, "and we hope you'll come again."

Stone caught sight of Lundquist moving down the bar.

"I see you're about to leave," Stone said to Wilkes. "Please let me send over some after-dinner drinks before you go." He didn't wait for an answer, but summoned a nearby waiter and told him to bring the Wilkes party whatever they wanted and to send the bill to him. That would keep them in their seats for another few minutes, Stone thought. He made his goodbyes and, instead of returning to his table, walked toward the front of the restaurant and the men's room, dialing Dan Griggs's cell phone number on the way. He caught Dino's eye and patted his side, where Bartlett was wearing the gun. As he passed the bar, he caught Lundquist's eye, frowned and shook his head, whispering loudly, "Stay where you are."

He pressed the send button on the phone as

he turned a corner, out of sight of Bartlett. Griggs answered immediately.

"It's Stone. I've bought them an after-dinner drink, so they'll be a few minutes."

"Okay."

"But listen. I think Bartlett is armed, and he's already seen Lundquist flash his badge. Why did you let him come in here?"

"I didn't. He just ignored me and walked in before I could stop him. I feel like arresting *him*."

"I'm going back to my table. When they leave you'd better take Bartlett quickly, before he gets to his car, and you'd better be ready to disarm him. He's packing on the left side, at his belt."

"Got it. Are you armed?"

"No, but Dino is. Don't worry, he won't do anything stupid."

"Okay, just go back to your table, and we'll handle it."

"I'm on my way." Stone punched off the phone and put it away. He stepped back into the dining room, and as he did, he was horrified to see Lundquist moving toward Bartlett's table. He looked back at his own group, and Dino was suddenly on his feet, making his way across the room and unbuttoning his jacket. Then everything seemed to slow down.

Bartlett turned to see Lundquist coming toward him and began to rise. Lundquist, who didn't know Bartlett was armed, had his hands at his sides, empty. Bartlett unbuttoned his jacket as he rose, and his right hand went inside it to his belt.

Stone saw his hand close around the butt of the pistol. He turned toward Dino and yelled, "Gun!" Dino stopped in his tracks, perhaps a dozen feet from the Wilkeses' table.

Bartlett never saw Dino; his attention was riveted on Lundquist, who now began to understand what was happening and went for his own gun. Four shots came in rapid succession.

Lundquist left his feet, the gun flying from his hand and knocking over a wine bottle on a nearby table. A woman at that table screamed as Dino fired. Bartlett was hit in his left upper arm, then a second time in the side of his neck, falling backward and out of sight, knocking over his chair.

Dino began running toward the table, his gun out in front of him, yelling, "Police, Police!"

Stone began running, too.

34

Pandemonium. A mass of diners abandoned their tables and rushed for the main entrance, knocking over chairs and elaborate flower arrangements. Women were screaming, and men were shouting at them.

Stone was swept sideways toward the door. In front of him a woman fell, and Stone grabbed her and yanked her to her feet before she could be trampled in the rush. He could see Dino at the Wilkeses' table, standing over Bartlett, who was out of sight on the floor behind the table. Dino was still pointing the gun.

He looked toward the front door and saw three uniformed Palm Beach police officers, one of them Dan Griggs, vainly trying to fight their way through the onrushing crowd. Stone grabbed a post next to the bar and hung on for dear life. Finally, when most of the crowd had fled the restaurant, he was able to make his way through the stragglers to Dino, who was now bending over Bartlett, feeling at his throat for a pulse.

Frank and Margaret Wilkes stood huddled against the wall, Frank cradling his sobbing wife's head on his shoulder. Margaret was spattered with blood. Bartlett's date was nowhere in sight.

"He's dead," Dino said, holstering his weapon.

Stone looked around the restaurant for Lundquist but did not see him. Thad and his party were standing against the opposite wall of the restaurant, having wisely not joined the panicked crowd. Thad waved and called out, "We're okay. Do what you have to do."

Stone resumed his search for Lundquist and found him under an overturned table. Lundquist had taken a round in the chest, and he had been trampled by the crowd. His nose was badly broken where someone had stepped on it, and there was blood everywhere, but Stone found a pulse.

Griggs and his men finally got into the restaurant and rushed toward Stone.

"We need an ambulance," Stone said as Griggs arrived. "Lundquist is still alive, but he's bad. Bartlett is dead. Dino shot him almost at the same time Bartlett shot Lundquist."

"There's an ambulance outside," Griggs said. He spoke into a handheld radio.

"There are probably some injured people in the crowd, too," Stone said. "It got pretty ugly."

A pair of EMTs made their way into the ruined room, toting a stretcher and equipment, and immediately began working on Lundquist. Stone stepped away to let them do their work. He followed Griggs over to where Dino stood.

Dino handed Griggs his gun. "You're going to want this."

Griggs nodded and examined Bartlett closely, picking up his weapon by its trigger guard and handing both guns to one of his officers.

Stone went to the Wilkeses, picking up a stray napkin along the way. He dabbed at the blood on Margaret's face, and she barely seemed to notice.

"I want to get her home," Wilkes said.

Stone turned to Griggs, who had heard, and nodded.

"Chief Griggs will want to talk to you in the morning," Stone said.

"I saw it all," Frank said. "Paul had a gun; it was all his fault."

"Griggs and his men were waiting outside the restaurant to arrest him quietly, but the Minneapolis cop ruined it all."

"Is he dead?"

"No, but he's pretty bad. His office had called to say that they have a witness who says Bartlett hired him to fix the seat belt on the car, so that Frances would be unprotected. It doesn't matter now, of course, but he would almost certainly have been convicted."

"We'll go, then."

"Do you need any help?"

"No, I can manage."

Stone watched them leave, then he crossed the restaurant to where Thad, Liz and Callie waited. "Everybody all right?"

They all nodded.

"I'm sorry you had to see that."

"See what?" Liz said. "I didn't see anything. I just heard a lot of noise."

"Paul shot a Minneapolis policeman, and Dino shot Paul. The cop is alive, but Paul is dead."

"Which Paul?" she asked.

"Aren't they the same?" Stone asked.

"I wish I knew," Liz said.

"Thad, why don't you take Liz and Callie home. Dino and I will need to give statements to the Palm Beach police. We'll probably be quite late."

"Sure," Thad said. "I hope to God the guy is Manning."

"We'll see," Stone said.

Thad ushered the women out of the restaurant, and Stone rejoined Dino and Griggs.

Griggs righted a table and motioned for Dino and Stone to pull up a chair. "You two are the best witnesses I've got. We might as well do this right now, then you two can go home." He pulled a small tape recorder from a pocket, turned it on and set it on the table.

"Okay, Stone, you first."

Dino stood up. "I'm going to go to the john. It's better if you interview us separately."

"Right," Griggs said. "All right, Stone, tell me what happened, and don't leave anything out."

Stone began at the beginning, and when he had finished, Dino came and took his place. Stone waited at the bar and discovered that one of Bartlett's rounds had hit some liquor bottles and the mirror behind the bar. A cop was digging it out of the wall behind the mirror.

When Griggs had Dino's statement, they stood up, and Stone joined them. "Frank Wilkes saw the whole thing," he said. "He'll back us up on what happened."

"I'm going to let my people finish here," Griggs said. "I'm going to the hospital to see how Lundquist is doing. I've got to call his department and his family, if he has one."

"Let's talk in the morning, then," Stone said.

"By the way," Griggs said, "I talked to the Minneapolis department earlier this evening. The guy who rigged Bartlett's car says the name he knew Bartlett by was Douglas Barnacle. They shared a cell in the Chicago federal detention center when they were both awaiting trial. He says Barnacle was a stockbroker in Chicago who got mixed up in a mob-backed stock scam and turned state's evidence. That was a little over five years ago. I'm running a check on the Barnacle name now, and I'll let you know what I turn up."

"Thanks," Stone said. "I want to hear about it." They shook hands and parted.

In the car on the way home Stone and Dino were both quiet for a while.

"You thinking what I'm thinking?" Dino asked.

"Yes. If Barnacle was in jail in Chicago five years ago, he couldn't be Paul Manning."

"Right."

They drove the rest of the way to the Shames house in silence.

35

One by one, Thad Shames's guests straggled on deck for breakfast on the afterdeck at mid-morning. Stone thought everybody looked tired, maybe a little shell-shocked. Not much was said, and he didn't feel ready to tell Thad and Liz what little he knew about Bartlett's background. He would wait for more information.

Stone was finishing his coffee when Juanito arrived with a fax of a dozen or so pages. Stone flipped through them, with Dino looking over his shoulder, occasionally pointing out something.

"What is that?" Thad finally asked.

"It's a copy of the criminal record of Paul Bartlett, aka Douglas Barnacle, William Wilfred, Edgar Chase and Terence Keane."

"He was all those people?" Liz asked.

"Those and maybe more. I'll summarize for you: He was born Robert Trent Smith, in Providence, Rhode Island, where he attended the public schools and the Rhode Island School of Design, which, incidentally, is very highly thought of. He was kicked out of school a month before graduation for running some kind of swindle that bilked nearly a hundred thousand dollars out of other students and faculty. After that, he chalked up half a dozen arrests for various confidence games. He was, apparently, a real bunco artist, and not averse to the use of violence, when he was caught. Five years ago, he got involved in a mob-backed boiler-room operation, selling worthless stocks at high prices. He ended up in jail and traded his testimony against his cohorts for his freedom and the federal witness protection program. While he was there, he shared a cell with a car thief and insurance scam artist. After that, he apparently left the program and took up a new identity as Paul Bartlett, in Minneapolis, where he eventually married a wealthy widow. Then he got his former cell mate to tamper with the seat belt on his car, and he wrecked it, killing her, but only after she changed her will in his favor."

"Then he's not Paul Manning?" Thad asked.

"No. Five years ago, Paul Manning and his wife were sailing in Europe, right, Liz?"

"That's right."

"And Bartlett was in jail at the time."

"So Bartlett was just a waste of your time?" Callie asked.

"Not entirely," Stone said. "At least you and I managed to get him caught for murdering his wife."

Dino spoke up. "And I managed to save the State of Minnesota the cost of a trial."

"I don't want you to feel you've wasted *my*

time, Stone," Thad said. "You were perfectly right to follow that lead, and I'm glad that it came to some good."

"But now we're right back where we started," Stone said. "Liz, let's talk about this sighting of Paul Manning in Easthampton."

"All right," she said.

"Tell me exactly the circumstances under which you saw him."

"I was in a shop on Main Street, pointing to something in the window for the saleslady to get for me, and I saw him outside the window."

"Did you see his face?"

"Not entirely, just partly. I caught a glimpse of his nose, which was straight, and that threw me off for a moment. Then, as he was walking away, he did this thing with his shoulders that he used to do." She demonstrated with a sort of shrug. "As if his jacket weren't resting comfortably on his shoulders."

"I remember his doing that in St. Marks," Stone said. "What else?"

"That was it. I waited until he had gone on down the street, then I got into my car, made a U-turn and got out of there. You're looking at me as though it were my imagination."

"No, no," Stone said. "I believe you. I just wanted the details."

"And," Thad said, "there is the matter of the vandalizing of Liz's house."

"Of course," Stone said. "I know the threat is real, and I think Paul Manning is just as dangerous as Paul Bartlett was."

"So," Thad said, "where do we go from here?"

"I'll have to give that some thought," Stone said. "I'd feel better if we had some bit of information that would give us a basis for a search."

"What sort of information?" Thad asked.

"Well, for instance, a man made several phone calls to my office and wouldn't give his name, making my secretary suspicious. Caller ID told us the calls came from a Manhattan hotel." He pointed to the stack of computer paper that rested on a deck chair nearby. "A friend of mine managed to print out the guest list, and Liz and I went through it carefully. I was hoping a name might ring some sort of bell. One name seemed plausible, but it didn't work out, and neither of us saw another familiar name on the list."

"I did," Callie said.

"You did what?" Stone asked.

"I saw a familiar name on the list." She got up, went to the stack of paper, riffled through it and ripped off a page. "Here," she said, handing it to Stone.

Stone looked at the sheet. "Frederick James? Does that mean anything to you, Liz?"

Liz shook her head. "No."

"It should mean something to you, Stone, and you, too, Dino," Callie said.

"Doesn't ring a bell," Dino said.

Callie picked up the novel Dino had been reading and tossed it to him.

"*Tumult,* by Frederick James," Dino read aloud.

239

"I'd forgotten the name," Stone said.

"And he's a novelist, like Paul," Liz said.

"Why didn't you mention this before, Callie?"

She shrugged. "I meant to, but somebody changed the subject, and I forgot about it until you mentioned the hotel guest list just now."

Stone looked at the sheet. "His home address is on Gin Lane, in Easthampton. That's interesting." Stone took the book from Dino and turned it over, opened the back cover. "No photograph. All the dust jacket says is, 'Frederick James travels widely around the world, never staying in one place for long. This is his first novel.'"

"Usually there's some sort of biography," Thad said. "Who published it?"

Stone looked at the book jacket. "Hot Lead Press. Linotype machines used to use hot lead to set type. Never heard of this outfit."

"Liz," Dino asked, "have you read this book?"

"No."

"Read it, or at least some of it. See if you think Paul Manning wrote it."

Stone handed her the book.

"All right," she said. "God knows I've read all of Paul's earlier novels; I ought to know his work."

"Well," Stone said, "now we've got some information — James's home address and his publisher's name. We couldn't ask for a better start. Dino, while Liz reads the book, let's you and I make some phone calls."

They went into the saloon, where there were two extensions. Stone was about to pick up a phone, but Dino stopped him.

"Listen, want to make a little bet?"

"About what?"

"I'll bet you a hundred bucks that after Liz reads the novel she won't be sure of whether Manning wrote it."

"I'm not sure I'd take that bet," Stone said. "She's been equivocal every time she was in a position to nail something down. I mean, you'd have thought she could tell us right away that Bartlett wasn't Manning."

"Yeah, I would have thought that," Dino agreed. "Of course, there could be a really strong resemblance. I mean, you knew Manning, and you weren't much help."

"You knew him, too, and you were no help at all, until shooting was required."

"You saying I'm trigger happy?"

"Dino, as far as I'm concerned, you can shoot anybody anytime you feel like it, because usually, when you shoot somebody, he's trying to shoot me."

"I'm glad you noticed."

"So, you suspect Liz of something?"

Dino shrugged. "Not yet. I'd just like to have a straight answer from her now and then."

"So would I," Stone said, half to himself.

36

Dino picked up a phone. "I know a guy on the Easthampton force; let's start with the home address. Maybe we won't have to go any farther." Dino made the call and waited. "I'm on hold," he said, then waited patiently. "Hey, yeah, I'm here." Dino listened and asked a couple of questions, then hung up and turned to Stone. "Frederick James rented a house on Gin Lane up until a week ago. He spoke to the real estate agent, and they didn't have a forwarding address. His address when he rented the place was a Manhattan hotel, the Brooke."

"Dead end," Stone said. "I'll call the publisher." He called New York information and was connected.

"Good morning, Hot Lead Press," a young woman's voice said.

"Good morning," Stone said. "This is Lieutenant Bacchetti, NYPD. I'd like to speak to the editor of Frederick James. Can you find out for me which of your editors that is?"

"That's easy," she replied. "We've only got one editor. I'll connect you."

This time, a man, also young: "Pete Willard."

"Good morning, Mr. Willard. This is Lieutenant Bacchetti of the NYPD. I'd —"

"No kidding? A real live cop?"

"That's right. I'd —"

"Listen, I'll bet you've got some great stories to tell. Have you got an agent?"

"No, and —"

"Great. And no publisher, either?"

"Mr. Willard, I'm calling on police business."

"Oh, okay, shoot. Not really. I mean, go ahead."

"I understand that you edit Frederick James?"

"Edit and publish. He was our first author."

"I take it you're new in business?"

"That's right. Opened our doors ten months ago, and already we've got a best-seller. That is, this Sunday we will. Frederick James's novel *Tumult* opens at number eleven on the *Times* list."

"Congratulations."

"Thanks. We're very excited."

"Who's we?"

"Molly and me. And baby makes three. No, Molly is . . . Well, she does everything I don't. And she's my wife, and she's pregnant."

"Congratulations again."

"Thanks. We're very excited."

Back where I started, Stone thought. "Mr. Willard, I need to get in touch with Frederick James."

"Oh, I'll bet you're one of his cop sources. He has all kinds of sources."

"Not yet," Stone said. "I'd just like to find him."

"Well, Mr. James is pretty reclusive," Willard

said. "I'm not supposed to give out any information."

"This is a very serious police matter," Stone said. "I'd rather not have to come down there with a search warrant."

"Hey, just like on *Law and Order*, huh? Except they always screw up the warrant, and the judge throws out the evidence from the search."

"I won't screw up the warrant, Mr. Willard. And believe me, it will be much simpler for you just to give me Mr. James's address and phone number than for us to come down there and start tearing your office apart."

"Actually, I don't have either an address or a phone number for him. I know it's peculiar, but like I said, he's reclusive."

"How do you communicate with Mr. James?"

"E-mail," Willard said. "And through his agent."

"What's his e-mail address?"

"FJ at frederickjames dot com."

"And his agent's name?"

"Tom Jones."

"The singer or the novel?" Stone asked dryly.

"No kidding, that's his name. I'll give you his number."

Stone wrote it down. "By the way, Mr. Willard, if Mr. James should communicate with you, please don't tell him I called It might make you a co-conspirator."

"Oh, jeez," Willard said. "I won't say a word."

Stone hung up, laughing. "This is some kind

of publishing house," he said to Dino. "Just a kid and his pregnant wife. But I've got his agent's name." He dialed the number.

"Tom Jones," a voice said — middle-aged, husky from booze and cigarettes. No operator, no secretary, just Jones.

"Mr. Jones, this is Lieutenant Bacchetti of the NYPD."

"I didn't do it!" Jones cackled. "She swore she was over eighteen, anyway." He roared with laughter. It took him a moment to recover himself.

"Mr. Jones, I'm trying to find a client of yours."

"And which client would that be?" Jones asked, clearing his throat loudly.

"Frederick James."

"What a coincidence," Jones said. "He's my only client!" This time, he nearly collapsed with laughter.

The man has to be drunk, Stone thought. "Mr. Jones . . ."

Jones continued to laugh, cough and clear his throat. "Yeah?" he said finally.

"It's very important that I see Mr. James."

"Well, if you can do that, pal, you're way ahead of me. I've never seen him."

"He's your client, and you've never seen him?"

"He's reclusive."

"And how do you communicate with him?"

"E-mail," Jones said. "FJ at frederickjames dot com."

"How about a phone number?"

"Don't have one. I've never even spoken with him."

"And how did you become his agent?"

"Manuscript came in over the transom," he said. "Literally. I came to work one morning — I was just about to close up the shop for good — and the manuscript was lying on the floor. Tell you the truth, Lieutenant, I was all washed up as an agent. But when I read *Tumult*, I knew I had a winner. Trouble was, nobody in any established house would even take my calls, let alone read the manuscript. So I called my nephew, who was an editorial assistant at Simon and Schuster, and he read it and went nuts. His dad loaned him some money, and he packaged the book and got S and S to distribute it for him. He's making out like a bandit."

"Would that be Pete Willard?"

"That would be he."

"Mr. Jones, did you ever know a writer named Paul Manning?"

"Sure, I knew him for twenty years; got him started and I represented him right up until his untimely death."

"You haven't heard from him lately, then?"

"Not likely. I don't have those kind of connections!" Jones laughed hysterically again.

Stone waited him out. When Jones had recovered himself, Stone tried again. "Mr. Jones, how do you send Mr. James contracts to sign, checks from his publisher, that sort of thing? You must have some kind of address."

"You promise not to tell him where you got it?"

"I promise."

"He lives at One Vanderbilt Avenue, right here in New York."

"Phone number?"

"Doesn't have one; not even an unlisted one."

"Mr. Jones, when you hear from Mr. James, it's important that you don't tell him I called."

"But he's my client. I represent him."

"Believe me, Mr. Jones, you don't want to get in the middle of this."

"Has he done something wrong?"

"Not that I know of. We just want to talk to him."

"Well, okay. Whatever you say."

"Thank you, Mr. Jones, and if you do hear from him, please call me at this number." Stone gave him the cell phone number and hung up.

"What?" Dino said.

"This looks real good," Stone said. "This guy Jones was Manning's agent before he 'died.' Jones has no idea who he is, I think."

"Did you get an address?"

"Yep. One Vanderbilt Avenue."

Dino looked at Stone as if he were a retarded child. "Stone, One Vanderbilt Avenue is Grand Central Station."

"I knew that," Stone replied.

37

Dino looked thoughtful. "Haven't we run across One Vanderbilt Avenue as an address before? It sounds familiar."

Stone slapped his forehead. "Mail drop! I tracked it down once, roamed around Grand Central until I found this wall of mailboxes. They're unattended, except when somebody shows up to sort the mail. Can you call the precinct and detail a man to watch it?"

"Stone, Frederick James has committed no crime that we know of, and he's not a suspect in any case. You trying to get me fired? Why don't you get Bob Berman to do it?"

"That's a thought, but I just had another one. If I were James, and I didn't want to be located, for whatever reason, I'd rent a box at One Vanderbilt, then I'd go to the post office and have the mail forwarded to another address, and then, if I *really* don't want to be found, I'd have it forwarded from that address. I might get my mail a week late, but what the hell?"

"So it would be a waste of Berman's time."

"Yes, it would. Mr. James has built himself a fire wall, and I can't think of a way around it."

"He must get paid," Dino said.

"Yes, but the checks go to the mailbox."

"But they have to be deposited, or the guy gets no money, right?"

"Right!" Stone said. He called Tom Jones back.

"Tom Jones."

"This is Lieutenant Bacchetti again."

"We've got to stop meeting like this. My wife will catch on." He roared with laughter.

Once again, Stone waited. "Mr. Jones," he said when he could get past the laughter. "How do you pay Frederick James?"

"He takes checks," Jones said. "If *I* were dealing with me, I'd demand cash!" This time it was a high-pitched giggle.

"Mr. Jones, when was the last time you paid Mr. James any money?"

"Last month, when *Tumult* came out. His contract calls for a payment on publication."

"All right. Dig out your most recent bank statement."

"It's right here in my bottom drawer, with all my bank statements," Jones said.

Stone heard the man struggling with a desk drawer.

"Got it," Jones said.

"Now, go through the canceled checks until you find the one to James."

"Okay, let's see: laundry, phone bill, liquor store — hey, that's a big one!" More laughter. "Here it is!"

"Turn the check over."

"It's over."

"There is a bank's name stamped on the back. That always happens when a check is deposited."

"Right, there is. It's kind of dim, though. Let me turn on a light and get my glasses."

Stone had visions of the man sitting in a dark office strewn with empty liquor bottles.

"Okay, I can see it now. It says, 'First Cayman Bank.'"

"Swell," Stone said.

"You like that, do you?"

"It's no help at all, I'm afraid. Mr. Jones, imagine for a moment that you absolutely *had* to get in touch with Mr. James. How would you go about it?"

"I'd e-mail him," Jones said. "I'm not much on computers, but my nephew set it up so that I can get to my e-mail without screwing it up. You want the e-mail address?"

"Thanks, but you already gave it to me."

"I did? Well, okay. Good luck finding him." Jones hung up.

"What?" Dino asked.

"His bank is in the Cayman Islands, well known for banking secrecy. We're not going to find him that way."

"What about his e-mail address? We could call his provider. Who is it? AOL or Hotmail? One of those?"

"Nope. He's got a domain of his own:

250

frederickjames dot com."

"Then it's got to be registered somewhere."

"Yeah, but even if we could track it down, we'd find that his address is One Vanderbilt, or some hotel where he stayed for a few days."

"We could see if he has a phone number in New York."

"If he does, it will be unlisted."

"If it's unlisted, I can find out the number."

"I just had a thought," Stone said. He picked up a phone and called Dan Griggs.

"Griggs."

"It's Stone. How's Lundquist doing?"

"He made it through the night, and he's stable. The doctor says we can probably ship him home in a few days."

"Good. Listen, Dan, we've got another line on Paul Manning. He may be using the name Frederick James. James is a novelist with a new, best-selling book out, and he's something of a will-o'-the-wisp. Can you check the local hotels and see if he's registered?"

"Okay, Stone, but I have to tell you, I'm wearying of Mr. Manning, and I can't keep putting resources into finding somebody who did nothing but trash somebody's house."

"I understand, Dan, and I appreciate your help."

"I'll get back to you." Griggs hung up.

Stone called Bob Berman. "How you doing?"

"Okay. What's up?"

"The hotel guest list turned up the name of

251

one Frederick James, an author. Can you do the whole skip-trace thing — address, phone number, credit report?"

"I don't suppose you've got a Social Security number?"

"No, but hang on." Stone dialed Jones again.

"Tom Jones."

"Mr. Jones, I need Frederick James's Social Security number. I know you've got it. You can't pay him without it."

"Sorry, the checks are made out to a corporation."

"Why didn't you tell me that before?"

"You didn't ask me." Jones laughed loudly.

"What's the name of the corporation?"

"Frederick James, Limited; it's a Cayman Islands firm."

"Thanks," Stone said, and hung up. He punched the button for Berman. "Sorry for the delay. No SSN; he deals through a Cayman Islands corporation. I don't suppose you can get anything on that."

"Probably not. You have any idea where the guy lives?"

"Until recently, he lived in Easthampton, New York. That's all I've got."

"Okay, I'll get back to you."

Stone hung up to see Liz appear in the doorway, holding the copy of *Tumult*. "What do you think?" he asked.

"Well, I've read enough of it to say that it *could* be Paul's work. But you have to understand, he was something of a chameleon as a writer. He changed styles from book to book, depending on the plot and characters."

"Thanks for trying, Liz."

She returned to the afterdeck, leaving Stone and Dino alone.

"What'd I tell you?" Dino said. "She's going to be useless in finding this guy."

"I'm feeling pretty useless myself," Stone said.

"I don't think we're going to get anywhere with the Frederick James name," Dino said. "My guess is, he's just using it as a pen name, that he's living his life under an entirely different name, maybe even more than one."

"That's a depressing thought," Stone said.

As if on cue, Dan Griggs called back. "I've had a whole squad calling around to the hotels," he said, "and there's no Frederick James registered anywhere."

"Thanks for your help again, Dan. I won't bother you unless we turn up something concrete." Stone hung up, and the phone rang.

"Hello?"

"It's Berman."

"Anything?"

"Mr. James has an American Express card, and that's it — no debts, not even a bank account."

"American Express wouldn't give somebody a card who had no credit record," Stone said.

"Then he must have applied under a name

253

that does have a record, then asked them to put another name on the card. By the way, I have a friend at American Express. I called him and he looked up James's address."

"Great! What is it?"

"One Vanderbilt Avenue, New York City."

"Thanks, Bob." Stone hung up. "Another dead end."

"You got any other ideas?" Dino asked.

"No."

"Neither have I."

"Well, we're just going to have to wait until he has another go at Liz," Stone said.

38

Everybody seemed to be taking a nap, except Dino.

"I need some things from the drugstore," Stone said. "You want to come?"

"Nope," Dino replied. "Married men don't need things from the drugstore."

"Toothpaste and dental floss," Stone said.

"Whatever you say."

"I'll be back in half an hour, if anybody calls."

"See ya."

Stone walked to the parking lot and got into his borrowed Mercedes convertible, putting the top down. He pulled out of the driveway, behind a passing Ford, which was driving rather slowly. Stone edged up behind the car, hoping to pass, when, suddenly, the Ford came to a screeching halt, and Stone plowed into it with a crash.

"Oh, shit," he said aloud. Now he had smashed up Thad's car, and it was his own fault. He got out of the car and walked toward the Ford. As he did, a man got out of the Ford, and to Stone's surprise, he was smiling.

"I'm sorry I hit you," Stone said, "but why did you slam on your brakes like that?"

The man looked like a salesman of some sort. He was dressed in a white short-sleeved shirt and necktie, and his shirt pocket contained a plastic pen guard and several writing instruments. "Don't worry about it," the man said, and very quickly, there was a gun in his hand.

Stone looked over his shoulder for some way out of this, but as he did, a silver Lincoln Town Car with darkly tinted windows screeched to a halt beside him.

The man with the gun opened the rear door. "Inside," he said, "and don't let's get blood on this pretty street."

Stone got in, followed by the man with the gun, and the car moved forward, leaving the other two cars stopped in the middle of the street. The whole thing had taken less than thirty seconds, he figured, and more disturbing than the gun in the man's hand was the fact that he was wearing rubber gloves. "What's this about?" he asked.

"First, let's get you all secured, and then I'll tell you," the man said. "Get down on your knees, rest your head on the armrest and put your hands behind you." He nudged Stone's ribs with the gun barrel for emphasis.

Stone did as he was told, and in a moment, he was handcuffed.

"All right, now you can sit back up here," the man said.

His accent was Southern, sort of educated

redneck, Stone thought. "So what's this about?" he asked again.

"First, let's get the introductions out of the way," the man said. "You can call me Larry, and the feller driving is Ernest. And you would be one Mr. Stone Barrington."

"How do you do?" Stone said.

"I do pretty good," Larry replied. "Now, as to what this is about, we're going to take a little drive out in the country, and then we're gonna make a phone call." His tone was pleasant, conversational. "I don't enjoy putting violence on folks, so I'd 'preciate it if you wouldn't make that necessary. I *can* do it, if the need arises."

"All right, I'll behave," Stone lied. He was going to get out of this at the first opportunity, and he was beginning to regret that he had gotten into the car without a fight. The rubber gloves were weighing heavily on his mind.

Shortly, they were in West Palm, driving west on one of its broad boulevards. "You were saying?" Stone asked.

"Oh, yeah. A friend of mine called me a couple of days ago and asked me to come down here and shoot your ass."

"What friend is that?"

"Does it matter? He's paying me and Ernest, here, fifty big ones to deal with you, and that's the most I ever got for a hit."

They stopped at a traffic light, and a police car pulled up next to them.

Larry stuck the gun in Stone's crotch. "Don't

you even think about it," he said. "They can't see us, and if they hear something, then I'm going to have to do you *and* the cop. Besides, wouldn't you rather die with your dick still on?"

Stone didn't answer that. "I'd like to know who your friend is," he said.

"I don't think you'd recognize the name," Larry said. "He uses a lot of them."

"What does he look like, then?"

"Tall feller, going gray."

"Ah, yes, Mr. Manning."

"Manning? If you say so."

"Funny thing is, I was about to try and give Mr. Manning a whole lot of money. Tell you what: Why don't you call him right now and tell him that? It might have an effect on the outcome of your day and mine."

"And why would you want to give him a lot of money?" Larry asked.

"I'm a lawyer. I represent a lady he knows. She's willing to pay a large sum to get him to go away."

"How much money we talking about?" Larry asked, clearly interested.

"She's willing to give him a million dollars," Stone said, "maybe more." *But not now,* Stone thought. *She won't give him a fucking penny, if I have anything to say about it.*

"You really expect me to believe that."

"You don't have to. Just make the call, and I'll make *him* believe it."

"What's in it for me?" Larry asked.

258

"How much has he paid you so far?" Stone asked.

"Twenty-five thousand," Larry replied. "There's another twenty-five due when he shoots you."

"When *he* shoots me? I thought he hired you to do that."

"Well, yeah, but only if you give me any trouble. He wants to do it himself, if he has the time. Something personal, I don't know."

"Tell you what. You make the call. If I can get him to agree to a settlement, I'll give you another fifty, on top of the twenty-five he's already given you."

"I don't know," Larry said.

"What have you got to lose? Tell you what. Drive me to the nearest bank, and I'll give you the fifty right now, in cash. Any bank will do. I just have to make a phone call."

"Well, see, I've got a lot of problems with that," Larry said. "You could make all sorts of trouble for me in a bank."

"You've got a point," said Stone, who had been planning on making a lot of trouble for him.

"And that wouldn't be the honorable thing to do, see? I mean, my deal is with Doug, not with you. Word got around about that, and I'd be short of clients."

"So, call him and let me speak to him."

"What the hell, why not? Ernest, give me the phone."

Ernest passed back a cell phone, and Larry dialed, mouthing the numbers from memory.

Stone heard the electronic shriek from the phone, and the announcement that the cellular customer being called was unavailable or out of the calling area.

"No luck," Larry said.

"Try him again in a minute," Stone replied. They were out of West Palm, now, headed west on a narrowing, increasingly empty road that seemed to be heading straight into the Everglades. He didn't want to go there.

"Okay," Larry said.

"You do a lot of this work?" Stone asked.

"You bet. Make a nice living at it, too."

"How'd you get into it?"

"Fellow offered me five grand once, when I was broke, so I got myself a mail-order book that tells you how to do it and get away with it."

"The work doesn't bother you?"

"Naw, it's just business. I mean, I don't have anything against the people I hit."

"You know, in my line of work, I have clients who sometimes have need of somebody with your skills. Maybe you should give me your number?"

Larry grinned broadly. "Well, first, let's see how this goes, okay?"

"Why don't you try the number again?" Stone said.

"Sure thing." Larry punched redial, then held the phone away from his ear, so Stone could hear the recorded message again. "Hey, Ernest," Larry said. "It's your next left, right?"

"Right," Ernest said, and a moment later, he turned left onto a dirt road. A moment later, they were winding down a track that ran through scrub pines. To their right, mangrove grew in swamp water. Shortly, they came to a small clearing, and Ernest made a U-turn and stopped.

"Okay, out of the car," Larry said, opening the door and helping Stone out of the rear seat.

"Let's try the number again," Stone said.

Larry punched redial, and again, the dreaded message repeated.

"Well, I guess you're just shit out of luck," Larry said, pocketing the phone. He pushed Stone toward the mangrove. "My instructions were, if I couldn't reach him, to do the deed and meet him tonight."

"You're doing this on credit, then?" Stone asked, trying not to panic.

"Don't worry," Larry said, "me and Mr. Barnacle go way back. We did a little stretch together."

Suddenly the name rang a bell. "Barnacle? *Douglas Barnacle?*"

"That's his name."

Stone realized that he was about to be murdered by a dead man. "Hang on," he said.

"Listen, Mr. Barrington, there's no use stretching this out. You don't want to think about this any more than you have to."

"Don't you read the papers? Watch television? Listen to the radio?"

"What are you talking about?"

"Didn't you hear about the shoot-out in a Palm Beach restaurant last night?"

Ernest, who had gotten out of the car, walked up. "Yeah, I heard something about that," he said.

"What shoot-out?"

"The guy you call Doug Barnacle was living in Palm Beach under the name of Paul Bartlett. The police killed him last night."

That brought Larry up short. "Ernest, that was the name, wasn't it? Paul Bartlett?"

"That's what he was using yesterday," Ernest said.

"Turn on the car radio," Stone said. "Find an all-news station."

"Do it, Ernest," Larry said.

Larry went to the car, turned on the radio and found a station. Farm report, bank robbery in West Palm, weather.

Larry looked at his watch. "Ernest, we got a plane to catch."

"I know it," Ernest said.

Larry turned and marched Stone back to the mangrove. He put a foot against his backside and shoved him into the swamp. Stone kept his balance and ended up thigh-deep in the black water. A large snake slithered past no more than a yard away. "Mr. Barrington, that was a real nice try. I admire it, but it's time for you to say bye-bye." He raised the pistol and pointed it at Stone's forehead, no more than five feet away.

"Hey, Larry!" Ernest called.

"What?"

"Listen!" He turned up the radio.

". . . chaotic scene at La Reserve, a Palm Beach restaurant last night, ended up with one dead, and a Minneapolis police officer seriously wounded."

"Don't Doug live in Minneapolis?" Ernest asked.

"Shhhh."

". . . have identified the police officer as Lieutenant Ebbe Lundquist, of the Minneapolis PD, and the dead suspect as Paul Bartlett, also of Minneapolis. Bartlett had been wanted in Minnesota for the murder of his wife, Frances Simms Bartlett, nearly a year ago, and Lieutenant Lundquist was trying to effect an arrest in the restaurant, backed up by the Palm Beach Police Department."

"Well, shit," Larry said. "You're not lying, Mr. Barrington."

"No," Stone said, "I'm not."

"I mean, you got no idea what some folks will tell you in circumstances like this, you know?"

"I'm sure. But the fact remains, Larry, that you're not going to get paid for this one, so why do it? You've already got the twenty-five thousand, so you haven't wasted your time, but Bartlett isn't going to pay off, now." Stone did *not*

263

like standing in this swamp, with *things* slithering around in it.

"He's got a point, Larry," Ernest said.

"Maybe," Larry said, thoughtfully.

Ernest looked at his watch. "And we haven't got all that much time before our plane."

Larry looked at Stone. "I don't guess you'd really pay me the fifty grand, would you?"

"Give me your address, and I'll send you a check," Stone replied.

Larry burst out laughing. "Come on, Ernest, let's get outta here!" He got into the car, and Ernest drove off, spinning the wheels and throwing mud everywhere.

Stone stood in the swamp for a minute, trying to get his heart rate down, then the snake appeared again, and he started struggling for the shore.

Once on dry land, he lay down and, with the greatest possible effort, got his handcuffed hands under his ass and finally over his feet. Now, with his hands in front of him, he was able to get to the cell phone under his sweater on his belt. He punched in the number.

"The Shames yacht," Dino said.

"Dino," Stone said, "I need you to come and get me, and bring your handcuffs key."

39

Dino found the whole story hilarious. "I don't believe it," he cackled. "Bartlett bites you on the ass from the grave! I wish I had been there!"

"Dino, it wasn't funny, even if you were there."

"And you thought it was Manning who bought the hit!" He cackled again.

"And it *still* isn't funny."

Stone went to his cabin, showered and changed, retrieved his laptop computer and brought it into the saloon.

"What are you doing with that?" Dino asked.

"The only address we have for Frederick James is an e-mail address, so I'm going to e-mail him."

"Will he be able to tell you're in Palm Beach?"

"No. The return address will be the same as if I'd sent it from New York."

"Okay, why not?"

Stone made some adjustments in his telephone dialing program, logged on to his Internet provider and went to e-mail.

TO: FREDERICK JAMES
FROM: STONE BARRINGTON

DEAR MR. JAMES:

I UNDERSTAND YOU HAVE BEEN TRYING TO
GET IN TOUCH WITH ME. IF SO, YOU MAY
REACH ME AT THE ABOVE E-MAIL ADDRESS,
OR TELEPHONE ME AT (917) 555-1455. I
THINK YOU AND I MAY HAVE SOMETHING
TO DISCUSS THAT WOULD REACT TO YOUR
BENEFIT.

Stone sent the e-mail. "Let's see if that raises
him."

"And what if it does?"

"All I want to do is buy the guy off. Maybe
he'll listen to reason."

"You think he's interested in money?"

"I don't think he's interested in anything else.
He's doing this because he's pissed off at his
wife for taking all his money. I'm going to propose that she give some of it back."

"I think the guy's a fruitcake, Stone, and . . ."

A chime from Stone's computer interrupted
him. "You have mail," a notice on the screen said.

"That was quick. The guy must have been
working on his computer." Stone opened the e-
mail.

TO: STONE BARRINGTON
FROM: FREDERICK JAMES

DEAR MR. BARRINGTON:

WHY DO YOU THINK I AM TRYING TO GET IN TOUCH WITH YOU? I DON'T EVEN KNOW WHO YOU ARE.

Stone was annoyed. He immediately wrote back.

TO: PAUL MANNING
FROM: STONE BARRINGTON

PAUL:

ALLISON HAS ASKED ME TO REPRESENT HER IN COMING TO TERMS WITH YOU. SHE IS WILLING TO PART WITH A SUBSTANTIAL SUM OF MONEY IN ORDER TO AMICABLY END ALL TIES WITH YOU. LET ME KNOW IF YOU ARE INTERESTED.

"Let's see if that has any effect," Stone said. Considerable time passed while they waited. Stone and Dino chatted about nothing in particular for a while, then the computer chimed again, and Stone opened the mail.

TO: STONE BARRINGTON
FROM: FREDERICK JAMES

SIR:

YOU SEEM TO BE SUFFERING UNDER THE DELUSION THAT I AM SOMEONE ELSE. HOW

DID YOU GET THIS E-MAIL ADDRESS?
Stone immediately wrote back:

PAUL, THERE IS NO POINT IN CONTIN-
UING WITH THIS. IF YOU HAVE NO IN-
TEREST IN A SUBSTANTIAL SETTLEMENT,
THEN YOU AND ALLISON CAN GO YOUR
SEPARATE WAYS, WITH YOU EMPTY-
HANDED AND EXPOSED.

There was an immediate return message:

SIR:

JUST WHAT DO YOU THINK YOU CAN EX-
POSE ABOUT ME? YOU DON'T EVEN KNOW
WHO I AM.

Stone wrote back:

PAUL, OF COURSE I KNOW WHO YOU ARE.
HOW ABOUT THIS: I CALL SOMEBODY I
KNOW AT 60 MINUTES AND SUGGEST THEY
DO A PIECE ON PAUL AND ALLISON MAN-
NING, WHO EVERYBODY THINKS WERE
HANGED IN ST. MARKS A WHILE BACK.
THEY COULD INTERVIEW ALLISON, WHO
COULD TELL THEM HOW SHE BRIBED
GOVERNMENT OFFICIALS FOR HER OWN
RELEASE AND YOURS. THEN SHE COULD
TELL THEM HOW YOU ARE NOW CALLING
YOURSELF FREDERICK JAMES, AND AS

SOON AS THE SHOW IS OVER, EVERY JOUR-
NALIST IN AMERICA WILL BE TRYING TO
FIND YOU, WHICH SHOULD MAKE YOUR
LIFE FUN. YOU SEEM TO HAVE MADE A
NICE NEW LIFE FOR YOURSELF, WITH A
BOOK ON THE *TIMES* LIST. WOULDN'T YOU
LIKE TO CONTINUE TO LIVE THAT LIFE,
UNDISTURBED?

ALL WE ASK IS THAT YOU TAKE SOME
MONEY AND LEAVE ALLISON UNDIS-
TURBED. TALK TO ME.

James's answer:

SIR: I DON'T KNOW WHAT KIND OF MANIAC
YOU ARE, BUT YOU ARE FLIRTING WITH
THE BIGGEST LAWSUIT YOU EVER HEARD
OF, PLUS MAYBE CRIMINAL CHARGES OF
EXTORTION. THIS CORRESPONDENCE IS AT
AN END. I DON'T WANT TO HEAR FROM
YOU AGAIN.

Dino, looking over Stone's shoulder, read the
e-mail. "Well, that was certainly indignant. You
think he's bluffing?"

"Yes," Stone said. "What's more, I think we
may have smoked him out. I don't think we've
heard the last of Mr. James."

40

Stone was reading the papers the following morning, when Thad appeared on deck, carrying two briefcases. He gave them to Juanito. "Put these in the car, will you, please?"

"You leaving?" Stone asked.

"Yes. I've got to go back to New York, then back to the Coast again."

"Thad, it might be a good idea if you took Liz with you."

"Why?"

"Well, I don't know if or when Paul Manning is going to turn up, but if he does, it might be better if Liz weren't here."

"What am I going to do with her in New York, lock her in a hotel suite? I'm going to be very busy for the next week or so, and I'd have little time to spend with her. And from what she tells me, I think she'd be afraid to go out shopping or anywhere else on her own."

"You have a point," Stone said.

"I'd feel much better if she were here with you and Callie and Dino."

"For how long?" Stone asked.

"For as long as you'll stay, or until you reach

some sort of accommodation with Manning."

"Thad, I can't stay forever, but I'll give it another week or two. Maybe we'll hear from this Frederick James again. If he really is Manning, I can't think why he wouldn't not want to talk to me. After all, he's already called my office three or four times."

"Does James know where you are?"

"No. At least, I don't think so."

"You want me to hire some private security to back you up?"

"No, not at the moment. If it gets bad we can always do that."

"If you want help, just tell Callie. She'll know who to call."

"All right."

The two men shook hands, and Thad left the yacht.

Dino, who had been having breakfast during this conversation, now spoke up. "Listen, Stone, I'm beginning to think you're taking this too seriously. I mean, all that's happened is the lady's house has been messed up a little. That's kid stuff; it's hardly a threat on her life. And if James is really Manning, then he can't be completely a fruitcake. He's made a life for himself, he's writing again, and if his book is on the bestseller list, he must be doing okay at it."

"Dino, you only met this guy when you arrested him. I got to know him a little in St. Marks, and he made this very angry scene in New York right before you picked him up. He

271

wanted his money, and he wanted it bad. I've got a feeling he still does."

"A feeling? What's that? Your hunches were never all that good, you know."

"Liz feels the same way, and she knows him better than anybody."

"So now we're operating on *Liz's* hunches? Don't get me wrong, I'm getting used to living on a big yacht and having my every wish catered to; I always knew I could. I'll stay here until the chief of detectives sends somebody down here for me with an extradition warrant."

"She's not a stupid woman. She and Paul pulled off quite an insurance fraud, you know."

"Pulled off? You think nearly getting herself hanged is pulling it off? The whole thing completely backfired on them. They're stupid, both of them."

"Okay, so it didn't work out. She's still pretty smart," Stone said stubbornly.

"Anyway, she may not be your only problem."

"What are you talking about?"

"I haven't mentioned this, but yesterday we got followed around town by a car."

"*What?*"

"You heard me. Somebody is tailing us."

"Why didn't you tell me?"

"It didn't seem related to Liz and her problems."

"And what do you think it's related to?"

"I think it could be the former Mrs. Barrington."

"Oh, shit," Stone said. He had nearly forgotten about Dolce. "What kind of a car?"

"Sort of an anonymous-looking sedan, probably Japanese. The windows were tinted dark. I couldn't see who was inside."

"Everybody's windows are tinted dark down here; keeps out the heat."

"I think you should take Dolce seriously."

"You think I don't?"

"I think you don't take her seriously enough."

"And how do I do that? Carry an automatic weapon at all times?"

"You could do worse. And I'm worried about Callie."

"What about Callie?"

"If Dolce sees you with her, she could be in trouble."

"Oh, God," Stone moaned. "When is this going to be over?"

"As far as Dolce is concerned, it'll be over when one of you is dead, and she might want that sooner than later."

"You think she's suicidal?"

"Homicidal, more likely."

"Thanks, I needed that."

"Anytime."

The cell phone on Stone's belt vibrated. "Hello?"

"Mr. Barrington?"

"Yes."

"This is Frederick James."

"Good morning, Mr. James," Stone said loudly,

so that Dino would get it. "I didn't think I'd hear from you again."

"I changed my mind. I want you to answer a question."

"Go ahead."

"How did you know that I know Paul Manning?"

"Let's not be cute, Mr. James. I think you *are* Paul Manning."

"Well, I'm not, but I've been in touch with him."

"When?"

"Recently."

"How recently?"

"Recently enough. I know about his past with Allison, and the business with the insurance company. Quite frankly, I know more about him than I want to know."

"Don't we all?"

"I got to thinking about what you said in your e-mail. Does Allison really want to buy him off?"

"Yes, she does."

"For how much?"

"I don't know that I can discuss that with you, since you claim not to be Paul Manning."

"Tell me this, then. Why do you think I've been trying to get in touch with you?"

"You really don't know?"

"No, I don't, or I wouldn't have asked you."

"A man called my office several times and wouldn't leave his name. I suspected it was Paul Manning. I managed to trace the call back to a

Manhattan hotel, and you were the only guest whose name I recognized."

"That's pretty tenuous, isn't it?"

"Is it? Wasn't I right?"

"Actually, you may well be. Paul Manning was in my hotel suite a couple of times, and he made some phone calls."

"Well, I'm glad you admit, at least, to being in the same room with Manning."

"Have you ever met Manning, Mr. Barrington?"

"I got to know him rather well, but he was using another name at the time."

"Listen to my voice. Does it sound like the voice of Paul Manning?"

Stone admitted to himself that it did not. "Manning's is deeper," he said.

"Exactly. I have rather a light voice, wouldn't you say?"

"I suppose."

"And Manning's is a sort of bass-baritone."

"Yes."

"Does that do nothing to convince you that Manning and I are not the same person?"

"It helps. Of course, we can resolve the question of identity very easily."

"How?"

"We can meet, face-to-face."

"Where are you, at the moment, Mr. Barrington?"

"I'd rather not say."

"I'd rather not say, too."

"Then we might as well be on different continents."

"We may very well be."

"How are we going to resolve this?"

"I may be able to help you deal with Manning."

"Deal, how?"

"You're trying to buy him off, aren't you?"

"Let's just say that I'm trying to bring a difficult situation to an amicable close."

"Then I'll take him your offer."

"You know how to get in touch with him?"

"How could I take him your offer, otherwise?"

"All right. Tell him that Allison wants to come to an arrangement with him to get out of her life. If he agrees in principle, then we can discuss it in more detail. Or just get him to call me."

"I don't think he'll do that."

"Why not?"

"He's very shy these days, and he's not fond of you."

"Tell him I can arrange for him to live his life more openly, without fear of legal difficulties."

"Now *that* might appeal to him. Can I reach you at this number?"

"Yes. How can I reach you?"

But Frederick James had hung up.

Stone turned to Dino. "You heard that?"

"I heard it."

"What do you think?"

"I think this is getting very weird," Dino said.

41

Callie came on deck. "And what have you two planned for the day?" she asked Stone and Dino.

"Zip," Dino said. "But I wouldn't mind some golf."

"I'll book you a tee time at the Breakers," she said.

"I don't want to leave you and Liz alone," Stone replied. "We'd better stick close."

"Liz and I will be just fine," Callie said. "I have your gun, and Juanito and a couple of crew members will be around. Besides, if you have to spend all your time here, you might get tired of me."

Stone snaked an arm around her and kissed her on the neck. "Not much chance of that," he said.

"I know," she replied, "but unless you and Dino get out of here and allow Liz and me some girl time, I'm going to start getting sick of you both."

Stone threw his hands up. "Golf, it is. Come on, Dino."

The starter cleared them from the first tee. Stone drove his usual slice into the next fairway, and Dino hooked his into yet another fairway.

"How're we going to handle the cart on this?" Dino asked, getting in.

"Well, I'm not giving it to you. You're away, so we'll go to your ball first."

Dino addressed the ball with a fairway wood, took a practice swing and sent the ball two hundred yards over a stand of palm trees, back into the fairway. "Take that!" he said.

Stone drove to his own ball, took a long iron and hit it to within five yards of Dino's ball.

"Looks like we're back in the game," Dino said.

"Back in the fairway, anyway."

They both parred the hole. A bit later, as they were crossing South County Road, Dino spoke up. "You are the most unobservant person I know."

"What brought that on?" Stone asked. "And how does being observant help my golf game?"

"Nothing can help your golf game," Dino replied, "but if somebody had told *me* that my former wife and lover was hunting me down to kill me, I'd take a look around me once in a while."

Stone tensed. "Where?"

"Over your left shoulder, parked at the curb, about two hundred yards down. Don't look yet!"

Stone tried to keep his eyes ahead. They stopped to tee off, and he took his driver out of the bag and tried a couple of practice swings, which allowed him to look at the car. "I can't see who's inside," he said.

"That's kind of the point, isn't it?" Dino asked. "If she'd wanted you to see her, she could have parked twenty yards from us."

"We've already made the local papers this week, as a result of the scene in the restaurant," Stone said. "I don't think I want to read a story that says I was shot dead on the golf course at the Breakers."

"Don't worry," Dino said, "you won't. I may, but not you."

"How do you know she doesn't want to kill you, too?"

"Because *I* never married her, then dumped her when an old girlfriend called," Dino said. "I've always been nice to Dolce."

Stone teed up and swung at the ball, hitting it straight, for a change. "I remember once your telling me that Eduardo was the devil, and that Dolce was his handmaiden. Is that what you call being nice?"

"I didn't say it to *her*," Dino pointed out. "You think I have a death wish?"

"But she must know what you think of her."

"I don't know how she could. I've certainly never told her."

"What about Mary Ann?"

"Mary Ann and I have not yet come to the point in our marriage where she wants me dead. Someday, maybe, but not yet." Dino drove the ball, and they got back into the cart.

"What is it with Sicilians, anyway?" Stone asked.

"Well, speaking as a scion of the more elegant north of Italy, it has always been my opinion that all Sicilians are totally batshit crazy. I mean, the vendetta thing would be counterproductive anywhere else but Sicily, but they've made an art of it. Do you have any idea how many more Sicilians there would be in the world, not to mention in this country, if there were no vendetta? If you took all of them who've been knifed, shotgunned, garrotted, blown up, and poisoned, married them off and had them produce, say, four point five children each? Millions."

"And you're saying that's not counterproductive?"

"Nah. It just concentrates more ill-gotten wealth in fewer hands, and it prevents a Sicilian population explosion. And that can't be a bad thing."

"But you married a Sicilian."

"How do you think I know all this? It's been an education, I can tell you." Dino curled a thirty-foot, breaking, downhill putt into the cup.

"How'd you do that?" Stone asked, astonished.

"I just thought about how a Sicilian would do it, if the ball would kill somebody."

Stone laughed. "How can I make it up with Dolce, without getting killed?" he asked, serious again.

"Make it up? You mean marry her again?"

"No, no, no," Stone sputtered. "I mean just make peace with her."

"You don't make peace with Sicilians, unless there is a threat of death on both sides. You know, like the nuclear thing: mutually assured destruction. Where do you think the Pentagon and the Kremlin got the idea?"

"There has to be another way."

"Eduardo could call her off."

"Yeah? He could do that?"

"If she wasn't crazy. Nobody can call off a crazy person, not even with a threat of death."

"You're such a pleasure to be around, sometimes, Dino."

"I'm just telling you the way things are. No use kidding yourself."

"I guess not," Stone said glumly. They were on a tee that faced the road, now, some four hundred and fifty yards away. Stone hit his first true drive, now, two hundred and sixty yards straight down the fairway.

"Everybody gets lucky sometime," Dino said.

"That's the thing about this game," Stone said, getting into the cart. "Even the worst duffer can go out and, maybe two or three times in a round, he can hit a shot that's the equal of anything a pro could do under the circumstances. And it gives you the entirely irrational hope that, if you worked at it, you might get pretty good at this game."

"That's what keeps us coming back," Dino

said. He hit a good drive, too, but short of Stone's.

"I like you keeping a respectful twenty yards back," Stone said. "Shows a certain deference."

Stone chunked his second shot, hitting the ground before striking the ball. It fell short, some forty yards from the green.

Dino hit the green. "Sorry about the lack of deference," he said.

Stone got out of the cart and looked toward the green, lining up his shot. Then he saw the car, sitting and idling at the side of the road, a hundred yards away.

"What club do you want?" Dino asked, standing at the rear of the cart beside the bags.

"Give me the two-iron," Stone said.

"Yeah, sure," Dino laughed. "You mean a wedge, don't you?"

"Give me the two-iron," Stone said again.

"Even you will hit the two-iron a hundred and eighty yards," Dino said. "I'd use a lob wedge, myself, to clear the bunker."

"Give me the two-iron," Stone said, an edge in his voice.

Dino gave him the two-iron.

Stone took the club and lined up on his target.

"You're aiming twenty yards to the left of the pin," Dino said, standing behind him.

Stone took a practice swing.

"Stone, if you take a full swing, you're going to hit the ball onto a neighboring golf course."

"No, I'm not," Stone said.

"Then you can kiss that ball goodbye."

Stone lined up with the ball. He took a short backswing and abbreviated his follow-through to keep the shot low. He connected solidly, and the ball flew straight and true, twenty yards to the left of the pin, across the road, narrowly missing a passing Rolls-Royce, and straight at the idling car with the blacked-out windows. The ball struck the driver's window with a *thwack,* but it did not shatter. Instead, it cracked into a hundred pieces, held together by the safety glass and the tinting film applied to the window.

Stone hoped somebody would get out, but instead, the car sped away, its tires squealing on the pavement, leaving a puff of black smoke.

"Nice shot!" Dino yelled.

42

Dino watched the car speed away and laughed aloud. "That ought to make the guy keep his distance!"

"Guy? What guy? You said it was Dolce."

"I said I *thought* it was Dolce. For all I know, it may be one of your groupies."

"I don't have groupies," Stone said.

"Okay, maybe it's one of your many enemies."

"Come on, let's finish the round," Stone said. "I assume you're going to let me take a mulligan on that one."

"Yeah, I guess."

Stone took his sand wedge, choked down on it, opened the face and flopped the ball onto the green, within three feet of the pin.

"You should have taken my advice in the first place," Dino said.

They were driving back to the Shames estate, with Dino at the wheel, when Stone's cell phone vibrated. "Hello?"

"This is Frederick James."

"Good day, Mr. James."

"I've spoken with Paul, and he's willing to deal, through me."

"Not through you," Stone said.

"Why not? He's chosen me as his representative."

"How can I trust you?" Stone asked. "You've already lied to me at least once."

"When did I ever lie to you?" James asked, sounding offended.

"You told me you'd never heard of Paul Manning, and then you told me you knew him. One of those was a lie."

"But —"

"I'll deal directly with Manning."

"For whatever reason, Paul doesn't wish to deal with you."

"Then I'll deal with a reputable lawyer who represents him."

James was silent for a moment. "I am Paul Manning's attorney," he said finally.

"You're a novelist," Stone said.

"So is Scott Turow, but he's a lawyer, too."

"I take it your name is not Frederick James, then?"

"A *nom de plume*."

"What is your real name?"

"I'm not prepared to divulge that."

"And you think I'm going to deal with somebody who says he's an attorney but won't tell me his name? Either get serious, or go away."

"But I —"

"I don't know who you are, where you are, if

you're an attorney or even if you really know Paul Manning."

"I assure you, I do."

"That's not good enough."

"What exactly do you want, Mr. Barrington?"

"I want to know that I'm dealing with the real Paul Manning and that he's represented by an attorney whose identity I can confirm."

"And what proof of those things would you accept?"

"Bring Manning to a meeting, and let him authorize you to represent him in my presence."

"Paul won't meet with you."

"Then I'm not going to remove the threat of his arrest on insurance fraud, and I'm certainly not going to give him any of my client's money."

"There must be some way we can resolve this."

"I think you understand my concerns, Mr. James. Why don't you go away and think about it for a bit, discuss it with your client and get back to me?"

"All right," James said and hung up.

"He's playing games?" Dino asked.

"I don't know what the hell he's doing."

"Manning's afraid you're going to set him up for an arrest."

"A reasonable fear," Stone said.

"Can you really get him off on the insurance fraud charge, or are you just blowing smoke up his ass?"

"I've *already* gotten him off," Stone said. "But

I'm not going to tell *him* that."

"How did you get him off?"

"I negotiated a deal for Allison with the insurance company, whereby they agreed not to prosecute in order to get some of the money back."

"And the deal includes Manning? Why?"

"I didn't want to admit to them that Allison was still alive, so I wrote the agreement without reference to names. Now they can't prosecute *anybody.*"

"That's pretty slick, Stone."

"I'm a pretty slick lawyer," Stone replied.

"Yeah, sometimes," Dino admitted.

They were back on the yacht, having a drink with Callie, when Stone's phone buzzed again. "Hello?"

"It's Frederick James."

"What did you come up with?"

"I propose that you and I meet, in order for me to establish my credentials."

"Okay, where?"

"Where are you?"

"Where are *you?*"

"I'm in New York, but I have to go to Miami on business later in the week. Is there someplace between New York and Miami we can meet? Preferably in an airport?"

"I'm on the west coast of Florida," Stone said. "How about Palm Beach International? It's a couple of hours' drive for me."

"Agreed. Now, what do you need from me?"

"In what state are you licensed to practice?"

"New York."

"Okay. Bring a copy of your New York law license, your New York driver's license and your United States passport. Also, I'll need a photograph of you with Paul Manning, taken no earlier than today and no later than tomorrow, and I want a copy of the day's *New York Times* prominently displayed in the photograph."

"I can do all that, I think, although Paul doesn't like to be photographed."

"I can imagine. Then I'll need a copy of Manning's U.S. passport, with his current identity recorded therein, and I want that clearly visible in the photograph, too."

"Whoa, whoa, he's not going to go for that."

"I'm giving him nothing unless I'm convinced he's who he says he is, and in order to do that, I'll need to know who he says he is. He's going to have to prove it to me."

"You're throwing in a whole lot of stuff, here," James said.

"If you're a lawyer, you'll know very well that I have to protect my client, just as you have to protect yours. That's all we're talking about."

"I'll get back to you," James said and hung up.

"Any progress?" Liz asked.

"By inches," Stone said. "Manning is being *very* cautious."

"He's got a lot to be cautious about," Liz replied.

An hour later, Stone's phone vibrated again. "All right," James said. "The day after tomorrow at one P.M., at Signature Aviation, Palm Beach International."

"Fine," Stone said. "I'll see you then, but if my concerns are not met, there'll be no discussion of terms."

"I understand," James said.

Stone hung up. "We're on."

43

Late that night, after a big dinner and more wine than he had intended to drink, Stone fell into bed, exhausted. He had barely fallen asleep, when he was wakened by a knock on the door — at first, softly, then loudly. Annoyed, he got out of bed, put on a robe and went to the door.

"Good evening," Dolce said. She stood there with two brandy snifters in one hand and a pistol in the other. "May I come in?" she asked, unnecessarily.

Stone looked at the gun and backed into the room. "Of course," he said.

Dolce kicked the door shut and offered him a snifter. "I brought you a drink," she said.

"Thanks, but I've already had too much to drink this evening," he replied.

"I said, *I brought you a drink*," she said, through clenched teeth.

Stone took the glass.

"Sit on the bed," she said, "where I can see you."

Stone sat on the bed.

Dolce lifted her glass. "To many more happy moments like this," she said.

Stone sipped at his brandy. It had an uncharacteristically bitter taste.

"Drink it!" she said, tossing down her own drink.

Stone tossed down his own. "To what do I owe this pleasure?" he asked.

Dolce smiled, revealing her startlingly white teeth against her olive skin. "A pleasure, is it? I had somehow gotten the impression that seeing your wife was no longer such a pleasure. How long has it been?"

"Too long," Stone said. He felt dreadful; the brandy on top of everything else he had had to drink at dinner was too much. He moved to set down his glass on the bedside table, and to his astonishment, he missed the table entirely. The glass dropped to the floor, missing the rug, shattering into tiny pieces. "I'm drunk," he said.

"Not exactly," Dolce replied. "You're just feeling the first effects of the Thorazine."

"What's Thorazine?" Stone asked, and he had to try hard to pronounce the words.

"It's a little something that an enlightened medical profession has devised to help those of us who are — how shall I put this? — *psychiatrically challenged* easier to manage. Do you know that one of Papa's doctors actually said those words to me? *Psychiatrically challenged!* You have no idea what those of us who do not meet society's standards of behavior have to endure at the hands of those who wish to make our company

291

more acceptable." She smiled. "But you're about to find out."

"Huh?" Stone said, dully. His mind seemed fairly sharp — certainly, he could understand her — but there was something blocking the connection between his brain and his lips, something that slowed everything to a molasseslike flow.

"Don't worry, my darling, it won't last long," she said, rising and approaching the bed. Her shoes ground the broken snifter into the floor with a loud noise. She placed a finger in the middle of Stone's forehead and pushed gently.

Stone fell back onto the bed. It was where he had always wanted to be, here on this bed, staring at the beautifully crafted ceiling of his beautifully crafted cabin.

Dolce lifted his feet onto the bed, untied his robe, then rolled him over and stripped it off his body. She rolled him onto his back again and tucked two pillows under his head.

Stone lay there, naked, indolent to a degree he would not have dreamed possible. He had no wish to do anything except lie there and let this happen.

Dolce went back to her chair, picked up the handbag that had hung on her arm, opened it, took out a wad of something and returned to the bed. She sat down on the edge and shook the little bundle into long lengths. "You know," she said, smoothing them out, "science has never solved the problem of what to do with old nylon stockings. There's no recycling of them, and they seem too good to throw away. One little run, and they're useless." She smiled again. "Or are they?" She rolled Stone's limp form through three hundred and sixty degrees, until he was centered on the bed, then she tied one end of a stocking to a wrist and the other end to a bedpost.

Stone watched her do it, unconcerned, and continued to watch as she tied his other hand and both feet to bedposts. He was spread-eagled, naked, on the bed, before a trickle of concern made its way from somewhere in his brain to his forehead, where it manifested itself in beads of sweat that popped out. *Wait a minute,* he thought, *something is wrong here.* He tugged at the bedposts, but the sturdy mahogany bed would not move, and neither could he.

"Well," Dolce said, "I believe your tiny dose of Thorazine is beginning to wear off. A psychiatric dose would have lasted much longer. It took me several months to learn to control my dosage — without the knowledge of my nurses, of course — to the point where I could manage a clear thought sooner, rather than later." She drew back a hand and slapped him smartly across the face. "There, feel that?"

"Yes," he said, and his lips moved better than they had a few minutes before.

"Oh, good, because I want you to be wide awake and feeling everything that is going to happen now."

"Dolce," Stone said, "what are you doing?"

"I thought it would be good," she said, "if you had some personal experience of a loss of control over what happens to you, and, particularly, if you experienced a sense of loss over, oh, I don't know, maybe a body part or two?" She opened her handbag and removed an old-fashioned straight razor.

Stone tried harder to free himself from the stockings and the bedposts, but to no avail.

"You're wasting your time, my dearest," she said, daubing the sweat from his brow with a corner of the sheet. "Nylon stockings make excellent restraints; they're extremely strong, stronger than you, in fact." She opened the razor, and the blade caught the light.

"There's a very nice little shop in town," she said, "that sells men's shaving products, and they had this very beautiful example of German steelmaking." She pulled a hair from Stone's head and let it fall on the blade. It separated into two pieces and fell to the floor.

"It has never been used," she said, "and it will never be sharper than it is at this moment. Just as well, too, since I didn't manage to steal a local anesthetic from my captors, only the drug. You'll hardly feel a thing, just the warm trickle — or rather, gush — of blood as it flows across what I believe the poets call the loins." She reached out and took hold of the tip of his penis. "Let's get it excited," she said. "It makes a better target." She drew back the hand holding the razor and swung it in a slow arc toward its destination.

Then Stone was screaming, and someone was hammering on the door.

"Stone, open the door!" a woman's voice called.

Stone was sitting straight up in bed, still dressed in his robe. He stumbled to the door and opened it.

"What's wrong?" Callie asked, alarmed. "You've been screaming at the top of your lungs."

Dino appeared behind Callie. "You all right, Stone?"

Stone went and sat on the edge of the bed, while Callie got a towel and wiped the sweat from his face and upper body.

"I had a dream," he panted.

"More like a nightmare," Callie said.

"Yes, more like a nightmare."

44

The following morning, Stone made the call he had been dreading and could no longer postpone.

"Hello, Stone," Eduardo Bianchi said.

"Good morning, Eduardo. I hope you're well."

"I have been better," Eduardo said, then was silent.

It was up to Stone. "I understand that Dolce has . . . left your house."

"I am afraid that is so," Eduardo replied.

"Do you have any idea of where she might be?"

"Stone, my friend, I think she would *like* to be wherever you are."

"I'm in Palm Beach, Florida, on business," Stone said. "Dino is with me, and he feels that Dolce may be in Palm Beach; that she may have been following me."

Eduardo heaved a sigh. "I will send people at once," he said.

"Eduardo, I cannot guarantee you that she is here. It's just a feeling."

"I respect what you feel, Stone, and if there is any chance at all that she is in Palm Beach, then that is where I must look for her."

"Eduardo, speaking as an attorney, I must ask if you have taken any legal steps toward guardianship?"

"No. This is a family problem, you understand, and I have no wish to bring the courts into it."

"I understand your feelings, but simply sending people to find her and return her could present legal difficulties that might be more invasive of your family privacy than taking steps to have her declared incompetent."

"She is not an incompetent person," Eduardo said stiffly.

"I'm sorry, I meant incompetent in the legal sense, not otherwise. Unless you are willing to make a case to a court that she is not currently able to account for herself and her actions, then she is legally entitled to do and go as she pleases. Removing her to New York from another state could pose problems."

"Stone, I understand this, and I am grateful for your advice, but you must understand that, in my family, we are accustomed to solving our problems without the help of, ah, public officials. If I can locate Dolce, I can achieve the reunification I desire."

"Of course, Eduardo. I don't doubt for a moment that you can."

"You say that Dino is with you? I had not heard this."

"Dino came down to help me with another

297

matter, one not connected to Dolce."

"I see. Well, it is good that he is there; you may well need his help. I need hardly tell you that Dolce may be a danger to herself and to you."

"I hope you are wrong, but I understand," Stone said. "If I should locate Dolce, what would you have me do?"

"Simply call me, and I will do the rest," Eduardo said. "Please don't try to deal with her yourself. From what her doctors have told me, she could be very dangerous."

"Eduardo, if Dolce should be traveling under a name not her own, is there a name she might choose to use?"

Eduardo was silent while he thought. "Once, when she was sixteen, she ran away after a quarrel with me. At that time, she used the name Portia Buckingham. It was a ridiculous name for a schoolgirl to choose, I know, but it was a kind of fantasy identity she made up as a child. She might possibly use it again."

"Would you like me to make some discreet inquiries?" Stone asked.

"Only if you can do so without involving the local police," Eduardo replied. "I do not wish for Dolce to be brought to the attention of the authorities, unless she tries to harm someone."

"There's not much I can do on my own," Stone said, "but I'll try."

"Ask Dino for his help. She is his sister-in-law, after all."

"I'll do that." Stone told Eduardo how he could be contacted.

"Goodbye, Stone, and thank you for your concern for Dolce."

"Goodbye, Eduardo." Stone hung up.

Dino sat down beside him. "You called Eduardo?"

"I felt I had to. He's sending people down here."

"Great, now we'll have goombahs roaming the streets of this piss-elegant town."

"Dino, you know Eduardo is more subtle than that."

"We'll see."

"He wants your help in finding her."

"What can I do?"

Stone handed him a Palm Beach classified directory. "Start calling hotels. Flash your badge. Inquire about her under her own name and under the name Portia Buckingham."

"*Portia Buckingham?* Give me a break!"

"It's a name she used to fantasize about having when she was a child, Eduardo says."

Dino shook his head and took the phone book. "I'll use the phone in the saloon," he said.

"Don't alarm anybody, just find out if she's registered."

"Thanks, Stone. I needed that advice." Dino went into the saloon.

"Leave a description with the desk clerk, too," Stone called after him.

Stone called his office. "Hi, Joan, it's me. What's happening?"

"Amazingly little," she said.

"Patch me into the dictator," he said. "I have some documents I'd like you to type up and FedEx to me today."

"Sure. Anything else?"

"Not at the moment."

"Here you go."

Stone heard the beep and began to dictate. When he had finished and given Joan her instructions, he hung up and went into the saloon. Dino was just hanging up the phone.

"I need the phone book for a minute," Stone said.

Dino tossed it to him. "I've called half a dozen places, starting with the Breakers."

"No luck, I suppose?"

"She's already checked in and out of two — the Breakers and the Brazilian Court, under Rosaria Bianchi."

"You're kidding. That was easy."

"Not so easy, pal. She's moving every day, and that's going to make her harder to find."

"Oh. Well, at least we know she's really in town."

"That, we know."

"Will you call Eduardo and tell him that?"

"Okay, I guess." Dino did not like dealing directly with his father-in-law, but he seemed willing to make an exception this time. He picked up the phone and dialed the number.

Stone began looking in the phone book under airports, and when he found what he was looking for made the call.

Dino finished his conversation with Eduardo. "What are you up to?" he asked Stone.

"I told our friend Mr. James that I was on the west coast of Florida, a couple of hours' drive from Palm Beach airport. I want him to go on thinking that until we get this settled." He made the arrangements he required, then hung up. "There, I guess I've done what I can." He picked up the phone again. "I'll make some of the hotel calls. You don't mind if I use your name, do you?"

"When did I ever mind?" Dino asked. "When did you ever care if I mind?"

45

At mid-morning, Stone drove north on I-95 and took the well-marked exit. Soon he was at North Palm Beach County airport, a small general aviation field a few miles from Palm Beach International. He found North County Aviation and parked his car.

Inside, he told the receptionist why he was there, and she made a quick phone call. "Don will be right with you," she said. "You're taking the Warrior, is that right?"

"That's correct."

"Then if you'd like to give me a credit card we can take care of that while Don is on his way."

Stone gave her his American Express card and watched as a Piper Warrior taxied up to the apron of North County Aviation and a young man got out and came inside.

"Mr. Barrington?"

"That's right."

"I'm Don. There she is."

Stone looked at the neat little airplane. "Looks very nice."

"Can I see your license and medical, please?"

Stone handed the man his private pilot's license and his third-class medical certificate. They were inspected and returned to him.

"How many hours do you have in type?" Don asked.

"A little over a hundred, but it's been a while. I did most of my private ticket training in a Warrior, and I'm real comfortable with it."

"Come on, then, and let's do a little checkride."

Stone signed his credit card chit, pocketed the card and followed Don outside.

"You do the preflight," Don said, handing him a fuel cup.

Stone put his briefcase into the airplane and walked slowly around it, running through a mental checklist. He drained some fuel from each wing and inspected it for dirt or water, checked the oil and handed Don back the fuel cup. "Looks good to me," he said.

"Take the left seat, then."

Stone climbed into the airplane, followed by Don. He started the engine, listened to the recorded weather from PBI, checked the wind sock and taxied to the active runway. He pulled into the runup pad and did his final check of the airplane, then, looking for traffic, he announced his intentions over the unicom frequency and taxied onto the runway. He pushed the throttle forward and, watching his airspeed, started down the center line. At rotation speed he pulled back on the yoke and left the ground. It was a fixed-gear airplane, so he didn't have to bother retracting the landing gear. Announcing his intentions at every turn, he climbed cross-wind.

"Just stay in the pattern," Don said, watching his every move closely.

Stone turned downwind, reduced power and prepared to land. He turned onto the base leg, then onto final and set the airplane lightly down on the runway.

"Okay," Don said. "You can fly it. Just drop me back at the FBO, and you're on your way. How long will you be gone?"

"Just a couple of hours," Stone said.

"You understand there's a four-hour minimum on the rental?"

"Yes."

Don hopped out of the airplane, and Stone taxied back to the runway and repeated his takeoff. He climbed to a thousand feet, listened again to the recorded weather, then called the PBI tower. "Palm Beach Tower, this is November One-two-three Tango Foxtrot," he said, reading the airplane's registration number from a plaque on the instrument panel. "I'm ten miles to the northwest, VFR, looking for landing instructions. I have the ATIS."

The tower called back. "Enter a right base for runway niner. Traffic's light today. You're cleared to land."

Stone followed the instructions and ten minutes later he was taxiing up to Signature Aviation, between a Gulfstream III and a G-IV. He wondered how long it had been since anything as small as his rental had parked here.

He got out of the airplane. "The brakes are off," he told the lineman, knowing they wouldn't leave it where it was. "No fuel. I'll be about an hour."

He went inside the handsome lobby and walked up to the huge desk. "I'm looking for Mr. Frederick James," he said to the young lady behind it.

"Oh, yes, you must be Mr. Barrington," she said. "Mr. James and his associate are in the conference room, right over there." She pointed. "You won't be disturbed."

"Thank you." He walked across the reception room to the door and knocked on it.

"Come in," a man's voice said.

Stone opened the door and entered the room. A man, who had been seated alone at the conference table, stood up to greet him. Stone recognized him immediately.

"Mr. Barrington, I'm Edward Ginsky," he said, offering his hand. He was dressed in a beautifully tailored, double-breasted blue blazer and white linen slacks, his shirt open at the collar.

Stone shook it. "Of course. I'm glad to meet you." Ginsky was a famous New York lawyer, known mostly for his expertise in representing women in divorce cases. He had handled a number of high-profile divorces, and his clients had always done very well from his representation.

"I've heard of you, too," Ginsky said, sitting down and motioning Stone to a chair. "Bill Eggers speaks well of you, in fact."

"That's kind of Bill," Stone said.

"Well," Ginsky said, "enough chitchat. Shall we get to it?"

"Let's," Stone replied.

"I trust that now you won't need the identification you requested."

"No, not for you, but for your client."

"Ah, yes. Trust me when I tell you that, before our meeting is concluded, you will have adequate proof that I represent Paul Manning. May we proceed on that basis?"

"For the moment," Stone said, "but I should tell you that I will not come to any agreement until I am satisfied who I am dealing with."

"Understood," Ginsky said. "Now, what do you have to propose?"

"Are you acquainted with Mr. Manning's activities with regard to the island of St. Marks some years ago?"

"I believe I have all the relevant facts."

"Then you will know that your client and mine were married at that time and, in the absence of a divorce, still are."

"You could put that light on it," Ginsky said.

"I hardly know what other light to put on it."

"I think you are aware that my client is, if not dead, then no longer legally alive."

"You could put that light on it," Stone said.

Ginsky allowed himself a smile.

"Still, he exists, my client exists and legally, as I'm sure you're aware, their marriage still exists."

"I assume your client would like that marriage to end," Ginsky said.

"You assume correctly. She wishes the marriage to end and she wishes not to see her husband again or hear from him."

"I think that could be arranged," Ginsky said. "Under appropriate circumstances. What is your offer?"

"My client is willing to pay your client one million dollars in cash, wire-transferred to any bank in the United States, in return for a signed property settlement to that effect and a contractual agreement that your client will never contact her again, nor knowingly inhabit the same city at the same time as my client." Stone knew that he had already put several stumbling blocks in the way of a settlement, one by omission. The two lawyers were circling each other, metaphorically, feeling each other out.

"I see," Ginsky said. "Of course, hardly anything you've said is acceptable."

"Tell me what you're willing to accept, and let's go on from there."

Ginsky threw his first punch. "Your client achieved a windfall of twelve million dollars as a result of my client's efforts. He wants half that."

"Your client masterminded a criminal conspiracy, and when it went wrong, left my client to hang by the neck until she was dead," Stone parried.

"She did not hang," Ginsky said.

"Neither did your client," Stone reminded him. "And, when your client murdered three people and was arrested in New York and extradited for his crimes, and was sentenced to hang himself, my client interceded on his behalf, paying half a million dollars to save his life. She could have done nothing, and we would not be having this conversation." Stone heard the door behind him close; he had not heard it open. He did not turn around. "It seems to me that your client is deeply in my client's debt."

"I don't owe her a fucking thing," Paul Manning's deep voice said from the door. "And don't turn around."

Stone felt cold steel pressed to the back of his neck.

46

Stone didn't move, nor did he allow himself to show any concern.

"Paul," Ginsky said, "that is entirely unnecessary, and moreover, unacceptable. If you want me to represent you in this matter, put it away and sit down."

"I'll put it away," Manning replied, "but I'll stay where I am. And, Barrington, if you turn around I'll use it on your skull."

"Mr. Ginsky," Stone said, "perhaps it would help if you explained your client's tenuous position to him."

"Let me explain something to you, Barrington," Manning said.

"Shut up," Stone said. "I will not deal with you, but with your attorney. If you can't accept that, then I'll leave now."

"Get in your little airplane and fly away, huh? Maybe I should have a look at that airplane. You know how good I am at fixing them."

"Paul, be quiet," Ginsky said. "If you say another word I will withdraw from this meeting, and we'll all be right back where we started. Mr. Barrington, you have not mentioned your previous offer to resolve any legal difficulties Mr. Manning might have."

"No, and I won't mention that until we are agreed on all other points, except to say that to resolve the legal difficulties is within my power."

"Very well," Ginsky said. "The offer on the table is for one million dollars in cash, a signed property settlement and, I assume, a divorce, and an undertaking not to see or speak to Mrs. Manning again. Is that correct?" He looked toward the door and held up a hand to stop Manning from speaking.

Ginsky had not mentioned that the transaction would take place through a U.S. bank. "You left out a couple of points, but I won't quibble," Stone said. "That's substantially it."

"The money is not enough," Ginsky said. "Let's cut to the chase. Make your best offer."

"A million and a half dollars," Stone said.

"If you will offer two million dollars, I think I can recommend the deal to my client."

"My client has already paid half a million dollars for his benefit; that makes a total of two million."

Ginsky looked at his client, then back at Stone. "Surely she can do better. She walked away with twelve million, tax free."

"My client has had many expenses over the years, and she has paid her taxes." He had advised her to, anyway.

"A U.S. bank is not acceptable for the transaction," Ginsky said.

"Then we'll wire it to your firm's trust account, and you can disburse it."

"Still not acceptable."

"What's the matter, doesn't your client want to pay *his* taxes?"

"That's beside the point."

"Speaking of points, you haven't addressed all of mine," Stone said.

"He can hardly agree not to be in the same city with her; he won't know her movements."

"All right, he stays out of Florida and New York City, except to change airplanes."

Ginsky looked at his client, then back at Stone. "We won't give you New York, but you can have Florida."

"Let me enumerate," Stone said, counting off on his fingers. "Two million dollars. I won't wire it abroad, but to your trust account. You can disburse it abroad, if you want to. He stays out of Florida, or he goes to jail for contempt of court. He signs a property settlement and a document acceding to a divorce petition, here and now."

"Let me see the papers," Ginsky said.

Stone unlatched his briefcase, selected the set of documents with the two-million-dollar figure typed in, then slid them across the table.

There was five minutes of silence while Ginsky speed-read the documents. He looked at his client. "This is good," he said.

"I expect there's a notary at this FBO," Stone said, "and I want him to sign twice, once as

Manning and once as whatever his current passport says."

Ginsky nodded.

"Let me see the passport."

Ginsky spoke to his client. "Paul, please ask the girl at the desk to send a notary in here."

Stone heard the door open and close.

Ginsky slid a U.S. passport across the table.

Stone opened it, anxious to see the photograph. A postage stamp covered the face. He looked up at Ginsky. "How do I know this is Paul's passport, if I can't see the face on the photograph?"

"Do you doubt that the man who was just in this room was Paul Manning?"

"No, I know the voice."

"Then you don't need to see the face for purposes of identification, do you?"

"Your client is very shy."

"He has his reasons," Ginsky said.

Stone copied down the information on the passport: William Charles Danforth, a Washington, D.C., address. He riffled through the visa pages and saw a number of entry and exit stamps — London, Rome, other European cities. "He's pretty well traveled." He slid the passport back across the table.

Manning returned with the notary, and Stone pulled out additional copies of the agreement.

"Both names," Ginsky said to his client.

Manning signed the documents on a credenza behind Stone, and the woman notarized them.

"When do we get your client's signature?" Ginsky asked.

"She'll sign today, and the documents will be FedExed to your New York office right away."

Ginsky gave Stone his business card.

The notary left. "What about the money?" Manning asked.

"To be wire-transferred as soon as the judge signs the divorce decree," Stone said.

"It's in the documents, Paul. He'll provide a release from the insurance company at the same time. The deal won't be final until we're in receipt of those two items."

"I don't like waiting," Manning said.

"It can't be helped," Ginsky replied. "It's how these things are done. Trust me."

Stone heard the door open and close behind him.

"Sorry, my client's a little edgy today," Ginsky said.

"How'd you get mixed up in this, Ed?" Stone asked.

"I've known him since college. He popped up in my life only a short time ago, when he got the e-mails from you."

"Can you make him hew to the terms of the agreement?"

"I think so. He wants out of the marriage, and he wants the insurance matter off his back."

"I'll tell you, off the record," Stone said, "that if he doesn't stick to the letter and the spirit of the agreement, I'll take it upon myself to expose him for who he is, and in a very public way."

"Are you threatening me, Stone?" Ginsky asked.

"No, Ed, I'm threatening Paul Manning, and I mean it. You should know that he's a dangerous man, and my advice to you is, when this matter is concluded, to stay as far away from him as you can."

"That may be good advice," Ginsky admitted.

Stone put his copies of the document into his briefcase and stood up.

Ginsky stood up, too. "We saw you taxi up and get out of the airplane," he said. "I was expecting you to drive in. Where are you flying back to?"

"I'd rather not say," Stone said.

"I don't think you'll have any more trouble from Paul. Where do you want to do the divorce?"

"Anywhere in Florida will do."

"I know a judge here in Palm Beach, and I'm licensed to practice here."

"Fine with me. I'm not licensed here, so I'll get Bill Eggers to find somebody. He'll be in touch."

"I'll look forward to receiving the signed documents tomorrow." Ginsky held out his hand.

Stone shook it. "Thanks for getting him to see sweet reason, Ed."

"See you around the courts in New York, I expect."

"I expect so."

The two lawyers walked out of the conference room and into the lobby. Paul Manning was nowhere in sight.

They walked out to the ramp together, shook hands again, and Ginsky got into a Hawker 125, parked near the door.

Stone assumed Manning was already on it. He walked a hundred yards to where his less imposing aircraft had been parked by the lineman. He did an especially thorough preflight inspection before climbing into the airplane.

He remembered Manning's remark about knowing how to fix airplanes, and he wanted to be sure the one he was flying would keep flying. He started the engine, and he listened to it carefully before starting to taxi.

All the way back to North County airport, he listened to the engine. It got him back safely.

47

When Stone arrived back aboard the yacht, Liz, Callie and Dino were all waiting for him.

"Did you see him?" Liz asked.

"Not exactly," Stone said, "but we were in the same room."

"Did he sign the papers?" she asked anxiously.

"Yes."

"How much am I giving him?"

"Two million dollars."

Liz collapsed in his arms, laughing. "Oh, Stone, you are a wonder. You saved me three million dollars!"

"Don't ever tell Paul that," he said.

"I hope I won't ever have to talk to him."

"I think we can avoid a court appearance for the divorce."

"Where will we do the divorce?"

"Here in Palm Beach. I'll find you a Florida lawyer for that, but since we have a signed settlement, there won't be much work for him to do. Now you have to sign the documents, and we have to find a notary."

"I'm a notary," Callie said. "I have to witness

stuff for Thad all the time."

"Great. Go get your seal."

Callie left them, then returned with her seal and stamp. Stone handed Liz a pen, she signed and Callie notarized.

"That's it," Stone said, handing the documents to Callie, along with Ed Ginsky's card. "Will you FedEx these to him right away?"

"Sure. I'll call for a pickup now." She picked up a phone.

"I have to call Thad and tell him," Liz said, running for the phone in the saloon.

Stone sat down beside Dino.

"Is this all over, Stone?"

"I hope so," Stone replied.

"But you're not sure?"

"It's not going to be over until it's over." He thought about that for a moment. "And maybe not even then."

"What's the problem?"

"The problem is Manning. He's still just as angry and, apparently, as nuts as he was the day you arrested him in New York. He's got a good lawyer — Ed Ginsky — but I don't know if Ed can control him."

"I know who Ginsky is," Dino said. "He's had a lot of experience dealing with angry spouses."

"I wonder how much experience he's had in dealing with crazy ones?"

"Everybody who's getting a divorce is crazy for a while," Dino said.

Stone picked up the phone. "I'd better call

Bill Eggers and find Liz a local lawyer."

Liz came running back from the saloon. "Thad's coming back tonight!" She ran toward her cabin.

Stone placed the call to Eggers and told him what he wanted.

"I don't know the Florida law offhand," Eggers said, "but it sounds pretty straightforward."

"That's what I think. You know somebody in Palm Beach?"

"No, but somebody here in the shop will. I'll have somebody call you."

"Okay."

"How's everything going?"

Stone gave him a recap of recent events.

"This is kind of messy, isn't it?"

"As divorces go, yes; but we might conclude a nasty case as well."

Thad Shames came aboard his yacht late in the afternoon in high spirits. He swept Liz into his arms, kissed her, then shook hands with Stone and Dino, then he turned back to Liz. "Right here, in front of these witnesses, I want to ask you: Will you marry me?"

"Oh, yes!" she cried, and they kissed again.

Dino glanced at Stone and rolled his eyes.

"Isn't this romantic?" Callie asked Stone.

"Oh, yeah," Stone replied.

"Let's do it this weekend," Thad said enthusiastically.

"I'd love that!" Liz said, tears of happiness streaming down her cheeks.

Stone and Dino exchanged glances. Stone was horrified, Dino amused.

Liz went to repair her makeup, and Stone made Thad sit down with him and Dino.

"Thad," Stone said seriously, "don't you think you ought to wait until Liz is divorced before you get married?"

"Oh, that's just paperwork," Thad said. "You've already got the signed property settlement and divorce papers, and anyway, legally, she's a widow — twice, in fact. Both deaths are a matter of public record."

"Thad, rushing into this could make your life a lot more complicated. Why do that? I haven't looked into the Florida law, but with signed papers and a settlement, it shouldn't take long to get a decree. Relax and enjoy being engaged for a while."

"Listen, Stone," Thad said. "I've waited a long time for this girl, and I'm not going to let her get away. I'm not going to relax until we're married and on our honeymoon."

Callie came with drinks for all of them.

"Callie, we're having a Sunday afternoon wedding," Thad said. "Invite everybody who was at the housewarming, plus the New York list. Call the caterers and find out how I get a marriage license and, if necessary, a blood test."

Callie grabbed a pad and started taking notes.

"And, Stone, Dino, I want you both to stay for

the wedding," Thad said.

Stone looked at Dino, and they nodded.

"I wouldn't miss it," Dino said.

"And, Thad," Stone said, "we're going to need some outside security for this occasion."

"Callie, take care of it," Thad said. He got up. "I'm going to get a shower and change for dinner. Please book us a table somewhere, Callie." He departed for the house.

Callie sat down next to Stone. "How much security are you going to want?"

"Let's see," Stone said, looking toward the house. "We'll want two men, dressed like the car parkers, out in front of the house. There should be two men in each public room in the house, dressed as guests, four in the garden and two on the yacht. How many is that?"

"Eighteen."

"Ask for twenty-four, and I want them to have radios."

"Do you want them armed?"

Stone thought about that.

Dino spoke up. "I'm not sure it's a good idea, having that many armed men in a crowd. After all, we don't know these guys, don't know how good they are."

"We'll have one armed man in each room, in the garden and on the yacht," Stone said. "Tell them we want only their best-trained and most experienced men carrying."

"All right," Callie said.

"And I want them here an hour before the

party, so I can brief them."

"Okay." She made a note of that.

"Anything else you can think of?" Stone asked Dino.

"Well, let's see," Dino said, "we could have a couple of machine guns mounted on the roof, and maybe a bazooka or two."

Callie laughed.

"Why do you think he's kidding?" Stone asked.

She laughed again. "I'd better go book us a dinner table," Callie said, "and I've got a lot of phone calls to make." She headed toward her cabin.

"Thad is completely nuts, isn't he?" Dino asked.

"He's nuts about Liz, no doubt about it."

"I've never seen anybody move so fast."

"It's the money. The superrich are accustomed to having what they want, when they want it, and that usually means *right now*."

"It's a pretty short time to put together a big wedding."

"Frankly, I'm surprised we're not doing it tonight. But don't worry, this is what Callie does, and she's used to doing it Thad's way."

"Sounds like it's going to be a hell of a party," Dino said.

"Or a hell of a mess," Stone said.

They had dinner at an Italian restaurant, Luccia, on a covered terrace, and Stone was gratified that gunfire did not break out. He did not enjoy himself very much, though. He was preoccupied with Paul Manning, and he didn't even understand why.

Everything Manning was doing made sense. He was making money, he was removing the possibility of prosecution for insurance fraud, he was getting on with his life. So why was Stone so worried?

When he got back to the yacht that night, he started to crawl into bed with Callie, then stopped and went to the phone.

"This is Berman," the voice said.

"Bob, it's Stone. I hope I didn't wake you."

"Nah, what's up?"

"Got a pencil?"

"Shoot."

"I want everything you can find — and I mean *everything* — on a William Charles Danforth." He read him the P Street Washington address. "I want a full bio, and I want to know how far his credit history goes back. Do a criminal record check, too, and I want a photograph. I especially want a photograph."

"Will do. How soon?"

"Tomorrow, as early as possible."

"I'll call you." Berman hung up.

Stone got into bed and snuggled up to Callie. Now that he felt he was doing something, he could pay her the proper attention.

48

Dino finished his coffee. "How are we dressing for this shindig on Sunday?" he asked.

"Black tie," Callie replied.

"In the afternoon?"

"The wedding's at six, with a small group of invited guests. Everybody else arrives at seven."

"Oh, good, for a minute I thought we were going to be gauche and wear black tie in the afternoon."

Callie laughed. "You gauche, Dino? Never!"

Dino gave her a sweet smile. "Stone, I gotta go shopping. You come with me."

Stone looked at Callie.

"We'll be all right," she said. "I've already got two security men in the main house."

"You anticipate me," Stone said.

"I try."

"Okay, Dino, let's go shopping." He led the way toward where the cars were parked. A man who was obviously a security guard paid a lot of attention to them.

"You're one of the two men on duty?" Stone asked.

"That's right."

"My name is Barrington. This is Lieutenant Bacchetti, NYPD. You armed?"

"Yes, sir."

"Try not to shoot anybody, if you can help it."

"I'll try."

They got into the car and drove away.

"What are you shopping for?" he asked Dino.

"A dinner jacket."

"Why don't you ask Mary Ann to ship yours down here? There's time."

"That's a question only a lifelong bachelor could ask," Dino said. "If you're in Palm Beach, and she's not, you don't call home and say, 'Honey, send my dinner jacket, will you?' It would take too long to explain why to her, and in the end, she'd never believe you. Besides, I need a new one, anyway. Somebody threw up on the last one at a wedding last year, and the cleaners could never get it all out."

"Where you want to shop?"

"They got an Armani here?"

"They do."

"Giorgio always does my dinner jackets."

Stone found a parking spot on Worth Avenue. He put the top up to keep the sun from over-heating the black leather upholstery, and they walked to the shop.

Dino conferred with a salesman, and shortly, a fitter was marking up a white dinner jacket. "You like the white?" he asked Stone.

"I like. Very elegant."

"I thought you would. I'm getting this just for you."

"You're sweet."

The fitter looked at them oddly. "What about the lump, sir?" he said, nodding toward the pistol on Dino's belt.

"Allow for that," Dino said. "I'll be wearing it to the party."

"Well, this is a first for Palm Beach," the man muttered, but he did his work.

When they returned to the car, the driver's side window was a web of pieces, held together by the lamination.

"Looks like a golf ball hit it," Dino said.

Stone looked up and down the street. "That's not funny."

"Sure it is," Dino laughed.

"You see her anywhere?"

"No, but a silver Volvo sedan has been following us."

"Why didn't you mention it sooner?"

"What good would it have done? It would have just ruined your day."

"You're right about that," Stone said, flicking small shards of glass out of the driver's seat.

They drove back to the house and walked to the yacht.

"A message for you, Stone," Callie said, handing him Bob Berman's number.

Dino glanced at the piece of paper. "What have you got Berman on?"

Stone led him into the saloon and picked up a

phone. "One William Charles Danforth of Washington, D.C."

"Who's that?"

"It's the passport Paul Manning is using these days."

"Oh."

Stone called Berman. "It's me. You got something?"

"I got a lot," Berman said. "You want me to FedEx it to you, or you want to hear it now?"

"Let's hear it."

"Okay. Mr. Danforth is all over the Internet, just like you'd expect a substantial person to be. He's got a credit history going back only four years. It's little stuff, credit cards, couple of department stores — Saks, Macy's. There's apparently no Mrs. Danforth, and there are no mortgages on the reports. He rents an apartment in the P Street house in Georgetown, has for four years."

"So Mr. Danforth is only four years old."

"Right."

"What does he do?"

"He lists his occupation as business consultant."

"Whatever that means."

"Yeah. His credit card spending is consistent with a man making less than a hundred thousand dollars a year. I got one of the credit card statements for the past year, and he's traveled to Europe and Florida."

"Where, Florida?"

"Miami, twice; last time ten days ago. He rented a car there, too."

"Okay, what else?"

"He seems pretty ordinary. His phone number is listed. Nothing jumps out at you."

"Did you find a photograph?"

"Nope, wasn't available from any of my sources."

"What about a driver's license photo?"

"I checked D.C., Virginia and Maryland. Nothing there."

"If he rented a car, he must have a license; if he has a license, there should be a photograph on file somewhere."

"You want me to check all the states?"

"The contiguous forty-eight will do."

"Okay, but it's going to take a few days. There's no federal registry of driver's licenses; it's purely a state thing."

Stone had a thought. "How about a pilot's license? He knows something about airplanes."

"There's no photograph on pilots' licenses; you ought to know that."

"Oh, right," Stone said, thinking of the license in his own pocket.

"You suspect this guy of being wonky in any way?" Berman asked. "There's no criminal record."

"Yes."

"Well, if he's wonky, he wouldn't have any trouble picking up a driver's license that would get him a rental car."

"Good point, but do the search anyway."

"Whatever you say, Stone."

"Does he own a car?"

"Yes, a six-year-old BMW 320i, registered at the P Street address."

"Strange that he has a car and a passport with that address, but no driver's license."

"Maybe he doesn't want his picture taken any more than necessary. Does he know you're looking at him?"

"Probably not, but he might guess."

"Maybe, if he's wonky, he figured that someday, somebody would be looking for a photograph of him."

"He has a passport, and you need a photograph for that."

"Yeah, but the State Department is a lot harder to get a photograph out of than a state driver's license office."

"Once again, you have a point."

"Anything else?"

"Not that I can think of at the moment. Let me know about the license."

"Will do," Berman said.

"And, Bob?"

"Yeah?"

"Put your mind to other ways to find a photograph."

"I already did." Berman hung up.

49

Stone sat on the afterdeck and nursed a gin and tonic. "Dino," he said finally, "when you arrested Manning that time in New York, you fingerprinted him, didn't you?"

"Yeah, why?"

"Because that gives us a possible way to find out what Manning has been doing for the past four years to earn a living. I can't see him doing it honestly."

"What do you need?"

"I need for you to run his prints against unsolved crimes with no suspects."

"Stone, you're about to be rid of the guy. Why do you want to press this?"

"Because I have the awful feeling I'm *never* going to be rid of him. If he's committed a crime somewhere in this country, and I can prove it, then I'd have something on him, something that would either keep him in line or put him in jail."

Dino picked up a phone, called his office and asked them to run the Manning prints against unsolved crimes. "Shouldn't take long," he said. "Why do you think he might have committed a crime?"

"Because he's apparently been earning less than a hundred thousand dollars a year, and I don't think that's enough to keep Paul Manning in the style to which he long ago became accustomed."

The phone rang, and Stone picked it up.

"Mr. Barrington?"

"Yes."

"My name is Fred Williamson. Somebody in Bill Eggers's office at Woodman and Weld in New York asked me to call you about some divorce work."

"Yes, of course. How do you do, Fred?"

"Very well, thanks, and divorce is a specialty of mine."

"Glad to hear it. What I've got here is a petition from a Mrs. Allison Manning against Paul Manning. Mr. Manning has already waived a response, and we have a signed property settlement."

"Where do the Mannings live?"

"In Palm Beach." Stone gave him Liz's West Indies Drive address.

"Shouldn't be a problem, then. It'll probably take a month to get it heard."

"Do the Mannings have to appear?"

"Not necessary, as long as they're in agreement on the terms and they're both represented by counsel. Who's his lawyer?"

"Edward Ginsky, of New York, but he's licensed to practice in Florida." Stone gave him Ginsky's address and phone number.

"I'll call him and get us on the court calendar."

"Fred, is there any way to get this heard right away? And in chambers, if possible? I don't want it to make the papers, even in the legal notices."

"I know a judge who might hear it in chambers sooner, rather than later," Williamson said.

"I'd appreciate it if you could handle it that way. Ginsky has his own jet. I'm sure he could appear on short notice, or appoint someone local to do it."

"Who's got the paperwork?"

"I have. Can you send a messenger for it?"

"Sure. Where?"

Stone gave him the address.

"I'll have somebody there inside an hour."

"Thanks, Fred. Call me if you need any further information." Stone hung up. He went to his briefcase, extracted the documents, stuffed them into a manila envelope, wrote Williamson's name on it and gave it to Juanito to leave with the security man guarding the front door.

"Maybe I can get them divorced before Sunday," Stone said.

"Would that make you feel better?" Dino asked.

"Yes, indeed. I'm uncomfortable about witnessing a client — two clients, in this case — committing bigamy in front of the crumbs of Palm Beach's upper crust."

"When they get to that part about 'if anybody can show just cause why these two people

331

shouldn't get married,' shouldn't you, as an officer of the court, stand up and yell, 'It's bigamy!'?"

"Probably, but this lawyer says he might be able to get it heard quickly."

The phone rang again, and this time it was for Dino.

"Hello? Yeah, this is Bacchetti. Hang on, let me get something to write with." He motioned to Stone for a pen.

Stone handed him one, and a pad.

"Yeah, yeah. Where? How many? And there's no other clue? Why the hell didn't this match pop up before? Oh, yeah, I see. Thanks. I don't know yet. Sit on it until I get back to you." He hung up.

"What?" Stone asked.

"You were right, pal. Our Mr. Manning knocked over a branch bank in Arlington, Virginia, four years ago."

"I knew it!" Stone said.

"He left a thumbprint on a note that he handed a teller."

"Why didn't the match turn up at the time?"

"I asked about that. It seems that when we printed the guy at the Nineteenth, whoever did it didn't put the prints into the system because he figured, what the hell, the guy's being prosecuted in another country. It was stupid, but it happens."

"This is wonderful," Stone said, meaning it.

"It gets better. A man answering the description — at least height and weight — knocked over three other branches within fifty miles of D.C. Two in Maryland and one more in Virginia. He was smart enough not to leave any prints on those jobs."

"What sort of money did he get?"

"Between a hundred and a hundred and fifty thousand at each bank; never more than that. Still, he had to do some planning or have some inside information to get that much out of a walk-in-and-hand-the-teller-a-note job. Usually those bring more like twenty-five or thirty grand a pop, and the banks don't even bother to prosecute if there was no violence involved." Dino stopped and looked at Stone.

"Why the smug little smile?"

"Gee, I don't know. I just have this warm fuzzy feeling inside."

"You've got the guy by the balls."

"You bet your sweet ass I have," Stone said with satisfaction.

"So what are you going to do?"

"I'm going to get Liz and Manning divorced and see her and Thad married, then I'm going to call the FBI and sic them on Paul Manning, and I'm going to take the greatest pleasure in doing it."

"I hope it's that easy, pal," Dino replied.

50

Stone was woken from a sound sleep by the phone next to his bed. He picked it up. "Hello," he said, sleepily. He looked at the bedside clock. It was shortly after ten A.M.

"Stone? It's Fred Williamson. Can you have Mrs. Manning at the courthouse at three o'clock this afternoon?"

"Why?"

"We've got a hearing before Judge Coronado in his chambers at that time."

"Why does Mrs. Manning have to be there?"

"This is an unusual situation, and the judge wants to talk to the couple face-to-face."

"But why? I thought we could do it with just their attorneys."

"He wants to know what the big rush is, I guess; whether these people are for real."

For real? Stone thought. *They are definitely not for real.* "Have you spoken to Ed Ginsky?"

"Yes. He says he can have his client there."

"Well, okay," Stone said. "We'll be there."

"The judge is going to ask some questions, like how long have the Mannings lived in Florida. You know the answer to that one?"

"I'll have to ask Mrs. Manning."

"This whole petition is based on the fact that they're Florida residents. Be sure you tell her that."

"All right. Have you told Ginsky about this?"

"Yes. He says his client will bring proof of Florida residency. The judge is going to ask these people why they want a divorce, and there shouldn't be any disagreement between them about that."

"You told Ginsky that, too?"

"Yes."

"All right."

"I'll see you at three o'clock in Judge Coronado's chambers, which are behind court-room A."

"Good, see you then."

Stone got dressed and found Liz and Thad having breakfast on deck. "Good news," he said.

"I'm always up for good news," Thad said.

"Liz, you're getting divorced this afternoon."

"Wonderful!" she nearly shouted.

"You and I have to appear in the chambers of a Judge Coronado this afternoon at three. Paul and his attorney will be there, too."

"I don't want to do that," she said.

"I'm afraid you have no choice in the matter," Stone said.

"I won't be in the same room with him."

"Look, this is not the first divorce this judge has heard. He's accustomed to people who aren't speaking to each other."

"Liz," Thad said, "Stone has gone to a lot of trouble to get this thing resolved this week. This is only going to take a few minutes, right, Stone?"

"That's right. I shouldn't think it would take more than half an hour, at the most."

"Oh, all right," Liz said. "I don't have to talk to him, do I?"

"No, but you'll have to talk. The judge will ask you both some questions, and be warned, he's not going to like it if you argue about the answers. Just don't disagree with Paul."

"That may be difficult," she said.

"Liz, this is the quickest, quietest way possible to get you out of this marriage. Just do what you have to do," Thad said.

"All right, darling," she said, and put her hand on his.

"Can I be there?" Thad asked. "Liz might feel better."

"Absolutely not," Stone said. "You're a very recognizable figure in Palm Beach, and I don't want you anywhere near that courthouse."

"Oh, all right," Thad said. "Sit down and have some breakfast."

Juanito appeared, and Stone ordered. "Now, Liz, tell me: How long have you been a Florida resident?"

"Since I married Winston, I guess. Three years. He was a Florida resident well before that, for tax reasons."

"The judge will ask you that."

"What about Paul? He's not a Florida resident. At least, I don't think he is."

"His lawyer says he can show proof of residency. The judge will ask you things like how long you've been married, and he's going to ask you why you want a divorce. What are you going to tell him?"

"That my husband led me into a life of crime and that, when he murdered three people, I didn't want to live with him anymore."

"No, no, no," Stone said. "You want to be general, not specific."

"You mean like, we just grew apart over the years?"

"That's better. And if he asks Paul first, just go along with whatever he says. Don't worry, he has a very good lawyer, and he will have been well briefed."

"Whatever you say," she said.

"That's the right answer, too. Now, another thing. Your agreement with Paul requires you to wire-transfer the money into his lawyer's trust account as soon as the divorce is final. What I'd like is for you to transfer the money to my trust account today, and I'll take it from there."

"The two million dollars?" she asked.

"That's right."

"God, but I hate to give that son of a bitch any money."

"Liz, get a grip. You've already signed an agreement to that effect. Yesterday, you were delighted to get off so cheaply."

"Liz, honey," Thad said, "two million dollars is small change to me. Let me take care of that."

"I couldn't let you do that," Liz replied.

"No, really. I'd consider it a great favor if you'd let me do that."

"Oh, Thad," she said, putting her hand on his cheek. "You're so sweet."

Thad turned to Stone. "I'll move the money this morning."

"You're sure that's the way you want to do this?"

"Yes, I am."

Stone watched, amazed, as they kissed.

Later, when they were driving to the golf course, Stone brought Dino up to date.

Dino's mouth fell open. "He's giving her two million bucks?"

"Like Thad says, it's small change to him."

"Holy mother! She's good, isn't she? She meets this guy, what, three weeks ago, and now he's paying her ex-husband two million bucks to go away?"

"You've got it."

"Well, Thad is either the sweetest guy in the world or the dumbest, or both," Dino said.

"Don't talk about my client that way," Stone said.

"Yeah, yeah, I know; he pays his legal bills."

"That's very important," Stone said.

"And you don't even know if he's really going to go away."

"Oh, I know that," Stone said. "When the FBI takes him away, he'll be gone."

"How do you know they can get a conviction?" Dino asked. "After all, when he gets Thad's two million, he's going to be able to afford a *very* good lawyer."

"I thought you said they have his fingerprint on a note he handed a teller."

"Sure they do," Dino said. "Gee, I hope the FBI hasn't misplaced it during the years that have passed since the robbery. They would never do that, would they?"

"They'll have the tellers' identification of Manning," Stone said.

"How do you know? Maybe he dressed up like Ronald McDonald. And it's been four years since the last robbery. I'd be willing to bet you that at least one of the four tellers is dead, and a couple more are retired and living in Costa Rica or someplace, and that the remaining one has come down with Alzheimer's. And even if one of them is still around and can identify Manning, Ginsky is going to turn him inside out on the witness stand. 'But, sir, it's been four years since you say you saw the robber, and you also say he was wearing a red wig, a big nose and floppy shoes. How could you possibly say that man is my client?' "

"You're starting to annoy me, Dino."

"Oh, yeah? Well, you're not nearly as annoyed

as you're going to be when Manning gets off scot-free and hires somebody to put his ex-wife at the bottom of Lake Worth in a concrete bikini."

Stone ran a red light, thinking about that.

51

Stone got Liz to the courthouse half an hour early. He wanted to talk to Ed Ginsky before they went into the judge's chambers. There was too much happening this morning over which he had no control, and he didn't like it.

They had been sitting in the empty courtroom A for ten minutes, when a balding man in his mid-thirties came in.

"Are you Stone Barrington?"

"Yes."

"I'm Fred Williamson."

"Hello, Fred. This is Mrs. Manning."

"Don't call me that," Liz snapped.

"Everybody's going to call you that today, Liz. Just get used to it."

Williamson shook her hand as if he were afraid she might bite it.

"I want to speak to Ginsky before we go into chambers," Stone said.

"Why?" Williamson asked. "I think we've got all our ducks in a row." He took a sheaf of papers from his briefcase and handed them to Stone. "I've taken the liberty of making a few changes so that they more closely follow the Florida form."

Stone flipped quickly through the papers. Ten minutes to three. Where the hell was Ed Ginsky and his client? "They look fine to me, but everybody will have to sign again. We'll need a notary."

"The judge's clerk can notarize them," Williamson said. "I've also written the decree for his signature. Judge Coronado is leaving on vacation today, and I don't want to have to wait for his signature."

"Neither do I," Stone said. He was looking forward to seeing Paul Manning's face at last, and he wished to hell the man would arrive.

At one minute before three, Ed Ginsky and his client strolled into the courtroom. Paul Manning looked like hell. He was wearing bandages that covered his nose and much of his face, and at the edges, both his eyes seemed blackened. Surgery, Stone thought as he stood up. He and Ginsky shook hands. "I'm glad you're here, Ed. I want to . . . ."

At that moment a door behind the bench opened and a solidly built, handsome Hispanic man stepped into the courtroom. His hair was completely white, and he was not wearing a jacket but sporting loud braces. "Everybody here, Fred?"

"Yes, Judge. All present and accounted for." He shepherded everyone into the chambers and made the introductions. Coronado waved them all to chairs.

"Now," the judge said, "you have a request, Fred?"

"Yes, Judge. We're here in the matter of a divorce between Paul C. Manning and Allison S. Manning. Mr. Manning is represented by Mr. Ginsky, and I am representing Mrs. Manning, with the consultation of Mr. Barrington, who is a member of the New York bar and Mrs. Manning's attorney in that state." He handed the judge a stack of documents. "The parties have agreed on a property settlement. Mrs. Manning's petition and Mr. Manning's waiver of response are all in order. We ask for a decree based on their mutual desire for a divorce."

The judge glanced through the papers, then returned them to his desktop and leaned back in his chair.

"Mr. Manning, are you a legal resident of the State of Florida?"

"Yes, Your Honor," Manning replied.

Ed Ginsky offered a sheet of paper. "Judge, this is a copy of Mr. Manning's declaration of residency, filed at the Dade County courthouse two and a half years ago."

"This seems to be in order." The judge turned to Liz. "Mrs. Manning, are you a legal resident of the State of Florida?"

"Yes, Your Honor, for three years. I own a house in Palm Beach."

The judge nodded. "Mrs. Manning, Mr. Manning, you're both obviously mature adults. Mrs. Manning, is it your desire to end your marriage?"

"Yes, Your Honor," Liz replied.

"Mr. Manning?"

"Yes, Your Honor."

"Are you both completely satisfied with the terms of the property settlement on my desk? Mrs. Manning?"

"Yes, I am, Your Honor."

"Mr. Manning?"

"Yes, Your Honor."

"I would certainly assume that you are satisfied, since you are receiving a settlement of two million dollars. Mrs. Manning, does that sum represent a part of your net worth that you can afford to part with?"

"It does, Your Honor."

Especially since she isn't parting with it, Stone thought.

"Has any duress been brought upon you to part with such a sum?"

"No, Your Honor," Liz replied.

"Very well, then, I . . ." The judge stopped and looked oddly at Liz. "I beg your pardon, but have we met before, Mrs. Manning?"

"No, Your Honor," Liz replied. "I think I would remember," she added, flatteringly.

"Wait a minute," the judge said. "Aren't you Winston Harding's widow?"

Uh-oh, Stone thought. *Here's trouble.*

"Yes, Your Honor," Liz replied, as if it were the most natural question in the world, in the circumstances.

"I'm confused," the judge said. "Mr. Harding

344

died only late last year, didn't he?"

"That's right, Your Honor," Liz said, still not getting it.

"And when were you married to Mr. Manning?"

Stone opened his mouth to speak, but nothing came out.

Liz had no such problem. "Oh, Paul and I were married before Winston and I." Then she realized what she had said and froze.

Stone still couldn't think of anything to say, and Fred Williamson was looking at him in panic.

Then Paul Manning spoke up. "Your Honor, may I explain?"

"I wish to God somebody would," the judge replied.

"Your Honor, Mrs. Manning and I were married eight years ago. Then, four years ago, I was accused of murder in a Caribbean country — unjustly, I might add. I was tried, convicted and sentenced to death. Then, at the last moment, the truth came out, and I was pardoned."

Stone looked at Ed Ginsky and thanked God it was Ginsky's client who was lying to the judge and not his own. Ginsky seemed, as well, to have lost the power of speech.

"Congratulations," said the judge, but he still looked baffled.

"Mrs. Manning had already left the island, having done everything she could, and she was under the impression that I had been executed.

By the time I was released, we had lost touch, and it was only recently that she learned that I was still alive. So, you see, she married Mr. Harding in good faith, believing that I was dead. In fact, she had been given a death certificate."

The judge looked back and forth between Paul and Allison Manning as if they were escaped lunatics. "So this divorce is merely a matter of legal housekeeping, is that what you're telling me?"

None of the lawyers would speak, so Liz did. "Yes, Your Honor. I think you can see what a horrible series of events this was and how Paul and I, having parted long ago, would not like this hanging over our heads."

"Yes, I can see that," the judge said. "Fred, I hope you brought a decree for me to sign, because after today, I never want to hear about this again."

Williamson set the decree on the desk, and the judge signed it. "I'd like your clerk to notarize the property settlement, please," Williamson said.

The judge pressed an intercom button and spoke: "Amy, come in here, please." A woman entered the room. "I want you to notarize some documents for these people." He stood up and put on his jacket. "I've just signed a divorce decree, and I want you to see that nothing is published about it, do you understand?"

"No, Judge," the woman said, baffled.

He handed her a copy of the decree. "Just give

these people copies of this and file it, and forget you ever saw it. I intend to." He turned to the group. "Fred, you can use my chambers to sign these papers, then get these people out of here. I don't ever want to hear a word about this again. Is that clear?"

"Perfectly clear, Judge," Williamson said.

The judge walked out of his chambers, slamming the door behind him.

Williamson whipped out a pen, and everybody started signing. Five minutes later, the group broke up.

As they were leaving, Paul Manning approached his ex-wife. "Well, nice knowing you, Allison."

"There was nothing nice about it," Allison said, and stalked away.

"Wait for me in the car," Stone called out. He shook Fred Williamson's hand. "Thanks, Fred, for all your help."

"Can you tell me what the hell that was all about?" Williamson asked softly.

"Just forget it and send us your bill," Stone said. "Ed, Paul, a moment, please?"

The two men stopped. Stone waited until Williamson had left the room. "I've got something to say to you, Paul, and I want to say it to you in front of your attorney."

"Do I have to listen to this, Ed?" Manning asked.

"Give Stone a minute, Paul."

"First of all, the two million dollars will be

wired into your trust account immediately, Ed."

"Thank you, Stone."

Stone removed a sheet of paper from his pocket. "And this is a release from the insurance company."

Ginsky looked at it. "Why, this is dated . . ."

"Yes, it is," Stone said.

Manning snatched the paper and read it. "You mean, I was already . . ."

"Yes, you were, Paul, but you're not out of the woods yet."

"What do you mean?" Ginsky asked.

"Ed, your client participated in four transactions in Virginia and Maryland a while back that you don't know about and don't want to know about. But I know about them, Paul, and I'm happy to tell you that you left a fingerprint on a note you handed somebody. I've never expected you to adhere voluntarily to the terms of the agreement you signed, so let's just call this insurance."

"It sounds a lot more like blackmail," Ginsky said.

"That's exactly what it is, Ed. Paul, if you ever so much as speak to Allison again," Stone said, ignoring the attorney and speaking directly to his client, "one phone call will make you a fugitive again. On the other hand, if you keep your word, you're in no jeopardy."

"I don't know what he's talking about, Ed," Manning said.

"Sure you do, Paul, and Ed shouldn't know.

348

But I know, and don't you ever forget it. Ed, thanks for handling this so well. Paul, you can go fuck yourself."

Stone turned and walked away.

52

Stone drove Liz back to the yacht, feeling relieved and relaxed for the first time since he had
arrived in Palm Beach. His relief lasted only
until he walked up the gangplank.

A short, stocky man with iron-gray hair, wearing slacks and some kind of Cuban or Filipino
shirt, stood up from a chair, where he had been
sitting next to Dino. "Are you Stone Barrington?" he asked.

"That's right," Stone replied.

The man didn't offer his hand. "My name is
Guido. A friend of yours sent me." As he spoke,
a puff breeze blew the loose shirt against his
body, revealing the outline of a pistol at his
waist.

It took Stone a second to register what the
man had said and to interpret it. He looked at
Dino questioningly.

"Yeah, that friend," Dino said.

"Oh, sorry. What can I do for you, Guido?"

Guido looked around at the other people.
"Can we talk?"

"Let's go into the garden," Stone said, leading
the way off the yacht and to a bench among

some flowers. "Okay," he said, "tell me."

"I'm here to bring the lady in question home."

"All right," Stone said.

"Where is she?"

"Did you talk to Dino about this?"

"He didn't seem too interested in talking to me."

"She's moving from hotel to hotel, every day," Stone said. "We know she's already been to the Breakers and the Brazilian Court."

"How many hotels in this burg?" Guido asked.

"Lots."

"Anything else you can tell me?"

"She may be driving a silver Volvo sedan, but I can't swear to that."

"That ain't much," Guido said.

"I know, but it's all I've got. Do you have any help?"

"I got a couple guys and a Lear waiting at the airport with a doctor and a nurse."

"Good. Want some advice?"

"Why not?"

"She seems to have been following me. I suggest you follow me, too, but from a distance."

"Yeah, that sounds good."

"Do you know her?"

"Since she was in diapers; I used to change them."

"She knows you, then?"

"Oh, yeah; since she's old enough to talk she's called me Uncle Guido."

"Well, Guido, if she's that fond of you, she

might not be so inclined to take a shot at you."

Guido nodded solemnly. "And she's a hell of a shot," he said. "I know. I taught her in her papa's basement, when she was fourteen."

"I noticed you're carrying," Stone said.

Guido threw up his hands. "Don't worry, I'm not here to off her. Those are not my instructions."

Stone didn't doubt that if those were his instructions, Guido would carry them out with alacrity. "I'm glad to hear it," he said. "Suppose you see her? How are you going to handle this?"

"Decisively," Guido said. "I'm not here to fuck around."

"Are the people with you good?"

"The best. They'd do anything for the old man."

"I suggest you lose the hardware. If I can spot it, anybody can spot it, and the local cops aren't going to take kindly to out-of-towners packing iron on their streets."

"What are the local cops like?" Guido asked.

"Professional. They've got a smart chief, and you don't want to mess with him or any of his men."

"We'll play it cool, then," Guido said.

"Guido, please don't take this the wrong way, but on the streets of Palm Beach, you're going to stand out."

"Don't worry, I tan fast."

Stone sighed. "I'm not talking about your lack of a tan. People around here can spot an outsider in a split second, and any cop in town would make you as a foreigner from a block away."

"I ain't a foreigner," Guido said hotly. "I was born in Brooklyn."

"My point is, Guido, nobody else in Palm Beach was born in Brooklyn. And if they were, they'd have learned long ago to look like they were born on Park Avenue. I hope you're getting my drift."

"Yeah, I get your drift," Guido said, "and if you were anybody but a friend of my friend I wouldn't take it too good."

"I'm trying to help you, Guido. Your friend would not like it if I had to bail you and your pals out of the local can, would he?"

"I guess not," Guido admitted. "How can we fit in better here?"

Stone thought about an honest answer to that question, but thought better of giving it. "Go down to Worth Avenue, to the Polo store or Armani and buy some nice quiet sports clothes. Jackets, too, like blue blazers with brass buttons?"

Guido nodded, but he was watching Stone closely to see if he was being had. "You think that'll do it, huh?"

Stone bit his tongue. "It can't hurt."

"Okay. How can I get in touch with you?"

Stone gave Guido his cell phone number. "And you? Where are you staying?"

"I don't expect to be here that long," Guido

said, and gave Stone his own cell phone number. "Listen," he said, looking around as if he might be overheard. "My people are not going to feel good about shedding their hardware, you know?"

"Guido, nobody in Palm Beach is going to give you a hard time, let alone shoot at you — with the possible exception of the young lady. And if that were to happen, I think you'd be better off taking a round or two than shooting her. Her father would not think well of that."

Guido nodded. "You got a point," he said.

"One other thing," Stone said. "What kind of cars are you driving?"

"Cadillacs," Guido replied.

"You might rent something more anonymous."

"Why? Don't nobody drive Cadillacs in Palm Beach? I thought we'd fit right in."

"I'm not thinking about the general public, I'm thinking about the young lady. I think it will be to your advantage if you see her before she sees you."

Guido nodded slowly. "I get you," he said.

"Another thing," Stone said. "There's going to be a wedding here on Sunday evening, starting at six o'clock. There'll probably be a couple hundred people. If you haven't found her by then, you should probably have your people here."

"Yeah, okay, we can do that."

"It's going to mean renting or buying some evening clothes."

"You mean, like, suits?"

"I mean, like, tuxedos. It's going to be that kind of wedding."

"Yeah, okay, I'll look into that."

"And tell your guys no pastel tuxedos or ruffled shirts. Keep it discreet."

Guido looked at Stone closely. "You think we don't know how to dress?"

"I thought we already covered that point, Guido. This is Palm Beach; it's different."

He nodded. "Different from Brooklyn."

"Different from anywhere you've ever been before. Give me the names of your people, and I'll get them on the guest list."

Guido took a notebook from one of his many shirt pockets and jotted down some names, then ripped off the sheet and gave it to Stone.

Stone read them aloud: "Mr. Smith, Mr. Jones, Mr. Williams and Mr. Edwards?"

"I'm Mr. Edwards," Guido said.

"Got it." Stone put the piece of paper into his pocket and stood up. "Thanks for checking in, Guido. I appreciate your help with this."

"I ain't doing it for you," Guido said, then walked away.

Stone watched him go, then walked back to the yacht and found Callie. "Please add these names to the guest list for Sunday," he said, handing her the paper.

Callie looked at it. "Do these people have first names?"

"No," Stone said.

53

Stone walked down Worth Avenue with Dino at his side, trying not to look behind him or at the reflections in windows.

"What are we doing, Stone?" Dino asked.

"We're trolling."

"For Dolce?"

"Yes."

"Which one of us is the bait on the hook?"

"I am."

"So what am I?"

"You're the cork."

"I must remember to stay out of the line of fire," Dino said.

"Don't worry, Guido and his buddies are on the job."

"Oh, that *really* makes me feel better: protection from goombahs."

"You're a goombah," Stone said.

"You say that again, and I'll shoot you myself."

"Come on, Dino, the only thing separating your life from Guido's and his chums' is the entrance exam to the police academy."

"You're really trying to piss me off, aren't you?"

"Can't you take a joke?"

"I'm going to sic the Italian-American Defamation League onto your ass," Dino said.

"Didn't the people who ran that fine organization all get gunned down while eating clams?"

"Only some of them. Are we trolling for Paul Manning, too?"

"No, I think Mr. Manning has retired from the field."

"And what makes you think that?"

"I explained to him that I knew about his little bank escapades, and that I could very easily cause the FBI to know about them, too, if he should annoy me."

"And you think that will get rid of him."

"I do."

"I expect it pissed him off, too."

"Oh, yes, I took some pleasure in pissing him off."

"Stone, you don't want to piss off crazy people with homicidal tendencies."

"I think he's smart enough to stay out of my way, now."

"Smart doesn't enter into it," Dino said. "Revenge has a way of doing away with smart."

Stone stopped and looked into a jewelry shop window. "See if you can spot Guido and his friends."

Dino didn't even turn around. "You mean the three goombahs in the red Cadillac, parked across the street?"

Stone sighed. "Tell me you're just saying that to annoy me."

"I'm just saying that to annoy you," Dino said. "They're really parked about fifty feet up the street."

"I told him to stay well away from me," Stone said.

"Goombahs like Guido don't listen, unless it involves an illegal profit, or the fun of shooting somebody in the head."

"I don't understand why Eduardo would send people like that to do this."

"Who else is he going to trust?" Dino asked. "They're his people. He's not going to ask his fellow board members at the Metropolitan Opera to come to Palm Beach and bring his crazy daughter home."

Stone started to walk again. "Once again, you have a point, but couldn't he have hired some private security people? Somebody with a little more discretion?"

"Then strangers would know his business," Dino said, "and Eduardo doesn't want anybody outside the family to know his business. To tell you the truth, I'm a little surprised he hasn't had *you* capped. After all, you're not exactly family, although you almost were."

"I guess I dodged that bullet," Stone said.

"Not yet, pal," Dino replied. "But at least you're not bound to them by a Catholic marriage and family obligations."

"I still feel obligated to Dolce."

"Eduardo doesn't feel you have any obligation to her, so why do you?"

"He has been very apologetic about this," Stone said.

"You're lucky he's Italian," Dino said. "If you'd been through the same experience with the daughter of some high Episcopalian, the old man would be out there ruining your reputation, even as we speak. He wouldn't have you shot, but you'd never get invited to dinner again by anybody with an Anglo-Saxon name, and you'd be kicked out of your clubs — if you belonged to any clubs."

"Yeah, keep telling me how lucky I am," Stone said. He turned into Tiffany & Company. "Come on, I've got to find a wedding present for Thad and Liz."

"Listen, those people ought to be giving *you* a wedding present," Dino said.

"Nevertheless." Stone looked, first at crystal, then moved up to sterling. "What do you think of this?" he asked, holding up a handsome silver bowl.

"What would they keep in that, their money?"

"Fruit."

"Oh."

"I'll take this," Stone said to a saleslady. "Could you gift wrap it?"

"Of course," the woman said. "I'll just be a moment." She vanished into a back room.

Dino went rigid. "Don't turn around," he said. "Dolce's looking in the window."

Involuntarily, Stone turned around and looked. He saw a disappearing flash of color.

"You stay right here," Dino said. "Don't move." He walked quickly to the front door and outside, looking up and down the street.

Stone waited impatiently until the saleswoman returned, then waited even more impatiently while she rang up the sale and had his credit card authorized. Finally, blue shopping bag in hand, he hurried to the front door. He looked up and down the street as far he could see, then stepped outside. Dino was nowhere in sight, and neither was the red Cadillac.

Stone stood in the bright sunlight, feeling helpless, not knowing which way to turn. He waited for five long minutes, then made a decision: He turned right and walked rapidly along the street, checking shopwindows for Dolce and looking up and down the street for the red Cadillac.

Suddenly, Dino stepped out of a doorway and ran head-on into Stone. "Didn't I tell you to stay where you were?" he demanded.

"I did, for a very long time," Stone said. "Did you lose her?"

"Yeah, and I don't understand it."

Then, from not too great a distance, they heard three rapid reports.

"Gun!" Dino said, and started running toward the noise.

Stone followed, and the two of them turned a corner and ran toward a parking lot behind Worth Avenue. Stone could see the trunk of the red Cadillac protruding into the street.

Dino got there first. Women were screaming, and people in cars were trying desperately to get out of the parking lot. The Cadillac sat, blocking the entrance, three of its four doors open, with three bullet holes in the windshield. It was empty.

Dino flashed his badge at a parking attendant, who was crouching in a booth at the entrance. "What happened?" he asked the trembling man.

"I don't know, exactly," he said. "I was about to give the man in the Cadillac his parking check when the windshield seemed to explode."

"Anybody hit?"

"I don't know. I dove in here in about half a second."

"Call nine-one-one," Dino said, then he turned to Stone. "Let's get out of here."

As they walked quickly away, Stone looked around the lot and the street for a familiar face, but Dolce was gone, and so were Guido and his two goombahs.

54

They got back to the yacht without sighting
Dolce, and Stone was in his cabin, putting away
his wedding gift, when Juanito knocked on the
door.

"Yes?" Stone called.

"Mr. Barrington, there's somebody to see you
on the afterdeck."

"Be right there," Stone said. He retrieved the
9mm automatic from under his pillow and
tucked it into his waistband in the small of his
back. He wasn't expecting visitors.

His visitor turned out to be Dan Griggs, and
Stone was relieved until Griggs started to talk.
He looked very serious. "Stone, there was an at-
tempted shooting in a parking lot downtown,
and one of my people saw you leaving the scene.
You want to tell me about that?"

"Don't worry, Dan, they weren't shooting at
me."

Griggs didn't smile. "I thought maybe it was
you doing the shooting."

Stone shook his head. "No, Dino and I were
shopping on Worth Avenue, when we heard
gunfire. Dino was armed, and we ran around

the corner and saw the car with the bullet holes in it. That's all we saw. We told the parking lot attendant to dial nine-one-one, then left."

"Did you see the occupants of the car?"

"No."

"Did you see the shooter?"

"No."

"Witnesses said there were three men in the car, out-of-towners, by the look of them, and the shooter was a good-looking woman."

Stone said nothing.

"Why did you leave the scene?" Griggs asked.

"We didn't see anything. It's not like we were witnesses. There was nothing there for us to do." Stone was relieved that he could tell the truth about this, even if he was withholding information.

Griggs sighed.

Stone was about to say something, when he looked over Griggs's shoulder and saw Dolce standing in the garden, maybe two hundred feet away. Griggs was about to turn and follow his gaze, but Stone took him by the shoulder and led him toward the afterdeck banquette. "How about a drink, Dan?" he said.

Griggs pulled away from his grasp, but did not look toward Dolce. "Are you nuts? I'm on duty. I thought that was obvious."

"How's Lundquist?" Stone asked, desperate to keep Griggs looking in his direction instead of Dolce's. He couldn't allow himself to look that way, either.

"I put him on a medivac plane for Minneapolis this morning. He's recovering, and his department sent the aircraft."

"He's going to be all right, then?"

"Didn't I just say that?" Griggs asked, irritated.

"Sorry, Dan. I just wanted to be sure."

"Something else: You still looking for that Manning fellow?"

"Not really," Stone said. "I pretty much straightened that out in a favorable manner."

"Favorable? Did you shoot him?"

"No, no, I just sorted out the differences between him and Liz, and I think he's out of our hair now."

"Maybe not," Griggs said.

"What do you mean?"

"I've had two reports from my men of a man answering his description being in town."

"Well, if he's in town, I've got no quarrel with him, nor him with me."

"Does he have any quarrel with Liz?"

"Not anymore. That's all settled."

"Then you don't want me to pick him up?"

For a moment, Stone considered blowing the whistle on Paul Manning, and the hell with their agreement. "No. You wouldn't have a charge, anyway. He's clean."

"How do you know that? I thought you said he was the criminal type."

"As a result of our settlement, he's now too rich to be criminal."

"You paid him off?"

"Let's say he walked away in very good shape."

"Well, I'll leave him alone, if that's the way you want it, but I intend to keep an eye on him."

"That can't hurt, I suppose, if you have the manpower."

Stone thought of something. "Tell me, Dan, did the description of the man include a bandage on his face?"

"A bandage? No, nobody said anything about that. He's clean-shaven, with dark hair, going gray."

"Oh."

"Why did you think he might be wearing a bandage?"

"When I saw him he was. I thought maybe he'd had an accident or something."

"Well, I've got to get going," Griggs said, turning back toward the house.

Stone looked up to see that Dolce was nowhere in sight. "I'll walk with you," Stone said.

"Don't bother, I can find my way," Griggs replied.

"I was going to the house, anyway."

"Suit yourself."

They walked down the gangplank and toward the house, with Stone casing every shrub and tree they passed.

"Did I tell you it was stolen?" Griggs asked.

"What was?"

"The Cadillac, the one that was shot at."

"Sounds like a drug deal gone wrong," Stone said.

"Maybe, but we don't get a whole lot of drug dealing in broad daylight around the Worth Avenue shopping district."

"I guess not," Stone said, still looking for Dolce.

They reached the house and walked through the central hallway and outside to where Griggs had parked his car.

Stone looked around for the silver Volvo, or for any other strange car, but saw nothing.

"You know, Stone," Griggs said, his mood still somber, "I've got a strong feeling that you know something I ought to know."

"Me? I can't imagine what."

"When I find the guys in the Cadillac, I hope I don't find out that they know you."

"Since I left the force there are no drug dealers in my life," Stone said honestly.

"We didn't find any drugs in the car," Griggs said. "It was stolen from the airport, by the way."

"I guess they couldn't get a cab."

"I hear Thad Shames is getting married on Sunday," Griggs said. "You want me to send a few people down here to help with the traffic?"

"Couldn't hurt," Stone said. "Thad has hired some security for the wedding and the reception, but I don't think he's done anything about traffic."

"I'll send a couple of men," Griggs said. He was about to get into the car, but he stopped. "Why does Mr. Shames need private security?" he asked.

"Gate-crashers, that sort of thing."

"Oh." Griggs got into his car. "I'll see you around, Stone."

"Thanks for stopping by, Dan."

Griggs drove away, and Stone began to walk slowly through the gardens, expecting at any moment for Dolce to pop up. He passed through the hedge and had a look around the swimming pool, then walked back to the yacht.

Dino was having a drink on the afterdeck.

"Has Griggs put two and two together?" Dino asked.

"Just one and one. Apparently, a cop saw us leaving the area, and he thought we might be involved. He doesn't really know anything."

"I wish I didn't know anything," Dino said. "I'd really be happier that way."

"I'll devote my life to keeping you ignorant," Stone replied.

"I wish you would. It's tiring, knowing too much."

"Tell me about it."

"When are we getting out of here?"

"After the wedding, I guess. How about bright and early Monday morning?"

"Sounds good to me. It's too cold down here."

"I know what you mean," Stone said truthfully.

55

Stone and Dino were having dinner alone together on the yacht. The crew had been given
the night off, and Callie, after preparing dinner
for them, had gone to work in her new office in
the main house. Stone had seen little of her
since Thad and Liz had decided to get married
on short notice; there didn't seem to be enough
hours in the day for her to get her work done.

"Gee, it's kind of nice here, just you and me,"
Dino said. "We never get to have dinner alone
anymore."

"Oh, shut up," Stone said. "You're worse than
a wife."

"That's something only a bachelor could say,"
Dino replied.

"You know, Dino, I've been thinking about
marriage."

"Oh, no," Dino groaned. "Not again."

"What kind of crack is that?"

"Stone, every time you start thinking about
marriage, you get into terrible trouble."

"Nonsense," Stone snorted.

"Stone, when you were thinking about marrying Arrington, look what happened: She mar-

ried somebody else, and you got involved with this flake Allison — excuse me, Liz. And look at all the trouble that came out of that."

"Well, that time, yes."

"Then there was the English girl — what was her name?"

"Sarah."

"You sure?"

"I'm sure."

"That didn't go so good, either, right?"

"Not so good."

"And then you actually *married* Dolce — well, sort of, and against all the advice I could muster. And now she's out there stalking you with a gun, and frankly, I wouldn't give you good odds on making it back to New York without taking along some excess baggage in the form of lead in your liver. Now, I ask you, what happens when you start thinking about marriage?"

"All right, I get into trouble," Stone said gloomily.

"Stone, you're my friend, and I love you, and that's why I can say this to you: You're not cut out to be married. Never in my life have I known anybody who was *less* cut out to be married. Marriage is very, very hard, and believe me, you're not tough enough to handle it."

"Callie is an awfully nice girl," Stone said mistily.

"I'll grant you that."

"I think it would be nice to be married to her."

"I'll even grant you that, up to a point. As far

as I can see, the only thing wrong with Callie is that you're thinking about marrying her."

"What, you think I'm the kiss of death, or something?"

"I didn't say that, you did."

"The sex is wonderful."

"I'm glad to hear it," Dino said. "Let me tell you something somebody told me when I was young and single. This was a man who had been married three times. He said to me, 'Dino, tell you what you do: When you get married, you keep a piece of chalk in your bedside table drawer, and every time you make love to your wife, you take out the chalk and make a hash mark on the wall. Then, after you've been married for a year, throw away the chalk and keep an eraser in your bedside drawer, and every time you make love, take out the eraser and erase a hash mark.'"

"What was his point?" Stone asked.

"His point was this: 'It'll take you ten years to erase all the hash marks.'"

Stone laughed in spite of himself.

"So, pal, my point is, if you're going to get married, you'd better have something going on in the relationship besides sex."

"I knew that," Stone said.

"No, you didn't," Dino sighed. "You still don't."

"No, I do, I really do."

"Tell me this," Dino said. "What makes you think she'd marry you?"

"Well . . ."

"You think all she's looking for is a great lay? Not that you're all that great."

"I could offer her a pretty good life," Stone said.

"Yeah, sure. You're traipsing all over the country, doing this very strange but oddly entertaining work. You think she's going to like that? You going to take her along when you have to drop everything and go to Podunk, Somewhere?"

"Why not?"

"Because women get rooted in their homes. I guarantee you, a month after you're married, you're going to find that your house has been totally redecorated."

"I like the way my house is decorated," Stone said. "I did it myself."

"Yeah, but Callie doesn't like it."

"She hasn't even seen it."

"You think that matters? She doesn't like it because *you* decorated it, dumbo. She won't think of it as her home until she's changed all the wallpaper and carpets and had a big garage sale and sold everything you love most in the house."

"You really know how to make marriage attractive, Dino."

"I'm telling you the truth, here."

"Did Mary Ann redecorate your place?"

"No, she *sold* my place one day when I was at work, and I had nothing to say about it. Then we bought one *she* liked."

"Oh."

"Yeah."

"This conversation is making me tired," Stone said.

"I don't blame you. Reality is always tiring."

Stone drained the last of the wine from his glass. "I'm going to bed."

"Good idea. The very least you should do about this marriage idea is to sleep on it. For about a month."

"I think I could sleep for a month," Stone said, yawning. "I could do that."

"Then go do it, pal," Dino said. "I'm going to finish my wine and look out at the night." He settled himself in a big leather chair and turned on the TV.

"Good night, then." Stone went to his cabin, undressed and got into bed. He stared at the ceiling, thinking about Callie redecorating his beloved house, until he fell asleep.

Then, seconds later, it seemed, Dino was shaking him.

"What?" Stone mumbled sleepily.

"Get up. You gotta see something."

"Jesus, Dino, what time is it?"

"A little after two."

"Don't you ever sleep?"

"I *was* sleeping, in the chair in front of the TV. Then I woke up."

Stone turned over and fluffed his pillow. "Then go back to sleep."

"Stone, get out of the fucking bed right now and come with me."

Stone turned over and tried to focus on Dino,

then he realized that his friend had a gun in his hand. He sat bolt upright, now fully awake. "What's wrong?"

"Put your pants on and come with me."

Stone got out of bed and put his pants on, then padded along behind Dino as he led the way to the afterdeck.

"Look," Dino said, waving an arm.

"Look at what?"

"Look at the shore."

"What about the shore?"

"We aren't tied up to it anymore."

"Huh?" Stone looked quickly toward where the seawall behind Thad Shames's house should have been. It wasn't there. "We're adrift," he said.

"*That's* the word I was looking for," Dino said. "Adrift!"

"Why?"

"How the hell do you think *I* know? What do I know about boats?"

"This is crazy," Stone said. "The engines aren't running. Where's the crew?"

"Ashore, probably drunk," Dino said. "What do we do?"

Stone grappled with that problem for a minute. "We stop the yacht," he said.

"Great. How do we do that?"

"Come on," Stone said, "let's get up to the bridge."

"The bridge," Dino said, following Stone at a trot. "I like that. It sounds real nautical."

56

Stone ran up to the bridge, which was completely dark. "Find a light somewhere," he said to Dino.

"I'm looking, I'm looking."

Stone began feeling along the bulkheads for a switch. Suddenly, the lights came on, but dimly.

"I found it, but it's not very bright," Dino said.

"That's okay, it won't ruin our night vision."

"What do we do now?"

"We've got to get the engines started," Stone said. "Look for the ignition switch."

"Right here," Dino said, pointing. "Trouble is, there's no key in it."

"Then look for the key," Stone said, starting to open drawers in the cabinetwork. He found no key. "We've got to get an anchor out."

"How do we do that?"

Stone looked over the instrument panel. "On a yacht this size, there's probably an electric windlass. Here it is!" He pressed the button, but nothing happened. "We need engine power for that, too."

"What about the radio?" Dino asked. "Call somebody."

"Good idea." Stone found the VHF radio, switched it on and picked up the microphone. "Channel sixteen is the calling channel." He changed the channel to 16 and pressed the switch on the microphone. "Coast Guard, Coast Guard, this is the yacht *Toscana*, *Toscana*. Do you read?"

Instantly a voice came back. *"Toscana*, this is the U.S. Coast Guard. What is your request?"

What was his request? He thought about it for a moment. "Coast Guard, *Toscana*. We're adrift in the Intracoastal Waterway, and we need a tow. We have no power."

"Toscana, Coast Guard. Sorry, you'll have to call a commercial towing service for that kind of help."

Stone looked at the ship's clock on the bulkhead. "But it's three o'clock in the morning," he said. "Where am I going to get a tow at this time of night?"

"Sorry, but we can't be of any help," the Coast Guard operator said. "Good night, and have a good trip." Then he was gone.

"Now what?" Dino asked.

"I'm not sure."

"Well, why don't we just wait until morning and flag somebody down?"

Stone pointed out the windshield. "See that?" he asked.

"What, the bridge? Sure, I see it; you think I'm blind?"

"We're drifting down on it."

"So what? We hit it, we'll stop. Isn't that what we want?"

"Dino, this is a two-hundred-and-twenty-foot yacht, and it weighs God knows how much. If we hit that bridge, either the yacht or the bridge is going to be very badly damaged, maybe both."

Dino blinked. "Well, do something, for chrissakes!"

Stone pressed the button on the microphone again. "Any ship, any ship, this is the yacht *Toscana*, in need of assistance. Anybody read me?"

Nothing. Silence.

"It's three o'clock in the morning," Dino said. "What did you expect?"

Then a voice came over the radio. *"Toscana, Toscana,* this is *Winddrifter.* Do you read?"

"Winddrifter, Toscana. I read you loud and clear."

"What's your problem?"

"We're adrift in the Waterway with no power, and we need a tow, fast, to keep from hitting a bridge."

"Sorry, *Toscana,* I'm halfway to the Bahamas. Afraid I can't be of any help. Good luck."

"You get the feeling we're all alone?" Dino asked.

"Well, shit, we've got to do *something,*" Stone said.

"I'm wide open to suggestions."

Stone looked outside the bridge and saw a large inflatable dinghy on deck. "There," he said. "We've got to get that thing launched right now."

"You mean we're going to abandon ship?" Dino asked.

"No, no. Come on, follow me." Stone opened the outside door and left the bridge. He ran forward to the dinghy, which appeared to be a good seventeen feet long. A big outboard motor was bolted to the stern. "Look, it's already hooked up to the davit," Stone said.

"To the what?"

"The davit, the cranelike thing." Stone yanked a cover off a pedestal. "Here we go," he said, switching on the electric motor. He tried the up switch, and the dinghy rose six inches, bringing its cradle with it. "Thank God it's got its own power." He set it back down on deck. "Quick, let's get this thing unlashed." He glanced at the bridge. It was beginning to look very large.

Dino fumbled with the ties. "Got this side undone," he said.

"Mine, too," Stone said. "Now, I'm going to get into the dinghy. You raise it higher than the rail, there, and use this joystick thing to swing it over the side. Then you push the down button."

"I've never operated anything like this before," Dino said.

"Think of it as a computer game."

"I can't do those, either."

Stone hopped into the dinghy "Okay, let's go."

Dino started to work the controls. He raised the dinghy three feet off the deck.

"Right, now use the joystick."

Dino did something, and the dinghy began to move sideways at an alarming rate. Stone nearly fell out. "Slowly!" he yelled.

"I thought you were in a hurry," Dino said.

"Gently. Don't throw me out of the dinghy."

Dino tried again, and this time the dinghy moved smoothly over the rail and hung, suspended, six or eight feet above the water.

"Great, now with the down button."

Dino found the switch, and in a moment the dinghy was in the water. Stone unhooked the cable and was adrift. "Put the davit back in the same position we found it in," he called to Dino.

Dino followed Stone's instructions. "Now what?" he called.

A light breeze had sprung up, and Stone was drifting rapidly away from the yacht. "Find a long rope!" he yelled, "and go to the bow!"

"Where?"

"Up front to the pointed end." Stone felt around the instrument panel for the ignition key and found it. He tried starting the engine. It turned over but didn't start. He made his way to the stern of the dingy, found a gas tank with a fuel line leading to the engine, and pumped the attached rubber bulb a few times. Then he returned to the controls and tried again. The engine started.

Stone put the thing in gear and headed for the

bows of the yacht, which was now turning side-ways. Then he glanced over his shoulder and found that, in the time it had taken to launch the dingy, they were nearly to the bridge. The yacht was about to hit not one, but two of the bridge's supports.

He did the only thing he could think of. He gunned the engine and attacked the bows of the big yacht, as if the dinghy were a tugboat. Grad-ually, the bows of the yacht began to turn up-stream, and a moment later she passed, backward, under the bridge.

Stone could see Dino standing on deck. "Did you find a rope?"

"Yeah, a big one, too."

"Make one end fast and throw me the other end." A moment later, a large coil of heavy rope hit Stone in the back of the head, knocking him down.

"You trying to kill me?" he yelled at Dino. He struggled back to his feet.

"You said throw you the other end."

"I didn't mean two hundred feet of it!" Stone paid out forty feet of rope, then made it fast to a stern cleat. "Okay, I've got it," he yelled.

"What do I do now?"

"Go back to the bridge and steer the boat."

"Steer it where?"

"Just keep it headed upstream behind the dinghy!"

"Okay, okay." Dino went aft toward the bridge.

"And when we pass back under the bridge,

don't let the yacht hit it!" Stone screamed.

"Thanks," Dino called back. "I needed to be told that!"

Stone put the engine in gear and slowly went forward until the rope was taut. For a long moment nothing happened. He applied more power and finally, the dinghy began to move forward an inch at a time, then a foot. The bows of the yacht fell into line behind him, and he aimed at the center of the bridge.

Slowly, with the outboard engine making a loud racket, the yacht moved under, then away from the bridge.

"What now?" Dino yelled from the bows.

"Go back to the wheel! I'm going to try to bring the yacht alongside where we were tied up before. Find some more ropes, and as soon as we're by the seawall, make one end fast to the yacht and jump ashore with the other end!"

"Okay!" Dino yelled, and went aft again.

The seawall came into sight now, illuminated by a dock light and the lights on the garden paths ashore. Stone could see Juanito and the yacht's skipper standing on the wall, looking at them. He towed the yacht past the seawall, then, very slowly, made a 180-degree turn and started back toward the yacht's berth.

"Easy!" somebody yelled from ashore. "Cut your power, and she'll drift in."

Stone did as he was told. Gradually, the big yacht drifted toward the seawall, then Dino was throwing ropes to the men ashore. Five minutes later, the yacht was secure.

Stone scrambled up a ladder to shore and tied the dinghy to the ladder.

The skipper approached. "What the hell happened? Did you decide to go for a cruise?"

"Don't be ridiculous," Stone said. "I was asleep, and somebody cut our lines."

"Untied them," the skipper said.

Dino walked over. "Yeah, they were just hanging in the water."

"I tried to start the engines," Stone said, "but we couldn't find the ignition key."

"In my pocket," the skipper said, holding up the key. "Well, she's secure, now. Why don't you go back to bed, and we'll try to figure this out in the morning."

"Good idea," Stone said, and he and Dino trudged back aboard.

"Are you thinking Dolce?" Dino asked as he paused at his cabin door.

"Maybe. Or maybe our friend Manning."

"Some friend."

"Yeah."

The two men said good night and went to bed. It took Stone a long time to get to sleep.

57

Stone and Dino barely made it on deck in time for lunch the following day. They had the after-deck to themselves, and they had just finished their omelettes when two men in suits emerged from the house and made their way toward the yacht.

"Ten to one they're FBI," Dino said.

"No bet," Stone replied. He knew how Dino hated FBI agents, and his own experience with them as a cop had not been wonderful.

"Nobody else looks quite like that. What the hell do they want?"

"I think we're about to find out," Stone said, as the two men came up the gangplank.

"Either one of you Lieutenant Dino Bacchetti of the NYPD?" one of them asked without preamble.

"Who wants to know?" Dino asked.

Both men whipped out ID.

"Wow, I'm impressed. I'm Bacchetti. Why are you disturbing my vacation?"

"We want to ask you some questions," the first agent said.

"See me in my office in New York," Dino said.

"I'll be back next week."

"It's in connection with a bank robbery in Arlington, Virginia, four years ago," the man said.

"I didn't do it," Dino said, "and I can probably come up with an alibi."

The man turned to Stone. "Who are you?" he demanded.

Stone started to reply, but Dino interrupted. "None of your fucking business," he said. "Now get off my yacht."

The agent looked around. "Yours, huh? Pretty fancy for a New York cop. I wonder what your Internal Affairs people would have to say about this."

Dino began laughing, and so did Stone.

"What's so funny?" the agent asked, annoyed.

"You be sure and mention my yacht to Internal Affairs," Dino said. "I'd enjoy their reaction. Now, will you people go away?"

"Look," the agent said, "maybe we got off on the wrong foot, here. My name is Miles, and this is my partner, Nevins. We'd really appreciate your help, Lieutenant Bacchetti."

"Why didn't you say so?" Dino said expansively. "Have a seat." He kicked chairs in the agents' direction, and they both sat down.

"Can I get you something?" Dino asked, the generous host, now that he had brought the two men into line.

"No, thanks," Miles said.

"What can I do for you?" Dino asked.

"A couple of days ago, your office in New York ran a match on some fingerprints in our computer."

Dino said nothing.

"Isn't that right?"

"If you say so. We probably run prints a dozen times a day."

"You ran a set of prints that matched with a thumbprint we got from a note passed to a teller in a bank robbery in Virginia."

"So?"

"We want to know where you got the prints."

"Didn't you ask my office?"

"They wouldn't tell us. They said we had to talk to you, and you were in Palm Beach, so we drove up here from Miami this morning."

"How much did the bank robber get?" Dino asked.

"About thirty thousand, I think. I'm not sure."

"Let me get this straight," Dino said. "You two guys got into your government car and drove all the way up here from Miami, using government gas, in pursuit of a guy who got thirty grand from a bank four years ago?"

"That's right," Miles replied.

"Well, Agent Miles, I'm not too sure I approve of the way you people are spending my tax dollars," Dino said.

"I don't understand," Miles replied.

Stone spoke up. "Neither does Lieutenant Bacchetti. He can't figure out why you fellows are making this kind of effort to track down a penny-ante, walk-in bank robber who the bank won't even make the effort to prosecute."

"I'm sorry, I didn't get your name," Miles said.

"Stone Barrington."

"Well, Mr. Barrington, bank robbery is a very serious crime."

"Gee, the bank doesn't think so. When you catch this guy, they won't even send somebody down to court to testify against him."

"No matter what the banks think, the FBI considers bank robbery to be a very serious crime," Miles said. "It eats away at the roots of our economic system, if we let people get away with stealing even what you consider a small amount from a bank."

"No kidding?" Stone said.

"What else did this guy do?" Dino asked.

"I'm sorry?"

"Come on, Agent Miles, you're not here about a bank robbery. What did the guy do?"

"That's confidential."

"I'm a police officer. Mr. Barrington, here, used to be a police officer, and now he's a distinguished member of the bar. You can tell us."

"Those are not my instructions."

"What *are* your instructions?"

"I'm, ah, not at liberty to say."

"Well, Agent Miles, if you want information from me, you'd better be at liberty to trade a little information."

"Lieutenant, why are you being so difficult

about this? All we want is to catch a bank robber."

"No, that's not all you want. You want to catch an entirely different animal, and I want to know the species."

Miles took out a handkerchief and wiped his brow. "Lieutenant, you're interfering with an FBI investigation."

"Oh? Well, I'm terribly sorry. Did it ever occur to you that you might be interfering with *my* investigation?"

"I think a federal investigation takes precedence."

"That's what you guys always think," Dino said. "You never think that something the NYPD is investigating might be as important as what the FBI is investigating."

"That's not true," Miles insisted.

"They're not going to tell us anything, are they?" Dino asked.

"Doesn't look like it."

"Then why should *we* tell *them* anything?"

"I can't think of a good reason," Stone said.

"This is obstruction," Miles said indignantly. "You obviously know something about this perpetrator."

"I didn't say that," Dino replied.

"Neither did I," Stone said.

"Look, Lieutenant, I could take this to your superior," Miles said.

"Oh, my captain would love that," Dino said. "Assuming you could even get him on the phone, he'd love you wasting his time about some dime-a-dozen bank job. He'd really call me in on the carpet about that."

"How about this, Agent Miles," Stone said. "Why don't you just tell us why the checking of this guy's prints would raise a flag on the FBI's computer system? It can't be just this bank robbery."

"If I told you that . . ." Miles stopped and thought better. "I can't tell you that," he said.

"Agent Miles," Dino said, "I'm trying hard to see some reason why I should help out the FBI, which wouldn't cross the street to help *me* out on an investigation."

Miles produced his card. "Here's my number," he said, handing the card to Dino. "I'll owe you one. A big one. Anytime you need a favor from the Bureau, you can call me."

Dino took the card. "How about you, Agent Nevins? Are you going to owe me one, too?"

Nevins produced a card and handed it over. "Yes, yes, I am."

"Well, now we're getting somewhere," Dino said. "Stone, tell the agents what you know about this guy."

"His name — or at least, one of his names — is William Charles Danforth, of a P Street address in Washington, D.C., a town with which you are no doubt familiar. Some years ago his name was Paul Manning, and he was a well-known author."

"Have you ever seen this man?" Miles asked.

"Yes, a couple of days ago."

"Can you give me a description?"

"Late forties, six-three or -four, two hundred pounds, dark hair going gray."

"Facial characteristics?"

"I haven't a clue."

"But you say you saw him a couple of days ago."

"That's right, but he had a big bandage right in the middle of his face. I had the distinct impression that he didn't want me to know what he looked like. Maybe he was afraid I might be talking to the FBI."

"Do you know his present whereabouts?"

"A man answering his description has been seen in Palm Beach, but I've no idea if it's the same man."

"Anything else you can tell me?"

"Nope."

Miles and Nevins stood up. "Thank you very much, Mr. Barrington, Lieutenant Bacchetti. We owe you one."

"You already said that," Dino pointed out.

"We'll be going, then," Miles said.

"Don't let the doorknob hit you in the ass on your way out," Dino said.

Miles looked at the gangplank. "There isn't a doorknob," he said.

Dino looked at Stone. "You can't fool the FBI, can you?"

"Nope," Stone agreed.

The two agents left.

When they had gone, Stone turned to Dino. "I'm surprised you cooperated. Why did you want me to tell them about Manning?"

"The sonofabitch set my yacht adrift," Dino said.

58

No sooner had the FBI men left than Liz came out of the house and walked to the yacht. She came aboard and gave both Stone and Dino a big kiss. She was carrying an envelope and two gift wrapped boxes.

"I just want to thank you both so much," she said, sitting down.

"You're welcome," Stone said. "Glad to be of service."

"Same here," Dino echoed. "Only I haven't been of all that much service."

"Of course you have," Liz said. "And I want to thank you. First of all," she said, handing Stone the envelope, "here's a check for your legal services."

Stone slipped the envelope into a pocket without looking inside. "Thank you, Liz."

"Second," she said, handing Stone the larger of the two packages, "this is to express my personal thanks for your friendship and your concern for me. Even though your job as my lawyer is done, I think of you as my friend."

"Thank you again," Stone said, accepting the box.

"And, Dino," she said, handing him the smaller of the two boxes, "this is for you, for taking the time and trouble to come down here and help out Stone. And for stopping that horrible man from hurting anyone else in that restaurant shoot-out."

"Thank you, ma'am," Dino said.

"Don't open them yet," she said, holding up a hand. "I'd be embarrassed." She stood up. "I have to run, now. Callie and I are going to town to look for dresses for the wedding." With a little wave, she departed the yacht and headed back toward the house.

"You first," Dino said.

"No, you."

Dino opened his gift. Inside was a handsome gold pen from Cartier. "Very nice," he said. "I'll be the envy of the precinct. What'd she get you?"

Stone opened the package to find a large, red Cartier box inside. He opened it and held the contents up for Dino to see.

Dino took the box from Stone and gave a low whistle. "Hey, now, that's *really* nice."

Stone took back the box and removed the wristwatch from it. "Certainly is," he said. He took off his steel Rolex, put it into his pocket and slipped on the new watch.

Dino picked up the red booklet that came with the watch. "Cartier Tank Francaise," he read. "You pick the best clients."

"I guess I do."

Juanito approached with the telephone. "For

you, Mr. Barrington."

"Hello?"

"Stone, it's Dan Griggs. Did some FBI agents come see you?"

"Yes, they just left."

"Now I've got a guy from the Houston PD wants to talk to you."

"Houston, Texas?"

"One and the same. What the hell is going on down there?"

"I don't have the foggiest, Dan."

"I'm sending the guy to you right now. His name is Fritz Parker."

"Okay. I'll be here." Stone hung up.

"What?" Dino asked.

"A Houston cop wants to talk to me."

"You committed any crimes in Houston?"

"I've never even been to Houston."

Twenty minutes later a middle-aged man in a seersucker suit walked up the gangplank. "Lieutenant Bacchetti?" he asked.

"That's me," Dino said.

"I'm Fritz Parker, Houston PD. Can I have a word with you?"

"Sure, pull up a chair. This is Stone Barrington."

"How do you do?" Parker said, shaking hands. "Lieutenant, do you mind if we talk alone?"

"You can talk in front of Stone," Dino said. "He used to be my partner, before he became a rich lawyer."

"All right." Parker sat down.

"In fact, Dan Griggs said you wanted to see Stone."

"No, I wanted to see you. Chief Griggs told me you were Mr. Barrington's guest."

"Okay, what can I do for you?"

"A couple of days ago, your precinct ran some fingerprints that matched an unknown perpetrator from a bank robbery in Virginia, four years ago."

"Jesus," Dino said. "The FBI was just here about that."

"They were? I asked for their help, but I didn't know they were coming."

"Typical," Dino said. "They liked what you told them, so they're poaching on your territory."

"It's what they do," Stone said.

"What's this about?" Dino asked. "Can't be the bank robbery."

"No. At least my department has no interest in that; the FBI might. I'm here about a possible homicide."

Dino and Stone looked at each other.

"Manning has been a busy guy," Stone said.

"Manning?" Parker asked.

"The fingerprint belongs to a man named Paul Manning. Or, at least, that used to be his name."

"Tell us about the homicide," Dino said.

"It was last year," Parker said. "A Houston businessman died of an apparent heart attack, but our medical examiner wasn't entirely satisfied with that as a cause of death."

"What did he suspect?" Stone asked.

"Poisoning, of a very special kind. Apparently, there are two common household products which, when mixed, create a poison that can't be analyzed."

"I've heard about that poison," Stone said, "but I don't know what the household products are."

"Neither do I," Parker said, "and the ME wouldn't tell me. Said it's not the sort of knowledge that should be spread around, and I think I agree. He did look around the house and said both products were present."

"But why do you think Manning had anything to do with this?"

"Because this guy Manning, if that's who he is, left a thumbprint on a bedside glass, right next to the body."

"And these two chemicals were in the glass?"

"No, the glass was clean, except for the thumbprint. The ME theorizes that the murderer removed the glass containing the poisons and substituted a clean one."

"And what was the outcome of the case?"

"It's still open," Parker said, "until we can find the owner of the fingerprint and question him. Do you have any idea where I can find Paul Manning?"

"He may be in Palm Beach," Stone said. "Two of Chief Griggs's men have seen a man in town answering his description. Lately, he has also gone by the name of William Charles Danforth." Stone gave Parker the Washington address. "I gave that to the FBI agents, too." He gave him Manning's description.

Parker made a note of everything.

"I'd suggest you tell Chief Griggs that you have a good reason for him to pick up the guy," Stone said. "We didn't have a reason before now."

"I'll do that right away," Parker said. Stone handed him the phone, and he made the call. Parker spoke to Dan Griggs, then handed the phone to Stone. "He wants to talk to you."

"Hello?"

"Stone, I hear you've finally got something on this guy."

"Well, Parker has, anyway."

"It will give me the greatest pleasure to put out an APB on him."

"He may be carrying ID saying that he's William Charles Danforth, of Washington, D.C."

"Got it. I'll let you know if we pick him up."

"Thanks, Dan." He hung up the phone. "Fritz, you're doing me a very great favor."

"Glad to be of service. Lieutenant, running those prints was a very great favor to us. I'd love to clear this case."

"I hope you clear it before the weekend," Stone said.

"Why the weekend?"

"Because there's going to be a big wedding

here, and Mr. Manning might just try to crash the party."

"I'll see what I can do," Parker said. He stood up and shook Stone's and Dino's hands. "Thanks for your help. I'll let you know if we find the guy." He turned to leave.

"Fritz," Stone said, "what was your victim's name?"

"Winston Harding," Parker replied.

59

Stone watched Thad Shames leave the house and walk through the gardens toward the yacht.

"Maybe I should talk to him alone," Stone said.

Dino got up. "I'll be in my cabin if you need me."

As Dino departed, Thad came up the gangplank and walked to the afterdeck, where Stone waited for him. "Hello," he said.

"Hello, Thad. Have a seat." Stone wasn't going to enjoy this.

"What's up? Why did you want to see me alone?"

"Because what I have to tell you is for your ears only. You must not share this with Liz, or even Callie."

"You sound very serious," Thad said.

"This *is* very serious."

"Tell me."

"Today, Dino and I have had visits from two FBI agents and a detective from the Houston, Texas, police department."

"About Liz?"

"No, about Paul Manning."

"What about Manning?"

"One of the problems with finding Manning was that, for a long time, he had never been fingerprinted. Lots of people haven't. If you have never been arrested, applied for a security clearance or served in the armed forces, then you've probably not been fingerprinted. The Bureau maintains a huge database of everyone who has ever been fingerprinted, and it can be accessed by authorized law enforcement agencies."

"I understand. And Manning has never been fingerprinted?"

"He has, once. After the business on St. Marks, Manning paid me a visit in New York. He wanted money. Fortunately, I had been expecting him, and Dino showed up shortly after his arrival and arrested him on charges of insurance fraud. Since he was wanted in St. Marks on three murder charges, and since the insurance company had no hope of retrieving any funds from him, they waived their claim on Manning and allowed him to be extradited to St. Marks. But first, he was taken to Dino's precinct, the Nineteenth, in Manhattan, and routinely fingerprinted."

"And then his prints went into the FBI computer?"

"No. Whoever handled the fingerprinting at the Nineteenth considered Manning's arrest as a foreign matter and didn't forward his prints to the FBI. But they remained on file at the precinct, and earlier this week, I remembered that Manning had been printed.

"The FBI also maintains a database of fingerprints that are associated with unsolved crimes. If a perpetrator leaves a print at a crime scene, it's run against all known prints, and if there's no match, it goes into the unsolved crimes database under a file number that relates to the case. I asked Dino to run a match of Manning's prints against that database, and it turned up a match with a bank robbery in Arlington, Virginia, four years ago. That crime was also matched by modus operandi and description of the perpetrator to three other bank robberies in Maryland. All the robberies took place near Washington, D.C., where Manning kept an apartment under the name of William Charles Danforth."

"So Manning is a bank robber, as well as a murderer?"

"Yes. It appears that he had been supporting himself in that manner while he was writing a novel, which has now been published and has become a best-seller."

"Busy guy."

"Yes, he has been. Which brings us to today's visit from the FBI and the Houston detective. The FBI told us they were interested in the Virginia bank robbery, which was patently nonsense because the Bureau would never spend its resources on such a small crime, especially when they know the banks won't even prosecute small robberies unless violence was employed."

"So what were they really interested in?"

"The Houston PD, in investigating a suspected homicide, also came up with a fingerprint, which they ran against the FBI's databases. They turned up the Virginia bank robbery, too, and then, when Dino's precinct turned up the same thing, it alerted both the FBI and the Houston department that somebody else had a match. What's more, Dino could attach an identity to the prints, as well, and that's why we had these visits today."

"Did you or Dino tell them who the prints belonged to?"

"Yes, we did."

"So they're looking for Manning, now?"

"Yes. And we think he may be in Palm Beach."

"Well, this is very good news, Stone."

"It is. I hope they'll have him in custody soon, which would prevent Manning's trying to disrupt the wedding."

"Why do you think he would try to do that?"

"Last night, while the yacht's crew was off duty, and Dino and I were asleep on the yacht, somebody let go all her mooring lines and removed the gangplank. If Dino hadn't woken up, the yacht would almost certainly have collided with a bridge south of here and done great damage; maybe even have sunk the yacht."

"Jesus. And you think it was Manning?"

Stone avoided mention of Dolce. "He seems

400

the likely candidate. It was hardly the prank of a roving band of juvenile delinquents."

"And you think he might try to disrupt the wedding?"

"Yes. We've taken security precautions against that possibility."

"So everything that can be done has been done?"

"Yes."

Thad stood up. "Then I'm going to put it out of my mind."

"Please sit down, Thad. I'm not finished."

Thad sat down.

"The Houston PD is interested in Manning because one of his fingerprints was found on a bedside glass of a man they believe may have been poisoned."

"So he killed somebody in Houston, too? Good God, the man's a maniac."

"That certainly appears to be so. But what's important to us here, today, is that the man the police think may have been poisoned was Winston Harding, Liz's late husband."

Thad seemed to freeze in place. "Oh, my God," he said, finally.

Stone felt he had finally made his point.

"The poor girl. This man has made her life hell, and now we learn he murdered her husband, too?"

Maybe he hadn't made his point, after all, Stone thought. He was going to have to spell it out. "That is a very distinct possibility," Stone said. "And it has implications for you."

"You mean, you think Manning may try to kill me?"

Stone nodded. "It's a possibility we can't ignore."

"But you've already taken security precautions."

"Yes, but how long are you willing to live under those circumstances?"

"I see," Thad said. "You mean that he might try to kill me at some time in the future?"

"Yes." Stone was having trouble getting the rest of it out. "Thad, I think that, under the circumstances, you should postpone the wedding."

Thad looked alarmed. "For how long?"

"Until Manning is caught and . . . interrogated."

"Gosh, I don't know if we could do that at this point without causing a major hullabaloo in town. We've already invited two hundred people from Palm Beach and all over the country. Some of them have already arrived."

"Of course, Manning may be arrested today or tomorrow."

"That would certainly solve the problem, wouldn't it?"

Stone took a deep breath. "Not necessarily."

Thad looked at him for a long moment. "You mean Manning might have help? An accomplice?"

"It's a very real possibility." Thank God, Stone thought, he's got it at last.

"Do you have any idea who it might be?"

No, he hadn't gotten it. "Thad, I want you to understand that what I'm about to say is conjecture, but it's a conjecture that has to be made."

"So, make it."

"There's only one person that we're aware of who knows both Manning and you."

Thad's brow wrinkled, then his face relaxed, and his mouth fell open. "You can't mean . . ."

"As I say, it's only conjecture at this point. We won't know more until Manning is arrested, and it's entirely possible that he won't say anything then."

"But that's completely crazy," Thad said.

"You may be right. But ask yourself this: Who profited from Winston Harding's death?"

"Well, Manning, I guess. In some way. Revenge against Liz, maybe."

"That's a possibility. But there's only one person who actually profited from Harding's death."

Thad didn't seem to be able even to think it.

Stone finally said it aloud. "That person is Liz."

"No, no, no, no . . ." Thad's voice trailed off.

"And if the two of you are married and anything should happen to you, she would profit a great deal more than she did from Winston Harding's death."

Thad's body sagged as if air had been let out of it. He seemed unable to speak.

"So, I think you should postpone the wedding

until all this has been resolved."

Thad seemed to collect himself. He sat up straight. "No," he said. "I love her, and she loves me. If I know nothing else, I know that. The wedding goes on as scheduled. Do what you can to protect us from Manning, but you are not to say a word about this to Liz, is that understood?"

"Thad . . ."

"Stone, you have to either do as I wish in this matter, or leave. There's no in between. What's it going to be? Are you with me?"

Stone sighed. "All right," he said.

60

Stone watched Callie leave the main house and, with a man in tow, come toward the yacht. She looked particularly beautiful today, he thought, and he had missed seeing her the past few days, when she had been so busy with the wedding.

She came up the gangplank. "Stone, this is Jeff Collender of Rightguard Security Services. He'll be helping us with the wedding, and I thought you'd better brief him."

"Yeah, I know," Collender said, shaking hands. "The name sounds like a deodorant; it was my wife's idea."

"Glad to meet you, Jeff. Have a seat."

"I hear you're throwing quite a shindig, here," Collender said.

"That describes it very well," Stone said.

"So, what do we need, here? You want us to keep out the gate-crashers, and like that?"

"Jeff, we may have more of a problem than gate-crashers," Stone said.

"Oh? You expecting a lot of big drinkers, then? We've had experience with that. We know how to quietly eject the drunks."

"Let me explain as fully as I can," Stone said.

"We have to be ready to handle an armed intruder."

Collender blinked. "*Armed?* You mean with a gun?"

"Well, yes. You do have the capability of supplying armed security people, don't you?"

"Sure we do, but we've never had to actually shoot anybody."

"And I hope you won't on this occasion, but we have to be prepared for anything."

"Okay, we'll be prepared."

"Earlier, I had estimated that we'd need only a few armed men, but now I think they'll all have to be armed. I assume your men have had some standard training?"

"Well, most of them are ex–law enforcement, so they've been trained by whatever department they worked for."

"Are there any that haven't had training?"

"Maybe one or two."

"Let's drop them. We need men who know how to handle weapons in a crowd."

"Mr. Barrington, why don't you tell me exactly who you're expecting?"

"His name is Paul Manning. He's tall and slender — six-three or -four, two hundred pounds, dark hair going gray."

"Would you recognize him on sight?"

"Only by his size and shape. I haven't seen his current face."

"His *current* face?"

"We believe he's had some cosmetic surgery."

"So you don't have a photograph?"

"No."

"Ooookay, no photograph."

"There aren't too many people that tall. He should stand out in a crowd."

"How big a crowd are we expecting?"

"About two hundred," Callie said.

"There'll be a tight guest list?"

"Pretty tight. If a guest wants to bring someone along, we're not going to make a big thing of it."

"And how many of these guests are likely to be armed?"

"Just the one," Stone said dryly.

Dino came out of his cabin, and Stone introduced him to Collender.

"Nice to meet a fellow officer," Collender said. "I used to be the sheriff of Palm Beach County."

"Mmmm," Dino said. "Don't let me interrupt, just keep going."

"So," Collender said, "how many people do you want here?"

"Twenty-four ought to do it," Stone said.

"All armed?"

"Yes. Can you manage that?"

"Yeah, I can manage it. How do you want me to manage this Manning character, if we spot him?"

"Isolate him as quickly as possible, pat him down, check whatever name he gives you against the guest list and do it all very, very politely and apologetically. There are going to be some important people here, and we don't want to annoy them any more than absolutely necessary."

"Believe me," Collender said, "we're used to dealing with the rich and powerful in this town. We know how it's done."

"Good."

"How do you want my people dressed?"

"Black tie. I don't want them immediately identifiable as security. Do you have any women?"

"I've got four, all ex-officers and good."

"Put them with men. Couples are less noticeable than single men."

"Got it," Collender said, taking notes. "If Manning starts shooting, what do you want done?"

Stone and Dino exchanged a glance. "Stop him in the most expedient way possible."

Collender nodded sagely. "I get you."

"I hope so," Stone said. "I don't want Manning to be able to hurt anybody. I think you can imagine how big a mess that would be."

"Oh, yeah, I read you completely. Are we going to have any cops here?"

"I'm talking to Chief Griggs in a few minutes about that. I'll let you know."

Collender stood up. "Anything else?"

Stone shook his head.

"I'll be going, then." He gave Stone his card. "Call me if you think of anything else; there's office, home and cell phone on the card."

"Thanks, and it was good to meet you," Stone said.

Callie escorted Collender off the yacht.

"You think this guy knows what he's doing?" Dino asked.

"I hope to God he does. Callie says he's the best around here."

"Twenty-four guys with guns at a party? Let's hope they don't shoot each other."

"Let's hope," Stone said.

Dan Griggs sounded amenable on the phone. "I'm glad we've got a charge against this guy, now," he said. "I'd like it if we could snatch him off the street before the wedding."

"I'd like that, too, Dan," Stone said.

"I think we ought to have a meeting of all the security people and my people the afternoon of the wedding, and we're going to need some kind of lapel pin to identify everybody. I'll bring some."

"Good idea," Stone agreed. "There's no way everybody is going to know everybody else on sight."

"You know, we've covered a lot of parties in this town, mostly off duty, but this is the first time we're actually expecting an armed intruder."

"I hope we're being overly cautious," Stone said, "but we've got to be ready for anything. The more I learn about Manning, the more he worries me."

"Let's meet at four tomorrow afternoon, then," Griggs said. "I know Jeff Collender. I'll call him."

"See you then, Dan." Stone hung up.

Dino called to him from the saloon, where he was watching a golf tournament on television. "Quick, come here."

Stone hurried into the saloon.

"Edward Ginsky was a prominent attorney in both New York and Miami legal circles," a television reporter was saying. He was standing in front of a large house. "He leaves a widow and two grown children."

"What happened?" Stone asked.

"Ed Ginsky got himself shot."

"Any details?"

"Maid found him on his front steps this morning. He took two in the head."

Stone sank into a chair. "Where is this going to end?"

"It's not going to end until Manning is dead," Dino said. "And I think you and I ought to do whatever we can to see that that happens, if he shows up at the wedding."

"Dino, are you suggesting we just shoot him down on sight?"

"As much as I'd like to, I think we have to be a little more subtle than that," Dino said. "But not much."

61

Stone stood in front of the living room fireplace in Thad Shames's house and regarded the decidedly mixed group of men and women who stood around him, dressed — or half-dressed — in what each of them understood to be evening clothes.

Behind him, propped on the marble mantel, was a crude drawing of the house and grounds that he had done himself with a Magic Marker in black, with other colors for various personnel. He felt quite proud of it, in fact.

"Okay, everybody listen up," he said. "You see here an outline of the place — house, gardens and yacht. There are sixteen small circles, in red, denoting employees of Rightguard Security. Jeff Collender will assign each of you to stations, and, once we've swept the grounds, you are to maintain those stations. Pick up a drink from the bar so you'll look at least a little like a guest, and the drink will be iced water, soda, tonic or soft drink — no booze. Eight of you, four men and four women, will roam the house and grounds as couples. Jeff will assign you areas to patrol.

411

"The green circles denote Palm Beach police officers — two at the curb to control traffic, one at the door to display a little authority to anyone contemplating gate-crashing, especially unauthorized members of the press, and to handle the metal detector. Authorized press people will be wearing photo IDs on strings around their necks. If you see anybody taking notes or photographs who is not wearing this tag, firmly request the ID card and, if it is not immediately forthcoming, escort him or her from the premises. If possible, take such people either through the center hall of the house or around the sides to the street. If they become obstreperous, turn them over to a police officer on the street, who will arrest them for trespassing and place them in a police van."

He pointed to his colleagues as he listed their names. "Chief Dan Griggs, Jeff Collender of Rightguard, Lieutenant Bacchetti and I will be known as the 'management group' and will be roaming the house and grounds. Everybody has been issued a lapel pin — green for Rightguard Security, red for Palm Beach Police, black for management group. You may also see some people with yellow lapel pins, but they are separate. Each of you has been issued a two-way radio, tuned to channel six. You understand that the use of radios is to be confined to sightings of Paul Manning. There is to be no unnecessary chat on the radios; there are too many of us for that. Paul Manning is six feet-three or -four, two hundred pounds, dark hair, going gray, moderately long. We have no photographs or sketches of him. If you spot a man answering that description, say the word 'bogey' into your microphone and give the specific location. If you see a weapon, either in his hand or on his person, say, 'gun,' into the radio. Keep it as short as you can while conveying the information you need to. After that, speak into the radio only if the subject changes position or if you are asked questions by one of the management group.

"Each of you has two sheets of paper with the entire guest list printed on them. If you have reason to suspect that a visitor is uninvited, politely request his or her name and refer to the list. If the name does not appear, ask the person to accompany you to the front door by one of the routes already mentioned, and turn him or her over to a police officer, who will determine if that person is, in fact, invited. It is possible that some invited guest may bring along another, uninvited guest. If an invited guest intercedes on behalf of such a person, do nothing, but make a note of the name on your guest list. Apologize for any inconvenience.

"Everybody insert the radio earplug for a sound check." He waited while they did this. "This is a test," he said into the microphone concealed in his left hand. "Anybody didn't hear that, raise your hand." No hands went up. Thank God the equipment was working.

"Now, let me tell you the policy on firearms.

You are all carrying concealed weapons. You are not to take out that weapon, unless you see a weapon in the hand of someone not in this room now, such as the subject, Paul Manning. If you do see a weapon and produce your own weapon, you are not to fire unless you feel sure that the subject is threatening to fire. You are not to fire unless you have a clear shot. You are not to shoot any guest. I hope that is perfectly clear." That got a laugh. "You might remember that if you fire a weapon this evening, you are going to have to answer to the police and, maybe, the courts for your actions. If you are in doubt about whether to fire your weapon, keep that in mind.

"Finally, if you spot the subject or any other threat, do not head for the bride and groom. Four Palm Beach detectives will be assigned to accompany them everywhere they go. Instead, head for the subject, and be ready to use physical force to disarm or disable him. Any questions?" Stone looked around at each face. Nobody spoke.

"All right, if you don't already have an assigned station, get one from one of the management group. As soon as you have your assignments, we're going to start at the seawall, and in a straight line, at arm's length, we're going to sweep the entire property, check every bush, every flower bed for any unwelcome person or weapon." *Or bomb,* he thought, but didn't say. He walked over to where Jeff Collender stood. "Jeff, the man standing over to the side of the group, there." He nodded toward a man in his twenties, barely encased in a white dinner jacket, with a head that had recently been shaved.

"Yeah, he's one of mine. Jason."

"Assign him to the seawall, to watch for anyone approaching the property in a boat. I don't want him mingling with the guests. He'll scare them to death."

"Will do."

"All right, everybody, let's go out to the seawall and start back toward the house." Stone led them out of the house and toward the yacht. When they were stretched out at arm's length, he called to them, "Commence your search, and when you get to the house, re-form farther down that way and come back to the seawall. When that's done, take up your assigned positions." He looked at his watch. "It's ten minutes to five. Guests will start to arrive at six, so move quickly but carefully.

"Dan, Jeff, Dino, the four of us will search the house, starting at the top floor. When we get downstairs, Dino and I will take the kitchen."

The four men walked back to the house, climbed the stairs to the third floor and went down hallways, knocking on every door, checking every room.

"Dan, your men at the door know that nobody enters the house except through the metal detector?"

"They know."

"Okay, Dino, let's check the kitchen." Stone

led the way, and they walked into a large, restaurant-style facility, teeming with people. He found the caterer, spooning caviar into a crystal bowl. "Mr. Weems?"

"That's me."

"My name is Barrington. I'm in charge of security."

"How do you do?"

"I'd like you to walk around the room with me and confirm that every one of these people is known to you as a member of your staff."

"Okay," the man said.

Stone walked him around the room, then took him into the dining room, where a bar was being set up. "Do you know every one of these people?" he asked.

"Every one of them. They're all mine. At the reception, we'll have half a dozen people serving drinks who are not my regular employees, but they all come well recommended."

"Thanks for your time."

"Don't mention it." The man returned to his work.

"Looks like you've got it covered," Dino said.

"I hope so," Stone replied. "Can you think of anything we haven't done?"

"Nope, not yet, anyway. If Manning gets in and shoots Thad or Liz, then I'm sure I'll think of a couple of things we should have done."

"Great," Stone said.

"By the way," Dino said, "have you read the guest list?"

416

"I glanced at it. I don't know anybody who's coming except Bill Eggers and a couple named Wilkes."

"Check it again," Dino said, "under C."

Stone removed the list from an inside pocket and ran a finger down to the C's. He felt a light sweat break out on his forehead. "Mrs. Arrington Calder," he read aloud.

"Did you know about that?" Dino asked.

"No, I didn't."

"I didn't think so. You've been too cool."

"And why do you think her name on this list would make me less than cool?" Stone demanded.

"Well, you're raising your voice," Dino said, "and, all of a sudden, you're sweating."

62

Stone and Dino took one more walk around the property, then, at six o'clock, they headed for the front door to check out the arrival procedures. Guests were already pulling up in Bentleys, Rollses and Mercedes-Benzes, and Stone was pleased with the efficiency with which the cars were being taken away and parked by the attendants.

He watched as a couple moved through the metal detector, which had been disguised as a rose arbor. A quiet beep was heard, and a smiling police officer approached the couple.

"Excuse me, sir," he said, and quickly ran a handheld wand over the man's clothes.

"Probably my house keys," the man said, holding up a large clump.

"I expect so, sir," the cop replied. "Sorry for the inconvenience."

"That was handled well," Dino said quietly.

"That's the Palm Beach Police Department for you," Stone replied.

The three dozen wedding guests had been asked to arrive early, and by six-thirty they were all present with drinks in their hands. At six thirty-five, there was a murmur from the group as Liz descended the main staircase, resplendent in a beautiful ivory lace wedding dress. She was met at the bottom of the stairs by Thad, who towered over her a good eighteen inches, Stone reckoned. He escorted her into the living room to the fireplace, where a judge was waiting to perform the ceremony.

"Let's go out back," Stone said.

"What, you want to miss the wedding?"

"Nobody in that room is going to bother them. If there's a threat, it'll come from outside."

"Okay."

They walked into the garden and had a look around until Stone was satisfied. There was applause from inside, and Stone turned in time to see, through a tall window, the bride and groom kissing. "That's one possibility down," Stone said.

"What do you mean?"

"If Manning wanted to stop the wedding, he'd have already made his move."

"I guess so," Dino replied. "But if he wants to create a very rich widow, he's got all evening."

"That's the scary part," Stone agreed. He looked up to see Guido and two other men approaching. They were carefully dressed in rented tuxedos, and Stone was relieved to see that the jackets were sufficiently loose-fitting not to reveal any weapons. "Evening, Guido," he said.

"Yeah, you, too," Guido said. "Everything cool?"

"So far." Stone dug into a pocket and came up with three yellow lapel pins. "Put these into your buttonholes," he said. "They will let security know you're okay."

The three men complied.

"Where you want us?" Guido asked.

"Wherever you think best. All the security people are looking for a tall man, but not for a beautiful woman, so you're on your own, if she turns up."

"Way I figure it," Guido said, "if she's coming, she's coming for you. We'll stick close."

"Not too close," Stone said. He didn't want to have to explain to anybody who they were.

"Got it." They wandered off.

At seven, the reception guests started to arrive, and the crowd became thicker.

"Jesus," Dino said, "this is a hell of a lot of people."

"Just two hundred of their closest friends," Stone said. A big dance band began to play tunes from the thirties and forties in the garden. Stone liked the music. It was a beautiful night, and a handsome crowd of people. They wandered through the house and gardens, sipping champagne and chatting with people they knew, and everybody seemed to know everybody. Stone began to relax a little.

The party wore on into the evening. The guests talked, danced, congratulated the bride and groom and did all the other things people did at parties. Some were drunk, but not too drunk. Then, late in the evening, Stone turned toward the house and saw Arrington. She was leaving the main house on the arm of a tall, handsome man of about forty, beautifully dressed. After the shock of recognition, Stone's next reaction was jealousy.

"Easy, pal," Dino said. "You look like you want to shoot the guy."

The tall man had already attracted the attention of a couple of security people, who looked at Stone inquiringly. He shook his head.

"Yeah, that's all we need," Dino said. "For security to shoot Arrington's date."

"Yes, that would be too bad," Stone said. Arrington saw him and started toward him, leaving her companion at the bar.

"Hello, Dino," she said, beaming at him and giving him a kiss on the lips.

"Hiya, kiddo," Dino said, beaming back.

"Hello, Stone," she said, almost shyly. She leaned forward and kissed him on the cheek. "I behaved badly the last time we saw each other," she whispered. "I know we can work this out. I'm at the Breakers. Call me late tonight, I don't care how late."

Stone nodded, then a voice entered his ear.

"Crasher at the front door," the voice said.

"Arrington, please excuse me," Stone said. "I have to attend to something. I'll call you later, I promise." He made his way toward the front door, closely followed by Dino.

"Don't you want me to handle the thing at the front door?" Dino asked. "Wouldn't you rather stay here and talk to Arrington?"

"I just want to see what's going on," Stone said. They arrived at the front door in time to see two Palm Beach PD officers hustling a man into a van.

Another cop approached. "Unauthorized photographer," he said. "We know him. He's a stringer for one of the tabloids."

"Good work," Stone said. "You had any other problems at the front door?"

"Not really. We've had to frisk a few people, but no problems. Nobody as tall as the guy you're looking for. An old man in a wheelchair set off all the alarms, but he was on the guest list."

"Wheelchair?" Stone asked. "What kind of wheelchair?"

"One of those electric jobs, almost like a scooter. He arrived in a van and had to be helped with it."

"What's his name?"

The cop consulted his list. "Walter Feldman."

"Describe him."

"White hair, kind of hunched over and frail-looking."

Stone turned to look at Dino.

"A wheelchair is a good way not to look tall," Dino said.

Stone lifted his left hand to his mouth. "Everybody, listen up. This is Barrington. Without leaving your stations, find a man in an electric wheelchair and report his position." He released the talk switch. "Come on, Dino."

They quickly checked inside the house, but did not see the man. "He must be in the gardens," Stone said. He spoke into the microphone again. "This is Barrington. Anybody got a position on the man in the wheelchair yet?"

Nothing.

"Jesus, how hard can he be to find?" Stone asked.

Then a voice came over the radio. "Mr. Barrington, I've got the wheelchair."

"Where?" Stone asked.

"At the pool, behind the hedge."

"Describe the occupant."

"There's no occupant. The wheelchair is sitting empty by the pool."

"Everybody, listen up," Stone said. "Our subject has arrived. Locate him quickly."

They were near the seawall, now. Dino spoke up. "Where's the guard you put on the seawall, the bald guy?"

"Nowhere in sight," Stone said. He arrived at the wall, walked to the stern of the yacht and looked at the water. The big security guard, Jason, was floating facedown in Lake Worth, a trickle of red coloring the water around him.

"Oh, shit," Dino said.

Then gunfire broke out.

63

Stone turned around to find a mob of people rushing toward him, many of them screaming.

"Shots fired!" he said into the microphone. "Secure the bride and groom in the master suite now!" Then he and Dino did what cops always do, and other people don't: They ran toward the gunfire.

They had trouble making headway against the onrushing crowd, but after a couple of minutes they were nearing the house. A man and woman were huddled behind a huge shrub. "On the roof!" the man yelled at Stone, pointing.

"Detail at the front of the house," Stone said into the mike. "Subject on the roof of the house. Watch the front drainpipes and apprehend."

"He's not coming this way," Dino said. "There must be a way from the roof into the house."

"Oh, God," Stone said. He spoke into the mike. "Bride and groom detail. Where are you?"

"On the main stairs," a voice replied. "We'll have them secured in a minute."

"Oh, no," he said to Dino, "we've been suckered. Let's get up there." They started to run. "Don't take the bride and groom upstairs!" he said into the microphone. He raced into the house and headed for the stairs. From the bottom, he could just see the wedding party disappearing down the upstairs hallway. "Wedding group," he said into the mike. "Stop, and come downstairs." No one came down. He ran up the stairs.

At the top he came to a sudden halt because the stairs were blocked by the bride, the groom, several guests and four Palm Beach police officers. They were standing there, rigidly, and Stone couldn't see past them. He stopped a few steps from the top and listened.

"Step away from the bride and groom," a man's deep voice said.

Manning. Stone tiptoed up the remaining stairs. Then, blocked from Manning's view by the group above him, he clambered onto the stair handrail and grabbed the banister built around the stairwell. He was holding onto the banister's vertical risers, trying to pull himself up, and it wasn't working very well.

"I said, clear away from the bride and groom," Manning's voice commanded.

Stone could see a couple of guests peel off from the group, but the cops stood their ground.

"Listen, Mr. Manning," a cop said. "There's more of us than you. More firepower, too. Why don't you —"

"If any of you touches a gun, I'll start firing," Manning said, "and I've got thirteen rounds left. The happy couple will be the first to go."

Stone swung his legs sideways and got a toe on the landing. Slowly, painfully, he muscled his way up until he could get a grip on the handrail. Then, as silently as he could, he pulled himself to the top of the railing and let himself down on the other side, striking the floor with a muffled thud.

"What was that?" Manning demanded.

"What was what?" the cop said. "Come on, Mr. Manning, you're not getting out of here. Just drop the gun."

"For the last time, step away from the couple, or I'm going to start shooting."

Stone had the 9mm automatic in his hand by now, and he slowly pumped the first round into the chamber. On his hands and knees, he crawled to the edge of the group and, very quickly, stuck his head out and withdrew it. What he remembered seeing was a white-haired man in a dinner jacket who had assumed the combat position, pistol in both hands, at arm's length.

The odds were not good on hitting Manning before he could fire, Stone reflected. He crouched, ready to leap to one side of the group and start firing.

Then Manning changed everything. He fired a single shot into the group, and everybody scattered. The women were screaming, and a cop had thrown Liz to the floor and was lying on top of her. The group parted like the Red Sea, leaving Stone exposed, but also leaving him a clear shot at Manning. He took it, firing four rapid rounds down the hallway.

Manning fired twice more as he was spun backward, but Stone was sure the rounds had gone into the ceiling. Stone rushed him, pistol out before him, yelling, "Freeze, Manning!" He could hear people moving behind him.

As he ran down the hallway, he saw Manning struggle to one knee and start to raise his gun. Stone stopped and aimed. "Don't!" he yelled.

But Manning wasn't listening. His hand kept moving upward.

Stone fired once more, and Manning fell backward. Two Palm Beach officers were all over him, kicking his gun away, rolling him over and handcuffing him. Stone put his gun away and walked forward. "Is he alive?" he asked.

An officer knelt beside the man, his hand at Manning's throat. "I've got a pulse," he said.

Stone looked down at Manning. He reached out and pulled the white wig off, then turned his head. At last, he had a full frontal view of the man's face. It was unrecognizable, and for a moment he thought he had the wrong man, but he remembered that voice. He held the mike to his lips. "The subject is secured. He needs an ambulance, now." He turned and looked back down the hallway. Liz and Thad were sitting on the floor, a Palm Beach officer leaning against Thad, holding his upper arm. "Make that two ambulances," Stone said into the mike. He walked over to where the three sat, moved the cop's hand and looked at his arm. He found a clean handkerchief and pressed it onto the wound. "Hold that," he said to the man.

Then he turned to Thad and Liz. "Is either of you hurt?"

"No," they both said, simultaneously.

"I'm okay," the cop said. "Get them out of here."

Stone helped them up and led them to the master suite.

"Is anyone else hurt?" Thad asked.

"A security guard is dead, back at the seawall," Stone said. "And Manning doesn't look so good. He got into the house in a wheelchair, then abandoned it at the pool. From there, hidden by the hedge, he must have gotten to a kitchen door and made his way up the back stairs. He fired a couple of shots into the garden to cause chaos and to get us to bring you two upstairs. You'll be all right here. There's no danger now. I want to get back downstairs and make sure no one else was hurt."

"You go ahead, Stone," Thad said. "We'll be fine."

"Is Paul dead?" Liz asked.

Tears were streaming down her cheeks, and Stone thought she looked very worried. "No," he said, "but he took two or three bullets. An ambulance is on the way. Don't go out into the hall." He left the room and closed the door behind him, then he started down the stairs. Where the hell was Dino? Stone had been sure he was right behind him when he entered the house.

He walked into the back garden and surveyed the damage. The members of the band had abandoned their bandstand, and a couple of instruments lay on the ground beside it. A large table used as a bar had been overturned, and the air smelled of spilled booze.

He saw Arrington and her date come from behind a huge banyan tree, where they had apparently been hiding. Then he saw Dolce.

64

She looked very beautiful, he thought. She was wearing a short, tight dress of dark green silk. Her hair, nails and makeup were perfectly done, and she was smiling slightly, showing the tips of her perfect, white teeth. For a moment, he thought she had an evening bag in her hand, but on further examination it turned out to be a small semiautomatic pistol with a short silencer affixed to it. *Where the hell did she get that?* he wondered.

She was not looking at Stone but at Arrington, and her smile became broader. Stone squeezed his left arm against his side, to be sure the pistol was still there. *I could shoot her right now, and this would all be over,* he thought. Instead, he managed the best smile he could, in the circumstances. "Hello, Dolce," he said, trying to work some delight into his voice. He held out his arms and walked toward her. *I'll just hug her, then I'll take away the gun,* he thought.

She turned toward him, and her face lit up with a burst of recognition. "Stone!" she said. "It's you!"

Then, to Stone's horror, she brought the pistol

up before her and aimed it at him.

"I could shoot you, and this would all be over," she said.

Where have I heard that before? Stone wondered. "I'm glad to see you," he said. "Don't shoot me."

"Why not?" she said. "I don't want *her* to have you." She nodded toward Arrington.

"I don't want him, Dolce!" Arrington cried.

Stone looked at Arrington. Her handsome escort was edging away from her toward the banyan tree.

"Of course you do, Arrington," Dolce said. "You've always wanted him. You only married Vance because you thought I wanted *him*."

"That's crazy, Dolce," Arrington said, then realized her choice of words was poor. She pressed on, though. "I didn't even know you knew Vance, when we were married. Come to think of it, I didn't even know *you*."

Stone took the opportunity to edge closer to Arrington, his arms still outstretched.

"That's a gorgeous dress," Arrington said. "Where did you get it?"

Trust Arrington to bring up fashion at a time like this, Stone thought.

"At a little place on Worth Avenue. The shopping is very good in this town," Dolce replied conversationally.

Stone edged closer.

Without taking her eyes from Arrington, Dolce said, "Stone, if you come any closer, I'm

431

going to have to make a decision."

Stone stopped moving, but he was afraid to lower his arms.

"You really don't want Stone, Arrington?" Dolce asked, wrinkling her brow.

"I wouldn't have him on a silver platter," Arrington said with conviction. "I'm with Barry, here." She turned to introduce her escort and discovered that he had vanished. "He must have had to go to the powder room," she explained.

Stone was beginning to wonder which of them was the crazier.

"Did you get the shoes here, too?" Arrington asked.

"Oh, yes," Dolce replied. "At Ferragamo."

What's going to happen when they run out of clothes to talk about? Stone wondered.

"And those earrings are a knockout," Arrington said.

"I got those at Verdura," Dolce said. "It's down a little alley off Worth Avenue, and up a flight."

"Wonderful shop," Arrington said. "I know them from New York."

"Dolce," Stone said, "can we —"

"Shut up, Stone," she replied. "Arrington and I are discussing shopping. I'll get to you in a minute."

"I'm so sorry," Stone said.

"Yes, you are, and we have to talk about that." She turned back to Arrington. "I love your handbag."

"Oh, thank you," Arrington said. "I got it at

Bergdorf's, at that little boutique just inside the Fifty-eighth Street door. I can't think of the name at the moment."

Dolce pointed the pistol at her. "Think of it, or I'll shoot you."

Arrington thought desperately. "Suarez!" she said, looking relieved. "That's it." She held out the handbag. "Would you like to have mine? Please take it as a gift."

"Why, that's very kind of you, Arrington," Dolce said.

I've got to do something, Stone thought, but he couldn't think what. If he rushed her, she'd shoot him, and then only Arrington would be left, and Dolce would shoot her, too. He remembered what Guido had said about Dolce's shooting skills. *Where the hell is fucking Guido?*

Then Stone saw a movement behind Dolce. He dared not take his eyes from hers and look at it. Instead, he tried to identify it with his peripheral vision.

Dolce swung the pistol back to Stone. "I may as well get this over with, so Arrington and I can talk seriously about clothes," she said, raising the pistol.

"But . . ." Stone started to say, then the pistol in Dolce's hand went off, with an evil *pfffft,* and he staggered backward. Almost simultaneously, the shape behind Dolce turned into a billowing sail, which fell over her head, and Dino, who had thrown a tablecloth over her, wrestled her to the ground.

Stone felt a searing pain in his left armpit and put his hand under his jacket. It came back covered in blood. Stone had always disliked the sight of his own blood.

"Will somebody give me a fucking hand?" Dino yelled.

Guido and his two friends materialized from behind a bush and went to Dino's aid. Or, that was the way it seemed at first. As Stone watched, the largest of the three men grabbed Dino by the collar and tossed him a few yards into a flower bed, as if he were an oddly shaped bowling ball. Guido picked up the shrouded Dolce, wrestled her gun away and threw her over a shoulder. Then he started toward the house, followed by his cohorts.

He nodded at Stone's bloody hand. "You oughta get that looked at," he said to Stone as he passed.

"Thanks," Stone said, and watched them walk through the house and out the front door. Painfully, Stone put the microphone to his lips. "Detail at the front of the house: Three men are coming out with a woman in a sack. Do not detain them. Repeat, do not detain." Then he fainted.

65

Stone came to in the backseat of a car. His head was in Dino's lap, and Dino was pressing something against his armpit.

"You awake?" Dino asked.

"Yes," Stone murmured.

"You want to know what happened?"

"I think I know what happened," Stone said.

Thad Shames spoke up from the driver's seat. "How are you feeling?"

"I'm not sure," Stone said. "Why aren't you with Liz?"

"Liz left the house," Thad said. "I came downstairs and went out into the garden to look for you, and she must have left the master suite then."

Dino spoke up. "The cop at the door said she insisted on getting into the ambulance with Manning."

"Are you sure I'm not still unconscious?" Stone asked, then he passed out again.

He came to again on a bed surrounded by curtains. Dino and Thad were standing beside the bed. Stone was not wearing a shirt anymore, there was a wad of gauze and tape in his armpit and his arm was in some sort of rubber sling, which seemed to be filled with ice. On a stand next to the bed, a plastic bag of blood dripped into a tube attached to Stone's other arm. He tried to sit up and started to speak.

Dino held a finger to his lips. He found a switch and the bed rose until Stone was in a sitting position. Dino pointed to the curtain and cupped a hand behind his ear.

Stone tried to focus. He could hear a woman's voice from behind the curtain.

"Don't you die on me, goddammit," she was saying. "Don't you leave me in this mess. We're going to get out of this together."

Stone recognized the voice, and he looked at Thad, whose face was drawn and whiter than usual.

"I'm going to need some time to heal," Paul Manning's voice rumbled, surprisingly strong.

"They're taking you to surgery in a minute," Allison Manning said. "But I've got to talk to you first. Thad told me they know about Winston."

"Do they know about you, or just me?" Manning asked.

"I don't know, but I can get Thad to tell me. Don't worry, I can deal with Thad. He'll believe whatever I tell him."

Stone looked at Thad. *He looks worse than I do,* he thought.

"The money is already in the Caymans," Manning said. "You know the account number.

Wait until I've recovered; but before they move me to some jail ward, find a way to get me out of here. Charter a plane and bring me a gun."

"All right," Allison said. "I hear a gurney. They're coming for you."

"Better get out of here and back to Shames."

"I love you," she said.

Thad stepped over to the curtain and drew it back. Allison spun around and looked at her husband and the other two men. It took her only a moment to recover. "Thad! Thank God you're here!"

"Hello, Liz," he said. "Or, perhaps I should say, Allison."

"Did you hear all that?" she asked. "Paul is crazy, you know. I was trying to find out what he did with your two million dollars."

Dino left the cubicle.

"Were you?" Thad asked. "Well, I guess you found out, didn't you? It's in the Cayman Islands, and you know the account number."

"Thad . . ."

Thad held up a hand. "Don't. You'll just embarrass us both."

Dino returned with Dan Griggs and the Houston detective, Fritz Parker.

"Mrs., ah, Shames, I guess it is," Griggs said. "You're going to have to come with me. This detective has some questions he'd like to ask you, and I have a few, myself."

Allison looked at Thad. "You've got to help me," she said.

"I don't see how I can," Thad replied. Then he turned and walked away.

"Stone," she said, "you've got to represent me. I need your help."

"You don't need me, Allison," Stone said. "You can afford the very best. Paul probably has a phone number in his pocket."

"Please, please," she begged.

"Goodbye, Allison," Stone said. "I expect I'll see you in court."

They led her away, then Griggs came back. "We took a nine-millimeter away from Manning," he said, "but it looks like the security guard was shot with a smaller caliber. You have any thoughts on that?"

Stone thought about that for a moment, then he shook his head and closed his eyes.

"We didn't recover the slug."

Good, Stone thought.

"I understand there was some sort of scuffle in the garden after Manning was stopped. You know anything about that?"

Stone opened his eyes. "A drunken guest," he said. Apparently Griggs thought he'd been shot by Manning. "She had to be removed." He closed his eyes again and kept them closed until Griggs went away.

Stone was comfortable in a reclining seat on the G IV. His arm was still numb, and he was still in a slight morphine haze.

Callie put a pillow behind his head. "Anything else I can do for you?" she asked.

"Yes," he said, "but not right now. Could I have a telephone, please?"

"I'll get you one."

Stone looked at his watch. Just past seven A.M. He had been taken to the airplane on a stretcher, but he had managed to walk up the airstair steps on his own. Callie had packed his clothes. They had been in the air for half an hour, and Dino was dozing across the aisle.

Callie brought him the phone. "After your call, you should get some sleep."

"Have you got the phone number for the Breakers Hotel?" he asked.

She took the phone, dialed the number for him, handed the phone back and walked back toward the front of the airplane.

"The Breakers," an operator said.

"Please connect me with Mrs. Vance Calder," Stone said.

"One moment." The phone began ringing.

"Hello," a sleepy voice said.

Stone thought for a second, then pressed the off button on the phone.

Dino stirred and turned toward Stone. "Who was that?" he asked.

"Good question," Stone said.

"Why did you hang up?"

"Isn't that what you're supposed to do?"

"When?"

"When a man answers."

439

ACKNOWLEDGMENTS

I want to express my gratitude to my editor, David Highfill, and my publisher, Phyllis Grann, for their continuing care and contributions to my work.

My agents, Morton Janklow and Anne Sibbald, and all the people at Janklow & Nesbit, continue to manage my career, always with excellent results, and they, as ever, have my gratitude.

I want to thank my friends, David and Carolyn Klemm, for sharing their Palm Beach existence with me and for showing me the town, its restaurants, golf courses and shops.

My wife, Chris, is my first and most critical reader, and I thank her for her strong opinions and her love.